THE LIGHT OF BEATHRA CHRONICLES

THE WARRIOR ARISES

By Holly S. Ruddock

Art credit © littlemagic

A message to the reader.

Dear friends, young and old, who may feel like a square peg,
the odd man out or a bit displaced; it gets better.
Learning to celebrate who you are and who you were created to be
will come.

Do not let the negative voices be your influence.
They are afraid of your strange, wonderful, rare self, and that's ok.
Your uniqueness is what this world needs for bringing change.
You, who you are right now, is enough.

So, you might as well start liking yourself.
You have to live with *you* for a very long time.
Learn to love who you are now and keep growing in who you
are meant to be.
The best is yet to come.

Holly

Dedication.

To my children and their families: Cody and Whitney, Ryley, Sydney and Kyle, and Jessey. You, my darling children, are my inspiration. Thank you for your service to our country. So few understand the life you have lived at such a young age. You are all my heroes.

To my sweet little neighbor girls that this story was written for: Ginny, Meredith, and Millie. May you forever see yourselves the way I see you, brave and beautiful with a touch of wild.

To my sweet friends and daughter that helped edit and guide me. Sydney, Liz, Sonja, Rhonda, and MaryKay. I owe ya all big. Thanks for believing in the book and its message. I love each of you so very much. Here's to more crazy ideas.

To my brother Tim, who advised and encouraged me in my writing, editing, and wondering what the heck I was trying to say. Thanks for challenging me.

To my husband, Joe, who had to listen to each chapter and rewrite and rewrite. You have never veered from encouraging me to be myself. You have always loved me for exactly who I am. You are the Sebastian to my Ruby. And I thank God for you.

To my grandchildren, Charlie Melia, Everett Paige, and Avery who is still in the oven. I thought loving your parents was my deepest love, but you three princesses have dug that well a little deeper. You are my greatest joy.

CONTENTS

PROLOGUE

Escape with me to a realm you never knew existed. A world that is beyond our imagination. Call it another dimension if you'd like; Havengothy is a place all to itself. With two loving spirits that created and rule the enchanted land, this magical place is like no other. The inhabitants of Havengothy are rare and only exist in this mystic forest. To call these creatures strong would be misleading because strength is measured only by the heart.

The remarkable realm is filled with unique animals you have never heard of and an atmosphere that will give any and all goosebumps. But everything extraordinary and beautiful always has an enemy. And this wicked rival is consumed with destroying all the good of the land and its two rulers.

However, heroes rise up from the most unlikely places. For what others might view as unusual or irrelevant, just might be the surprising weapons needed to defeat an enemy.

Eighteen years ago:

She woke up in the middle of the night, drenched in sweat. "What in the world was that about?" She thought.

Ginny was a young miniature fairy who ran a magical beast farm. She lived alone but never felt lonely and loved her job and all it entailed. She rescued and raised enchanted beasts who were wounded or abandoned. Hiking the foothills of the Hyperion Mountain Range or scanning the forest floor and branches of Havengothy, Ginny was compelled to nurture the unique and unusual inhabitants of her world.

She laid in her dark root contemplating her dream. She was catching a newly bloomed gidgie falling from her King Tree, Beathra. The little one nearly toppled Ginny. Being a mini, Ginny was half the size of other fairies in her garden. If the vision was real, it meant her King was asking her to adopt a freshly blossomed gidgie. "Who am I to raise a new bloomling on my own? I am too young, too small, and too single to tackle such a responsibility." She said out loud to a vacant room.

Yet, she couldn't shake the feeling of needing to adopt. She tried to go back to sleep, but the dream hounded her again. She gave up on slumbering and shuffled to her kitchen to make a mug of spicy pinkle pepper brew and considered what her King was asking. "I know nothing about raising a child." Commenting to an empty chair across from her. She then had a picture of a little girl looking back at her from that same chair, smiling a crooked grin.

Ginny walked over to her kitchen window and watched the sunrise over the horizon. She looked out over her small, enchanted farm and knew; she had to catch the pink winged fairy that would fall from the branches of Beathra. Putting her cup down, Ginny prepared for the four-hour flight to the center of the garden. If this dream was to be fulfilled, she needed to be present at the Bloom Festival to witness the magic of a fairy's beginning.

The Bloom Festival was teaming with gidgies, all enjoying the spring carnival. The yearly festivities celebrated life, growth, and the wonders of new fairies blooming. Ginny waited under the giant King Tree. "What am I thinking?" she thought to herself, about adopting a baby fairy.

As Ginny stood in the midst of a crowd of other families anticipating catching their first or fifth child, Ginny was the only one who stood alone. And though she was a dwarf gidgic, her smallness was not a handicap; it was her motivator.

Ginny was an independent fairy with a tenacity to tackle any mammoth task. Still, the enormous job of being a single mother caused her to doubt her abilities.

She was about to talk herself out of the madness; suddenly, she spotted the bright pink petals of a flower begin to cascade towards her. The bloomling's pedals formed into wings in the night sky and developed their vivid color. They were a brilliant pink and shimmered like a precious gem glowing as they floated towards Ginny.

Upon seeing the radiant wings, Ginny heard Beathra say, "This one's yours." As the little one floated downward, she landed in Ginny's arms, and she nearly fell over catching her. The new fairy reached up and grabbed her mother's face with her tiny hands, and that was that. At that moment, Ginny knew she would do anything for her little girl. She named her Ruby because her wings resembled the precious jewel.

Unable to fly home, Ginny carried Ruby in a sling of sorts and tied her to her back. Then Ginny rode Prince, her skypony, back to her farm. This was the beginning of her most excellent adventure yet.

Growing up on the farm, Ruby was celebrated in her uniqueness. She was as rare as the enchanted creatures Ginny rescued. Ruby was a busy little girl that was incredibly excited to learn, frequently getting ahead of her own two feet.

When Ruby fell or tripped, Ginny would scoop her up, dust her off and say, "Slow down, little one, there's plenty of time to learn." But Ruby wouldn't listen, she was wiggly and uninhibited. Which led to several scraped knees, bumps, and bruises. Ruby was full of zeal, and her busyness kept little Ginny on her toes, and she loved every minute of it.

Ginny's heart of compassion hated to see anything suffer. Which may have been why she had such a tender heart towards Ruby's clumsiness. Ginny knew her daughter was special and would do anything to nurture and protect her rareness.

At bedtime, Ginny would lay with Ruby in her canopy bed and tell her how Beathra picked Ruby just for her. The two would giggle, and Ruby would ask for more stories, and Ginny would always oblige.

"You were the most unique and remarkable bloomling I had ever laid eyes on. There were no other gidgies with wings like yours. And those rose gold curls of your stole my heart."

Ruby loved it when her mother recounted her adoption. With bouncing curls and giggles, she would ask her mother to tell her more stories of her growing up. And Ginny always gave in.

After five beautiful years on the farm, Ruby left for Havengothy Gardening University, a live-in school created to prepare fairies for the gardening world. But when she started University, she had a crash course that not all celebrated what her mother called *unique*.

Her clumsiness drew attention to herself, along with her bright wings and wild hair. Her locks would have been the envy of all who lived in the enchanted forest if it weren't for the tangles, tree bark or twigs that knotted her lovely mane. The years of bullying would have been unbearable had it not been for her faithful friends, Sebastian, and Elle.

Ellie was a cute gidgie with long yellow hair that the older girls loved. But poor Ruby wasn't as favored. Her nickname was *weirdo* or *Ruby the weirdo*, and *mop head*. The harsh names did not hurt nearly as much as the stares or rejection that she felt for being different. She was jeered at by students and teachers because she was strange, and *different* scared some gidgies. But one day, a young fairy named Sebastian came to Ruby's rescue.

Ruby was being teased by a group of cheerleading gidgies. She only wanted to hang out with the squad; they had embraced Ellie, so Ruby thought she would naturally be invited into their click. She was wrong; she was not quite the beauty queen they approved of for their circle.

The older girls sat on the bench and hissed at Ruby to go away. Laughing at her weird personality, mocking her embarrassing unruly hair, and detesting her presence. Ruby was devastated and flew away in humiliation.

When Ellie saw the rejection, the squad had inflicted on her friend, she immediately left the caddy girls. What Ruby and Ellie had missed was Sebastian had seen the whole thing.

He sympathized with Ruby's pain and rejection; he had felt it from his family. First by his parents, Jake, and Betty, then by his older brother Jared, who dropped out of school. He bullied Sebastian with cruel acts, such as rolling him up in carpet rolls until Sebastian couldn't move. Then Jared and his friends would put ants on Sebastian's face and head and watch him struggle, trying to escape the insects. Often times Jared would threaten to cut Sebastian's ears off in his sleep.

One day, Sebastian had his belly full of being tormented. One punch to Jared's face, and he spun around and fell face forward into the dirt. Jared never told Jake and Betty how he got his black eye, and he never harassed Sebastian again. So, when Seb (his preferred name) saw Ruby being bullied, something rose up inside of him that compelled him to help.

He quietly snuck behind the mean girls and tied all their uniform belts to the bench. When the bell rang, they tried to launch from their seat, but they all flopped to the ground with a giant thud, some even ripping their school uniform clean off, leaving them in nothing but their bloomers.

It was after this incident that the three became inseparable and could be found helping Ruby pull off her pranks of retaliation.

It was near the end of the year, and Ruby and her friends were set to graduate in a few short months. But what she thought was to come after graduation would not be.

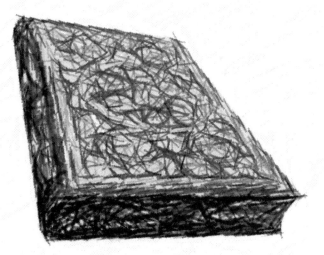

The Secrets Scrolls of Havengothy

Chapter One
The Mystery book.

It was late at night. Ruby silently snuck out of Professor Hill's office in a bit of a panic. She didn't intend to steal the antique book. She had only crept into his office to peak at a few questions for next week's test. But when she saw the tattered volume that looked hundreds of years old, she had to see what was written on its pages.

Professor Hill's small root office was filled with artifacts from all over their enchanted world. Stuffed magical creatures, ancient weapons, scrolls of historical documents, and bookcases filled with small dusty relics.

The old, tattered book sat on Hill's desk, just begging for Ruby to read it. She had just opened the musky pages when she heard someone coming. Ruby quickly hid under Hill's desk until the voices faded down the long root hall. She then stuffed the book under her shirt, and as soon as the coast was clear, snuck from the professor's office and flew back to her root dorm.

Fascinated by the archive, she laid in her bed reading into the night. The book felt different, magical. But now she had a new dilemma. She may not have swiped the questions for the test for Sebastian, but how on earth would she ever return the book? And did she even want to?

The next day: Ruby was drifting off in class. She tried to disguise her sleepiness by placing her face in her hands as she propped herself up on her desk. She had stayed up way too late reading the magical pages, but now she was falling asleep in geography class.

Ellie kicked Ruby's chair to wake her. Surprised by the jerk of her chair, Ruby jolted awake with a snort and then fell over backward in her chair, somersaulting. Ellie watched in horror as Ruby tumbled awkwardly, head over heels.

Frantically acting, she grabbed Ruby's arm and pulled her upright in an attempt to save her dignity. It was too late; the class saw the disaster and was now roaring in laughter.

Ruby sat back down before the professor saw the fiasco, but the class was in a chaotic uproar of hilarity. The upside: Ruby was wide awake.

"Settle down, class! Settle down," Professor Hill squeaked with his gentle voice. "I will release you in just a few minutes. Until then, why not rest your wings as I recount our marvelous beginning." With a twinkle in his eye, he began…

"There are wonders all over Havengothy. Even its name is wonderful, meaning *Haven of Hope*. When one walks the lands or flies through the atmosphere of this hallowed place, goosebumps crawl up the arms of visitors and residents alike. You can feel the hope hovering. Life is felt like a tingle in the air. The spirits that rule our land are good but fierce. Our creators, the Great Tree King, Beathra, and The Whisper, are the ones who fashioned and gave life to our world. All us gidgies come from Beathra. Our gift of flight, sense of purpose and our precious fire seed all come from the King of Trees."

Professor Hill paused for a moment to take a sip of his hot pinkle pepper brew, then he cleared his throat and continued. "Beathra and The Whisper come from one source: the heart of the Mighty Ghost Warrior, a fierce and mystical God, full of fire and joy. Moses, the oldest elder of our time, tells of the Great Ghost Warrior who lives in the clouds high above the Hyperion Mountain Range and uses the summit as a footstool. When the Ghost Warrior laughs, sparks fly from his mouth like little embers that ignite joy, creating the stars, planets, and new worlds. When you see a falling star, the chances are, there is a celebration in his world. Returning from a great victory, this Mighty Ghost Warrior was in a full belly laugh the day The Whisper came to be. The sparks of his life-giving laughter were caught by a mystical wind blowing in from the southern sky. It was an ancient cry from the Ghost Warrior himself that had been floating in the atmosphere from a former battle that he lost years ago."

The lesson was suddenly interrupted by a bellowing, "ACHOO!! ACHOO!! ACHOO!!" Lewis, a blonde-haired and winged, gidgie had a sneezing fit just as Professor Hill was about to explain the great collision.

"The weeping…"

"ACHOO!"

"The weeping…"

"ACHOO, ACHOO, ACHOO!!!"

In frustration, Professor Hill squeaked, "Lewis, please go see the Healer's station to take something for your cold."

"It's not a cold pwofessuh, it's allogeez." The stuffy nosed Lewis tried to explain.

Billick, another classmate, remarked in a snarky tone, "Who has ever heard of a gidgie allergic to his own garden? That's ridiculous. You just need to drink more water and workout Lewis." Billick then flashed a smile, flexed his muscles to show off his biceps, and winked at the girls.

The class all bellowed in laughter. Then, Trixie, a lavender winged gidgie with short dark purple hair, shot back, "Maybe he's allergic to Ruby, she *is* sitting right next to him. Perhaps something died in that nest on her head. Lewis should be grateful he can't smell the weirdo."

Trixie was always teasing Lewis, and his horrible allergies made him an easy target. And if she got a chance to bully Ruby, even better. However, Lewis always looked at Trixie in a way that made her feel guilty about how she treated him.

"Very funny, Trix, everyone knows it's your foul perfume that makes him hack like an old man." Sebastian snapped. Trixie darted Sebastian a dirty look, but she shut up.

Ruby ignored Trixie's insult this time. Ruby had just gotten out of detention from her last retaliation when she replaced Trixie's toothpaste with ink. Trixie's teeth were as purple as her hair for a week.

Ruby was sentenced to a month of detention, helping Professor Whitmore with the larva nursery of Havengothy. The awful job made her queasy. She had to handle maggots, grubs, larva, and earthworms.

Professor Hill clapped his hands loudly and, at the top of his feeble voice, yelled, "ENOUGH OF THIS NONSENSE!" It wasn't often that Hill raised his voice, so when he did, it got everyone's attention. He then proceeded with his lesson.

"Now, where was I? Oh yes! The weeping wind collided with the spark of laughter from the Ghost Warrior, which triggered a bright flash and a burst of embers. As the flame of the Mighty Spirit and the mystical wind wandered, they drifted from atmospheres and planets until they merged together as one. Perhaps you have felt one of those gusts over you before. If so, it's possible you felt the presence of The Whisper. When the warm breeze finally landed on the mountain range of Darphea, it made the sound of a low, hushed voice, like that of a whisper. Longing for companionship, The Whisper took a portion of the fire that lived within her from the Warrior Spirit himself and used it as a seed and planted Beathra, the King of Trees. The life-giving fire grew into the most magnificent and majestic tree. And when we bloom, we too receive a piece of the warrior's spark, known as our fire seed. To this day, in the center of The King of Tree's glows the flame from the Great Ghost Warrior."

The bell rang interrupting the professors lesson. All the students bolted from their desks, papers flying everywhere behind them. Professor Hill had to raise his small voice over the noise of the excited class to give them their homework assignments. "I want a five-page essay on the Banishment War and turned in by next Monday at the start of class."

Trixie flew by Lewis, knocking him down and causing him to topple his pile of books. She looked back at him, and he gave her one of his soul-piercing gazes. Trixie looked away, ashamed, and rushed to catch up with her love interest.

Ruby and Ellie were dashing out of class to find Sebastian when Ruby was stopped by Billick. He was a year older than her but was held back last year. Billick loved to tease Ruby. He taunted her about her messy hair, crooked smile, her strange imagination, and so on. It didn't matter, he was relentless with his poking fun, and it always got the best of Ruby's temper.

"Hey ya, little red-haired weirdo!" Billick shouted as Ruby walked by, "I think Trixie was right; a critter has made a home in that nest of yours." Billick flashed a grin.

He thought he was clever. He then looked at the group of girls that followed him around and gave a charming smirk. They all started giggling at the joke made at Ruby's expense, and they swooned. Trixie laughed the loudest of them all.

Billick was handsome, with his dark green wings, green eyes, and broad frame. Sure, he was easy to look at, and he always had a way of making the girls laugh, but to Ruby, he was impossible to tolerate.

"Billick, you're a grub eating snout nose. And you smell like atto-glider poop!" Ruby yelled. Her hands were in fists, and she was poised to punch him in his perfectly straight teeth when Instructor Kay was spotted coming down the long hall.

Ellie grabbed Ruby's elbow and said, "He's not worth detention again, let's go."

Ruby looked at Billick with fire in her eyes. Every fiber in her wanted to punch his flawless grin. But Ellie continued to pull at her. She looked back at Billick, with a finger sliding across her neck, and mouthed the words, "next time."

He smiled and winked at her just to taunt her more. This always made Trixie resent Ruby. Trixie could never understand why he teased the little freak.

"I hate him so much," Ruby muttered. "One of these days I'm going to get even with that weasel. Ooooh, and that horrible flock of hens that follow him around hanging off his every word, will finally see him for what he is, a big phony! I don't understand what they find so appealing about the dung heap," she seethed.

Ellie knew exactly what they saw in him, she saw it too. Billick was cute, funny, confidant, and had a way of winning everyone except Ruby. He was also arrogant and could subtly manipulate others to get what he wanted. Billick often teased Ruby just to get a laugh from Instructor Kay and the following flock of girls. If it made himself look good, he didn't care who paid the price. And that's what Ruby despised about him; he had no loyalty.

Ellie has had a secret crush on him since she started learning at Havengothy Gardening University as a young gidgie. She saw what most saw; a handsome fairy that was smart and athletic. But she could never tell Ruby this, it would be the biggest betrayal of all time. Billick and Ruby had always had bad blood.

To like someone that her best friend despised would destroy Ruby. Devotion and loyalty meant everything to her. Ellie stuffed her crush deep down inside and hated Billick for Ruby's sake.

The only one who was equal to Billick in athletics and academics was Sebastian. Billick never bullied Ruby in front of Seb, he would not stand for it. Instead, Billick always waited for her to be alone or with Ellie. He knew Ellie wouldn't confront him because he saw the way she looked at him. Even instructor Kay, who everyone called I.K., frequently singled out Ruby to embarrass her, unless Sebastian was around. Most of her tormentors left Ruby alone when Seb was nearby.

Ruby and Ellie were meeting Sebastian at their favorite hideout, a secret fort in the fickle fruit bush. It was a twisty shrub with fuzzy green globes of fruit that was way too sweet and its seeds extremely sour, but when eaten together... perfection.

Sebastian was at the fort and had already picked some fickle fruit and snagged a few millie fruits from the Camillicent tree near Malcolm's root. Millie fruit was a favorite of the gidgies. Its ever-changing flavors gave the partakers a surprise with each orb they picked from sweet and flavorful, like a key lime pie, to horrid and putrid like rotting potatoes.

The two girls finally arrived at the hideout. To enter, they had to go through an ivy curtain that draped from the fir tree growing next to the fickle fruit. It was the lushest of ivy, and there was no other vine quite like it in all of the garden. This remarkable vine crawled up the fir tree and then cascaded downward as a green waterfall of leaves. This made the concealment of their hideout even more mysterious.

"Hello, beautiful, you are looking as gorgeous and green as always," Ruby said to the rich emerald, ivy. She pulled the greenery back as one would tie back draperies. Ellie loved it when Ruby held back the vines, they seemed to draw back before she even touched them.

"What took you guys so long?" Sebastian asked. He had eaten nearly half the millie fruit waiting for them.

"Sorry, Seb, that rotten Billick tried to detain us," Ruby explained.

"I hope you let him have it." Sebastian cheered.

"I couldn't, tomato face, I.K. was coming, Ellie had to pull me away before I got detention again," Ruby informed.

"It's a good thing I did, last time Ruby got under I.K.'s skin, she had to pull weeds for a week in the school's activity field." Ellie defended herself.

"Man, if I was in charge of Havengothy University, that I.K, would have been demoted to grub control. And will somebody please make him stop singing his blasted opera songs. My ears are bleeding." Sebastian stated emphatically.

"No, kidding! Last week when he handed out our graded assignments, he actually sang my grade out loud for everyone to hear. 'Ruuubeeee has a DEEEEEE' I could have died. I mean, good grief. I realize I struggle with my spelling, but does everyone need to know how bad I am? Sheesh!" Ruby shouted in frustration.

Ruby hated that she did so poorly in her writing and spelling assignments, and I.K. loved to humiliate her. He thought it might motivate her if he embarrassed her. All it did was make her loathe him more and cause her to have anxiety on her tests.

"Keep your voices down. This is supposed to be our secret hideout. With the way you guys are bellowing, we might as well put a sign out welcoming anyone and everyone. We need to focus! We have a serious paper to write, and I, for one, am not going to let anyone stand in my way of grades. Who's been studying the history of Havengothy and the Banishment war?" The ever-studious Ellie asked in a chiding tone.

Sebastian and Ruby conceded and went to join Ellie on the makeshift chairs, the three of them made from branches and rocks. "I have been studying, but I'm stumped on one thing; why didn't The Whisper strip Neeradima's powers when she turned evil. I mean, The Whisper created her to be the Forest caretaker, and she gave her all these powers. Why not destroy her? Or at least her ability to do magic when Neeradima grew jealous," Sebastian asked.

"Because, you blockhead, if you had studied further back, you would have seen that when a prophecy is given from The Whisper or Beathra, its irrevocable. It's part of an ancient prophecy from the Ghost Warrior himself. Honestly, how far did you read in the history book anyway," Ellie scoffed.

"I don't know." Seb shrugged. "But I do know she will have a day of reckoning, and I am going to be there," Sebastian said, sounding valiant.

"That prophecy is not in the history book. It's an old wives' tale. Nobody believes in that catastrophic legend." Ellie said, rolling her eyes.

"Joseppi does," Seb defended.

"Of course, he does, he's probably one of those conspiracists." Ellie taunted with a grin.

Ruby interrupted their argument. "You guys won't believe what I found in an old book."

"What?" both Sebastian and Ellie said in unison.

Ruby had their attention and began to relay what she had read the night before, acting out the details in a demonstrative way.

"Neeradima has planted corrupt seeds here, in Havengothy. Horrible plants that distort the minds of those who eat it or even handle its leaves. Apparently, the seeds cause the victim to be absorbed by their greatest fears or selfish desires. Not only that, but I also read in the book, she created this Tragedy Tree thing. It is so vile; its seeds drop and are covered in black sticky goo."

Ruby made sure as she told the story to be extremely dramatic. In her sensational way, she acted out the awfulness of the account with a gloom and doom tone. "It adheres to anything that comes in contact with it, and they can't shake it off. The seeds are covered in barbed hooks that burrow in, inflicting more pain trying to remove it."

She then put her hands around her throat to display the suffering. "choking the life out of its poor victim. The only pain relief is Meredith Barry's merrybare, berry bush brew." Ruby said in a serious tone.

Seb and Ellie sat in silence, thoroughly enjoying Ruby's theatrics. Then they both busted into laughter.

"You're making this up! That intoxicating brew is only for festivals. Plus, if this was the case, the University would teach this information to prepare us." Ellie snorted.

"It's true! The only way for them to endure the tragedy seed removal is the giggling effects of Meredith Barry's, merrybare, berry bush brew. Read it for yourself!" Ruby shoved the old book into Ellie's hands.

Ellie looked at the tattered volume and read who the author was then asked, "Who in the world is Melchizedek? I've never heard of him. And where in Havengothy, did you get this antique?"

Ruby shrugged, "I have no idea who he is, but he's written some remarkable accounts in detail. As for where I got it? It was sort of in Professor Hill's office. And I saw it tucked under some papers on his desk. Aaaand, I sort of borrowed it. Without him knowing. I mean, it practically called my name, how could I resist. And why wouldn't he want us to know about them?" Ruby replied sheepishly.

"How am I supposed to cover for you if I don't know what you are up to? And how in the world did you happen to be in his office? He has precious artifacts from all over our world he collects. He never allows anyone in there without permission. So, what were you doing in there?" Ellie asked, irritated.

Sebastian answered that for Ruby. "She was doing me a favor. I asked her to sneak into his office and see if she could find our next exam questions just so I could study them. I wasn't cheating, I didn't want the answers, just the questions." He said, defending himself.

"You two are the worst! And how in the world do you plan on writing a paper from a book you stole? Don't you think Professor Hill will figure out you swiped one of his antique collections? And how in Havengothy are you not cheating by knowing the test questions?" Ellie said in a raised voice.

"I borrowed it, and I'm not gonna write about it in our paper, but why would he be hiding this information from us? I'm just curious. I never did find the test, I had to hurry and get out of his root, but when I saw this old book title, "The Secrets Scrolls of Havengothy" I had to grab it. And anyways, Sebastian's not cheating. He just wanted a heads up on his studies. I thought you would approve of that." Ruby said defensively.

"This is driving me crazy. Can we just work on our papers like we came here to do? Using the actual books we are assigned?" Ellie emphatically asked.

"Fine." Ruby and Sebastian both conceded in unison. The three worked on their homework, sharing their studies, and chatting about life after the University.

"Are you going to Ginny's root this summer Rubes?" Ellie asked with a mouth full of fickle fruit.

Ellie never went home during the summer months. She either stayed at the school or went with Ruby to Ginny's farm. Ellie loved being at the boarding school more than going back to Walter and Wanda's root. They were nice enough but were loud and seemed to always argue about the smallest of things. Plus, Wanda was a hoarder who clashed with the very tidy, organized Ellie. She enjoyed her summers with Ruby and Ginny but would often stay at the school to progress her studies.

"Probably so. I haven't decided on my career yet. I like the idea of working with Gin on her farm. She wants me to move home after school and come work with her, but she's been dating this adorable guy named Duke, and I think it's pretty serious. I would just feel in the way." Ruby answered.

"You would be amazing working with the vines of Havengothy, Ruby. You're a natural." Ellie suggested with a sincere belief in her friend.

"You know what I want; I've talked about it for the past three years. All I want to do is be a professor at one of the branches of the University. Midyear, I applied to go to ALC, but haven't heard what branch I will be assigned for my teaching degree, that is if I'm accepted."

ALC stood for Advance Learning Center and was like a college. It's where gidgies went to continue their education. They were all over Havengothy, and different branches offered higher training in specialty areas. Due to a gidgies life span, they could continue to grow their education in a variety of centers if they chose.

Sebastian had been quiet while the girls were chatting about life after school. He had been waiting to tell them his news but wasn't sure how Ruby would take it. After graduation, Seb would only have the summer before leaving for training. He decided to interrupt their giggle-fest with some information he recently heard about.

"Did you guys know that Neeradima is trying to grow her army again? There have been sightings of her filthy liath servants near the edge of the Darphea Wilderness. In fact, there have even been a handful of abductions the council is keeping under wraps until they know more."

Ruby and Ellie looked at him in shock. "How do you know this, Seb?" Ellie asked.

"Does this mean there will be another war?" Ruby inquired with wide eyes.

"There's no way! The Banishment war prevented her from ever entering Havengothy again. She was stripped of using her power here. She can't even cross the Darphea Wilderness that separates us from her kingdom." Ellie replied emphatically.

"Well, I've heard from my recruiter that another war is coming," Sebastian said in a hushed tone.

Ruby and Ellie sat shocked. What was Sebastian saying? "What do you mean, your recruiter?" Ruby asked with a concerned look. "You said you were thinking of training as a Skyguard." A Skyguard was a policeman for Havengothy.

"I was accepted into the Skyforce. I passed the obstacle course, and I leave the end of summer for cadet training." Sebastian informed them with a sheepish grin.

"I thought you were considering a career as an engineer. Are you thinking of being an engineer in the Skyforce?" Ellie asked, interested.

"Joseppi really helped me with my future. I was having a hard time deciding, and the Skyforce seemed like a good fit. I want to help our gidgies and be a part of the rescue team." Sebastian answered, defending his decision to be part of a Special Task Force.

Ruby was not nearly as intrigued as Ellie. If she was honest, she felt a speck of fear tug at her heart the moment Sebastian mentioned the military.

"So, let me get this straight, you are joining the Skyforce, and there might be another war? Anything else you care to drop on our laps today, Sebastian?" Ruby asked, irritated.

Chapter Two
Ruby's scheme

Ruby and Ellie made their way back to their root dorms before dinner. Ruby was quiet; Sebastian leaving for cadet school weighed heavily on her. The anxiety she felt was more than just graduation. It was more than all three of them going separate ways. Something felt different.

And though Ruby was not given to fear, she could feel a change in the air. She believed what Sebastian said, or at least part of it; things were changing in Havengothy. Was it a war? She didn't know, but she did know something was coming.

"Are you going to come down for dinner?" Ellie ventured, noticing Ruby's melancholy mood.

"Nah, I think I'm gonna go to my room and read," she answered.

Ruby plopped on her bed and pulled out the tattered book she *borrowed* from the professor. "Why does Professor Hill have this book," she wondered. Cracking it open, she found a page that was dog eared. It was an ancient spell Neeradima used to grow the plants in Havengothy.

"She had everything she could ever want here in Havengothy. How could she betray the King and The Whisper?" Ruby thought to herself.

Just then, she heard Beathra speak to her heart, "Jealousy is a maddening seed. When it takes root, it will destroy even the most wonderful of my creations."

"You're telling me," She agreed out loud to an empty room.

Ruby was accustomed to hearing Beathra and the Whisper's voice. It started when she was very young and was hiding in a Merrybare berry bush. I.K. had humiliated her once again. He mocked her publicly making fun of her school picture.

It wasn't the most flattering painting of her, it was during her awkward years, and she tried a new hairstyle. She had cut her hair herself but went a tad too short. Curly hair shrinks after its cut, causing Ruby's bangs to coil up tight near the top of her forehead. And if that wasn't bad enough, she had run into a tree branch the first part of the week and had a horrible raspberry-like rash on her upper lip.

The artist rendition of her made Ruby look like a bald man with a red mustache. The eccentric artist could have painted her without the rash, or even made her hair look a bit longer, but he was all about "authentic" and Ruby's authentic awkward shone through like a sunbeam.

To top off this horrific day, when I.K. was passing out the portrait packages, he came across Ruby's and began to laugh out loud. Then, he flashed her dreadful picture to the rest of the class. Ruby was so humiliated; she snatched the canvas out of his hands and ran out of the room.

Hiding in the Merrybare bush, she wept. She hated how different she was. She asked Beathra why he would make such a mistake with her, giving her extremely bright wings and wild hair. She begged him to make her smart, pretty, or athletic. She was average in every way except her bold wings and messy hair. The combination of those two made her stand out all the more for others to witness her failures.

As she wept, she felt the presence of a warm breeze blow in. It wrapped around her, hugging her. Then, she heard The Whisper speak in a still small voice, "Ruby, you are precious to us. We love your uniqueness, and we made it for our delight. Your joy in the little things brings joy to us. The way you love your friends is as fierce as the great warrior himself."

Ruby then felt her fire seed speak inside of her heart. It was the oddest thing. She could hear Beathra's voice within her. And his answer to her questions washed over her like cleansing water. Removing all the shame, she felt for being different.

"Ruby, make no mistake, what you call different we call rare. What you think is a mistake, we call a masterpiece. Take heart little one; we have great and wonderful things planned for your life. If we removed all that was difficult, we would also remove all that helps you grow into your destiny. Lean into us, and we will show you the way."

Ruby rested against the foot of her bed, smiling at her wonderful memory of the great spirits. She had come a long way since that day. Back then, she was ready to run away and never return. Even though leaving Havengothy would be like a fish wanting to pack its bags and live on land, Ruby knew no one could make her stay.

Gidgies are free to leave their beloved forest, but they were made for their garden, and living outside of it was hard and cruel. Leaving also made them an easy target when they left the shelter of their King Tree.

To the north of Havengothy was the Darphea Mountain Range, and further north the gigantic Hyperion Mountains where mystical and magical beasts dwelled. To the south of Havengothy, the Quartz gulf and to the east, the Broad River, the home of the water gidgies. To the west was perhaps the most dangerous of all terrains to cross; The cursed land of the Darphea Wilderness.

To leave the garden, without proper supplies or training, could kill a gidgie. Outside of their sacred land, Neeradima's soldiers, the liaths, were always hunting, looking for wayward or isolated beings to snatch.

Now, here Ruby sat, having a casual conversation with her King. She is still learning to love who they made her, but at least she has finally learned to like herself.

She continued to read the old book and came across a chapter that included the spell that Neeradima used to sing over Havengothy. This charm was to encourage growth and help the garden to bloom. Though Ruby didn't know the tune; she could almost hear it in her head.

Reach towards the sky, crawl out of the earth.
Uncurl your leaves, and let your blooms burst.
The King and the Whisper made you for a reason,
now come forth all that's green, today is your season.
It's time to grow.

This spell was pure and good and filled with a deep love. But now, the only magic coming from the wicked enchantress was that of poison and hatred.

Ruby had that sinking feeling wash over her again; Havengothy was changing. She then felt a dread about Sebastian joining the Skyforce. "Why do I care so much about what he does? It's not like we're a couple," she chided herself.

If Ruby was honest, she would have admitted she did have feelings for Seb. However, she kept them concealed for fear of rejection. Ruby's stomach grumbled loudly. She wished she had at least gone to the kitchen and asked Yoli, the head fairy of the cafeteria, for some cake and some pinkle pepper brew. Oh well, she would just have to wait until morning.

There was a scratching on her root door, then a kick. She put her book down and went to see what the commotion was. It was Ellie with a tray of food for Ruby. Her faithful friend was trying to open the door to their root with her foot so as not to spill the pinkle pepper tea.

"Ell, you are the best! How did you know I would be starving? Did Sebastian ask where I was? Oh, forget that I asked that. Thanks for bringing me sustenance." Ruby took the tray from Ellie's hand so she could come in.

"I told Yoli, you were down with a headache, and she made you a tray of food. And yes, Seb did ask where you were. I told him you were studying. You know Ruby, you guys could just admit you like each other, rather than play this stupid game of *we're just friends*." Ellie suggested.

"We are just friends. At least I think we are. I don't even know how I feel. I do know *what* I feel; fearful for him to join the Skyforce. I have this sinking feeling that something bad is coming. I sound crazy, don't I?" Ruby asked.

"Not crazy, but maybe in love." Ellie ventured. Ruby gave her a darting look.

"Don't look at me like that, Rubes. Am I the only one that can see that you two like each other? This is ridiculous! You are feeling afraid because he will be going away for months to train, and Havengothy is huge. Who knows where he will end up being stationed? I think you are afraid of losing him. That's what I think, anyway." Ellie finished her thought with a matter-of-fact tone.

Ruby plopped on her bed. She looked at the tray that sat before her. Ellie had made sure she had plenty of honey for her pinkle pepper brew, and she even took the tomatoes out of her sandwich. Yoli always forgot Ruby hated tomatoes, but not her best friend. Ellie thought of everything.

Ruby went sullen for a brief second; how would she endure all the changes coming? She stirred the honey in her drink and washed down the lump in her throat, along with her sandwich. Taking a cleansing breath, Ruby smiled, "I have thought about how I want to get even with Billick for one last hoorah before school is out."

"Do tell," Ellie said with a smirk.

"It involves the needles from the pinkle pepper plant," Ruby explained her plot to Ellie. It would take all three of them to pull it off, but if it worked, it would be her greatest prank yet.

The Pinkle Peppers

Chapter Three
Pinkle Peppers

Ruby, Ellie, and Sebastian sat in their separate classes, watching the hours slowly tick away. They had scheduled an emergency meeting in their fort to plot Ruby's great practical joke against Billick. However, it seemed that warm spring days were the worst time to be sitting in class; the hours tended to pass at a snail's pace. Plus, the large root classrooms, though roomy, managed to hold the sun's heat when it was hitting it just right, torturing the students all the more, that a beautiful day awaited them.

Havengothy was in full bloom, and it was one of the loveliest springs it had experienced in ages. All the seasonal fragrances were exploding, and the air dripped of its wonderful, perfumed scent. Lavender, jasmine, vanilla, and lilacs were bursting as well as the sweet scent of the pine trees. Spring was not to be missed in the magical forest.

The highlight of the season was the Bloom Festival. It was just around the corner, and this meant one had a chance to see the visitation of The Whisper and possibly witness the bloom of new gidgies. No one knew when the exact year the blooming would happen, but they always happened during a spring carnival. This year was full of anticipation of things to come.

Finally, the bell rang, and the three friends rushed out of class to meet at the hideout. As Ruby was shoving her way through the crowd of students, she saw Ellie chatting with Billick. She was smiling all weird and batting her eyelashes.

"What in the world is she doing?" Ruby thought. "Is she flirting with him?"

Ellie is a tall slim fairy with golden hair and sunflower yellow wings. Ruby and Ellie endured teasing together when they were young. However, Ellie's transformation into a slender, beautiful fairy, hushed the harassers.

And there she was, leaning against the wall of Beathra's roots, with her knee bent back with her foot resting against it, as she held her books and slid her hair behind her ears, smiling at BILLICK!

"Cool down, Ruby," she told herself. "She may just be getting intel from him to help with the plan." Ruby looked back at Ellie and Billick chatting and decided to ignore it, she had too much on her mind. She made her way out of the school, towards the fort in record speed.

Upon arrival, Ruby flew down to the entrance and thought about trying the charm she read in the old book. She reached out to touch the vines and got exceptionally close to them as one would to tell a secret. She was about to whisper the spell when Sebastian landed next to her.

"What are you doing with the ivy? It looked like you were about to make out with it," Seb teased.

"I was going to do nothing of the sort! I was just admiring its beauty." Ruby said, hoping he bought her fib.

"You have always had a talent with the crawling stuff Rubes. Where's Ellie? Is she not coming today?" Seb inquired, secretly hoping for some time with just Ruby.

"I have no idea. When I left, she was swooning over Billick!" Ruby said, annoyed.

"Yeah, I've noticed she's been a little sweet on him. I hope this doesn't ruin the plan," Seb said.

"What do you mean she's been sweet on him? Are you saying Ellie likes Billick? That can't be. She would tell me. Why would she keep that a secret from me?" Ruby wondered and asked shockingly.

"Because you hate him. And Ellie is a loyal friend and would never want to betray you. Good grief Rubes, you're not too observant, are you?" Seb paused for a few seconds, then pushed past his nerves and mustered the courage to ask what had been on his heart this last year.

He did not know when things shifted exactly, he just knew his feelings for Ruby were changing. She wasn't like the other girls; she loved to laugh, be silly, and have adventures. Ruby wasn't the type to be primping in front of a looking glass. She was the kind of girl who loved to chase the wooly atto-gliders and watch their glowing hooves streak across the night sky. Ruby loved them and often tried to catch one to tame.

"Speaking of observant...I was gonna ask you something, and since Ellie's not here, this would be a perfect time." Sebastian was nervous but continued with his venture. "I was wondering if you were gonna go to the Bloom Festival, and if you wanted to, uh... well, uh, go with me?"

Ruby looked at him, and without thinking, blurted out, "We always go to the Bloom Festival together, dork. Of course, I'll…Oh, wait a minute. Are you…" Ruby was tripping over her words. It just dawned on her that Sebastian was asking her to the Bloom Festival, but not as a friend, as a date. Now she felt like a fool.

She looked at him, and his face was flush. He was a handsome gidgie, who was often guessed older than he was. And though he wasn't tall, he was broad and athletically built. His black hair had specks of blue that reflected his brilliant blue wings. And then there were the dimples in his giant smile. It was the best when Ruby was having a bad day.

Seb had a way of encouraging Ruby. One particular time was when I.K. was punishing Ruby for misspelled words on a test. He had her fly laps for every word that was spelled wrong.

It was a cold and rainy fall day, and Ruby had been outside for over an hour. As soon as Seb realized Ruby was being disciplined, he flew out with his coat to give to her, he then flew next to her, until her last lap was done. Often times putting his hand on her back, pushing her to finish. To say he has always been a devoted friend would sound trite. Sebastian was a steadfast and faithful friend. Ruby had to be honest with herself at this moment; she had been waiting for this day.

"I would love to go to the Bloom, Flestival…I mean, Bloom Flestival. Ugh, why can't I say it? Bloom Flestival!" Ruby yelled. "Sheesh! You know what I mean!" She blurted out.

Sebastian and Ruby laughed till their sides hurt. And in true Ruby form, her giggle fit led to her snorting. The two young gidgies laughed all the louder. Just then, Ellie walked into the hilarity. Sebastian and Ruby tried to compose themselves, but the tears of laughter were still falling, and stifling the chuckles made it worse.

"Don't stop on my account. What's so hilarious?" Ellie asked, smiling.

"Nothing, I just said something wrong, and it struck us funny," Ruby answered with a feeling of being caught at doing something wrong. "Where have you been anyway?" Asked Ruby a little too sharply.

"Oh, I had to stay after class for a few minutes to ask someone a question," Ellie answered vaguely.

"Would that someone be Billick?" Ruby fired out with a sharp tone, and her arms crossed.

Ellie looked mortified that Ruby knew, and she felt ashamed. "Don't worry, Ruby, nothing happened. If you must know, I asked him to the Bloom Festival."

"At least someone can say it," Sebastian said with a snicker.

"What?" Ellie asked confused by his sarcasm. She then continued her defense as to why she was late. "You may not have known, but I've had a little crush on him since our third year in school. I am embarrassed to even admit that now. I hate myself for liking the guy that all the weak-minded twits follow around like a puppy. And he's a poser, I know that, but there's this charm and charisma about him, and he winks at me sometimes. I just figured since we are all about to graduate, after fifteen years of school together, I would take a chance and ask him to the festival."

Ellie's eyes were glossy with tears from the embarrassment and rejection. "But he already had someone in mind. He was nice enough about it. In fact, he was extra nice. I had never seen him that kind before. It almost makes me feel bad that we're about to prank him…almost. But since he turned me down, I am ready to fry him."

Ruby ran to her friend and gave her a big hug. "You are too good for that swamp rat. Let's make him regret rejecting you. Sound good?" Ruby said with a smile.

"That sounds perfect. I picked up some long stems from the pinkle pepper bush in Mr. Ryster's herb patch. He was great about letting me take as much as I wanted. He was going to cut just the berries off the top of the plant, but I made sure he gave me stems and all. I didn't tell him why I needed the needles of the stalk; I didn't think he would approve of our use of them." Ellie explained as she carefully pulled the long stems from her bag.

Mr. Ryster had wrapped the stickery stalks in brown paper careful to preserve the bouquet of pinkle peppers. Seb, Ellie, and Ruby got to work cautiously, removing the long thin sliver like thorns from the stalks. It was delicate work, and they would often prick themselves with the sharp tips of the pepper needles.

"I just had a horrible thought. What if Billick is part of the small percent that's allergic to pinkle peppers or its needles? Has anyone actually seen him drink it?" Ellie said horrified, as she sucked the blood off the tip of her fingers after a nasty poke from the barbs.

"That's highly unlikely, Ell. The percentage of gidgies that are allergic to the favorite drink is pretty low." Sebastian informed.

"Plus, it's just the needle, not the actual pepper berry. What are the odds of someone being allergic to only the needles?" Ruby stated with more confidence than she felt.

Chapter Four
Billick's butt

"Ruby, you are such a nuisance!" I.K. muttered under his breath after she had run into the side of him. She was rushing to her next class and was frantically gathering the pinkle pepper needles from her locker when she ran out of time. She had to stuff the delicate bag of thorns in her book bag and fly as top speed for Geography class.

I.K. was fat, so fat in fact, Ruby's tiny body ramming into his flabby side made her bounce back and hit her head on the root wall, giving her a nasty bump.

"Young lady, there is no flying in the halls. I want to see you in my office after school. You need to learn a lesson or two on following instructions," he snorted. He then turned on his chunky heels and continued down the hall to yell at a group of fresh gidgies for laughing in a serious setting.

Going to I.K.'s office would throw a wrench in her plans. She, Seb, and Ellie were hoping to be long gone after the prank. They just had to make it to the last few minutes of Geography class, and that's when the three could execute the plan.

Plotting the prank had to be well organized. The last class of the day on a Friday afternoon was the perfect time for their practical joke.

Ruby was late to Geography class due to her blunder with Instructor Kay. Sebastian looked at her with wide eyes, as to question where she had been. She mouthed the words, "I'll tell you later."

Ellie saved a seat for Ruby near the front. Miss Milton, the professor, noticed Ruby's tardiness and turned to address her. "Ruby, you are tardy, I would like to see you after class. We are nearing the end of the year young lady, and it is no time to get lackadaisical."

"Get in line," Ruby mumbled and took an exhausted breath.

"What was that?" Miss Milton asked, pulling her glasses to the end of her long pointy nose. With her hair pulled into a tight bun and her incredibly tall, skinny figure, she looked like a skeleton.

"Nothing, ma'am," Ruby answered.

"I thought so. Now, where was I? Oh yes, the Broad River. The Broad River is east of Havengothy. And is known to us as the

Emperor of rivers. He is broad as he is wide. The river is alive and is a life form of its own. Many visitors mistake the Broad River for an ocean. Can anyone tell me where the Broad River flows into?"

Lewis raised his hand. Miss Milton looked around, hoping another gidgie would want to answer. No one did. "Go ahead, Lewis." She acknowledged.

Lewis sniffed a couple of times and then began, "Sniff, sniff. The Bwodd Wivuh flows into the Cotes Gofe, which is the home of the leviathan and singing whales." Lewis sniffed, then snorted a good long snort and then coughed. The magnificent spring was destroying him.

"That's the Quartz Gulf, for those who didn't quite... eh, hear Lewis. The Quartz Gulf opens to the Sequestia sea. Has any of you students visited the gulf or the sea on vacation with your family?" Miss Milton inquired of the class.

Lewis raised his hand again, but Miss Milton pretended like she couldn't see him. She then looked to Ellie and asked if she wouldn't mind sharing a little about the waters of Havengothy.

Ellie could practically teach this class. She knew everything there was to know about the topography of Havengothy and its streams. The only one who knew more at the school about the waters in the forest was Professor Hill. His job as an engineer for the Skyforce often had him building bridges, canals, and water ducts.

Lewis looked hurt that Miss Milton ignored him, but got over it quickly, he knew why she had little patience with him, and it wasn't his allergies. Miss Milton was jilted at the altar, and since that day, she became withdrawn and depressed. She had also picked up a bad habit to ease her pain.

He took his hanky out and blew a tremendous loud blow and then wiped his red nose. Lewis was a good-looking gidgie, but his allergies hid his handsomeness and made him despised due to all the gross sounds that came from him. He huffed a couple times on his puff-puff gourd and sat back in his chair with glassy, allergy eyes and looked miserable.

Ellie stood up and, being the ever prepared and studious fairy, didn't miss a beat to describe the Quartz Gulf and the Sequestia Sea.

"There are mystical creatures that live in the Broad River, gulf, and ocean. They are neither friends nor foes. They guard the waters and its creatures that live in it. The Whisper created the creatures of the waters by blowing over it. When she blew, the sparks from the Great Ghost Warrior, that lived in her, landed in the river. Rather than a sizzle, the embers bubbled and created life. Her breath was like the force of a hurricane, hitting the waters, thus creating the Quartz Gulf. Her exhale stirred the waters, and giant waves rolled and then began to gurgle. That's when the river gidgies emerged. They have fin-like wings on their backs, so it appears as if they are flying in the water. Their feet and hands are webbed, but no one knows or understands how they breathe underwater, they just do."

"Thanks, Ellie, that was informative. I can definitely tell you will make a great teacher someday." Said the exhausted professor. "Can I get my teachers assistant to come and pass out the lessons. Billick, would you also please make sure everyone has an information sheet on the waters of Havengothy?"

This was the time-of-day Miss Milton checked out. As the papers were being passed out, she sat at her desk and sipped her tea that made her sleepy. It was suspected her drink was laced with wizard weed to calm her nerves and ease her jilted heart. Whatever it was, she was sipping; it created the perfect opportunity to execute the plan. Miss Milton took a book in her hand and pretended to read as she nodded off.

That was the cue. It was now or never for the three to pull off this prank. Ruby looked at Ellie and gave her the nod. As Billick wandered around the room passing out papers, he also made sure he lingered where the pretty girls were sitting.

Sebastian went to the door to keep a lookout for I.K. Ruby went to find Billick's seat. Ellie approached him to make small talk and to distract him while Ruby sabotaged Billicks's chair.

"Hi Billick, do you want some help?" Ellie asked in a much too sweet of tone.

"Nah, I'm good." He said and continued with passing out papers. He looked past Ellie as if he was looking for someone. Ellie looked at Ruby, who had just found Billick's seat. Ruby waved her hands to gesture to keep going with the plan.

While Ellie followed Billick around trying to distract him, Ruby took her precious pinkle pepper thorns and carefully placed them on Billick's seat. Making sure to conceal the spikes under the fabric of the chair cushion.

Ellie was still detaining Billick, with nonsense questions about a reading assignment on underground critters when Ruby placed the last of the thorns under his seat. The timing was perfect, Billick was getting annoyed with Ellie's questions.

Breaking free from Ellie's rant about worms and why we need them, he swaggered back to his desk. Looking suave and winking at the girls as he flew by. He looked at Ruby with a flashy grin and smugly said, "Hey, when are you gonna make good on that threat you made. How about we meet after school." He charmingly said and then winked at her.

"No, thanks, my afternoon is already booked," referring to her meetings with I.K. and Miss Milton.

Billick made it back to his seat and proceeded to plop down. That was his first mistake, driving the pinkle pepper thorns into his rump. Bolting off his chair with a high-pitched scream, Billick grabbed his bum and rubbed his backside attempting ease the pain. That was his second mistake, driving the needles further into his rumpus.

With eyes as wide as a dinner plate, Ruby looked at Ellie and Sebastian. All of them realized at the same time that Billick was part of the percentage of gidgies who were allergic to the pepper's thorns.

The effect was immediate. Billick's rear-end tripled in size, blowing his butt up and turning it the color magenta red and splitting his pants. Billick held his hands over his behind and flew backward to hide his hiney.

Just then, Miss Milton woke up and saw the infirmed fat fannied fairy. She flew from her desk, spilling her tea all over her robe. Miss Milton clumsily grabbed Billick and assisted him to the Healer's station. She was a little tipsy from her secret brew, causing her to bumble and bump poor Billick's behind into the walls as they went. His yelps of pain could be heard down the long school roots.

Ellie was laughing so hard she peed her pants, creating an obstacle they had to hurdle. Ellie's fiasco made their getaway a tad difficult. Ruby looked at Sebastian, and he looked back and raised his hand in protest, "You guys are on your own, my job is done." Seb wanted nothing to do with this next disaster.

Ruby creatively escorted Ellie to the nursery, where seedlings were started. Professor Jinkles was on staff and worked in the greenhouse. She was the kindest of all the teachers.

As Ruby explained the situation, Professor Jinkles burst into laughter. In her high-pitched hilarity, she continued to bust a gut while escorting Ellie to the lost and found to find her a skirt. However, Professor Jinkles giggles carried down the long halls, catching the attention of I.K., who was looking for Ruby. He had just come from the Healer's station and saw poor Billick.

With Ellie with Professor Jinkles, it was only Ruby in the nursery when I.K. busted in and found her. Assuming she was the mastermind of the prank, he grabbed her by the ear and dragged her to his office.

Ruby was in I.K.'s office for hours being interrogated, but she never gave up her two friends and their involvement. She received detention until graduation and was also put on laundry duty. Ruby hated laundry duty. And she had to check in with I.K. every day. That was the worst of all the penalties. However, these horrible punishments were worth it to see Billick fly out of the class with a baboon butt.

Later that evening, after Ruby had finished laundry and folded what felt like thousands of towels, she met Seb and Ellie in the Great Root. Waiting for Ruby was a mug of hot pinkle pepper brew and shortbread cookies.

"Does anyone know how Billick is doing?" Ellie asked in genuine concern.

"I checked on him before dinner, his butt is pretty huge, but the Healers have tonics and ointments to put on his boils. He won't be sitting down for a week or two." Sebastian said with a snicker.

"Poor Julia, she has to smear ointment on Billick's behind. That has to be the worst job in all of Havengothy Healer's history." Ruby said and burst into laughter, snorting, and then laughing even harder. In her flailing of hysteria, she knocked her book bag off the table, and a letter fell out.

All three stopped and looked at it. Ruby looked puzzled and thought it was from Sebastian. She unfolded the parchment to read.

Dear Ruby,

We have been enemies long enough. I want to call a truce. Let's end this year as friends. Will you go to the Bloom Festival with me?

Hopefully yours,
Billick

Ruby's face turned hot. Ellie snatched the letter out of Ruby's hand to read it. Ellie and Sebastian leaned in and read it together. They both looked at it, then at each other and then at Ruby.

"Holy Havengothy Ruby, you were the one he was planning to ask when I asked him to the festival. I can't believe it." Ellie whispered.

"That's some terrible luck, Rubes. Billick calling a truce and you put boils on his butt," Seb said, trying to lighten the mood.

Ruby was shocked. What in Havengothy was she going to do?

The shadow of a liath

Chapter Five
The liath sighting

Ruby sat in a Merrybare bush holding Billick's note. She had a few minutes to herself, and she didn't want to be bothered by anyone, not even her best friends. She was confused and needed time to think.

Why would Billick call a truce at the end of the school year? What was his motive? In fact, the more she thought about it, the angrier she got. "He was probably only inviting me to the festival to stand me up, or make a fool of me," she huffed out loud to herself.

Graduation was a month away, and Ruby was nearing the end of her punishment of laundry duty and her detention. She sat in her secret hideout near the edge of the forest, trying to clear her head when she heard voices.

She peaked between two branches and saw a cloaked gidgie. The mysterious fairy was speaking low and hushed to a gray looking creature. "That must be a liath." Ruby thought in disbelief.

She had never seen a liath before, she had only heard about them in school. Ruby found it challenging to understand that there were gidgies who would leave Havengothy on their own free will. Over a third of Beathra's gidgies left with Neeradima during the Banishment war, forming the beginning of her army.

Ruby quietly watched the liath speak to the cloaked gidgie. She couldn't fully make out what the concealed fairy was saying. She thought she heard the word midge. "What is a midge?" Ruby wondered.

The liath looked over its shoulder, then he handed the cloaked fairy a small bag. The liath gave a horrifying grin. It was the most terrifying thing Ruby had ever seen. It was the kind of evil sneer nightmares are made of.

His skin was a flaky grayish-white. His nose looked like it was about to fall off his face, leaving him with just holes for nostrils, jagged yellow teeth filled his gross, purple lipped mouth, and his hair was nothing but a few wisps of greasy gray strands.

Gidgies live incredibly long lives, but without the fire seed, their youthfulness and beauty disintegrate as they aged. This was an old liath, perhaps one of the first of the gidgies to leave with Neeradima.

Ruby gasped in terror at the frightening creature, and both the gidgie and liath looked at the merrybare bush. Ruby tucked deep into the shrub and held her breath. Its pink leaves and fruit hid Ruby perfectly.

Startlingly, a fitternick fowl, (a flightless quail looking bird with lavender fur, mid-flight wings, and two short stubby legs), bolted from the merrybare bush. It was peeping and squeaking as it chased a grasshopper.

The liath and the blanketed gidgie looked at each other, assuming that the purple critter was what they heard. The wicked liath mounted its beast and flew toward the Darphea Wilderness. The traitorous gidgie pocketed the small bag and tightly pulled his cloak over him and darted towards the shadows of the fir trees.

Ruby sat in the pink bush in a panic. She just witnessed a gidgie conspiring with the enemy, at least that's what she thought he was doing. And what was in that bag? She had to do something, but what? She was afraid to leave the bush for the chance of one of them seeing her. She waited for about thirty minutes to make sure the coast was clear.

Ominous flew back to the dark forest after providing his distributor with the unique produce created by Neeradima. This dispensing traitor is a gidgie who will recruit future liaths.

Ominous was pleased with himself and was hoping his queen would reward him for his excellent work. He had been faithfully serving Neeradima since the revolt against Beathra and The Whisper in the Banishment war.

He had no recollection of the gidgie he used to be. That part of him is lost in a darkness that is as thick as the Skawlterrin marsh. His only motive and mission now were to please his queen and build her army.

He landed at a secret entrance of a cave in the Darphea Mountain Range. He dismounted his ride, a worn-out buzzard who had been enslaved to him for many years.

Ominous crept through the caverns towards the center of the mountain to the queen's chambers when he heard a familiar crack. Neeradima had snapped the wings off a gidgie who had been wandering in her forest for the past week.

The poor little creature had been drinking the tainted water and eating the corrupt fruit of the evil garden and was losing himself to the wickedness of the forest. This unfortunate soul had left Havengothy and had been tricked by the cloaked gidgie, Ominous had supplied.

The covered stranger approached the wandering fairy and convinced him of secrets that lie within the forest of Skawlterrin. Winning his trust and "sharing" his meal, the gullible fairy ate a morsel of fruit with an intended purpose, to destroy the mind of the consumer.

The corrupted fruit did what it was designed to do; magnify every anxious and shameful thought the partaker felt. A shadow moves into their soul, and every fear, insecurity, and doubtful thoughts become crippling. A flood of lies immerses them as the poison enters their body. Feelings of jealousy and anger rise, and then they become paranoid. They are convinced they are unloved and do not belong. They are confident their world is against them, and they need to escape.

Without any effort, the veiled gidgie points the confused victim to a new place that will love and receive them. He tells them they will be adored and worshiped in the land just on the other side of the Darphea Wilderness. The poisoned fairy is convinced they do not belong in Havengothy, so they run. They run towards the cursed wilderness to escape the false voices in their heads.

The wayward fairy suffered for nearly a week before a scout grabbed him and brought him to his queen. Neeradima's scheme was perfect when it came to deceiving her victims. The marvelous fruit that was being dispersed in her former home destroyed the common sense in a fairy.

They hated themselves and everything in their loving garden. Feeling rejected and ashamed, they ran away from home and, directly into Neeradima's next trap. The tainted waters and sinister vegetations that inflicted pain so intense, a victim would do anything to find relief.

Neeradima promised to end the tricked fairy's misery; the weary gidgie had only to denounce his love of the King. The queen wanted to hear him say, "I no longer serve Beathra, you are my queen."

With the prospect of pain relief, the tortured fairy uttered the words Neeradima, longed to hear. Afterward, she gave her victim a tiny black speck to ingest. This evil creation of the wicked queen numbed everything. It silenced the truth in their heart and created a false sense of pain relief. However, its intended purpose was more sinister than the searing the victims conscious; it was highly addictive, making the new convert dependent upon Neeradima and her creation, the very things that destroyed them.

With a sickening crunch, the wings came off, and the beautiful colors began to drain from the wayward fairy, turning him gray to match the environment. Hidden at the base of the wings was the fire seed. Neeradima held the seed for a moment. As the lovely glow of the speck began to dim, she screamed for silence. With an eerily hush, Neeradima waited until she heard what she called "the music."

And there it was, a faint but audible sound; it was the weeping of Beathra for his fallen gidgie. There was never a gidgie that Beathra did not grieve over its loss. Tossing the now dimmed seed aside, in a graveyard of them, Neeradima's gaze turned to her new devotee.

The latest liath was motionless. Showing little life, it stood silently waiting. No wings, no color, no fire. Just a shell of what he used to be. In a syrupy false tone, the wicked enchantress asked, "What was your job in Havengothy little one?" The empty-eyed gidgie just stared at her. "ANSWER ME!" she screamed.

Jolted by the violence in her voice, the new recruit replied in a monotone style, "I can't recall." Pleased with his answer, Neeradima split a menacing smile. Just then, she spotted the General of her army walking into her chambers. "Where have you been?" she screamed.

Ominous bowed low, "Serving your purpose, my queen," he said in a slithering tone.

"I have a purpose for you, and it's to be here when I call your name, you idiot! Now take this piece of dung and show him to his new quarters." she hissed. Ominous was unmoved by the mood of his queen; screaming and wailing were part of the caves.

Deep in the caverns of the Darphea Mountains, Ominous led the new liath into the darkness. The feeling of nausea kept flooding him. Pushing past his vomit reflex, this gray soul trudged forward. New to the sense of hopelessness, the black seed began its work of anguish. With his memories robbed, he became dull and numb to any and all hope. He passed several chambers that had one or more prisoners in them. These captives refused to deny their King. They waited in hope for their rescue, and they felt their fire seed give them the strength to persevere.

A newly converted liath would never think of calling for help from Beathra; they are overflowing with shame, emptied of hope, and immersed in dread and blame. They're plunged into a constant sensation of falling or sinking. However, even in the worst of situations, in their most betrayed state of mind, these woeful liaths are not without hope. For even in their lowest part of despair, hope still lives because they still have breath.

Ruby made it back to the University in record time. She had to tell Sebastian and Ellie, all she witnessed. She was making her way around the corner of the root halls when she ran into Billick. Billick went flying back, landing on his still swollen behind. He yelped in pain. Ruby flew to help him up, "Oh Billick, I'm sorry. I'm so sorry. I didn't mean to run into you." Ruby apologized.

Billick pushed her away. "Don't touch me!" he yelled. "You meant this!" Billick bellowed, pointing to his enlarged backside.

Ruby's eyes went wide, and she had to stifle a snicker. Billick's butt was enormous. And the swelling had gone down quite a bit. Ruby tried to muster a concerned look.

"Billick, I had not seen the note you wrote to me. I was just getting even from our last conflict. And I had NO IDEA you were allergic to the pinkle pepper thorns. I mean, who has ever heard of anyone being allergic to the thorns? How is one to know these things? Seriously, I never imagined your butt blowing up so bi…" Ruby stammered and stopped on the word big. Billick was not accepting her apology.

"Because of you, I may miss graduation. And just so you know, I have no interest in going out with you, it was a practical joke, to see if you would take the bait." Billick lied. "Why would I want to go to the festival with you? You are nothing but a clumsy weirdo that can barely spell her own name." Billick fired with the intent to hurt Ruby.

It worked, he hit all the points Ruby felt insecure about. Too angry to cry, she charged at Billick, knocking him down on his swollen bum. He yelled in pain, but Ruby didn't care, she left him there like a turtle on its back as she fled to her room.

Billick pulled himself up the root wall and made it back to his feet. He watched her rose gold curls bounce in her departure. "Billick, you idiot," he chided himself.

If he was honest, he's crushed on Ruby for nearly two years, but because of her awkwardness and her academic struggles, Billick would risk social suicide if he associated with her. He did ask her to the festival in the act of bravery.

Taking a chance, he wrote a note to call a truce. It was the end of the year, and everyone would go their separate way. He would be leaving for the Skyforce after graduation. His hope was that he and Ruby could write to each other and form a relationship apart from his peers. But his opportunity was gone. Ruby would never forgive him for what he just said to her. His injuries would heal, but he just inflicted a wound that would take years for Ruby to forgive. Billick wobbled back to his bed at the Healer's station with his hands on his butt and his mind swimming in regret.

Ellie was faithfully studying when Ruby burst into their room and draped across the end of her bed. Seeing her best friend was upset, she sat next to her. "You alright, Rubes?" she asked carefully. Ruby, a quiet sufferer, made little noise, but the hot tears ran down her red cheeks. Ellie put her arm around Ruby, and the two sat quietly at the end of Ruby's bed.

"Would you like me to make us some pinkle pepper?" Ellie ventured in hopes that a sweet, spicy drink would do the trick to help her friend. Ruby sat up, looked at Ellie, fell back onto her bed, covered her face with her hands, and groaned in despair.

Chapter Six

Ruby apologizes.

The next day Ruby quietly made her way to the Healer's station with the hope that all were still sleeping. She slid a note at the foot of Billick's bed reading,

Billick,

I truly am sorry. If you don't walk with our graduating class, I won't walk either, it's only fair.

Sincerely,
Ruby

Ruby snuck out of the room and ventured to the dining root, where breakfast was served. The long quiet walk down the root halls provided a therapeutic think session. Early mornings at Havengothy University were peaceful. Beathra's presence was tangible in the dawn hours before all the voices filled the halls.

The winding roots that led to different classes were empty. The sun poked through the tiny windows and cracks of the lengthy roots. It was silent. She could hear her shoes shuffle on the dusty floor, clanking dishes and silverware echoing down the hall.

As Ruby slowly journeyed to the kitchen, she felt physically sick from all that was swimming in her chest. She never meant to hurt someone and cause suffering. Ruby was the scorn of the school right now because of Billicks blown up bottom. Burdened with the liath encounter she witnessed; Ruby couldn't stop thinking about who the traitorous fairy might be.

The more Ruby pondered, the more she was convinced that the cloaked stranger's voice seemed familiar. She had a circus of thoughts going on in her head and heart. And her jawline hurt from clenching it from stress.

The end of the school year was supposed to be filled with joy and anticipation. The graduates were supposed to be cutting class, having fun, and making lasting memories. There were lots of "supposed to's" that were not happening.

Instead, Ruby was serving double detention. She was the blame for another's pain, and she could feel the changes in her beloved garden. And though the atmosphere still dripped with the wonderful scents of spring and the ever-presence of hope, there was another feeling that couldn't be pinpointed.

Sebastian leaving for the Skyforce cadet school and the possible war coming, tied her stomach in knots, and she could feel the lump in her throat grow more prominent. Her mind darted to Ellie, moving to the other side of the garden for advanced education training to become a professor. Ruby's shoulders went tense with the anxiety that was pulsing through her. Her days were going to get lonely; she knew that.

Ruby finally made it to the dining root. No students were up yet, and the only other fairies in the hall were the kitchen staff. Ruby sat down at the end of a long table and let her nose enjoy the fantastic aromas. The smell of smoked meats and freshly baked bread wafted in the air. "The bakers must be making something with blueberries," she thought.

She closed her eyes and inhaled her favorite smell, the spicy pinkle pepper brew. Opening her eyes, she then exhaled a sad sigh, and her shoulders and head slumped. The joy of all the smells faded, and the guilty feeling rose. "Stupid, stupid me," she scolded herself.

Humming, Yoli brought out a giant pot of the pinkle pepper brew and sat it on the serving bar. She saw Ruby and waved her over. As Ruby sauntered to the bar of beverages, Yoli made her a steaming mug of the spicy brew and loaded it up with honey. "Here ya go punk'n, just the way you like it, extra sweet, just like you." She said with a wink.

Ruby sat on the end of a bench with her bum barely resting on the edge. She placed her elbows on her knees and held her hot drink, staring at it. Yoli sat down on the bench next to Ruby. She was a wise and kind fairy who has worked at the University for decades, perhaps centuries. Her husband was part of a Special Task Force team with the Skyforce and has been missing in action for nearly seven years. Somehow Yoli persevered with joy. She had a deep trust in Beathra that she would see Jermaine someday.

The kind fairy looked Ruby in the eyes, and with a smile began, "You and Billick have been at each other's throat since you were very young. He's not innocent in this, so stop beating yourself up. I think he is milking this injury as long as possible. I.K. is feeling sorry for him, so Billick is getting out of the end of year projects. He even has his mob of swooning girls visiting him daily, doing his homework, and bringing him meals. He has no incentive to get better."

Yoli then plopped a fresh hot fruit tart in front of Ruby. "Now, stop this moping and useless guilt and enjoy my fresh baked millie fruit tart. It's not every day someone gets the pleasure of these treats right from the oven. Pretty soon, I.K. will come in and take a pile and try to blame it on a young student." Yoli said in an annoyed tone. She gave Ruby a side squeeze, kissed her on top of her head, and went back to the kitchen to finish getting breakfast ready.

Ruby started to cut into the gooey pastry when she heard I.K.'s thundering operatic voice bellowing down the halls. Ruby grabbed her tea and millie fruit tart and snuck away to hide. She did not feel like seeing tomato face this morning, or any other for that matter. He entered the root hall and poured himself a giant mug of pinkle pepper brew. Like Yoli said, he peered around him, and then when he thought no one was looking, wrapped eight pastries up and stuffed them in his jacket.

Yoli was bringing another platter of food out to the tables when she saw I.K. She looked for Ruby and could see her tucked away. Yoli noticed half her pastries were missing from one plate. Knowing full well who took them, she exclaimed, "Who in Havengothy snuck in here and swiped my fresh pastries?"

I.K. put his hand over his jacket pocket, where he hid the pastries and gave them a little pat. "It must have been Lewis; I just saw him in here a few seconds ago." Lied the instructor.

Yoli looked over to the corner where Ruby was hiding and gave her a wink, then in fake anger, said, "When I see that little thief, I'm going to put him on kitchen duty till his fingers bleed."

I.K. quickly turned away to lick his fingers and wipe his hands on his pants and then turned to Yoli and said, "I'll take care of Lewis, you leave him to me." He then turned on his fat heels and left the dining root.

Ruby came out from the corner, giggling. Yoli chuckled and went back to prepping for breakfast.

The council, made up of elders and high-ranking military, sat in a deep root on this early morning, discussing the recent sighting of liaths. Moses is the oldest gidgie on the board. His once chocolate brown wings are now dulled with age, and his head is as bald as a lava bean. His long beard hangs past his belt, and he loves to adorn it with colorful beads at its ends.

He and his wife Sylvia are some of the last of the first bloomed gidgies. Sylvia is an oracle and can see things from the past and future. She has beautiful opalescent wings and long silver hair that flows down her back.

"We have a traitor among us. Evidence has been found of a gidgie using Neeradima's brain-altering fruit to lure our fairies to Skawlterrin. Our Skyforce has rescued a few young gidgies who have attempted to cross the cursed land of the Darphea Wilderness. The conspirator is targeting our University students, as well as those who feel like an outcast. Still, we are unclear if the betrayer is a student, teacher, or an outsider," General Dax stated.

The General was a tall thin gidgie who had a receding hairline like mouse ears. His wings were deep mahogany and his eyes the color of amber. And He was as kind as he was fierce.

As the council discussed how to investigate the University, Sylvia's eyes began to flutter back and forth. The board took notice, and everyone went still. She floated up from her seat at the table, and her eyes twitched even faster. When she began to speak, it was a low feminine voice.

"There are dark days ahead. Neeradima is rebuilding her army, and she is targeting the youngest and the weakest of our gidgies. But her motive is more than abductions. It is to strike fear in the hearts of our residents. To cause them to doubt the goodness of our King and The Whisper. The betrayers among us have been fooled into an act of treason. Though they are not trying to overthrow Havengothy, their selfishness will start a war that will devastate our land. I see great loss and destruction because of reckless fairies. Our young ones will need to grow up quickly, for their garden is changing. Beathra is already stirring them to put away their childish ways and rise to the challenge of defending their land. There is a war coming, but there are also warriors rising. I see one being called to the front. It will take time to prepare the chosen, for there is much doubt in their heart and insecurity to overcome."

Sylvia then collapsed to the floor. Moses ran to her and took out a piece of honeycomb to help revive the older fairy. Visions always took an immense amount of energy from the prophetess. She waved her husband away, "I'm fine, Moses, stop fussing over me. I'm a Healer, remember?" Sylvia reminded her husband. She was not only a Healer; she was the greatest of Healers. With her prophetic instinct, she could treat the wounded and the sick with a skill that was beyond knowledge; it was practically supernatural. This remarkable yet rare gift is known as fire sight.

The council pondered on Sylvia's vision. "I propose we get an agent in the school to start doing some investigating." General Dax declared.

Captain Roland spoke up, "I have a guy who goes to the University once a month to teach a shop class and help recruit new cadets. First Sergeant Joseppi can be the eyes and ears for the next few weeks. There is also a veteran engineer that teaches there. I will check in with him this week and see if he has any suspicions."

The council all agreed to Captain Roland's suggestion, and General Dax closed the meeting.

Ruby sat in the dining hall as it filled up little by little. Ellie found Ruby at the end of a long table sipping on her pepper brew. Waving Sebastian over, the three went through the food line and filled their trays with all the delicious dishes Yoli and her crew had prepared.

"Where did you go so early this morning?" Ellie asked.

"I went to check on Billick. He was sleeping, but I left a note saying that if he didn't walk with the class, I wouldn't either," Ruby informed.

Seb and Ellie were mid-bite when Ruby dropped this information. Sebastian looked at Ruby hurt. "You would miss walking with Ell and me because you feel guilty about Billick and his big, ballooned butt?" he asked sharply.

"I'm having second thoughts about it now, but at the time it seemed like the right thing to do," Ruby said, doubting herself.

"That weasel will walk. Everyone knows baboon butt is stretching out his convalescent time!" Ellie stated firmly.

"Enough about Billick. I have been distracted by him long enough. I have to tell you both what I saw yesterday evening." Said Ruby in a whisper.

Ruby proceeded to tell them all about the cloaked gidgie and the liath. Ellie opened and closed her mouth to try to say something, but no words came out. Sebastian's eyes were huge with interest.

"I told you! I told you guys! A war is coming!" Feeling justified, he continued. "Joseppi even says it feels like something is coming with all the liath sightings. You gotta talk with him, Rubes. He's a weapons expert and is a First Sergeant in the Skyforce. He comes here once a month to teach a class on making gardening tools. He'll be here tomorrow as a matter of fact."

"That's perfect! However, I'm not in Tools and Devices class. I was never that interested, so how will I be able to talk with him? Do you think you can get him to stick around a little longer, Seb? I can leave my fertilizer class early; it stinks anyway." Ruby snickered at her own joke. "Then, I'll dash to Tools and Devices and share what I saw yesterday," Ruby said excitedly.

Sebastian smiled at Ruby. He loves it when she gets excited about something. She was animated in her speech and gestures. "Do you think he will take my information to the Skyforce council or the elders? What if I have to go before the council and relay my information?" Ruby said excitedly with bright eyes and a huge grin.

"Well, I think we should just start with Joseppi, he will know what to do with your information. He's a pretty cool guy and a very wise gidgie. Jo's been in the Skyforce for a long time and has fought a few liaths in his days," Seb informed admiringly.

Sebastian always spoke highly of Jossepi. From what Ruby knew, Joseppi's the one who encouraged Sebastian with a military career, but Ruby had never officially met him. She was curious to chat with the First Sergeant about what she saw but wasn't sure if she was going to like him. After all, he recruited her Seb.

Chapter Seven
Meet Joseppi

Joseppi was teaching on the use of lava beans in his weapon designing class. As a weapons expert in the Skyforce, Joseppi has the skills of a blacksmith. Though fire is illegal in Havengothy, there is this incredible plant known as the lava bean.

Lava beans are searing hot legumes that grow under the roots of Beathra. They are a heat and light source for the gidgies. Their location is marked with little white bellflowers. The lava bean miners dig deep for the hidden seed pods as one would mine for diamonds. Closely resembling a sweet pea. The pods are white with round, orange, beans inside. Once opened and exposed to air, the little peas begin to blaze with a searing heat. The hot beans are what is used for cooking with warming roots homes and blacksmithing. While enclosed in the pod, they glow and are used as a form of light. When opened, the heat can last up to 24 hours. If remained sealed, a pod can shine for days. When the beans cool, they are simply replanted near Beathra. If it is not planted near his roots, it will only produce a coffee-flavored seed. Although it is tasty, it is not a heat source.

Jo was explaining the importance of the lava bean and why they needed to replant them near the root when Billick entered the class. Billick was moving slow, and one could see his swollen rump sticking out past his thighs. He was wearing a pair of I.K.'s trousers due to the swelling. He went to find a seat and assessed the chair size according to his butt, he then looked around to see everyone watching him.

"Man, I wish Ruby was here to see this," Sebastian chuckled to himself.

Billick decided not to sit but lean against the root wall. Joseppi continued with his demonstration of using precious metals that were mined from Havengothy along with branches and wood from Beathra for making weapons.

"One of the most incredible things about us gidgies and our weapons coming from Beathra; our fire seed can communicate with us both. The handle of my sword is from the limbs of Beathra: therefore, I can combat with more power, wisdom, and insight. Our bows bend with agility, and the arrows are instinctive to their target.

Our daggers are precise and practically think for themselves. Thus, when we create our gardening tools with the same level of skill, using similar materials, our devices become an extension of Beathra and us." Jo finished with a smile.

Billick loved this class, he and Seb would be leaving for cadet school at the same time, and Jo had a way of inspiring them for military life. Since the pinkle pepper incident and his harshness with Ruby, there was a humility about him that no one had ever seen. Even Sebastian was noticing the once overconfident, flirty Bill was a bit more serious and reserved. "Perhaps his pain in his backside is making him more somber," Seb guessed.

Seb was wrong. Billick was self-conscious of his appearance and overcome with shame after his cruelty with Ruby. All he wanted to do was finish school and join the Skyforce. He wasn't interested in going to the festival anymore and didn't care if he walked with his class. The look of Ruby leaving after he spoke so brutally, leveled him. He never wanted to hurt her like that again.

Billick asked Julia for a release from the Healers to go back to class. He could have returned earlier but was too embarrassed to be seen in such a bulbous state. Julia was kind and encouraged him to be brave and to swallow his pride; she explained to him his reaction to the thorns was more of a disorder than an allergy. Billick was comforted by Julia's reasoning, even if it was a bit of a stretch. She saw how humiliated he was, and she was a Healer, after all. And that meant to heal one's self-esteem. Her words worked, and they gave him the courage to return to class.

Jo was finishing his lesson about how to handle the boiling heat of the lava beans when shaping and hammering a tool when Ruby snuck into class and slid in by Sebastian. He looked at her, then plugged his nose with one hand and waved his other hand over his face to fan a stink away. With eyebrows furrowed at her in disgust, he mouthed, "What is that Horrible smell?

"I spilled atto-glider fertilizer all down the front of me. Professor Jinkles had us gather their poo at their nesting grounds for the summer interns to use in the greenhouse. They really do have remarkable poop, with incredible benefits for growing practically anything. But, in the process of transfer, I spilled a bag. Is it really that bad?" Ruby whispered, trying to explain her stench.

"It's pretty bad, Rubes," Seb answered honestly. Just then, Ruby saw Billick leaning against the back of the class root wall. His butt was still inflamed, and he was looking at her. She looked away, she didn't want to see or talk to him.

"What is he doing here, isn't he supposed to be at the Healer's with his hiney in a sling or something?" Ruby whispered.

"I guess he's better. Well, betterish. His poor tookis is still a tad swollen." Seb said with a smile crawling across his face.

"Looks like I don't have to make good on my promise then, eh?" Ruby quietly said, feeling relieved.

Joseppi stopped teaching and asked someone to open a window. "I do believe a student has been down by the atto-gliders nesting grounds. I think we should end this class a little early and get some air in here."

The class let out, and Seb and Ruby walked to the front of the group to chat with Joseppi. Ruby had to walk past Billick to get there so, she kept her head down and did not glance up at him, certain he would say something about the stink she was covered in. She couldn't handle any more of his nasty comments. He cut her deeper than he ever had before, and she was done.

Billick tried to make eye contact, but Ruby kept her head down and walked swiftly. Billick never said a word about the atto-gliders stench. Seb, however, saw Billick look at Ruby, and it wasn't one of hatred or irritation, it was something else entirely. "I think he likes her," Sebastian noted to himself.

Walking by Billick, Sebastian put his hand on the small of Ruby's back. Not only to guide her past Billick but for Billick to see that Seb and Ruby were close. It worked, Billick looked away and left class quietly.

Ruby and Sebastian made it to the front of the class, where Jo was putting the lava bean in a bucket of water to cool it down. "Peeee yew, Seb, is that you that smells so bad?" Jo asked while he tried to wave the stink away. "Sorry, sir, it's actually me," Ruby said, embarrassed.

"Did Professor Jinkles have you gathering the atto-glider's poop?" Jo asked.

"How did you know?" Ruby asked, impressed.

"She always did prefer their manure to any other creatures here in Havengothy. I can't tell you how many times one of those old cloth bags of poo broke on me, but it really is a remarkable product," Jo commented with understanding.

"I agree. I tried to tell Seb, but he just rolled his eyes." Ruby teased.

Ruby liked Jo right away. All her apprehensions and concerns of him faded. She could see what Sebastian saw, a kind, honest fairy. He had stick, straight black hair, and kind, dark, button brown eyes with the thickest lashes. He also had a full black mustache and beard. And his wings were a stunning rich charcoal gray with flecks of silver. He flipped an empty bucket over and said, "pull up a chair miss and tell me what's on your mind."

Ruby sat on the bucket and tried to dust more of the dried stink off her. She then described what she saw to Jo all the way down to the voice of the cloaked gidgie that sounded familiar, but he spoke in such a low, hushed tone that she couldn't decide who it belonged to.

"The liath you're describing sounds like the General of Neeradima's army. He's a dreadful fellow, I'm surprised he's even here in Havengothy. We have only had sightings of his goons. Something is going on because the sightings are getting more frequent. Did you happen to see what was in the bag?" Jo asked.

"I didn't. I tried really hard to hide, and I waited for a long time before I even left the merrybare bush. I was so afraid they were going to see me." Ruby confessed.

"I will take what you've told me and relay it to my Captain. He will be very interested in this sighting. But I would like you to keep it to yourself and not share this with anyone, not even your professors. Can you do that for me?" Jo asked, concerned.

"Shoot, we gotta go, Rubes, our history class, starts in just a few minutes," Seb announced. With that, the two gidgies dashed out of class. Jo flew to the Skyforce Sky base to find Captain Roland. He would definitely want to know about the sighting of Ominous.

Ruby flew to her root dorm to change then made it back to history class in record time. As usual, Ellie saved a seat for the ever-tardy Ruby. Feeling a bit of guilt, Ruby realized she still hadn't snuck Professor Hill's book back to his office as the grades for the Banishment war papers were being passed out. If she were honest, she didn't want to let it go. There were far too many glorious things in this *borrowed* treasure. The most recent chapter she read was describing Neeradima's song to Beathra. It was positively beautiful.

Ruby had the song swimming in her head, she had memorized the lyrics because of how lovely they were.

"Who is like our King of Trees?
Who can compare to his Majesty?
With love, life, shade, and fire,
No other King of trees is higher.
Beathra, the King of Trees, is his name,
with life in his branches and power in his flame.
He loves us uniquely as a father loves a child.
And though he is kind, he is also wild."

Neeradima, at one time, adored her garden and the two spirits. She used to walk through the enchanted grounds, singing songs of charms to help things grow. "How can someone write with such love and adoration and then be filled with jealousy and hate, what changed, I wonder?" Ruby thought to herself.

Ruby sat lost in her daydreaming when she suddenly felt a kick to her shins. Ellie was trying to get her attention. Jolted to reality, she saw the small professor looking down at her with a stern face.

'Sorry, Professor Hill, I was lost in thought." Ruby said feebly.

"Care to share with us your daydreaming?" Hill asked.

She didn't dare. Her mind was flooded with the findings of the secret book she swiped from Hill's office. She decided to ask a question that pertained to the Banishment war.

"Professor, why did Neeradima change? I mean, what happened that caused her to hate our garden?" Ruby inquired.

Ruby's questions had the attention of the entire class, even her harassers. After much thought, the professor pondered how to answer, then carefully began to reply to the loaded question.

"That's an excellent question, Ruby. Neeradima was a faithful apprentice to The Whisper, but she thought the two spirits were keeping things from her. In the History of Havengothy volumes, you should have read that she felt she should have been considered as important as the King and The Whisper." Professor answered.

"I did read that, but with all the good inside of our garden, why did she go bad? Where did that "bad" come from?" Ruby pressed.

The brilliant Lewis shot his hand up with an interjection. "Wasn't she conspuh…conspuh conspuh...ACHOO. Sorry bout dat. My allerrr…allerrr...my allergeeeeez-Achoo, sniff, are gedding worse wid all duh bloombs. Wasn't she conspiohing with duh fallen gidgies to destroy Beathruh?" he said, sounding phlegmy. "I mean, I read it was dat, and because she'd stopped spending time wid the two Spuh...Spuh...Spuh...SPIWITS!' Lewis finished with a bellowing sneeze.

Billick got annoyed with Lewis and his allergies. "Spring allergies aren't real Lewis. Whoever heard of a fairy being allergic to his own garden?" he grumbled, still feeling sorry for himself.

Sebastian was quick with a sarcastic response, "About as many who have heard of those who are allergic to the pinkle pepper needles, Billick."

The room roared in laughter. Lewis felt justified with Sebastian's defense of him. Seb always looked out for the underdog. He didn't worry about being popular, he was far too confident for that type of pressure.

"It's not an allergy, it's a disorder. Even the Healer, Julia, says it's a condition few fairies suffer from," Billick shouted, trying to defend himself.

The class was getting out of hand, and it was nearing the end. The professor tried to take control of the crows by answering Ruby and Lewis.

"It's hard to say where Neeradima went bad. As you know, we gidgies are all bloomed from Beathra, but Neeradima was not bloomed, she was made from a song. When The Whisper sang, Neeradima took form. So perhaps, Neeradima feels equal to the Tree King and The Whisper due to her unique design and impartations of powers. As for where evil comes from, I believe it's born in the heart of a desperate being motivated by their own interest. Neeradima craved power and longed to be worshiped, but it was not hers to have. Misery is a motivator to get what you want; however, that looks". Professor Hill stated as he finished class.

The Darphea Wilderness

Chapter Eight

Lewis is missing.

It was the morning of graduation, and per tradition to years past, Yoli made a special breakfast for all the last years. "Has anyone seen Lewis?" Yoli asked at breakfast.

Ruby looked over at Sebastian with a questioning glance. Seb shrugged his shoulders and answered, "Last I saw of him, he was headed to the activity field. He and Billick had a big fight last night about what was a real allergy and what was a disorder. Billick was pretty harsh with him."

Yoli wiped her hands on her apron and flew directly to I.K.'s office. He was eating his stolen pastries and taking a big gulp of Pinkle pepper brew when Yoli barged in. Startled by the intrusion, I.K. spilled the drink all down the front of his crumb covered jacket.

"UGH! Woman, you better have a good excuse for charging in like that!" I.K. thundered as he sopped up the spill with his napkin.

Yoli was unmoved. I.K.'s outburst, he didn't intimidate her. She knew too much for him to ever make good on any threats of firing her.

"I want you to contact our security and have them search for Lewis. He's been missing since last night." Yoli demanded.

"Now Yoli, calm down. These young fairies don't always come down for breakfast. I'm sure everything is fine." I.K. mumbled as he took a bite of a soggy millie fruit pastry.

"I know something is wrong, I can feel it in my fire seed. If you don't send a search party out for Lewis, I'll. I'll... I will tell everyone what you use on your bald head for hair growth," Yoli threatened.

I.K. wiped his chin and looked at Yoli sideways, "You wouldn't dare."

"Try me! I've seen you leaving Professor Jinkle's office with a handful of..."I.K. stopped Yoli before she said atto-glider poop. "Alright, Yoli, I will go talk with the University security and have them walk and fly the grounds. Has anyone checked Lewis's room, before I make this big fuss?" I.K. asked, annoyed.

"Sabastian said he saw him near the activity field last night," Yoli informed.

I.K. was irritated his pre-breakfast was interrupted, but to keep

Yoli from blabbing about his secret hair growth formula, he went to the University security. I.K. spoke with Pete, a retired Skyforce combat veteran. When I.K. walked in, he didn't notice the two mugs of lava java sitting on Pete's desk. The stout hot beverage was something all military fairies got used to while out on a mission. It was practically a meal and had a great pick me up.

"Hey Pete, we may have a lost student, would you make a pass over the grounds? I've got Yoli in a tizzy, and I told her I would have you check on him. Let's keep this from that, Jo fellow. I don't need him giving a bad report about how I run the place." I.K. instructed.

"Keep what from me?" Jo asked as he was leaning on the root wall left of the doorway that Instructor Kay walked through. Jo overheard everything. I.K. did not know that Jo and Pete had met, and Jo had arranged to speak with Pete before breakfast about the school's safety procedure.

I.K. was flustered and stammered an excuse, "You know how these young fairies are; moody and unpredictable. It's close to graduation, and emotions are high. And then I have a hysterical female fussing over one gidgie, not showing up for breakfast."

"Don't you think you should be concerned with a missing youth? And if a faithful servant to the University, who has a trusting relationship with the students, says something is amiss: Don't you think you should respond according to the protocol? With the abductions becoming more frequent, don't you think we should react to every possible threat?" Joseppi stated, calmly but his demeanor was full of authority.

I.K. was embarrassed by Joseppi correcting him. "I'll have you know, no gidgie has gone missing under my watch! It has been after they have graduated or on their summer break," he said defensively with a raised voice and a red face.

Jo was not amused. "I don't have time for your insecurities, we have a possible missing fairy. I will deal with you later and your precious position as the Head Professor. Pete lets round up a search party, I am going to speak with Sebastian and find where Lewis was last seen." With that, Joseppi jetted from the security root and spoke with Seb.

Lewis was feeling hurt and angry after class and embarrassed from his severe seasonal allergies. "I mean, it's not like I can help them." He thought to himself as he blew his nose. Billick had harassed Lewis about his allergies, but the ever kind Lewis disregarded the insults. Still, he could not dismiss the hurt they caused.

He wandered to the edge of the activity field. He sat on the bleachers to watch the Havengothy track and field players practice. He was set to graduate with honors, yet few respected his intelligence. Lewis was not athletic nor popular, but he was brilliant. He memorized everything he ever read and could tell you every plant in Havengothy. He also knew precisely what time it was without looking at a timepiece or the sky.

Lewis also had an uncanny way of feeling the emotions in another. When Billick was healing, Lewis could sense Billick's embarrassment. However, Lewis was a fairy of integrity and would never use what he was discerning against someone. Perhaps, that's why Beathra shared with him the feelings of others because Lewis was kind, trustworthy, and full of compassion.

He sat on the bleachers, blowing his nose, wishing he could experience the magical scents of Havengothy. Lewis felt a presence behind him, and he turned to see who it was. He didn't see anyone right away, but then he looked into the shadows of the trees. He thought he recognized the man and hopped down to say hello.

He approached the veiled gidgie with his head sideways, trying to see the stranger's face. "Helloooo," Lewis said, all stuffed up "Who's dare?"

The stranger disappeared, then from nowhere, came from around him, and grabbed Lewis's face. Stuffing an orange morsel of the mind-altering fruit down his throat.

Once the orange fruit was ingested, the brilliant, brained Lewis became disoriented. The fruit began to do what it was designed to do, turning logic into confusion, and making the victims easily manipulated. The traitorous gidgie persuaded Lewis his answers to his allergies were on the other side of the Darphea Wilderness. Delirious from being drugged, Lewis was convinced he could fly over the barren land, unaware that the wasteland was cursed.

The bewildered Lewis tried to fly over the curse wilderness, but he was unsuccessful. The treacherous valley was void of all life, hope, and even moisture. Wings began to shrivel from dehydration. A sense of confusion enveloped the travelers and had the poor souls wandering in circles. Making them an easy target for a scouting liath.

The liaths had it down to a science. They knew if a spy could lure a foolish gidgie out of Havengothy, the Darphea Wilderness would hand the strays to them on a silver platter. Usually delirious from the curse on the land, and exhausted from going in circles, starvation, and dehydration set in. The desperate wanderers would be too tired to make an escape, or better yet, they would go willingly with the enemy.

Lewis wandered in the wasteland overnight and somehow was unseen by any scouting liath. He was discombobulated as he walked, his head spinning, and his body feeling strange. It had only been a few hours, but it felt like an eternity. Why couldn't he remember the face of the cloaked gidgie?

Lewis sat down on a rock and considered his situation; Did anyone know he was missing? There was this horrible feeling of guilt that would overcome a victim in the Darphea Wilderness. The land twisted one's mind and put a soul in such disarray they are overwhelmed with shame and humiliation. Calling for help from Beathra was a struggle. As if one was stuck in a dream and trying to speak, but the words feel strained coming out of one's mouth. They are stuck between the heart and the tongue, and it takes a sheer grit just to utter them. The pitiful wanderers are convinced the situation is their fault, and maybe sometimes it was.

Lewis brutalized himself in self-deprivation chatter. Speaking to himself, most awfully and negatively. That's what the cursed land does, though. It is drained of all things good, so all an unfortunate creature can do is feel misery and defeat.

Lewis only wanted to go home, but how? He could feel a longing in his heart for Havengothy, but his prayers to Beathra felt stuck in his chest. He sat down on the dry, cracked ground and wept. Through sobs, that the wilderness lapped up, he pressed out a cry for help, "Beathra, please help me."

Lewis felt a warm wind blow and then heard his King speak to his heart. "Lewis, my loved boy, I am here, you are not alone. You are not a fool, and you are not an inconvenience. I know you long to fit in and desire the acceptance of others. But you have forgotten how well you fit in my heart and in my plans. You are our brilliant boy who has been created with a special purpose. This time of frustration will pass, and your time of shining will come. Trust me little one, I have big things in store."

Lewis felt his heart lighten, and his hope renewed. All he wanted was to be loved and accepted. He knew his intelligence got him teased more than others, but oh how he wanted to be approved of by the popular fairies. The worst part has been these blasted allergies. "I can't be the only one who struggles with things that make a fairy feel different?" he thought.

"Sylvia has answers to your questions, and she is waiting for you," he heard in the wind. Lewis had only read of Sylvia and her great wisdom as a Healer.

He tucked himself between two small rocks and began to drift off from his weariness. Lewis dreamt of becoming a Healer and saw a vision of himself working in the greatest Healer's root of all, The Skyforce Healers station. "That's it, I'm meant to train as a Healer!" Lewis shouted as he jolted himself awake.

———————

Pete and Jo recruited Billick and Sebastian to comb the grounds of Havengothy as the two seasoned fairies ventured towards the Darphea Wilderness. Jo went southwest, and Pete went northwest. All task force members knew a charm to speak over themselves, enabling them to cross the cursed desert.

As they came upon the vexed wasteland, they both stopped mid-air and began to recite their charm.

From the Ghost Warriors fire to the whisper of the wind,
May I fly with faith and courage, where my King intends.
Let my life be guarded against the evil that exists.
May my wings and mind be strengthened with the wisdom to resist.

After reciting the charm, the two trained gidgies began their vigilant search. Praying for Beathra to help them find Lewis. Jo flew low, scanning the dead scenery when all of a sudden, he heard Lewis's faint voice yell, "That's it!"

Lewis's exclamation also got the attention of a liath scout who was searching for wandering gidgies. Pete spotted the liath that was aiming towards Lewis. At top speed, the combat vet flew with a violent force. Pete plowed into the liath knocking him off his flying beast. The two tumbled to the ground, and Pete and the liath engaged in a full-fledged brawl.

The skilled liath fought dirty, throwing sand and scratching Pete in the face with claw-like fingernails, causing blood to run into Pete's eyes, blinding him. But the liath was no match for the burly combat vet. Pete blindly threw a few bare-knuckle punches to the face of the liath, knocking him backward. He was able to wipe the blood from his eye and aim his sword ideally, beheading the wicked creature.

Jo nose-dived towards Lewis. The young gidgie was startled by the abrupt landing of the First Sergeant and panicked. Lewis started swinging at Jo and telling him to get away from him.

"Calm down Lewis, I'm here to rescue you. I need you to trust me. Can you do that?" Jo asked.

Lewis squinted in the dawn light and recognized Jo from the school and nodded yes. Jo grabbed Lewis with one arm and gripped his sword with the other. "We have to be as stealthy as possible. There is a liath not too far from us, and I don't know if he is alone."

Jo flew as low to the ground as he could, keeping out of sight of the liath who was searching for Lewis. Pete flew up next to them, covered in blood and dirt. "That is the most fun I've had since retirement. I just might re-enlist! I feel sixty-five again." He flew upward in a spin and then dove back down to Jo, who was still carrying Lewis.

"Oh, by the way, we're all clear. I took care of the stinky liath. I forgot how bad they smell." Pete was grinning through his blood-covered face. Lewis looked startled but could feel the elation in Pete's heart. He was going to need stitches, but Lewis sensed he would even like those.

Lewis then had the most fantastic thought; "My time in this horrible place actually directed me for my future. I was lost in the wilderness, and Beathra used it to help me find myself. I'm going to be a Healer." Lewis cracked a broad smile and took a deep, cleansing breath and sighed with this revelation. At that moment, Jo flew into the borders of Havengothy, and Lewis caught the scent of something marvelous. It was wildflowers.

A young Neeradima

Chapter Nine
Another abduction

Neeradima paced her chambers with an unmatched fury. She was greedy for revenge and wanted to strike against Havengothy. She had a bloodthirst to destroy the two spirits that denounced her from their garden. Her mind was consumed with hatred and twisted with a wicked desire to steal, kill, and destroy all that Beathra and The Whisper loved. And though it had been hundreds of years since her banishment, the sting of her exile felt like it was yesterday. It consumed her.

"How dare they think they are better than me. I grew that garden. I made it what it is today. If it wasn't for me, there would be no Havengothy." She seethed.

Of course, she was wrong, she was created by The Whisper and Beathra. But she did not have the connection that the gidgies had with the two great spirits, and that was the fire seed. The Whisper was part of the Great Warrior. She was a combination of his joy and his sadness. His spark of happiness and the weeping wind was life, and she was life. Beathra was a part of the Great Warrior because the fire seed was his heartbeat and the reason for his very existence. And the gidgies were part of the two spirits because they carried a piece of The Whisper and Beathra within them: the fire seed.

Neeradima did not have the fire seed. She was not linked to the spirits the way the "children" were. She was a loved creation, fashioned to assist, help, and advance the garden. But time eroded her heart to serve. Darkness within her grew as she spent less time with The Whisper and more time alone. She would distance herself from the two loving spirits, and with their absence, Neeradima was her own counsel. She soothed herself with her own words of warped wisdom. It wasn't until she rallied the compassion of Sunny that she plotted her revolt.

Sunny was a caring fairy who was sensitive towards others and their unhappiness. He brought a sense of joy and sunshine wherever he went with glorious, marigold-colored wings and hair. Sunny loved Neeradima and would do anything to make her happy. Neeradima knew Sunny was committed to her and, one day, asked the most substantial favor of her devoted friend.

"Sunny, would you do anything for me?" She asked in a much too sweet of tone.

"You know I would. I would even die for you," Sunny answered, hurt Neeradima would question his devotion,

"Would you give me anything I asked for?" She asked cunningly.

"Of course, my sweets. I would bring you the waters of the Quartz Gulf. I would mine the deepest treasures of Havengothy. I would climb the Hyperion Mountains to bring you back one of the enchanted beasts that live there." Sunny declared.

"Would you give me your fire seed? Beathra and The Whisper never gave me a piece of their heart, and I am alone and different from the rest of you. Perhaps if you gave me your seed, I could be like them, and they would finally view me as an equal." Neeradima was crying and working extremely hard to play on Sunny's compassionate nature.

"If it would make you happy and stop you from crying, I would take it out myself and give it to you. But the seed is in my wings, my darling, so I have no way to give you my fire seed," he said, hoping that would be the end of their conversation.

Sunny could hear his King telling him to run. However, his love for Neeradima was becoming more significant, and Beathra's voice was being drowned out by desire.

Neeradima assessed Sunny's tiny body and came to the sick conclusion that if she broke his wings off, she might be able to pluck the seed from his back and ingest the fire seed. She smiled her sweetest smile, and convincingly said, "I might be able to help you. Let me take your wings off and pluck the seed from your back. Perhaps we can share the seed. Then, when I have its power, I will heal your wings."

Sunny sat in silence, feeling the nudge of his King to getaway. But he was enamored with Neeradima. He walked up to her and turned his back and, with tears running down his face, said, "if giving you my fire seed will show my love for you, then it is yours."

Neeradima was elated, but she needed to keep her excitement under control. With her thin ribbon-like hands, she scooped Sunny up and, in the act of exciting greed, snapped his wings off Sunny. The sound of bones breaking echoed in Sunny's ears. Neeradima then viewed the tiny glowing seed at the end of his wings and plucked it from their golden base. It was beautiful. The little seed glowed with a fire that danced all around it. She held it in her hand, ready to pop it in her mouth when she heard a noise. She and Sunny were alone, so where could this voice be coming from? What was it? Who was it?

It was crying. It was the faintest of sounds, but Neeradima heard weeping. She held the seed next to her ear and recognized the voice. She then realized it was Beathra weeping over the loss of Sunny and his fire seed. Then the glowing little seed faded to a dull beige gray. Neeradima's anger flashed in her eyes. Her plan failed.

Sunny, lay motionless, flightless, colorless, and wings tossed to the ground like garbage. The weakened fairy pushed himself up from the ground, feeling pain as if someone stabbed him in the back. He reached behind himself to touch the wings that he knew were no longer there. All he felt was hollowness. He then began to feel himself drain. Not of blood, but of hope, emotion, joy, and life. The color poured from him like water from a bucket with a hole in it. The once vibrant, golden-toned fairy turned an ugly dead gray. Sunny stood before Neeradima, numb and altered, with its arms down and eyes fixed on Neeradima.

Neeradima wasn't quite sure what to do with this newly transformed fairy; however, she was delighted that it stared at her in reverence. "Well, hello there. Do you know who I am?" she asked.

"Are you my queen?" he responded.

A sinister smile cracked across her face, "I have made my own disciple." She thought wickedly.

She then answered. "I am your queen; you will serve me and me alone. Do you remember your name?"

The little gray soul stood there thinking; flashes of his life flew by his mind, but then faded as quickly as they came. And then, nothing. His body ached, and his head was swimming in the sense of utter failure and defeat. Joyless, he stood with no direction or purpose.

"I have no name," he answered. "Oh, but you do small one. Your name is," Neeradima thought for a minute and then decided on a title, rather than a name, "You shall be called Ominous," she said with a malicious grin.

Neeradima was getting excited, and her mind was spinning with a plan. "All I need to do is remove the piece of Beathra to create a new creature." The realization that she had made her own species delighted her malicious heart.

Neeradima knew deep down within she was not a creator, but

only a servant to grow the garden, but this new little being sure felt like her own design. And if she couldn't make something on her own, she would distort it to become her own.

She sat in her secluded place in the garden and turned the dirt and plants with her hands like one would stir something in a bowl. The innocent garden sensed the change in their forest spirit. The leaves around her began to curl away. The flowers closed, and the grass rolled up like a carpet. She didn't care, she was consumed with her recent discovery with the change of Sunny and obsessed with her new magic.

As she sat in a secret corner of the garden, she delighted in her evilness; stirring the earth, the greenery in her hands began to transform. Her head tilted back. All the energy that was once good started to flow in a wicked pouring of magic. Neeradima's toxic behavior surged out of her and into the plant that was in her grasp. Willingly but unwittingly, she used the magic that was given to her to grow the garden. Instead, she corrupted a piece of it. Amid her toxic, emotional descent, a small green shrub formed with tiny orange berries. The plants around it withdrew, and the new bush stood alone, with dead earth circling it.

Neeradima was startled at what appeared before her. For she had just made her first poisonous plant. She took the orange berry and could feel misery emanating from it. The leaves eeked with unhappiness. She had imparted all her wretchedness and discontent, into this small shrub.

Neeradima had a faithful following of gidgies that loved her, and like Sunny might even offer her their seed. If not, with her invention, she would be able to persuade them to follow her and revolt against The Whisper and Beathra.

"This new product has the power to change the minds of those stupid joyful gidgies," she thought.

With her new devoted subject, Ominous could help her build her army to take possession of the garden and claim it and its inhabitants as her own. All he had to do was to distribute the newly formed fruit. With this new plant, it would help convince them to join her. Their discontentment would be her opportunity to offer her solution. She named the evil plant a Liath bush, and she would grow her own followers with it.

Now, Neeradima sat, hundreds of years later, exiled from the forest she tried to overthrow, with no way to return. The Darphea caves became her refuge. The forest that rested beneath the Mountain Range became her playground, corrupting the foliage and the streams that existed in the Darphea forest. She renamed the land Skawlterrin, meaning terrain of torment. Any creature that lived in it before, either became her slave, her prisoner, or the land's fertilizer. The once lush Darphea valley was now her boundary. Cursing the land and its river that ran through it with her exit. All she had now was hate and time.

Neeradima reminisced about the beginning of her fall that was so long ago. She had developed several evil plants since her exile, each one a product of her black heart. Even though she was unsuccessful in overtaking Havengothy, she still felt a sense of accomplishment. Wounding the heart of Beathra and The Whisper thrilled her. "If I can't take the land, I will pick off your precious children, one at a time." She said to an empty cavern.

Ominous walked into Neeradima's chamber with a new recruit. "I found this unfortunate individual near the edge of Skawlterrin. Looks like my dealer is making good on his promise." He said with a sick grin, showing his jagged yellow teeth covered in bits of decay and food. "If he keeps this up, I might have to make good on mine. Too bad it's impossible to fulfill." He said with a snarled smile.

Neeradima was not amused. "Bring the piece of trash to me." She bellowed. Ominous dragged the terrified gidgie to Neeradima. She looked at the frightened soul. The fairy was writhing in pain from sipping from the waters of Skawlterrin. Shaking, she threw up all over Neeradima's cold chamber.

"You disgusting piece of filth! Ominous, clean this up!" she screamed. The obedient General jolted and then began to mop up the vomit.

The wicked enchantress then looked at the unfortunate fairy and made her an offer, "I can end your pain. All you need to do is swear allegiance to me. Just speak the words, 'Beathra is no longer my King', and I will stop your suffering."

Trixie shook in pain. She could not recall how she ended up wandering in the wilderness. "Who was it that convinced me that if I ate that orange fruit, it would help win Billick's heart?" her mind spun with questions and confusion. The stranger knew just what to say to her to persuade her to partake of his offering.

It was during the chaos of Lewis's absence that Trixie went missing. She, too, was out by the activity field to watch Billick practice but realized his swollen behind would have kept him from running drills with the team. Trixie was about to go back to her root dorm when she was approached by the cloaked gidgie. He was familiar, and he knew she was in love with Billick.

As Pete and Jo were returning with Lewis, the school had been put on alert for Trixie. That was the trouble with being a bully, her absence wasn't missed right away. But Beathra knew she was gone, and he placed it on Professor Jinkle's heart to ask about her. She went to find Professor Hill, who was speaking with General Dax about his thoughts on the recent abductions when Professor Jinkles entered his office. General Dax was quick to respond, and he dispatched a task force immediately to search for her.

Trixie stood in front of the evilest creature that existed in her world.

"Answer me, you fool! I can end this right now!" Neeradima raged.

Trixie shivered from the cold and shook from pain, but courage rose up from her like she had never experienced before. Beathra had spoken to her and revealed help was on the way.

She looked the wicked queen in the eyes and stated with a boldness that could only come from the fire seed, "I will never deny my King or The Whisper. Their love for me is far greater than life. And if they do not save me from this disaster, I am ready to meet the Great Ghost warrior!" Trixie grew louder, bolder, and stood taller as she finished her statement.

Her body was quivering in pain from the poisons of the forest water. It was an agony she had never experienced before. She felt like her muscles were on fire; her bones ached as if they were being bent to a breaking point, and her head was splitting with a migraine that caused Trixie's vision to blur. Yet, in the torment, Trixie dared to hear the fire seed.

It was a strength few displayed, but this young fairy showed a resilience and a sturdiness few grown gidgies exhibit. Trixie did consider taking the black seed just to end her anguish, but the flicker of hope burned in her to hold fast. She dug her heels in and bit the side of her mouth until she tasted her own blood. She was resolved. She would wait for her rescue or her death, but she would not deny her King.

The evil queen was infuriated at the fierce gidgie. She would have finished her right then and there but preferred to allow the sinister nourishment from her garden to torture this obstinate girl into submission.

Neeradima screamed for Ominous and his thugs to throw the stubborn fairy in the dungeon. Suddenly, a team of Special Task Force members stormed in the chambers. Led by Commander Sidney, the furious crew engaged in battle. Ominous escaped with the queen, leaving behind a team of liaths to contend with the skilled task force.

Grabbing Trixie, Commander Sidney bolted out of the cave, ordering her crew to find any other imprisoned gidgies before they returned to Havengothy. Trixie was draped over Sidney's shoulders as she went in and out of consciousness. "Hang on little one, we will be home soon," the Commander whispered to the weakening fairy. Trixie was dreaming of the cloaked fairy who deceived her. She could see his shoes and the color of his cape in her dream, but she could not make out his face.

Back at the University, Lewis was in the Healer's station. He had been there for nearly a day, being attended to by a young Healer named Julia when Commander Sidney landed with Trixie. The crew of Healers rushed to Sidney and scooped Trixie from her arms. The Commander was kind and watched as Julia was quick to gather the proper elixir and tonics. Sidney explained what Trixie had been rescued from, and the possible poisons she had ingested. The Healers made fast work of treating the traumatized fairy.

Lewis looked over and saw Trixie in her weakened state. She looked war-worn, and she was covered in dirt. He felt all the fear and anxiety Trixie had gone through at the wicked forest. He could feel the horror in the memory of Neeradima, crossing Trixie's mind. Lewis shuddered at the terror she endured. He got up from his bed and went over to Trixie. Putting his hand on her hand, he stroked the back of her arm to soothe the nightmare away.

Trixie was covered in the dust from the wasteland. She had a winding riverbed that trailed down her face where the tears ran. She looked over at Lewis, and he could feel her relief for being rescued, and her shame for being tricked. He held her hand, not saying a word. Simultaneously, Julia gave her tonics and blue liquids that were created to countcract the toxic waters of Skawlterrin. Then Julia called the head Healer over.

Melia was not only considered the chief of all the Healers at the University, but she was also a "head" Healer. With a unique way to speak over broken-hearted, anxious, or depressed gidgies, Melia was gifted by Beathra with a presence of peace to calm the mind.

Melia floated over to Trixie's bed. The lovely young Healer had striking, sapphire blue wings and long pearly white hair. She witnessed Lewis comforting his friend and smiled. "You are gifted with healing, young man." She said with a wink. Lewis smiled shyly, but he knew she was right. He was the first to experience his "gift" with the healing of his own allergies.

Melia tucked a strand of loose hair behind her ears and placed her hands over Trixie's forehead. While cupping Trixie's brow and head, Melia leaned in incredibly close to Trixie's face. This was done so Trixie could hear what Melia was about to whisper. The gifted Healer began to speak softly, a life charm over the scared, sick fairy.

"Let all the cares and burdens go.
Breathe in the air that freedom owns.
Rest in the truth you have always known.
You are never far from home.
Let your mind heal and your heart fly.
Let the shame fall, and the guilt die.
The King is near, and his love is real.
He forgives our failures, and he longs to heal.
Let the wind of peace blow across your soul.
Take heart child, you've been made whole."

It was practically a song, and Trixie and Lewis both felt the effect of the charm like a prayer. It soothed both of their minds and spirits.

Trixie laid on her side in the Healer's bed, still holding Lewis's hand. Cleansing tears flowed from deep within, and silent sobs escaped her as she allowed the life-giving words of Melia to do their work.

Lewis sat quietly, feeling the atmosphere seeped with healing and peace. A calming presence of The Whisper flowed over both of them like warm oil running down their heads. He squeezed Trixie's hand in reassurance. Lewis allowed his tears of compassion to fall, and he softly spoke to his friend, "We are gonna be ok, Trix. Better than ok, we were lost, but now, here we are, found, healed, and experiencing a part of our King we never knew existed." Trixie squeezed his hand back and looked at him. "Thanks, Lewis."

An extraordinary ivy

Chapter Ten

The Vine wakes.

A small tent was set up just outside the dining hall. I.K. was going to cancel the graduation ceremony altogether, but Yoli would not have it. "These young fairies need to be acknowledged for all their hard work. You can't penalize the lot because you feel the heat of the council breathing down your neck. Not to mention, the world they are facing outside our root walls is changing. They need this ceremony. It just might give them a wonderful memory to cling to during our trying times." Yoli barked at I.K.

As usual, Yoli got what she wanted, and created a small area to commemorate the graduates. The graduation was bumped for a week later than scheduled, which gave Yoli plenty of time to organize a safe ceremony. And it gave Jo time to rally troops to watch over the perimeters of the University.

Yoli put on an outside feast celebration and recruited the help of a few teachers. Professor Jinkles and Hill helped with the set-up, and Miss Milton was in charge of directing families to the new graduation sight. Joseppi and Pete stood guard with the assistance of a few Skyforce members that Captain Roland sent earlier that week.

Moses was set to hand the diplomas, and I.K. was to announce the fairies next step in life they had chosen to follow. Moses, Captain Roland, and the General had a meeting scheduled with I.K., who was in his office, eating everything in sight from nerves. I.K. felt the judgmental looks from Havengothy Council.

He was scheduled for a debriefing meeting to discuss the two fairies who were targets. His plan was to cancel the graduation, hoping it bore the appearance of protecting the students. But the council wasn't buying it. I.K.'s laziness with the school was about to be dealt with, and the two rescued gidgies were the justifying reason for his reprimand.

Moses glided into Instructor Kay's office with General Dax and Captain Roland. Before Moses said a word, I.K. spoke. "I would like to submit my resignation from Havengothy as a head professor. With the recent events that have occurred...."

General Dax interrupted I.K., "You mean, the recent abductions of two of your students, instructor? I am glad you brought that up. This is why we are here. We are not here to only address your lazy leadership, but also, your carelessness in protecting Beathra's youngest."

I.K was embarrassed by the General's corrections and attempted to cover his flippant remark with a heroic excuse, "Yes, of course, I mean abductions. It's a tragic, tragic thing to have our precious students targeted by the evil enchantress. I feel it is my duty to step aside and allow the council to come in and protect our Skyforce to the University. It is a sacrifice I am willing to make for the safety of our youngest gidgies."

Moses, General Dax, and Captain Roland all exchanged glances of disbelief. I.K's lame attempt to look valiant was worthy of all the eye rolls the council could give. Moses was first to speak after that ridiculous show of false humility. "That is quite generous of you I.K. considering you will be forgoing your retirement of a southern root near the Quartz Gulf. But being you are so willing to sacrifice your warm retirement; the council extends its gratitude. If you could have your office emptied by the end of the day, we happen to have a replacement ready to come in and reorganize the curriculum and safety of Havengothy University. All this will be done before the next school year."

I.K went red, first with embarrassment and then with anger. But he didn't dare argue with the top councilman. Instead, he shoved his humiliation down to his fat feet, swallowed his pride, and conceded. "Yes, of course, Moses. However, I don't think I could be ready to leave my root or living quarters until the end of the week. I need to decide on a new place to reside. I did so hope for my warm root near the water. Is there a possibility that the council could grant me a different retirement root? After all, I have been a faithful head professor for over one hundred years." I.K ended his request with pleading eyes.

Moses considered I.K.'s appeal, "I believe there are some open roots near the west side of Havengothy with a view of the Darphea Wilderness, or the northwest side of Beathra." Moses offered.

I.K. shrugged his shoulders, conceding. "I supposed the northwest will do. I do love the snow," he lied.

Yoli had done a remarkable job turning the outside dining area into a lovely venue for graduation. The security was tight around the school, and the Skyforce's presence was felt by all. Moses and General Dax found their way to the kitchen to find Yoli.

"It appears I will need a list of the graduate names." General Dax informed Yoli.

Yoli looked up from a bouquet of flowers she was adjusting. She gave a daisy a quick fix, then wiped her hands on her apron and met Moses and General Dax. "I am happy to get that for you, gentleman, but I.K. should have had that for you. Where is he? I do hope he isn't planning on opening with his singing."

"I.K. has decided not to join us for the graduation. Instead, he has opted to get a jump start on packing his quarters. Moses will be performing the entire ceremony. He will announce the graduate, and then hand them their diploma. We decided to have the graduates announce their own vocation," General Dax shared without explaining why I.K. would not be joining them.

"I am rather looking forward to this. It's been centuries since I have officiated graduation. I do so love hearing the graduate's career choices. Some of them really surprise you." Moses said with a smile.

Yoli looked confused and asked, "Did he at least give you the itinerary of today's events? We've already had to change our traditional field graduations to using the outdoor dining area. I hope they still get their launching moment from the entrance of Havengothy. There is nothing like watching a gidgie fly out of the same entrance they walked through some twelve years ago."

"We plan on adhering to the schedule you put into place, Yoli. We will follow your lead." Moses encouraged.

Moses was keenly aware of Yoli's service and sacrifice to Havengothy. He respected how she led the young fairies, all while serving them.

Lewis and Trixie stood side by side for graduation. The two had drawn rather close after the wilderness ordeal. Lewis reached down for Trixie's hand, and she slid her slender fingers to interlock with his. He gave it a little squeeze, leaned in, and asked, "Are you ready to shock everyone with your career choice?"

"I am. Everyone thinks I am advancing my training in the Beast of Havengothy. I can't wait to see the look on Billick's face when I announce my decision." Trixie smiled.

Trixie would have been hurt by the lack of concern Billick had for her, had it not been for Lewis's kindness and genuine friendship. Billick never visited Trixie at the Healer's root, even after she had done his homework and snuck him treats from the kitchen while his butt was healing. None of that mattered; she felt made new, with a fresh start and a true friend by her side, she was ready to face her future.

"Everyone was certain I would go on to an advanced learning center to become an instructor and possibly the next head professor." Lewis grinned. His rosy cheeks were still a bit chapped from the dry wasteland.

Yoli was fluttering around, getting the graduates in line. She was going down the path, checking names off her list, when she noticed how swollen Billicks behind still was. "Oh my," she thought, but she proceeded with her work.

Yoli arranged the graduates in two lines, boys on the left girls on the right. She checked the line-up she had organized: Todd was escorting Barbara. Lester with Katie, Lee with Landy, Elisabeth with Colin, Jim with his twin Marlin, Billick with Ellie, and Lewis with Trixie. Yoli even arranged for Sebastian to escort Ruby, except Ruby, was nowhere to be found. "Oh, my Havengothy, where in this beloved forest is that girl!" Yoli exclaimed.

Sebastian looked over at Ellie, and she shrugged her shoulders. "Last I saw of her was this morning, she said she needed some time alone, you know how anxious she is in these things. If you think me peeing my pantaloons is bad, then a projectile vomit from Ruby will kill you." Ellie chuckled at her joke. "She'll be here, Seb, she won't miss graduation. And she will not want to miss me walking with baboon butt, here," Ellie whispered and nodded her head in the direction of Billick.

Billick pretended not to hear Ellie. He just wanted to get through this day, so he could put school behind him. With a few months before leaving for cadet school, he was hoping to leave all his mistakes, bad behavior, and bullying behind. He wanted, no, he needed a clean slate, and cadet school was just his ticket.

Ruby left early that morning to breathe a bit before the crowds suffocated her. Crowded events like these made her anxious. She wasn't sure if it was the hordes of fairies she had to greet or the relief of finally graduating; she just knew she would be sick if she didn't take a few moments to herself. Flying to the three's favorite hideout, she landed near the entrance of the fort. She placed her hands on the ivy; this was her chance while no one was around, she could practice the spell that Neeradima used in the garden.

She drew close to the ivy as if she was going to whisper to it, taking her left hand, she slid it behind the curtain of foliage and scooped it towards her face. Then, looking around to make sure she was completely alone, she began to speak the charm.

"Reach towards the sky, crawl out of the earth.
Uncurl your leaves, and let your blooms burst.
The King and The Whisper made you for a reason,
now come forth all that's green, today is your season.
It's time to grow."

Ruby was timid as she recited the spell. All of a sudden, Ruby felt a shaking beneath her feet. The garden trembled violently, and a loud sonic boom vibrated through the forest. The vines began to tremor like a gust of wind was blowing them. Then, she heard a song in her head, being sung to her.

"Your song of growth makes my roots take flight.
My limbs are your arms, and my leaves your delight.
Guide me as I crawl this land.
What you say is my command."

The vines wrapped around Ruby's legs and lifted her high, carrying her to the top of the tree, singing while it rushed Ruby from the ground. Ruby burst through the canopy of the forest into the golden morning sun. Dazed by what just happened, she yelled, "What in Havengothy is going on?" The Vine then answered her, "You woke me from a deep sleep. I haven't felt this alive in centuries."

"Holy crap, does this vine understand me? What is going on?" Ruby was freaking out. She was hearing voices in her head. A plant just spiraled around her to lift her high above the trees of

Havengothy. Ruby thought about what the vine said to her, "What you say is my command." So, she asked aloud, "Vine, does this song give me power over you?" feeling rather foolish, expecting an answer.

The vine answered, but not out loud. Ruby felt the answer as one would have a thought. "The song you sang is an ancient one. Long ago, it was used to grow and expand our beloved land. That was back when our Forest Spirit cared for us. But there is a new voice behind the melody. The lyrics of the song now have love and innocence behind them again, that is why I responded. But I do not necessarily obey, I surrender. If the voice goes against our King and The Whisper, I will not comply."

"Are you telepathic?" Ruby thought her question this time, waiting for a response.

"I am. There is no other vine like me in the forest," The vine answered.

"Blessed Beathra! I knew you were special. I could feel it every time I came to our hideout!" Ruby exclaimed.

"And I knew *you* were special. It is the only reason we are speaking now." Vine answered.

Ruby's head was spinning. This was beyond incredible. No wonder Professor Hill had this book, she thought, "So I just need to think towards you, and you will hear me?" Ruby questioned, not believing what she was experiencing. "Why would Neeradima give up such wonderful magic?"

"Because she fell in love with the power and not the purpose of the power. And that was to love Havengothy into its fullness and beauty." The vine answered.

"Vine, do you communicate with other vines around the garden? I mean, if I speak to you, can I speak to others as well?" Ruby excitedly asked.

"If the vine is part of me, then it will be I that answers," Vine informed.

Ruby sat on top of the enormous tree looking all across Havengothy, thrilled with this new bit of information, when she suddenly realized she was supposed to graduate. "Shoot, I gotta go, Vine. But I'll be back. Keep this safe." She shoved the ancient book into a hand-like leaf. Ruby then bolted. "I'm likely to get screamed at by I.K. and forbidden to walk with my class." She thought. But she didn't care, she just experienced a magic that has not been seen or heard of in centuries.

Torn, a young scout for Neeradima, had landed near a fickle fruit bush searching for wandering gidgies when she felt a small earthquake and heard a bass sounding boom. She jumped off her red-tailed hawk and assessed the land. What she saw astonished her. As she watched from the top of a tree, she witnessed a pink winged fairy, being lifted by a vine towards the sun. She had only heard of such magic by her enchantress, but here she was witnessing another sorcerer commanding the garden.

"My queen will want to know about this," she thought. She jumped on the back of Nash, her hawk, and made her way across the Darphea Wilderness to the queen's chamber. This information will move her up in rank quickly.

Torn was once known as Courtney, a lovely tangerine-colored winged gidgie who worked in the southern section of the forest as a seedling starter. But it had been years since she was called by her real name.

The plummet of Courtney started with the discovery of a suspicious plant. It was sown by Neeradima before her banishment. It was one of the toxic plants Neeradima was secretly sowing about the garden.

Courtney was curious about the leafy shrub she discovered. Knowing it was evil, she began to experiment with the plant anyway, namely the flowers and seeds. The rebellious fairy felt the nudge of Beathra to pull the plant and turn it into the council, but Courtney ignored the King's voice. She was captivated by the plant, and the more she worked with it and handled it, the more consumed she became.

Courtney fled to the wilderness in search of the creator of who developed the incredible shrubbery that fascinated her. She needed to know more. Courtney offered her wings and fire seed to Neeradima. But it was not because of love, it was a strange obsession that Courtney had towards the enchantress and her power.

Now, here she stood, many years later, a devoted servant to Neeradima, with no recollection of who she used to be. Torn's sick fascination with the queen delighted Neeradima, and she fed off it. If she takes an interest in a liath, it was for her own gain.

———————————

Neeradima felt a power surge through her like an electric current. She knew precisely what the tremble was; somebody knew her ancient charms and recited it.

"Those are my songs, my charms. MY MAGIC!" she screamed. "Who dares to speak my spells? Who dares to take my place?" The wicked enchantress fumed in a jealous rage. The electric current that pulsed through her burned her ribbon-like skin as if she was hit by lightning. Neeradima had never felt pain, but this was a sting like no other. It was a torturous feeling of being replaced.

As she sat in her venomous rage, a wicked thought came to mind, "If I can get my hands on the creature who can operate the spells, I may be able to corrupt them to do my bidding." She sat down on her granite throne and began to contemplate how to find the being who holds her book. She was rubbing her hands up and down her arms to soothe the strange pain that seemed to linger.

Back at the school, Yoli was about to leave the kitchen to find Joseppi and inform him that there may be a missing student when the root violently shook, and a low boom was heard. Captain Roland, Jo, Moses, and General Dax all looked at each other, each knowing what that sound and tremble meant. The last time that rumble and shaking were felt in Havengothy was when Neeradima was exiled, and a war broke out.

Moses spoke, "It appears the prophecy is being unfolded." Moses was referring to the day Neeradima was stripped of her authority in Havengothy and banished from the garden. Beathra and The Whisper cast a spell harnessing Neeradima's charms. This was to ensure the spells were sung in adorations and belief, and not self-serving. The one whose love is deep, loyal, and pure of heart, will be given access to the charms.

The mystery cloak.

Chapter Eleven
The Cloak

Yoli was grabbing glasses and plates that fell during the earth shake. All of her towered platters filled with sandwich squares, cookies, and pastries toppled. Her meticulous display of fruits, spelling Havengothy University, wcrc all jumbled and read *Hav e goht U sty*. Food was scattered everywhere, and all her precious pinkle pepper brew spilled out on the floor. Yoli was doing her best to bring order back to a disaster of a venue. "Why do I think that blasted girl has something to do with this?" Yoli thought to herself, referring to Ruby.

Several families left the ceremony to go home to check on their roots and farms. Havengothy had not experienced an earth shake since the banishment war, and this tremble had all the garden nervous.

The entire school and staff were scrambling to clean up after the rumbling and shaking of the garden. Books fell from shelves; pictures came unhinged or hung sideways in the long halls. I.K. came out of his office in a wild-eyed wonder. He was unsure as to the happenings due to his own miserable state. He was in his office throwing things, such as plaques, books, vases, and drawers from his desk, when all of Beathra shook. The entirety of his furious mess-making was combined with the earthquake disaster, and it looked like one giant pile of chaos.

He ventured out of his gloomy office to see what the ruckus was, but the Skyforce members were gathered in conversations, so he snuck back to his root. He had no desire to communicate with Jo or Moses. He went back into his office, took the heat from his lava bean in his stove, and lit his pipe. He didn't care if all of Havengothy burned to the ground.

Ruby landed at the entrance of the University to find Pete guarding it. "Yoli is going to be glad to see you, young lady. They are assembling a search team right now as we speak. I suggest you fly through those halls and make your presence known swiftly." Pete reprimanded.

"I know Pete, I am so sorry. I got..." Ruby paused and weighed her words carefully. "I got tied up." It was an honest answer.

"Well, you should know that a late gidgie around here sets off quite a few alarms. We can't be none too careful. Now scoot! The search team is congregated in the dining hall about to fly." Pete ordered.

Joseppi was in the center of a team of Skyforce, council, and school staff, giving directions as to where to look when Ellie glanced up from the hurdle and saw Ruby flying into the dining root.

"Ruby!" she yelled. Ellie flew to meet her. Jo looked up and saw the pink winged fairy and immediately darted towards her to question her whereabouts. But Sebastian was the first to get to Ruby.

"Where in the blazing Beathra have you been? The entire school has turned itself upside down, looking for you. And then there was an earthquake; you could have been crushed or snatched. Why in Havengothy do you insist on your bloody time alone?" Seb yelled.

He was scared Ruby was the most recent victim of Neeradima, and his scolding was out of fear more than anger. He admired Ruby's free spirit, but he worried it would get her in trouble in these changing days.

Ruby was trying to explain herself when Jo landed next to her. "I suggest we try to salvage what we can of this graduation, but when the ceremony is done, the council would like to meet with you, Ruby. Ginny and Yoli flew next to Ruby, and both clutched and hugged her "Praise be to Beathra!" Yoli exclaimed.

The ever gentle and kind Ginny pointed for Ruby to bend down to her level. Ruby obeyed her mother but knew what was coming. Ginny placed her petite hands-on Ruby's shoulders and began to scold her.

Ginny's motherly tone of displeasure caused Ruby's head to drop as Ginny laid into her. "You gave us quite a fright, Ruby. When Yoli grabbed me out of the crowd looking for you, I was shocked that you would venture out the day of graduation. You are wiser than this, and I believe you need to grow up. Your little adventures have set the entire school on alert, and if that doesn't beat all, our garden experienced a vicious shaking. Your carelessness could have gotten you hurt, or worse. I don't know what I would do if that happened. I agree with Sebastian; you could have been killed or kidnapped."

Ginny took a breath she then hugged Ruby and gave her the tightest of squeezes. She then grabbed a bobby pin from her purse, split it open with her teeth, and seized her fly away hair, pinned it back in place. That was that. Once Ginny got something off her chest, she was done. She was forgiving and loving and never held a grudge.

"I'm sorry, everyone. I never meant to cause any trouble or worry. I just needed some time to myself. I wasn't trying to be selfish; crowds just get me all anxious inside. And then, well, I don't know how to say this, but…I may be the cause of the earthquake." Ruby stopped and looked at the group of gidgies circled around her. She heard the gasp of Ginny and Yoli both, but she caught Ellie, saying, "I knew it."

"I have a handful of graduates and their families waiting to see if we are going to finish this production. I want you three," Yoli pointed to Seb, Ellie, and Ruby, "to go get in line with the other graduates. I am going to finish this day if it kills me."

With that, Yoli flew to Moses and ordered him to get on the platform that was covered in papers. Moses smirked at the bossy fairy and did precisely as she directed. He had to place the podium upright and gather his notes. They had been strewn all over with the earthquake.

It was a simple ceremony, the plainest Havengothy University had ever seen. But Yoli did a remarkable job organizing the celebration. Yoli asked Todd and Barbara to open with a song of their choice. Todd was an artistic gidgie with pumpkin-colored hair and wings to match. He was attempting to grow a beard for graduation, but it looked more like wisps of moss hanging off his chin.

With his guitar in hand, Todd adjusted his round wire-framed glasses, moving them back and forth from his eyes until the musical notes came into focus. He sat on his stool, positioned to accompany Barbara with her melody.

Barb was as lovely as they came. With light brown hair and sage green wings, she looked like Havengothy scenery. She was a natural beauty who loved flowers and anything in its purest form. She made a daisy garland to wear on her head with lovely blue ribbons that draped down her back. Her song was sweet, and her voice was soft, and it held the attention of all who attended the event. As soon as the two finished their tune, they got back into the line-up of graduates and awaited their name to be called by Professor Hill.

Moses stood on the platform with rolled certificates in hand, while Professor Hill announced the graduates. "Billick Bailey," Billick went to the stage and received his diploma. Moses congratulated him, then while handing him the rolled-up document asked for him to declare his next journey as a gidgie.

"I have enlisted in the Skyforce with the hopes of being part of the Special Task Force." Billick stood tall and proud. He was ready to start a new life. He scanned the audience for his family. There they were, in the front row, standing just as tall and proud with two younger gidgies his foster family adopted a few years ago. They were in their first year of University but were already standing tall like their father. Billick then looked back at the graduates and watched as Ruby smiled at him. He smiled back and felt a sense of relief. "I guess that's something," he thought, considering Ruby's smile.

One by one, Phineas Hill called the graduates. "Ellie Winn," Ellie stated she was accepted to ALC, the Advance Learning Center for her degree to become a professor, specializing in geography. She would be training in the east branch near the Broad River.

Ruby was excited for her best friend, but she knew the distance of the east branch would make spending time with her difficult. Braving a smile, Ruby looked at her friend and gave her two thumbs up.

Lewis shocked everyone. Deciding to become a Healer amazed the students and teachers alike. Everyone was sure he was going to study to become a professor. He was the smartest gidgie in school and was sure to be the next instructor to run Havengothy Gardening University or any other branch for that matter. His pronouncement was said clearly, with no sniffles, sneezing or congestion.

"Ruby May," Ruby stood on the stage and looked at the small gathering that remained for the ceremony. There was nothing lofty in her choice. She didn't want to join the military. She certainly didn't want to continue in school. The only real thing she was good at was gardening. She saw Ginny out in the crowd hanging on the arms of Duke, smiling proudly.

"My vocation will be gardening and the cultivation of Havengothy. I would like to live near a beloved fickle fruit bush," she looked at Moses with a hinting look, hoping that would incline him to help her secure a root." She then continued. "This is, of course, after I work the summer on my mother's farm," Ruby stated as she smiled at Ginny.

Ruby had initially secured a root near the Havengothy stream. After this morning, she had to live near the vine. Moses passed her the diploma and then quietly said, "I'll do what I can." And then gave her a wink.

Sebastian declared his choice as a Skyforce member and, like Billick, chose to pursue the Special Task Force. Joseppi asked to hand the diploma to Seb. Jo's mentorship and guidance had directed Sebastian with his career choice.

It was Jo's encouragement that gave Seb the guts to ask Ruby to the Bloom Festival. Seb wanted to make Jo proud, but there was no need for Seb to concern himself with such thoughts, Jo was already button busting proud as if he had raised Seb himself.

Sebastian's foster fairies were not your typical gidgies. He lived with Jake and Betty, the first five spring of his life. One day, after the Bloom Festival, he went home for summer vacation and found Jake and Betty had moved with Jarred. Leaving only a note on the door that read, "Found a new home." No forwarding address, no explanation. Seb didn't miss them. In fact, he felt relieved they wouldn't be there when he went home.

Seb would still go back to the root every once in a while, until new tenants moved in. But after that, he stayed at the school and volunteered. Seb never talked about being abandoned or rejected. Instead, he pretended as if it never happened. Sebastian met Jo during one of his recruiting visits. Jo was instructing a class on the making of tools and weapons. Sebastian volunteered to help with clean up. It was two years of watching Jo teach and serve his garden and King as a Skyforce soldier, which made Sebastian want to do the same.

Perhaps Trixie's vocation was the most shocking of all. She was joining the Skyforce to train as a sentinel. If she passed the grueling training requirements, Trixie would be the first female guardian of the Havengothy border. After her abduction, she knew; she would never want another gidgie or any other creature to endure what she went through. Her time of healing and secret time with Beathra led her towards a new career choice.

The small graduation ceremony was a success, even though it was amongst the broken glass, a disarrayed courtyard, and a sideways canopy, it was lovely. The feast was delicious. Yoli and her crew did a remarkable job with the spread. While the meats and the savory dishes were mixed up with the desserts, the remaining gidgies who stuck around did not seem to mind. The girls were gathered around Trixie, excited about her career choice.

"What made you decide the sentinel path, Trix? I've heard it's one of the worst training programs in Skyforce. It's only for the elite of the elites. You have to be strong enough to wield a sword that is tall and weighs as much as you." Barb exclaimed.

Then Kay chimed in, "And stand on the Skyforce platform for hours."

"Exactly, that's why it's always just been, men. The weapon alone is just too heavy for us girls." Barb commented as she was repairing a daisy that was slipping from her headband.

"I know it's going to be hard. Right now, I can barely lift a garden spade. But after my terrifying experience in the evil forest, I will do whatever it takes to stand guard over our garden and ensure the safety of our gidgies. As for why? It was after my rescue from Skawlterrin. The time was horrifying, but I never felt so close to our King. Beathra's voice burned inside me to hang on and not give up, even though I was partly to blame for being in that horrible queen's presence." Trixie explained. "and after my stay at the Healers, I had an audience with Beathra." Trixie paused and let that morsel of info penetrate the group around her. "It was in a secret knot in one of Beathra's branches, and from what I know now, the location is always changing."

"You are going to be Havengothy's first female sentinel!" Ruby exclaimed, genuinely excited for Trixie. Ruby was all about girl power, and Trixie's choice to join an all-male team was motivating and inspiring. And I can't believe you spent time in the actual presence of our King! You must tell us what it was like meeting with Beathra. I have only read about face-to-face encounters with his spirit." Just as Trixie began to explain her special meeting, Jo walked up behind Ruby and said, "Young lady, we would like to meet with you in Professor Hill's Office."

Ruby's stomach dropped. How could this day be filled with so much craziness already? Just a few short hours ago, Ruby was telepathically speaking with a plant. Now, she is, eating a millie-fruit-pudding filled cake and sipping fruit punch and chatting with a former adversary. Ruby was a mix of emotions due to the elated feeling of speaking with a vine and the devastation of the earthquake. The disaster she created with her tardiness caused a meeting with the council and the General of the Skyforce. Ruby looked over at Ellie and said, "I'll be glad when this day is over."

Ellie smiled to encourage Ruby, "I'm coming with you, and so is Sebastian, so don't worry about a thing." She then felt a raindrop hit her on the head, then another, and suddenly, a downpour. "Hey, be glad you have a meeting Ruby, we would have to be part of getting this shindig inside," Ellie said. She pointed her head towards Yoli, who was barking orders at anyone and everyone who could lift a table and gather the food.

Miss Milton was wrestling with the broken canopy when a gush of water came funneling down onto her face. Coughing and sputtering, she threw the poles that held the tent up and just grabbed a tray of meat and ran for cover. A crack of lightning, rumble of thunder had everyone scramble all the more.

The three young fairies dashed toward the root to get out of the rain. They followed Jo down the long, root hall. Jo seemed to be prepared for the storm before it even started. "How was that even possible?" Seb thought to himself.

It was Ellie who broke the silence. "Did anyone notice how cute Billick's butt was. It's shrunk down a ton; it looks like the pinkle pepper thorns did him a favor." Ellie and Ruby started giggling, and Sebastian rolled his eyes. Then Ruby added. "Yeah, he could crack a walnut with those two ham hocks." The girls burst into laughter, and it echoed down the hall.

Sebastian shook his head in disbelief. Then Jo turned around and faced the three, with his hooded poncho on, and piped in, "If you ask me, he could give a centaur a run for its money with his tookis. His hind end is going to be an eye-catching attraction for all the young ladies, for sure!"

And that was all it took, all of them were roaring in hilarity. Ruby even had a snort or two in her laughter when they reached Professor Hill's root door.

Then Ruby looked at Jo funny. "What is it, Ruby?" Jo asked, noticing her sideways glance. "Your rain poncho, where did you get it?" Jo looked at his old cape, it was patched in places and had served him well for years, "It was Skyforce commissioned, why?"

"Because it's the same kind of hooded cloak the mysterious

gidgie was wearing," Ruby said.

Jo's eyes widened, "That can only mean one thing, the traitor was or is in the Skyforce."

Chapter Twelve
The meeting

The rain was torrential, and the roots of Beathra could be felt stretching and thoroughly enjoying the deluge. The sound was that of wood creaking and squeaking. The graduation ceremony was moved quickly to the dining hall. Yoli conceded that this would be the first year that the graduates did not have a launching. There were too many variables that were interrupting the traditional University commencement. Starting with missing gidgies, then the earthquake, and now to this unusual downpour. Yes, Havengothy was changing, and the inhabitants would need to adjust as well for the garden's future.

Professor Hill was at his desk, straightening the earthquake mess. Moses and General Dax were sitting in the chairs near the root window watching the rainstorm while they waited to meet with Ruby.

"Moses, would you be able to find a lost Skyforce member for me?" Phineas Hill asked shyly. Moses looked at Phineas, his eyes were full of sympathy but did not answer him. General Dax was the one to reply, "We've been through this Hill, we have no knowledge of her whereabouts."

"Yes, I realize that, but I was hoping Moses might have some insight, with Sylvia being an oracle and all." Professor Hill ventured.

Their conversation was cut short when Captain Roland entered and saluted the General. "Afternoon General, Moses, Phineas. Where is the girl?" The Captain asked in a short-tempered tone.

He was soaking wet and went to warm himself at Phineas Hill's potbelly stove. "This blasted rain came from nowhere. I got stuck helping that bossy kitchen lady move everything to the dining root." The General and Moses had a chuckle, but Professor Hill was not amused. He was disappointed by the General's denial of his request.

Jo knocked on the door, and the four filed in the tiny office. Phineas' room was typically quite tidy, with well-organized books, files, historical documents, and hangings of maps and paintings of Havengothy. His root wall was the perfect example of an engineer turned history teacher. However, the quake made quite a mess of his lovely space. His books had fallen, the shelving had toppled, and files and pictures were strewn everywhere.

Seb noticed a small painting of Hill with a beautiful woman and elbowed Ruby to check it out. The professor quickly grabbed the fallen frame and laid it face down on his desk before Ruby had a chance to see it.

Moses and the General stood to greet Ruby and her friends. General Dax offered Ruby his seat, and Moses rose for Ellie to take his. The two girls sat down nervously. Dax then leaned against Hill's desk with his arms folded and with a kind yet stern demeanor, looked down at Ruby, "I hear you have a bit of information to share with us. Care to start?"

Ruby coughed and then cleared her throat, trying to figure out where to begin. It wasn't too long ago she was excited about an audience with the head of the Gidgie Council and the General. But today, she felt anxious. Does she tell them about the book? And what about the vine, how does she even begin to explain that? "They will think I'm crazy," Ruby mumbled to herself. Her head whirled with where to start when Moses interrupted her spiraling thoughts.

"Ruby, Jo told us about your liath sighting. We are curious, exactly where did you witness the exchange between the cloaked gidgie and the liath?"
Ruby explained everything she had seen at the Merrybare berry bush. Describing in detail the terrifying liath who Jo thinks might be the General of Neeradima's army.

"Ah, Sunny. At least that's who he used to be before he freely gave Neeradima his wings and fire seed. He was a beautiful golden fairy who, at one time, was filled with kindness and compassion. The Lewis boy reminds me of him." Moses stated out of the blue.

Ellie gasped. "A gidgie actually gave that wicked beast of a queen their fire seed and wings? How could they? I don't understand."

"Neeradima was quite convincing, and Sunny loved her, it was more of an obsessed love, but he loved her, nonetheless. And misdirected love can misdirect. Poor Sunny was enamored by Neeradima, and she played him like a fiddle. But make no mistake, young lady, Neeradima is no more a queen than I am." Moses stated thoughtfully, but with a small smile.

"Ruby also has some more recent news General," Jo interjected. "She recognized my rain poncho as the same kind of cloak the mysterious fairy was wearing."

"Well, that is interesting, isn't it?" Moses said with a curious tone.

"I agree that it's fascinating; however, I don't want us to read too far into it. It could be military gear that has been found, passed down or sold in a second-hand shop. It's hard to say who it belongs to unless Ruby noticed any badges or special markings?" Capital Roland said in a questioning tone and one raised eyebrow.

"I didn't. I was pretty scared and was only peeking through the shrubbery. I could tell the cloak was pretty worn out and faded, but I couldn't see any special markings. I was just really worn. Does that help?" Ruby asked nervously.

"Yes and no. It could mean the fairy is a retired Skyforce or an older member of the military. But it could also lead to a cloak that was found or passed down from fairy to fairy. There is just no way of knowing," General Dax interjected.

"Have you talked to Trixie and Lewis about it? Wouldn't they know more than Ruby? They saw the guy up close." Seb asked.

"Yes. We have interviewed the two, and both students have the same answer: they can't recall their abduction with a clear mind. Trixie says the gidgie had brown shoes on, Lewis says he had black boots. And neither one of them can remember his face. Whatever mind-altering drug they took caused them to lose any memory that would identify the traitor," General Dax answered.

"Perhaps there are two different fairies," Seb offered.

"We appreciate your help, uh, what is your name?" Captain Roland asked, annoyed.

"Sebastian James, sir," Seb answered, standing tall.

"Well, Mr. James, we are grateful for your interest in this case. I can see you will make a great cadet and Skyforce member one day. However, for now, why not enjoy your youth and leave the investigations to us." Captain Roland said gruffly.

"Yes, sir," Seb answered a little downcast.

"Captain, Sebastian has a point. What if we are dealing with more than one traitor?" Jo asked, defending Seb's inquiry, and agreeing with it as well.

"And what if we are dealing with confused young fairies?" Captain Roland barked."

"Captain!" General Dax raised his voice in irritation and addressed Captain Roland's grouchiness. "First Sergeant and

Sebastian have made a valid point that deserves our investigation. Now, if you are dry enough, I suggest you find your rain gear and make your way to headquarters."

Captain Roland gave a curt salute and a swift exit. Moses went to the door to leave, and General Dax followed him. But then General Dax turned back to Jo, "Do not pay any mind to the Captain. He's upset, but not at you. Sebastian's consideration of two fairies is smart. I, too, have thought of it, and we are checking into all possibilities." With that, the General left.

Jo turned to Sebastian, "Escort the girls back to their dorms, I have a business to attend to." Then Jo took his leave. He was suspicious of something he wasn't ready to voice.

Phineas Hill was nervously cleaning his desk, but Ruby thought he was looking for the book. She felt a twinge of guilt, but now she didn't dare tell him she had it. For starters, it was a magic book. Secondly, how did she tell him a plant was guarding it? The three younger fairies watched the stressed-out professor for a long minute when he finally looked up and caught their glance.

"I'm sorry students, these types of confrontations get me all befuddled. My office is a disaster and its late. I do believe we should all go back to our roots and get some rest. It's been a very trying day."

The new graduates walked the long hall, and then Ruby dramatically declared, "I'm starving! I'm so hungry, my stomach is eating itself. If I don't eat, I'm going to fade away. Let's go see if Yoli has any leftovers we can chow on." Seb and Ellie loved the idea, and the three made their way to the dining root.

The plans of feasting on piles of cold meat, cake, and millie fruit pastries were dashed. Poor Yoli was sitting in a kitchen chair in the corner. Her legs were stretched out in front of her, and her apron was still damp from all the dishes. With a dishtowel draped over her head, she was snoring. She was utterly exhausted from the day's event, and it still wasn't done.

The three stared at the faithful servant of the school with pity and gratitude. "Should we wake her so she can finish cleaning?" Seb asked in a low hush. Ruby and Ellie shot Sebastian the dirtiest of looks. "You are such a guy!" Ellie steamed.

"Change of plans," Ruby whispered. "Ellie, you help get Yoli to her room, and Seb and I will finish up here. We will meet you in our common area with a platter of leftovers." Sebastian grudgingly agreed. He hated cleaning, and the kitchen was the worst of all the chores. The two made quick work of it, and it allowed them some time alone to discuss life after graduation.

"Ruby, I know it's been whirlwinds around here with all the goings-on, but could we set aside the craziness of today and talk about us?" Sebastian asked nervously.

Ruby was elbow deep in lukewarm, dishwater trying to scrape dried cheese curds from a plate. She paused for a minute and felt butterflies in her stomach. She tried to answer as relaxed and casual as possible. But in classic Ruby form, she mixed her words up when she felt nervous. She wanted to say, "Certainly" or "Sure, not all." but instead, it came out, "Certainly snots small."

Sebastian looked at her, confused. Ruby giggled and quickly recovered, I mean, "sure, not at all."

Seb dried the dish Ruby had just finished washing. Then he grabbed her pruney hands. "It's important to me, with all these sightings of liaths and the dangers that we are experiencing in our land, that you use more wisdom on your little adventures. I was so worried today."

Ruby stood and stared at Sebastian. She thought he was about to declare his undying love. Instead, he has the nerve to tell her to use wisdom on her adventures. Who does he think he is?

"I'm not some wild animal; you have to tame Sebastian! And I am not an idiot. I know there are dangers in our forest, but I refuse to live afraid. Plus, I have ways to stay safe that you know nothing about?" Ruby stated, thinking of her recent experience with the vine. Then she yanked her hands from Sebastian's.

Sebastian was hurt, he wasn't trying to tame her, he just wanted her to use common sense when it came to venturing about the garden. He took a step back from her and put his hands in his pockets and said. "I don't think you're an idiot, I am just afraid when I leave for the Skyforce, I won't be here to protect you."

Ruby seethed at that comment. "Ooh, Ellie was right, you are such a guy! I don't need your protection! I need your friendship, your support, and your love!" Ruby yelled. Her eyes went enormous; she could not believe she just said the "L" word. She turned back to the dishes and started washing them in a frantic. She was utterly humiliated.

Sebastian began to smile, showing his dimples. Ruby didn't want to look at how cute he was, she was mad. "How dare he think I'm some sort of damsel in distress!" she fumed in her thoughts.

Sebastian reached in the dishwater and calmed Ruby's frenzied washing, "I'm sorry, Ruby. I don't know how to see you any other way. I have always wanted to protect you. From the harassment of I.K. to the bullying of Billick. And now, from the horrors that are coming to our world and the dangers that are increasing here. You do have my support, my friendship, and…"

Ellie came storming in the kitchen. "Are you two ever going to finish. I took Yoli to her room and even helped her put her nightshirt on; I'm pretty sure I'm scarred for life. And I've been waiting in the common root starving! What is taking you so long?" She was unaware of the exchange that was happening. All she saw was two gidgies doing dishes.

Sebastian stepped back from Ruby, smiled, took a hand towel, and dried the last of the dishes. Ruby took the dishtowel from Seb and wiped her hands. She didn't know what to say. Was Sebastian about to say he loved her? It sounded like it.

Ruby looked up at Seb and smiled. "Sorry, Ellie, Seb and I were discussing," she paused and had to think of something. "We were talking about the Bloom Festival," Seb reached for the towel in Ruby's hand, and their fingers touched. He took her hand under the concealment of the cloth for the briefest of seconds and gave it a little squeeze.

"That's right, the Bloom Festival is in two days! And then that's it; we are done. We will move out of our root dorms and start the next chapter of our lives." Ellie said, looking at her two best friends and sounding a little down.

"Ah, don't let that get you down, Ell, look on the bright side; we are now old enough to drink Meredith Barry's merrybare berry bush brew this year," Seb declared.

"You are such a guy," both Ruby and Ellie said in exasperated unison.

Chapter Thirteen
The dead gidgie

It was the day of the Festival. Lewis walked the garden grounds that were just outside the door of Professor Jinkle's greenhouse. Connected to the side of her root classroom was a large glass conservatory. This is where the professor had all her seedling starts, rare orchid collection, and specialty herbs used by the Healers.

Beautiful butterflies native only to Havengothy flew about. The professor stored the atto-glider poop under the shelving of her seedlings, where the butterflies love to lay their larvae. To the left side of the root were double doors that opened to a grand outdoor pavilion and flower garden.

Professor Jinkles taught all things gardening in these halls and grounds. However, Lewis was never healthy enough to sit in during the spring bloom. He was part of the seedlings start classes, the fertilizer course, and the importance of pruning. However, he never had the chance to thoroughly enjoy the fruits of his labor. And that was to experience the blooms of all his hard work. But since his time in the wilderness, and the remarkable healing he received, he was able to breathe in the intense fragrances. He instinctively reached for his puff-puff gourd, but then realized, he would never need it again. Lewis smiled at the thought of that and put the gourd back into his pocket.

Lewis enjoyed walking the pebble laid trails. Small benches were stationed about the garden to stop and enjoy the beauty of the place. Professor Jinkles had done a fantastic job creating paths and mazes that wandered through the fragrant paradise. The roses and peonies were as large as dinner plates, two stems of them, and the bouquet would be finished. Lewis was looking for more delicate flowers to give to Trixie. Professor Jinkles sent him towards the finer blooms.

As Lewis was clipping bluebells, jasmine, and pink and white dianthuses, he noticed Billick sitting on a bench alone. Lewis's healing gift began to perceive Billick's mood. It was loneliness, sadness, and humiliation. Lewis casually walked over by Billick and sat down next to him.

"Hey Billick, mind if I join you?" Lewis asked as he confidently plopped down next to his former bully.

Billick looked at Lewis, "I would think this place would kill you?"

He snickered. When Billick giggled, it sounded like a hissing sound. Billick was sitting with one leg crossed, resting his left ankle on his right knee, and leaning against the back of the bench with an arm draped over it. He wanted to apologize to Lewis, but how? He sat there, trying to figure out how to start the conversation when Lewis interrupted him, "Are you going to the Bloom Festival?"

"Nah, I just want to be done with everything. I- I've made a lot of mistakes here I'm not proud of. One of those is harassing you." Billick stuttered over his apology, but he felt lighter, confessing what was pent up inside of him. If only he could apologize to Ruby.

"You know Billick, you going to the Bloom Festival with this new attitude would show what the Festival is all about. Growth," Lewis stated with an ease that was new to him when speaking with Billick.

"Yeah, I guess so. But my last year here has not ended the way I imagined it would; humiliated and alone," Billick said, feeling a little sorry for himself.

"Those are two subjects I am very familiar with," Lewis said with a smile. Billick looked up in shame, but Lewis continued, "However, I've learned that my self-worth is not tied up in another's opinion. If that was the case, I would not be sitting here with you. You see, bully or nerd, we both have new opportunities to live life differently. Me? I am choosing to be braver. And living brave sometimes means forgiving those who hurt us or forgiving ourselves for failing."

Billick sat, holding his head with his elbows on his knees now as Lewis spoke. Flooded with feelings of regret, Billick turned to Lewis and said, "My beginning was so good, but my ending blew up just like my butt.

"Well, my friend, it's a matter of getting up, after disappointment or embarrassment, and facing a new day as your first day to begin again. Tonight, I am taking a beautiful girl to our Bloom Festival. If that doesn't scream, there is hope, I don't know what does." Lewis chuckled.

"That's right, you and Trix are seeing each other now. You know Lewis, she was hung up on me for a long time." Billick said with a smirk.

"Yup, I know. And I know you led her on and let her believe there was hope for you two. But Trixie and I have embraced something others need to grasp." Lewis said.

"Oh, yeah, what's that?" Billick asked.

"That there is life after hurt and mistakes, and we have a choice to look ahead to our future and embrace the new and let go of the old. It's all a matter of where I want my mind to live, Bill. I don't want to be trapped in a thought loop of misery and unforgiveness. I choose to live life in forward motion. Trix is doing the same, and that means letting go of you." With that, Lewis slapped Billick on the back and said, 'I hope you come tonight, and show others, you too chose to live life moving forward."

Lewis scooped up his flowers and sauntered out of the garden, throwing his puffing gourd in the waste bin on his way out.

Jo was at the Skyforce headquarters leaving General Dax's office when he ran into Captain Roland. "First Sergeant Joseppi, aren't you supposed to be at the Gardening University?" The Captain asked in a sharp tone.

"Yes sir, but I had something to discuss with the General," Jo answered.

"Do you care to elaborate?" The Captain asked curiously.

"I'm sorry sir, I have been ordered to keep the information to myself," Jo stated. With that, He saluted the Captain and flew back to the school.

The Captain was irritated with the lack of information but could not argue with Jo. He would just have to ask the General what that was all about. He approached the General's office only to be met by Corporal Garett, also known as Pocket, who was a young fairy who served as the General's assistant. He was known for all his strange collections and oddities that he kept in his pockets. Many of them useful to his work.

"Hey Pocket, is the General in?" Captain Roland asked, knowing the answer was yes because he just saw Jo leaving the General's office.

"Yes sir, but he is in a meeting." Pocket replied.

"Don't you mean he just finished a meeting? I saw Jo leave a minute ago." The Captain questioned with annoyance.

Pocket was nervous, "no, sir, he is in with the head of the council." Pocket said with a wince, preparing for the Captain's temper.

"Is that so?" Captain bellowed.

Here came the rage the Captain was becoming known for. Pocket steadied himself because Roland's fury wasn't finished.

"You mean to tell me that Jo and Moses had a meeting with the General without me?" the Captain yelled.

Moses suddenly opened the door of the General's office, and calmly said, "Captain, would you care to join the General and me?" Moses gave Pocket a nod of hello, and the Captain barged into the office, offended that he was not invited in the first place. The door slammed behind them, and General Dax's voice could be heard getting louder. Then Captain Roland's voice raised. The argument was a screaming match of accusations and defense.

Pocket reached into his front pocket and pulled a pair of earplugs out. These encounters with the Captain were happening more often, and the arguing would often turn to screaming. Pocket then took a snack from his side pocket and a scribble stick from his sleeve pocket and busied himself with his work. He knew this meeting was not going to end well for the Captain.

Many of the gidgies were busy setting up for the Bloom Festival. Several booths of games and food were being built. Lava lights were strung, and rides were being constructed. The smell of caramel corn, cotton candy, and millie fruit tarts was in the air.

Ginny had decided to run a booth with Duke. She would be selling her newest creation, a hot lava java drink with vanilla pod milk, honey, and lavender. Duke, a former Skyforce watchman, now ran an HBN, a honeybee network that was used for mail around the garden. He had shared with Ginny the hot lava drink with honey from his hives. Ginny liked the lava beverage but didn't love it. She felt it needed something creamy.

Her creative mind made it even better. She heated vanilla pod milk with sprigs of lavender and then added the honey to the Lava Java. She amusingly called Honey-Laven lava java, and it was served hot or iced. Duke made his famous fig and honey pastries and had several batches ready for the first night of the Festival.

Ruby, Ellie, and Sebastian were helping Ginny and Duke prepare for the opening night of the Festival when Jo landed next to Seb. He looked stressed and frazzled. "Gee whiz Jo, you look horrible," Sebastian said. Duke brought Jo a pastry and a mug of black lava drink. "Hey bud, you look like you just came back from a mission, this ought to revive you."

"Thanks, Duke, I have been on a mission, and I'm not done. I've been tracking down a suspicion of mine, but I am not at liberty to share it in case I am off track. I don't think I am, though." Jo said as he washed down a giant bite of the fig and honey pastry with a gulp of bitter tar-like liquid.

Duke pulled up a bench for Jo and the others to sit on and made himself a mug of steaming lava java and loaded the dark drink with honey. Duke was a larger gidgie with a potbelly and lemon-yellow wings that had black flecks throughout. His hair was dark brown with blond streaks, and he had a full thick mustache that hung over his upper lip. He sat down next to Jo with his drink and asked, "Is this about the dead gidgie they found near the north side of the garden?"

"What? No! I hadn't heard about that. I had been busy chasing down a different lead. When did this happen?" Jo asked.

"Last night. The information came in via HBN. It will more than likely be in the Havengothy Times come morning. They think it's a suicide, but I have a hard time believing that." Duke said with a swig of his drink. He then took his bottom lip and sucked off the lava java from his bushy mustache that was drenched in the dark liquid.

"Holy Havengothy, someone killed themselves? Who?" Ruby asked, overhearing their conversation. Ruby's outburst got the attention of Seb, Ellie, and Ginny. "OH NO, Duke, who is it?" Ginny asked with concern.

"It ain't no one we know, sweetheart, and it's not common knowledge just yet. But since it will be in the papers by morning, I will tell you what I do know." Duke said as everyone leaned in close to hear his whispered account of what he read.

"Apparently, there was a gidgie who was living near the northwest side of the garden working for Neeradima. He was cultivating one of her wicked plants. The letter said he went mad with the handling of seeds and hung himself in his own root. That is what is being reported at least."

Ginny had tears streaming down her face, "That's horrible, Duke.

Was he married?" Ginny was thinking of his wife living without her husband. Gidgies lived long and loved deeply, and any death was grieved for years.

"Who cares if he was married, he's a traitor, and he offed himself in the Beathra's roots. How is that even possible? Why didn't Beathra stop it? This makes no sense to me at all," Ellie said appalled.

"Man, this kind of stuff makes me want to join the Skyforce now! Why do I have to wait until fall?" Seb exclaimed.

Ruby just wanted to get to Vine and ask if she had seen anything. Still, she hadn't been able to get away since graduation, and she didn't dare tell Seb and Ellie her secret just yet. She asked Duke, "What is the council doing right now, did the letter say anything else about the death?"

"It did, it said the gidgie was found hanging from his root ceiling by an old Skyforce poncho. It was ripped to shreds and used as a noose, I guess. It sounds suspicious to me." Duke informed.

Jo dropped his mug of lava java, "None of this makes any sense. I have to go back to the General. Either I have made a horrible mistake, or someone is going to great lengths to make this look like a suicide," with that, Jo jetted from the group.

The five fairies all looked at each other, wondering what Jo was talking about. Sebastian finally spoke, "I think Jo might know who one of the traitorous gidgies is." Ruby had to get to Vine, how was she going to leave her friends? She was just going to have to tell them about the power of the book.

A liath bush

Chapter Fourteen
Confessions

Slipping away from Ginny and Duke, Ruby grabbed Sebastian and drug him behind a tent being set up for millie fruit tarts sales. Sebastian smiled and put both his hands on Ruby's waist. He was going to wait until after the Festival tonight to scoop her up in his arms for their first kiss, but Ruby making the first move was just fine with him. He pulled her into his arms, and she looked up at him.

Her mind was bent on confessing about the book's magical powers. Now, here she stood, Seb embracing her, smiling that ridiculous, cute smile that made her heart gush. "Get a grip, Ruby. Now is not the time to go all mushy," she thought to herself.

She shook off the emotion, "Sebastian, I have something to tell you."

Sebastian continued to grin with his arms around Ruby's tiny waist. "Go on." He said with a smirk.

"It's about the book I swiped from Hill's office," Ruby said with a cringe.

"Wait. What? You weren't about to…Oh, never mind. What about the book?" Sebastian was disappointed but didn't move away from Ruby.

Ellie was looking for the two. She found them in the embrace when she peered around the corner of the tent. "Am I interrupting something? Or should I just goooo?" Ellie said with her eyes wide and pursing her lips shut to not burst into laughter.

Ruby looked over at Ellie and then up at Seb, "Goodness, no, I was just about to tell Sebastian about the book I borrowed from Professor Hill's office. It's magic. When I used one of the charms from the book that Neeradima wrote, it made me able to speak with a plant." Ruby grimaced with this insane bit of news.

Sebastian released his grip from Ruby's waist but still held her hand. "What are you talking about, Rubes? How is it magic?"

Ruby looked at them, and then with Sebastian's hand still in hers, she said, "Follow me, I have to show you something." She bolted from the Festival, dragging Seb, leaving Ellie rushing to catch up.

In less than thirty minutes, they all landed at the fort. Ruby stood at the entrance of their hideout near the curtain of the vines. Seb and Ellie stood next to her. They were having a tough time comprehending what Ruby shared with them on the way to the fickle fruit fort.

"Hold on! You used one of Neeradima's old charms to speak to a vine, and it came to life?" Ellie asked in disbelief.

"Yes and no. I did speak to it, and it did respond, however, it is always alive and listening. I think that the spell Neeradima used for growth had a special magic that caused the vine to not just grow, but to grow where she wanted. And not just vines, other plants as well. Plus, the charm gave her the power to understand this special ivy. But the vine said the charm had to be spoken with love. And you all know how much I love any crawling plant, right? So, my fondness of vines, and the magic of the charm, caused me to be able to hear its voice. At least, that's how I think it worked." Ruby paused, then she continued. "We need to see if Vine saw anything last night. She's the only one who would really know what happened. Both of you look around and make sure we are alone. I'm going to speak to her."

Sebastian and Ellie's heads were spinning. They flew around the perimeter of their hideout, feeling crazy for even entertaining the possibility of Ruby being able to communicate with a shrub.

"We're all clear over here," Ellie informed as she landed next to Ruby. "Same here," Sebastian said as he settled back down on the other side of Ruby.

Ruby closed her eyes and began to direct her thoughts towards Vine. "Vine, are you there?" The leaves started to rustle as if a wind was blowing them, but there was no wind. Seb and Ell watched as Ruby cradled the branches of the old vine in her arms.

"I'm always here. I see you brought friends." Vine replied.

Ruby began to speak her question to the vine, so Seb and Ellie could follow half the conversation. "Something horrible happened last night, and we are wondering if you saw anything?"

"Are you speaking of the death of a fairy?" asked Vine telepathically.

"Yes, did you see or hear anything? They think it was suicide, but others are finding it hard to believe." Ruby informed.

"They would be right to doubt that conclusion," Vine answered.

Seb and Ellie watched the one-sided conversation in confusion and intrigue. "What is it saying?" Ellie asked.

"That it wasn't a suicide." Ruby shared in a hushed tone. She then asked for Vine to take the three to the dead fairy's root. Vine wrapped her thin leafy limbs around all three of the young gidgies and crawled across the tree's upper branches. Finally, making it to a very lonely looking area of Havengothy. The long skinny root home was swarming with the Skyforce. "Whose root is this? "Sebastian asked.

"This is the home of Emmet. He's a hermit and a wounded Skyforce veteran who had lost the ability to fly from his last battle. No one knows how he was injured or what battle it was he was fighting. It is just known that Emmet was injured on a mission, and he never spoke of it. He lives here alone with his pet chameleon. But since last night, the chameleon has been missing. I think it may have run away. I have never seen anyone visit Emmet, except Skyforce and council members." Vine answered. "His only friend was the little lizard."

Ruby shared with Ellie and Seb what Vine said and then asked, "Did he have a visitor last night from the Skyforce."

"Emmet did have a visitor, but I was unable to see who it was. It was dark, and the stranger was covered." Vine replied. As Ruby was telling Seb and Ellie about the cloaked fairy, Ellie pointed out General Dax near Emmet's root. "Did he just pick something up from the ground? It looks like a pin or broach of some sort."

"He's collecting evidence, Ell," Sebastian informed. "Then why did he just put it in his pocket and not give it to the Skyguard's?" Ellie asked with raised eyebrows. The trained General looked up in the tree, feeling the eyes of something on him. But Vine had them concealed in her foliage. He walked back toward the root where the investigating teams were and spoke to them in a low tone.

"Something strange is going on. Why would the General sneak a piece of evidence in his pocket?" Ruby wondered out loud.
The three sat nestled in the branches of Vine, tucked away watching the investigation for a few more minutes. "I think we've seen enough here. It's not like we can do anything about this right now," Ellie said nervously.

"Yeah, let's go. We need to talk with Jo about all of this, he will know what to do." Sebastian said.

"And just how do you think you're going to tell him what you saw and how you came to see it?" Ruby asked with a curious look. "I can hear you now, 'Oh, hey Jo, Ruby used a magic book stolen from Professor Hill's office to speak with a plant. That plant lifted us up and carried us to a crime scene of a murdered gidgie. And by the way, we saw the General steal evidence.' How does that sound?" Ruby asked sarcastically.

"A little nutty, I'll admit, but Jo's a good guy, and I think he will understand. We've got to trust someone, Rubes." Seb advised.

"I agree, Ruby. Let's tell Jo." Ellie looked uneasy. These adventures that Ruby and Seb liked were not her cup of pinkle pepper brew. "Can we go back now? I sort of promised to meet someone at the Bloom Festival, and I still need to get ready." Ellie looked around her and then said, "I don't even know where we are. How far away from the center of the garden are we?" Ellie asked.

"We are in a very isolated area. These roots are stretched a long way from Beathra's trunk. It might be best if I just take you back." Vine advised.

Ruby looked at Seb and Ellie and told them to hold on. "Vine is taking us back to the festival." Just as they were about to leave, Seb saw Jo land near the General. "Wait a minute, tell her not to go yet. That's right, Jo needed to talk with the General. Vine, can you get us closer to them to hear what they are saying." Seb asked sheepishly.

"You mean spy on them." Ellie accused.

"No, I just want to hear what they are talking about without them seeing me," Seb said, smiling.

"Seriously, you two need a moral compass, between Ruby's "borrowing" and your curiosity, you're practically criminals." Ellie smiled. But she had to admit, she was curious as well.

Vine obliged the three young fairies and crawled towards the two Skyforce men as they conversed.

"Good afternoon, Jo, what can I do for you?" asked the General.

"Sir, I hope you don't mind me tracking you down, Pocket told me where you were. About what we were talking about, I'm worried I may have jumped to a conclusion. Do you think this is a crime against oneself, or did someone kill Emmet?" Jo was direct with his question. The General preferred it when his Skyforce soldiers didn't mince words.

"We did find evidence of an intruder. And It does appear that there was a struggle. So, we will be ruling out suicide. If you are wondering if your suspicions are correct, no proof points to him. I did find something that was interesting; a Skyforce badge. It's a specialty badge, meaning whoever earned this pin graduated from a training course to advance their combat skills. This one appears to be for Gidjidsu combat. I think we should research the possibility of it being Emmet's. If not, we can conclude it's the murderers." The General stated handing the pin to Joseppi to inspect.

Jo observed the shiny bronze metal pin. It had the imprint of two hands clashing and was polished with pride. "It seems rather new, so it was either well cared for or recently earned, by its looks. So, it's possible, if it were the intruder that killed Emmet, he is currently serving in the Skyforce. If the pin belongs to him, that is." Jo inspected the pin and then handed it back to the General. "But why kill Emmet?"

"We believe Emmet witnessed something he shouldn't have. Commander, could you please join us?" The General waved Sidney towards him. "Please explain to Jo what your team has found near the edge of Emmet's property."

The lovely Commander stood confidently next to the General. She had dusty, light blue wings and short white hair. She pointed towards a small green shrub and began to describe what her team uncovered.

"We believe this is one of Neeradima's bewitched plants. We are taking every precaution to handle it, so our crew is not poisoned by it. However, we can't get too close to it. It emanates an evil we can feel in the air. The ashy dead circle around it is our indicator of a safe distance. It looks like the ground has been burned around it, but that's not the case. The poisonous fragrance from its fruit secretes an oily air that burns up the good in our land. Although it smells rather alluring, when you get in the circumference of the fragrance, there's a hint of rotting flesh. Early this morning, we had an incident. A young Skyguard handled the leaves, and the dunderhead tasted a berry. It seemed to cause him to become paranoid and suspicious of everyone around him, he began to act erratic, and he thought we could read his mind. He then tried to run away from us. My team tackled him, and he was rushed to the Skyforce Healer station. We should know more tonight about the contaminants that reside in and on the plant just by what the Healers gather from the infected Skyforce guard."

Commander Sidney walked Jo and the General towards the small toxic bush, stopping at a safe distance. Vine carefully and quietly slid the three spying gidgies towards the outer edge of Emmet's property. She ran out of space to crawl due to the isolation of Emmet's root and stopped at the last tree that edged his property. All other greenery had withdrawn from the tainted shrub. It had a broad, dead brown circle that encompassed it. However, the little green bush seemed to be thriving in a dry patch.

"Vine, can you hear what that Skyforce lady is saying to Jo?" Ruby asked. Vine leaned in a little closer, while still holding the three back in the tree she had them hidden. She extended part of her branch and crawled on the floor of the garden. She stopped just shy of a small, shed Emmet had near the edge of the dead circle. She listened in on the Commander's explanation of the wicked plant.

"We've contacted Moses and Sylvia for this situation. It is beyond our skill set. This wicked shrub radiates evil magic. All other life in the forest seems to recoil from it. Even the birds fly a safe distance in the air. Our animals have an instinct that deters them from consuming the leaves and fruit. We have found that if one lingers too long in the unsafe zone, it seems to unhinge their minds. This vile creation has changed part of our atmosphere of hope, and it creates a very confusing feeling as if your head is spinning. When I got near it, all the hair stood up on the back of my neck. We are trying to find a protective suit for its handling. It has the fingerprints of Neeradima all over it.

"We believe Emmet was a guardian of the plant. He would watch from that garden shed on the edge of his land, making sure no one touched it or partook of the fruit. However, that shack is where it appears Emmet was killed and then drug to his root, to make it look like a suicide." The Commander explained to Jo.

Ruby began to speak with Vine telepathically, asking, "What is that bush? I can sense the evilness radiating from it."

"It is one of Neeradima's corrupted plants that was born from her hatred while she was here in the garden. From the sounds of it, Emmet was guarding it. He was assigned by Beathra to keep others away." Vine answered.

Sebastian then asked, "Can anyone hear what that lady is telling Jo? They are too far away for me to make out what they are saying."

Ruby relayed what Vine had just told her about the shrub. "Emmet was keeping others away from the plant? I don't get it. Why not just destroy the thing?" asked Sebastian.

Jo looked distraught. "How could someone do this to a war hero? A guardian of our garden. Were there signs of liaths near the shrub?" he asked the Commander.

"Yes, this is clearly a place they have been trying to get control of, but Emmet's presence has kept them at a distance. His death was intentional, with the control of this corner of the garden in mind. That's my conclusion. Our question is, who killed Emmet? Was it a citizen of our garden, or was it a liath? And now I have to find someone with some form of expertise to stand watch over this area without it corrupting them, while we figure out how to destroy this awful thing." The Commander then turned to the General and saluted him. "If that will be all, sir."

The General saluted the Commander back and freed her to continue with her work. He then turned to Jo. "We need to keep this under our hats. He will figure out what's going on, and we will watch him closely. If he is a traitor, we will catch him. Now, I would like you to make your way back to the Festival, I have a sneaky suspicion that those three young gidgies are going to be a little bit of trouble."

"Yes, Sir." Jo darted towards the center of the garden, and Vine was quick to gather the trio and rush them to the festival grounds. Vine explained everything to Ruby as she rushed to drop them off at the Bloom Festival. Ruby then conveyed it all to Seb and Ellie as Vine rushed them through the garden to beat Jo to the festival grounds.

As a vine went, she was quite motherly toward Ruby and her friends, and she was growing fond of Ruby. She dropped the young gidgies off at the edge of the Festival. "You must go now, that Jo fellow will be looking for all of you. I will keep watch over Emmet's root and let you know if I see anything worth telling." Vine then quietly withdrew from the festival ground, leaving Ruby, Seb, and Ellie standing in bewilderment.

"Who is the 'he' Jo and the General were talking about?" Ruby asked.

"I have no idea, but we need to find Jo," Seb said.

"Find me for what?" Jo asked as he startled the three with his sudden appearance.

"Wow, that was fast!" Seb said. Jo looked at Sebastian sideways. Ruby then approached Jo, "I'm not sure if you will believe us, but we have some pretty interesting news to share with you."

Jo was sweaty and had clearly flown at top speed to get back to the Bloom Festival. "Why don't we go sit down and have one of Miss Violet's lavender lemonades, and you can tell me what's so unbelievable."

Ellie excused herself, "If you guys don't mind, I have a date I need to get ready for. You can tell Jo everything he needs to know without me."

"What? Who are you going to the Bloom Festival with?" Ruby asked, shocked.

"I tried to tell you, but all this craziness happened so fast that we haven't had a chance to chat. It's Theo." Ellie explained.

"Theo, the nerd who graduated last year? That's your date? Oh, Ell." Seb teased.

"He's nice, and he wrote to me and asked me to meet him. And he is smart. Plus, nobody else asked me. I don't want to be a third wheel with you two at the Festival. It's your date, and me hanging around with the both of you will make it, whatever it is that we are, when we are all together. I'll be fine. I'm looking forward to it." Ellie said with a smile.

Ruby hugged her friend, and then apologized, "I'm sorry I drag you into all my fiascos. As soon as we're done telling Jo about, you know what, I will join you in getting ready."

Ellie flew off to her root dorm, and Seb and Ruby sat down at one of the small tables Miss Violet was just setting up for the night's festivities. Jo sweet-talked her into serving them early. He bought three large drinks and sat down at the table with the tart beverages. He chugged the lavender lemonade, quenching his thirst from his frantic flight back to the Festival. Slamming the empty mug down, he said, "Now, what is it you have to tell me."

Ruby and Sebastian looked at him and then told him everything, from the book to them witnessing him at Emmet's root. Jo leaned back in his chair and slid his hair back with his hands. His sweaty head caused his hair to slick back, sticking to his scalp. He kept shaking his head.

Sebastian asked, "Jo, who is the 'him' you are suspicious about?"

Jo took a breath. He was stressed and wasn't sure if he should share with the young gidgies who he suspected of being a traitor? "They will find out eventually, that vine thing, will more than likely tell Ruby. Plus, Seb will be leaving for the Skyforce soon; so, he's practically a cadet." He thought to himself.

He leaned in and, in the quietest he had ever spoken, whispered who he thought might be behind the abductions, "Captain Roland."

Falling Blooms

Chapter Fifteen
The Bloom Festival

It was the first night of the Bloom Festival. Lava bean lamps were strung throughout the center of the garden causing every fairy to feel as if heaven was at their fingertips. There were tents of wonderful specialty foods and drinks, games, and competitions. There was even a Ferris wheel, operated by Buck and Barney. These twin gidgies wore overalls, straw hats and were known for their jovial nature.

Duke and Ginny's booth was an enormous hit, with a line that zigzagged the customers towards the counter. All were raving over Ginny's magnificent hot Honey-laven lava java. It was a perfect drink for the slight nip in the evening air. The smells of all the delightful booths mixed with the spring scents made the atmosphere magical. And though there was darkness looming, this night was filled with a celebration of life, hope, and community. It would take an act of Beathra to cancel a Bloom Festival. Gidgies were designed to love and celebrate life, even in difficult seasons.

Ruby was meeting Sebastian at Meredith Barry's Merrybare berry bush brew booth. The title was thought of by the giggling Meredith Barry herself. After a few drinks of her joy sparking brew, the patrons were in giggle fits.

Meredith would require the intoxicated customers to say the name of her establishment before she would allow them to leave. The brew booth had two sitting areas. One was inside the tent, and the other was an outside area roped off with small tables where it was legal to indulge in the drink. However, the brew was not allowed beyond the tent or ropes. If a customer was ready to leave, they had to prove they had the wherewithal. Thus saying "Meredith's Barry's merrybare berry bush brew booth" three times without falter. If they were successful, she allowed them to exit, if not, they were given a mug of pinkle pepper brew and could try again later. This ensured the partakers were steady enough to walk or fly about the garden with most of their wits.

Ruby entered the roped area looking for Sebastian, but he wasn't there yet. Billick was sitting at a booth, and he saw Ruby. Billick had one and a half of the three-drink minimum and was feeling quite happy. He waved Ruby over to his table. "Hey Rubes, join me for a mug?" the giggling Billick asked.

Ruby surveyed the intoxicated Bill. This was new for her; he was in a strangely good mood. Billick was doing his strange giggle, and it wasn't pleasant at all. He had the type of snicker that sounded like air being let out of a tire, with slow and interrupted hisses.

Ruby gradually made her way to Billick's standing table. Billick did a sliding whistle admiring Ruby's loveliness. She was wearing a secondhand dress Ginny had picked up at Miss Kitty's dress shop. It was an off the shoulder, pale yellow chiffon dress, cinched tight around Ruby's tiny waist and it fell just past her knees. Ellie had done her hair, pinning it up into a pile of curls atop her head. Ruby had a few wayward strands that refused to obey, but it only added to her natural beauty.

She had hoped Sebastian would have been the one to see her first, and now she is stuck at a table with a drunk hissing Billick. The tinge of guilt still lingered about her prank of blowing poor Billick's butt up, so Ruby obliged herself to join him.

"Hi Billick, are you waiting for someone?" Ruby asked as she gave her order to Edna, the waitress, of just water.

"Nope, the girl I asked is going with someone else," Billick said, sounding a little pitiful.

"Who did you ask Billick? Was it Trixie?" Ruby asked with sincere curiosity.

"Trixie went with Lewis. Lewis! Can you believe it? That snot-fest of a nerd has a date before me!" he yelled in disbelief and then did his weird hissing snicker.

"Yeah, I saw the two of them on Buck and Barneys Ferris wheel. They are an odd couple, but they look happy," Ruby said, attempting to soften the blow.

"I agree. Lewis is a good guy, and Trixie is a nice gal. Still, it wasn't her I wanted to go with, it was…" just as Billick was about to confess the note was not a practical joke, Sebastian entered.

He saw Ruby standing at Billick's table. Seb had never seen her in that flowing dress before, and he could not take his eyes off of her. Little ringlets of her wild hair fell down her back, and she looked stunning. He stood there, staring at her for a good ten seconds before he had to tell himself to move his legs.

Seb walked up behind Ruby and slowly slid his hand down her arm and linked his pinky with hers. Ruby jolted but did not pull away. She was horribly uncomfortable visiting with Billick, and Sebastian walked in at the right time and set her heart at ease.

"Hey, Bill. I see you have taken advantage of being the legal age of partaking of the Merrybare berry bush brew," Sebastian stated, noticing poor Billick's inebriation.

Edna came by to ask for Seb's order when she saw the state of Billick. "Poor sod, can't hold his drink. He hasn't even finished his second one," then she looked at Sebastian, "What will you have dear?" she asked.

"I'll have a pint of the Merrybare berry bush brew, make it two, one for my date," Seb said with a smile as he looked at Ruby.

"Well, look at the two of you. I was wondering if it was ever going to happen. Glad to see you didn't waste a minute, Seb. I asked Ruby here, to the Festival, but… well, my butt ended up making me the butt of the joke." Billick snickered his hissing laugh, then took a swig of the last of his brew and called for another round of drinks. "Drinks for everyone, my treat!" he hollered.

Edna looked at Billick's bloodshot eyes, "I don't think so dear, how about some pinkle pepper brew?" Both Sebastian and Ruby yelled, "No!" in unison. Edna looked confused, "Alright then, I'll just bring him some lemonade, she then grabbed a chair for Billick to sit on before he tipped backward.

"Poor Billick." Ruby thought to herself. The big guy on campus, Mr. Cool, was making a fool of himself. "We need to help him, Seb. We can't let others see him like this." Ruby suggested, filled with compassion.

Billick sat up and looked at Ruby and Sebastian. The two were openly holding hands. Sebastian was not embarrassed by the wild and unabashed Ruby, in fact, he seemed to admire it. Billick was not brave enough to embrace what he thought was different or a deficiency in Ruby. His plan failed in pursuing her because of his pride.

"I know just the thing for him, Dukes Lava drink!" Ruby announced, and she bolted to Ginny's booth to grab one of Duke's blackest java beverages. She explained to Duke why she needed it, and Duke was more than happy to whip up one of his eye-opening, hair standing, toe-curling swills. She carefully carried it back to Sebastian, but she couldn't find him in the outdoor sitting area.

Edna had walked by, with her arms full of brews and made eye contact with Ruby. The kind waitress tilted her head in the direction the two men went.

Sebastian had dragged Billick inside the tent and propped him up in the corner booth away from view. Ruby carried the black tar beverage and handed it off to Seb. Billick was still doing his hissing laugh when Ruby arrived with the lava java. "Hey, uh, Rubes! Welcome to the party!" Billick yelled across the room in a slurred speech.

Ruby winced and looked around to see if anyone had seen Billick's odd behavior. Thankfully, Sebastian had tucked Bill back in the tent just in time. Lewis and Trixie had entered and were sauntering to a tall table outside.

Sebastian was pouring the muddy lava java down Billick's throat when Ruby put her hand on Seb's arm and stopped him. She asked the question, "Billick, you said you asked me to the Festival, but you didn't. I think the brew is mixing you up."

Billick grabbed the mug from Sebastian's hands and chugged down the bitter drink. He then smiled at Ruby, "Nah, Rubes, it's not a mix-up. I asked you. It wasn't really a joke. I was sort of hoping we could start fresh as friends and maybe let it grow into something more, but then you inflated my tookis, and that was that." Billick said, in a somewhat sober tone, but then laughed, hissed, and hiccupped.

Ruby and Seb stood there dumbfounded, "Did Billick just openly say he liked you?" Seb asked.

"It sure sounded like it," replied Ruby.

Just as Sebastian was about to say something, Billick's head fell forward on the table, bounced like a ball, and then he started to snore.

Edna came to the table with the two mugs of the Merrybare brew and witnessed the scene. "Why don't you two kids take your drink to the outdoor patio, and I'll make sure this fellow sleeps it off."

Ruby and Seb only had one glass of the brew, but they were giggling like small children. And then in a burst of joviality, Seb grabs Ruby's hands and says, "Will you wait for me Rubes, while I train and serve?"

Ruby was lightheaded from the drink, but she knew he was serious. She held Sebastian's hand and said, "You know I will wait for you, just don't be gone forever, Billick here may be my backup plan." The two busted into Merrybare brew induced laughter. But from this point on, Sebastian was going to keep a closer eye on Billick.

The delightful drink's effect wore off, and they walked hand in hand, enjoying all the wonders of the Festival. They danced under the lava lights, ate popcorn, and drank Honey-laven lava javas. It couldn't have been a more perfect night.

Sebastian saw Joseppi at a Skyforce booth, and he and Ruby made their way to chat with him. They hadn't seen him since that morning. He had flattened them with his suspicions of the Captain, and Sebastian wanted to talk with Jo about their morning conversation.

As Ruby and Seb approached the tent, they were distracted by a young Special Task Force agent. He was telling a tale that mesmerized a small audience. In his arms was the tiniest creature known as a pompadour, a white ball of fluff that looked like a cotton ball with legs. These magical creatures were from the Hyperion Mountains and were known to change colors with their mood. White was a good sign; it meant calm, and that the little critter was at peace.

"How did you find it?" Came a voice from the small crowd. The animated Skyforce agent told of little Gertrude's rescue.

"All I can tell you is I was in the Hyperion Mountains tracking liaths. I was in a rocky ravine when I saw this little soggy pile of wet hair. I thought she was dead. She was a horrible blue color when I scooped her up. Underneath all this fur is the smallest, itty bittiest of frames. I wrapped her in my coat and started to warm her. I was hoping and praying she was still alive. And then she sparked a color of silver. Her fur started lighting up with all the colors of a rainbow. Then she got super skittish and buried herself deep inside my blanket. I knew she was terrified, but of what? The rest is classified." He said with a smile.

The audience was engulfed in the story of Gertrude's rescue.

Ruby and Sebastian had stopped to hear the tale. He continued, "I had only read about these enchanted critters. I had to go back to my days in the University under Professor Raj's class of enchanted beast. That is where I first read of the pompadours. They have magical powers to feel evil or sense danger, and their fur will begin to transition in color. I'm still trying to figure out all little Gertie's moods and colors." He smiled and looked at Gertie, then continued, "but I don't know who saved who. She certainly has helped me after my last injury, keeping me company as I healed." The young soldier touched his scar with his hand, and Gertie licked him as to say, "It's ok."

Ruby approached the Skyforce soldier and said, "I may know someone who can help you with little Gertrude. My mother runs an enchanted beast farm, and she is often rescuing creatures like Miss Gertie."

"That would be great!" the Skyforce soldier exclaimed, he then introduced himself. "My names Lieutenant C.J. and you know little Gertie here." C.J. was young but had an old soul look. One could tell he had seen more than most in his short years. Serving as a Special Task Force member, he was often sent on top-secret missions. He had a scar that drug across his face. It went between his eyes and down the left side of his nose. "That must be the last injury he was talking about." Thought Ruby.

C.J. shook both Seb and Ruby's hand. He was friendly and kind but had a certain ruggedness that seemed guarded. He asked where he might find Ginny to help him with Gertie. Ruby directed him to Duke and Gins booth but gave Gertie one last little scratch on her head. Gertie nuzzled Ruby's palm and licked her hand.

Seb found Jo at the recruiter's table. "I thought you might have the night off or at least be on guard duty with all the stuff going on, why are you in the recruiter's tent?" Seb asked.

"Captain Roland stationed me here at our information booth. He thought I would be a better recruiter than protector tonight," Jo said, annoyed. "I don't trust that guy, I know he's my Captain, but something isn't sitting right with me. But there is nothing I can do about it right now. I have no proof, just suspicions. No matter, I like seeing all the familiar faces here at the Festival." Jo said, trying not to sound disappointed. The three sat and talked about Sebastian's leave date and what to expect during his cadet training.

"It's going to be brutal, Seb. You will want to quit the first three weeks in, but once you hit your stride, you'll be alright. Just remember, the Drill Sergeants can't kill you. That's what got me through during training. That, and I was already pretty good at push-ups. You might think about doing a few of those every day before you leave." Jo's advice was noted. Ruby squeezed Seb's biceps and teased, "these are pretty puny Seb. You definitely need to work out."

Of course, that wasn't true. Sebastian was incredibly fit and was already doing his push-ups and pull-ups preparing for the excruciating courses at cadet school.

C.J. stood in the long line at Duke and Ginny's. As he progressively moved through the roped lane, Ginny saw Gertie in C.J.'s arms. The mini fairy was excited to see a pompadour and just had to get her hands on it. Ginny looked over at Duke, "I'll be right back, dear," she said as she stepped off her stool that helped her reach the counter. She quickly washed her hands, and left poor Duke with a mob of fairies vying for the lava java drink, while she beelined it towards C.J.

"You must be Ginny," C.J. said with a giant grin.

"How did you know?" Gin asked as she let Gertie smell her hand.

"I met Ruby, she said you might be able to help me with my little girl here," C.J. said as he held out Gertie.

Ginny scooped up the pompadour. Gertie looked twice as big in Ginny's small arms. "What do you want to know about this beauty?" she asked as she inspected the pompadour as a Healer would check out a patient.

"Well, I only know what I learned at the University, but that was years ago. I am aware they are very rare, change color with their moods, and have a keen sense of danger or evil. However, I have no idea what colors to look for, but I have assumed white means she's in a good mood." C.J. said as he scratched Gertie's tummy while Gin held her.

"You've guessed right," Ginny looked over at Duke, he was sweating profusely, trying to serve the large crowd. She then spotted Ellie; she was with a tall thin fairy.

"Ellie, would you and your fellow be a dear and help poor Duke out for a few minutes? Free drinks and food are all yours if you say yes." Ginny asked pleadingly.

Ellie looked over at Theo and smiled, "It's Ruby's mom. Do you mind helping?" Theo was more than delighted to be with Ellie. He had regretted not asking her out while they went to school. His shyness got the best of him. But as he has been away, training at the East ALC as an Engineer Professor, he became a bit braver. He couldn't believe she said yes to his proposition of them meeting up at the Bloom Festival. Ellie was out of his league when it came to looks, but the two were equal in intelligence.

"Not at all, if it means I can stand next to you all night, I will scrub the washrooms," Theo said with a wink and smile. The two jumped behind the bar and Ellie moved Ginny's stool. It was not needed; their height was almost too much for the little booth. Poor Theo had to hunch down just to view the customers.

"Now that that's taken care of, let's have a seat, and I will help you understand this thimble-size creature." Ginny sat down at a picnic table, and C.J followed, carrying Gertie under his arm.

"Pompadours are magical with their gift of sensory. Did you know evil creatures like to collect them due to their wonderful color making moods? I think it is because it strokes their ego, reminding them of their wickedness. They put the pitiful creatures in a cage and place them on display as one would a trophy. I saved a male from a group of trolls that dwelled in the caves near the base of Hyperion Mountain. Of course, that was before I adopted Ruby."

Ginny shared this story with zeal. She loved her adventures in the mountains, and though Ruby went with her on several occasions, she would never risk Ruby's life to rescue a beast.

"That's horrible. I had no idea pompadours were a prize for evil creatures. What did you do with the one you rescued?" C.J. asked.

"I rehabilitated him and then released it back into the wild. As you know, white is calm, purple is happy, and blue is scared. Pink can mean nervous and yellow, well yellow means, she's gotta pee."

"Ha ha ha, yeah, I figured that out a little late. Gertie peed in one of my boots. I didn't know it until I put them on." C.J. laughed.

Ginny discussed food and caring for Gertie when suddenly C.J. noticed Gertie's fur change. "What does this deep red mean?" C.J. asked as Gertie's fur began to transform before their eyes."

Ginny put her hands over her mouth, "Magenta means evil or danger is approaching. We need to alert the Skyforce."

"I'm on it, do you mind watching Gertie?" C.J. asked, but did not wait for Gins reply, he was already in combat mode. He bolted from the Festival to find Captain Roland.

Ginny ran back to her booth and asked Duke to lift her up on the counter. She announced that they were closed, and all were advised to gather their family and find a safe place to hide. Ginny then flew at top speed to see Ruby. Ruby was still at the Skyforce recruiting tent with Sebastian visiting with Jo.

Ginny was winded from her frantic flight. She grabbed Ruby and held her tightly. "What is it Gin, what's going on? Ruby asked, seeing the fear in Ginny's eyes.

"We need to hide, something bad is about to happen," Ginny said breathlessly as she held the red colored Gertie who was shaking.

Something evil indeed was coming.

The Darphea caverns

Chapter Sixteen

Abductions

Out of nowhere the enemy struck. The vile assault was swift and calculated and the aftermath of the invasion was devastating. The beautiful strands of lava bean lights were scattered and dispersed all over the grounds, looking as if the stars had fallen. Tents were torn and slashed. Neeradima's army struck hard and fast and the surprise attack was costly.

The liaths circled like a swarm of hornets, snatching up victims as they dove into the Festival. The lucky ones who escaped the enemy's clutches lay in pain, some suffering from the tainted swords that gashed them. Others were crying out from talon punctures left from the beasts the liaths rode. The Festival was destroyed, but the heart anguish was more profound than the injuries. The shock and fear gutted the garden inhabitants.

Had it not been for Ginny and C.J.'s quick actions, the casualties would have been much higher. Little Gertie saved more than just Ruby and her friends. No sooner had Ginny said something was coming, that the enemy's sound was heard thundering through the forest.

Sebastian grabbed Ruby, and Joseppi picked up Ginny as they ran for the nearest cover, a burrow at the base of Beathra's root. Jo secured the three of them and then charged out to battle the enemy. He was outnumbered, but his skills were unmatched. He knocked a few liaths off their birds and was able to capture the enemy for questioning.

C.J. was unable to find Captain Roland. The lieutenant flew to the sentinels and warned them just before the first wave of liaths invaded the Bloom Festival.

General Dax was leading a team searching the area, investigating as to where the enemy broke through. Interviewing each guard on duty, he discovered two sentinels were missing. The General was unsure if they were part of the invasion, snatched by the liaths, hiding in fear, or worse, dead.

These answers would unfold as he went deeper down the rabbit hole. He was stumped as to how an army of liaths could gain access to the garden center. It was mind-boggling. The General had garden sentinels, Skyguards, and watchmen keeping a lookout from the sky and ground. The liath strike was quick and precise, coming from several unknown areas. It was as if they came from nowhere.

Ruby, Sebastian, and Gin climbed out of the burrow. Ruby felt as if she had been hit on the head. None of this felt real. Her beloved garden was invaded. She looked over at Sebastian, who was helping a distraught wife look for her husband. Joseppi was preparing to escort Ginny to find Duke when he, Ellie, and Theo flew in. Ruby ran and grabbed Ellie.

"Thank Beathra, you're ok. I was so afraid something happened to you!" Ruby squeezed Ellie even tighter.

"I'm fine, Ruby. Duke's quick action saved everyone near their booth." Ellie informed. Theo put his arms around Ellie and added, "It's true Ruby, Duke hid and guarded all of us, he even joined the Skyforce and fought a few liath scum."

Ruby looked over at Duke and Ginny. Duke was bent down, ensuring Ginny he was fine. She kept running her hands over his head and through his hair, then kissed his face. Little Gertie was near Ginny and had turned a pink shade. It was a good sign, meaning she was nervous, but at least the danger had passed.

Jo was busy checking on as many fairies and their families as he could before leaving to find the General. Families were calling for each other. Buck was wandering the grounds yelling for Barney, but it was futile, Barney was gone.

Lewis and Trixie found Sebastian and Ruby and asked if anyone had seen Billick. "Oh my gosh, Sebastian! We left him in the corner of Meredith Barry's brew booth!" The entire crew of friends bolted to the tent. It was fallen over, and no movement was seen.

No one at the joyful brew booth saw the strike coming, and many were victims to the attack. Ruby called for Edna, but there was no answer, and there was no telling if she was taken or scattered from fear.

Lewis, Theo, and Sebastian began to move the debris to get to the back of the tent. They lifted the last pole that helped them gain access to the corner, and Billick was still sleeping. He had missed it all.

It was an act of terror filled with pure hate, and all of Havengothy was whirling from the enemy's strike. The Healer stations all over the garden were overflowing with the injured. The waiting roots were overflowing with gidgies searching for their loved ones. As of now, the count was thirty-four missing, and twenty-two injured.

Neeradima was elated with her plan. Ominous' insiders had given them information that provided them with the element of surprise, and to her delight, it worked. Standing before the wicked queen was thirty terrified fairies and possible new recruits.

"Welcome to my Kingdom, you insignificant tree lovers. I am going to make you an offer you cannot refuse. Not all my prisoners are brought to me in such," Neeradima paused to search for the words. Then she found them, "Awe yes, not all my prisoners are brought to me in such healthy conditions. I can offer you a painless induction into my Kingdom. If you should choose to attempt bravery, I can let my tormenting vittles convince you to join my side. Either way, you will be my slave, or you will be my soldiers." She sat in a secret cave of the Darphea mountainside and waited for their answer.

"Excuse me, ma'am," a frightened voice squeaked.

"You shall call me your queen or your Greatness!" Neeradima screeched.

"Sorry. Excuse me, queen, but what do you mean by 'tormenting vittles'?" the timid gidgie asked.

Neeradima stretched a wicked smile across her hardened yet beautiful face, "We have an ignorant little pup among us." She teased.

The assembly of liaths all jeered at the innocent question. "Weren't you told of the dangers of me in school, you dumb little waste of breath?" Neeradima asked in a condescending tone.

Yoli reached out and drew the questioning fairy to her side and whispered, "It looks like you are getting a crash course in it right now, Raymond. But don't worry, dear, Beathra will save us. I can feel him in my heart telling me to not be afraid."

Neeradima seethed, "How dare you say that name in my presence, in my Kingdom! How dare you mention that old piece of timber. He has no power here. This is where pieces of that relic of a tree, come to die!" She bellowed at the top of her lungs and then pointed to a corner where her precious music makers lay.

Yoli felt fear grip her heart, "Oh Beathra, please do not let one of those souls be my Jermaine," she prayed.

Neeradima saw the anguish in Yoli's eyes and knew immediately that Yoli was missing someone she loved.

"Does this pile of lifeless seeds scare you? Does someone you love, live here in this heap of hopelessness?" the wicked queen taunted.

Yoli's face went serious, "My only concern right now is the roast fitternick fowl in my oven." She said in a much braver tone than she felt.

The queen leaned in, face to face with Yoli. But the defiant Yoli met her gaze, standing tall and unflinching. Then the queen spoke low for Yoli's ears only, "There will be roasting, my courageous little speck. But it will be *your* goose that is cooked."

She then screamed in Yoli's face, "To the dungeons with them all!"

"Pardon me queen, but I think I would like to forgo the suffering and waiting, and just surrender now," said a shaking voice.

"No, Leon, don't do it, Beathra will send help." Yoli pleaded.

"If Beathra loved us, he never would have let this happen," Leon whimpered.

The wicked land was draining the little hope Leon did have. Five other gidgies offered themselves. Neeradima was practically dizzy with this offering. The brave Yoli blurted out, "Why don't you just kill us and take our wings and fire seed? Why do you have to torture us? Why do you need us to serve you?"

Ominous slapped Yoli across the face, splitting her lip and shooting pain through her jaw that felt like he broke it. "You'll be begging for her pain relief soon enough, you wench!" he hissed.

Yoli's question was valid, why didn't Neeradima just kill them? Because killing them did not wound Beathra, and Neeradima loved to injure her former master. And though Beathra grieved for the fallen, he knew a life lived holding on to hope, even unto death, was in and of itself a rescue. For death with your fire seed meant entrance into the Great Ghost Warriors Kingdom.

At the beginning of Neeradima's revolt, she waited near a dead fairy she had just executed in hopes of hearing the song she loved. But she did not hear any music that day. And if Beathra did not weep, she didn't win.

Neeradima wanted her captives as slaves to grow her army. She found out early on that if she killed a gidgie, the seed would not release from the fairy. It had to be relinquished for her to pluck it from their back. A gidgie could not serve two kingdoms. Therefore, Beathra had to be denounced before they could swear allegiance to the evil enchantress.

Neeradima has converted several creatures of the forest for her cause. Though she has many soldiers, not all are gidgies. They all serve her purpose; however, it is only a gidgie that can give her the rush of hearing the weeping of Beathra. It was her addiction, her drug, her high. To inflict a deep wound on the King of Trees and listen to him weep, sickeningly elated her.

"Get these prisoners out of my sight. Perhaps a little time in the darkness might help them see the light I have to offer!" Neeradima screamed.

She knew the captives would change their minds after some time in her dungeon. And if the darkness of the caves didn't cause them to submit, the meal rations would. If the prisoners still refused her offer, they were welcome to be her slave.

As Torn herded the prisoners to the secret cells deep in the heart of the mountain, Yoli tried to make mental notes of all the turns and canals, but it was impossible. If Havengothy's atmosphere was filled with hope, the Skawlterrin atmosphere lingered with despair. Hopelessness could be felt physically. It was going to take all her grit to hold onto it.

She drew Raymond next to her and whispered to him, "Do not stop speaking to Beathra, whatever you do, he is your connection to hope. He will rescue us, and if not on this side of the world, then the other."

Torn shoved Yoli into a dug-out cell. It was dark, and the only lights were small torches. The fumes of the oil that they burned gave Yoli an immediate headache. The stench in the caves smelled of brimstone and sulfur. She sat in the corner of her cell, shaking.

After a few seconds in the dark cavern, she heard a weak, "Hello?"

Yoli jumped up, shocked. She recognized that voice. "He can't be," Yoli said, as she slowly peered towards the darkness. "It's impossible... Jermaine, is that you?

Yoli couldn't see a thing. Her heart was racing as she ran towards the dark, slumped shadow in the corner. As her eyes adjusted to the sight, what she saw crushed her. The stink alone was more than one could stand.

Jermaine was thin and frail and covered in seven years of filth. Yoli held his bearded face in her hands. Her heart broke at the sheer sight of him. Scabs covered his forehead from scratching bug bites, and his hair was matted and long. She lovingly looked the pitiful fairy in the eyes and searched for her husband. And there he was. He cracked a smile showing a nearly toothless grin.

"Hello, sweetheart, it's been a long time. But what are you doing here? You shouldn't be here." Jermaine said as he forced his weak body to stand up. "Don't worry, I look worse than I feel." He said with a smile.

Yoli grabbed Jermaine and held him tight. She was afraid she would break him in half, he was skin and bones. "What happened? Where did you go? Why didn't you come home?" Yoli wept her questions. The tears fell like rivers. She collected them in her hands and used them to wash Jermaine's face.

Jermaine loved the feel of Yoli's warm hands. She wiped around his eyes first and then his cheeks. He leaned his head into her cupped palm and answered, "I was on a top-secret mission for Beathra. The liaths had snatched three young fairies. My rescue mission freed them, and several others before one of the guards caught me. Neeradima made me suffer for months, with beatings and feeding me her poisonous food. But I would not betray my King. In fact, even though Beathra did not rescue me, he offered me a strength outside of my own. Even her poisonous food couldn't torment me. I think it's because I kept singing. You know how I love to sing."

Jermaine looked at his weeping wife but continued, "One day, while working the marshlands, I was up to my waist in her toxic project, and I started singing songs from the school choir. I sang about The Whisper, Beathra, and Havengothy. That got others singing too, and before you knew it, our pain started to lift, and our hearts felt light. And even though we were chained, we felt free. I can't explain it. Needless to say, I got a good beating that day." Jermain chuckled.

"Oh, my darling, I knew you were alive. I never gave up hope." Yoli couldn't stop the tears from falling, but she didn't waste them either. She had torn a remnant from the corner of her dress and used it as a washcloth, sopping up her tears and then using them to wash

Jermaine. It was the most profound act of love that no one would ever have the chance to witness.

Yoli was washing away seven years of hurt, heartache, and filth with her tears. This is the exact meaning of cleansing tears. The kind that purifies. She continued to wipe away the grime that hid her handsome husband's face. With each cleansing dab, the Jermaine of old appeared. He stopped her hands from their loving work.

"Sweetheart, I overheard their plans for the invasion. I knew they were going to strike. I heard of traitors that are working for Neeradima. The liaths were using secret passages to get into the garden. And I knew I should have been worried about my home, but all I could imagine was you at the Bloom Festival. I pictured you in one of your pretty homemade dresses, sipping a pinkle pepper brew, sitting on a blanket, and staring at the lava beans that were strung about. And I prayed, 'Beathra, I would love to see my Yoli one more time', then I prayed for my rescue again."

Jermaine took a long breath, weary from standing and talking. "I can't believe you are here; it should have been the Skyforce. I never imagined my prayers would imprison you," Jermaine began to sob.

"Darling, it was just as you imagined. I was sitting on a blanket, but I was trying a new drink called a laven lava something. I know it sounds crazy, but it was delicious. I was staring at the lava beans, dreaming of our festival days when I heard someone yell to take cover. I looked up. I heard the enemy before I saw them. I began to gather young fairies and usher them into hiding places. I even hid some in outhouses, and that's when I was grabbed by a horrible creature. I can't believe they used to be one of us. They look nothing like us. I fought hard. I kicked and screamed and even helped free another gal with my flailing, but the nasty liath had me in a tight grip.

"I know Beathra did not cause the invasion, but I have no doubt that he will be the source of our rescue. And I believe, he used me to rescue those young gidgies from being snatched, and I trust he sent me to you." Yoli said with a wincing smile due to her fat lip and aching jaw.

Jermaine touched Yoli's face that was beginning to swell. He held it in his cupped hands and then whispered, "Let's sing, my love."

Chapter Seventeen

The Call

The Skyforce was assembling in their station high above Havengothy. General Dax was gathering several task force teams to rescue the captured when Moses entered the headquarters.

"General Dax, might I have a word with you?" Moses asked.

The General ordered his team to continue with their preparations when he stepped aside to meet with Moses.

"What is it Moses, I am in the middle of prepping my team to deploy?" he asked.

"The council convened, and we believe it is time to put into effect The Call," Moses said solemnly.

The Call was just as it sounds; it is calling all available gidgies who are old enough and strong enough to enlist and join the Skyforce or Skyguard.

"We also concurred that at this time, we should move up the date for those scheduled to leave for training. There is a battle coming, and we need to organize our gidgies for the days ahead. And we need all who are available, prepared to fight and defend our land." Moses finished.

"I agree with you, Moses; I can sense we need to plan for the coming days. I will have Pocket send out a letter to all our enlistees to arrange their sendoff in two weeks. I am about to deploy a search party to find our missing gidgies. Captain Roland is still unaccounted for; and I fear it is as Jo suspected." General Dax admitted.

"Jo is with Lieutenant C.J. and Sergeant Major Kody, interrogating the enemy. He will bring me a report as soon as he has found any information." The General stated.

"I just came from there. Sylvia is using her truth tonics to pull out information. The liaths have been given every opportunity to be restored to their former selves, but they are refusing. The horrible poison Neeradima has them on, is addictive. They are suffering more from the withdrawals than we could ever inflict with our truth remedies.

"You and I both know a liath cannot be forced to come home, but we will give them the opportunity to be restored. Let's just hope

Sylvia can work her magic and discover where they struck from and who their informants are." Moses finished and shook the General's hand then left swiftly. He was anxious to return to the interrogation.

The General sighed in exhaustion, then yelled, "Pocket!"

The small corporal ran to the General and saluted him. "Yes sir," he inquired.

Pocket was always nearby when the General was at headquarters. "I need you to compose a letter ASAP, calling all available gidgies to enlist. I also would like you to write a separate letter, moving the date for any enlisted gidgies scheduled to leave for fall training. Inform them that their new leave date is June fourteenth."

Pocket reached into his side pocket and pulled out his notebook and took a scribble stick from his upper pocket. He began to scribble as fast as he could, all the instructions the General was giving. He then paused, with wide eyes and asked, "Sir, are we putting The Call into effect? We haven't done that since the Banishment War. I wasn't even bloomed yet. Is it really that bad?" Pocket asked nervously.

The General knew Pocket was not questioning his order, but that the young corporal was afraid. The tall General looked down and called Pocket by his name, "Corporal Garret, I have always been truthful with you. You have written many letters for me; some with good news and others not so good. The days ahead we are facing can be confronted just fine by our well-organized military. However, we are going to need all hands and feet available to ready themselves. I would not say bad, but hard; yes. We are well equipped to snuff out the evil that would attempt to come our way. That is what the letter is about. Now write it in the best morale-boosting script you are capable of and send it off post-haste."

Pocket saluted the General and went off to write the letter of his lifetime. It would be a call to action. A message that did not strike the fear of an invasion but instead stirred their garden inhabitants to courage, resolve, and power. Bravery to stand, to fight, and to answer The Call.

Pocket grabbed a snack from inside his coat pocket and nibbled on some crackers while he walked to his desk, reciting in his head his epic letter.

Moses approached the room that held the liath captives and gently knocked on the door. He could hear the thrashing and hissing coming from one of them. Sylvia peaked out to see who was interrupting, "Hello dear, I'm afraid the one you are inquiring about is still unresponsive to my truth tonics. He is fighting something fierce. And I'm not sure if he is fighting to live or to die. He is in quite a bit of pain."

Moses felt compassion for the poor creature. "Sweetheart, do you think he will survive the withdrawals, of whatever it is that has its teeth sunk into him?" he asked.

"The pitiful creature is suffering something fierce, Moses. It is my belief; his addiction may kill him. We are doing our best to pull from him any information that might be locked inside his twisted mind. But for now, it's a waiting game. Kody believes this liath used to be Milton, the garden-spider farmer. He's been missing for years." Sylvia informed Moses.

She sat on a bench outside the interrogation room, gave a big yawn, and leaned against the seat. Moses sat down next to her and put his arm around his weary wife. "I remember Milton, odd fellow, nice, but odd. I've noticed a trend that Neeradima uses on her victims. She searches for that outcast, the lonely ones. That's why this strike is so unusual. Why now, what is driving her to wage war? Up until recently, she was just a fly in the ointment with small attacks, but she seems to be itching for a fight. This invasion is a message."

Moses was pondering out loud like he usually did, and Sylvia listened. She stood up and went to the small kitchen in the hall and poured the two of them a hot cup of pinkle pepper brew. They sat for a few minutes in silence, sipping their drinks. Both of them remembering the first war Havengothy saw, so long ago. And both of them knowing another one was coming.

"You'll figure it out, dear, but for now, I need to get back to Jo, C.J., and Kody. They are likely to have the poor sod in a headlock or tied up by his wretched toenails." Sylvia gave Moses a little peck on the cheek, then went back to work.

Moses sat for a little longer on the bench, listening to the suffering of what used to be Milton. And then he softly said, "Beathra, if there is a hint of Milton still there, please bring him back to us." He took another sip of his brew and exhaled in exhaustion.

Ruby and Ellie had been staying at Ginny's since the liath invasion. Ginny's root was cozy and quaint. Just outside her little root, she had pastures for her exotic creatures to graze on and stables for the flying skyponies. Down a small hill from her root, was a large pond with a dock that Ruby and Ellie loved jumping off of in the summer months.

But this summer break was different. The joy they felt a few days ago was fading fast. The girls were staying in Ruby's old room. Ginny never changed it. She always had it ready for Ruby to come home. Ruby sat on her canopy bed and looked at Ell, "It would be easy to just move back home and not go out on my own. But that just feels like I'm going backward."

Ellie sat down next to Ruby, "Be grateful you have a root to come home to. Walter and Wanda have already filled my room with whatever is Wanda's latest hobby or collection. I just hope it's not rescuing the Brindled needle snoutnose. You know how bad those smell." The two giggled about what life would be like living in a hoarder's root, surrounded by stray snoutnosed creatures. It was the laugh they needed.

"I want to get to Vine and ask her what she knows about the attack," Ruby confessed.

"Have you tried to speak with her telepathically?" Ellie asked.

"I did the day after the attack, but she was quiet. And I couldn't get to her because of the high alert our garden is in right now. Plus, Ginny won't let me leave her sight. I'll give it a go again."

Ruby closed her eyes and focused on Vine. "Vine are you there, can you hear me?"

It was a long few seconds, but then Ruby heard a feeble voice. "I'm here, but I'm not well. Do not come to me. There is a threat. Do not come to me." Vine's voice faded.

Ellie watched as Ruby's face twisted in concern. "What did she say?" Ell asked.

"She's sick, and she says there is a threat. I'm sure she is talking about the recent attack. But she told me not to come to her. She has the book, Ell; I hope it doesn't get into the wrong hands." Ruby said worriedly.

"You still know the spell to help our garden to flourish, and the only one who can use the magic is the one who's love is pure. So even in the wrong hands, the book is safe." Ellie comforted Ruby, but even she wondered what was going on.

Seb was staying with Jo but was helping Duke with his HB network. The Honeybee Network is really quite remarkable, and only qualifying farmers have a license to raise these types of bees. They have an intelligence antenna that enables them to read an address on the envelope or package.

A bee mail carrier has two stingers, ensuring that it can defend itself but still fulfill its duties if danger comes. They are also powerful and able to transport up to six letters or one giant package. The message is placed around the legs with a loose band. The brilliant little insect holds the attached envelope using his or her tiny foot as a stopper, almost like making a fist. Upon reaching the addressed locations, he simply points his toes down, and the letter slips off his leg. No other creature in Havengothy has this genius way of understanding.

Duke and Ginny had moved their wedding date up to next weekend. Rather than the fall nuptials, they decided to get married on Ginny's farm, with Moses performing the ceremony. Duke was preparing to move his hives to Ginny's after they got married, and Seb was helping him organize the transport. The recent attack made Duke extra protective of his precious Ginny and Ruby, and he did not want "his girls" out of sight during these challenging days.

Seb was carefully moving a barrel of honey so as not to upset those who worked so hard to make it. It was then that several HB carriers flew in, delivering the days letters for the west side of the garden. The buzzing was spectacular. They flew in a straight-line, diving towards the crates Duke had set out to catch the dropping mail. Each bee swooped down, just missing Sebastian's head and dropping the day's post in their bins. Then, in uniform, they flew back to their original station they were sent from.

Duke went to gather the new mail. He had to sort each letter according to the root address and then attach it to the bee assigned to the area. As he was filtering through the mail, he noticed a letter addressed to Sebastian. "Hey Seb, you got a letter from the

Skyforce." He yelled out so Sebastian could hear him over the hum of the bees.

Seb put the barrel down, feeling sticky from the honey. He grabbed the letter from Duke and opened it. His hands were having trouble letting go of the torn envelope, due to the honey residue. He shook his hand, trying to fling it off. Finally, it fell to the ground. Sebastian unfolded the parchment and read the message Pocket had fervently written,

Dear future Cadet,

    I am writing to inform you the date of your leave has been changed. Due to the recent events, General Dax is ordering all future enlisted to report to Skyforce Cadet School in two weeks. June fourteenth, you will depart for training. Please be advised that The Call has been put into action. The Council requires all able bodies to report to the Skyforce recruiting center. There is a separate letter for The Call that's been sent out.

    General Dax would like to thank you for your willingness to serve our magnificent garden. He is confident in his Skyforce and knows the bravery of his gidgies is fierce. We will meet this threat to our garden with an unmatched fury that will cause Neeradima to regret the day she touched the apple of Beathra's eye.

Respectfully,

Corporal Anthony Garret
Assistant to General Dax

Sebastian looked up from reading the letter, excited to leave early; he was anxious about it. He couldn't wait to leave for training and start his career as a Skyforce soldier. But how was he going to tell Ruby?

"Well, what did it say?" asked Duke.

"It says I leave in two weeks for cadet school. June fourteenth, to be exact. The General has activated The Call. Any able body that hasn't already enlisted will be required to answer it; at least that's what it sounds like." Sebastian felt a flood of nervousness wash over him. It was really happening. He would soon be leaving to train, but it was more than that, that gave him butterflies. He knew he was preparing for a battle that was coming.

"The Call, eh? That's pretty serious. I've never heard of it being activated in my lifetime, and I'm an old duff." Duke teased, trying to lighten the mood.

"I'm more nervous about telling Ruby about the early leave date than actually leaving for training," Seb admitted.

"When we have dinner with the girls tonight, you can tell her then. We will all be there to help both of you process this news. Heck, I would answer The Call, if I didn't already have bad knees from my service in the Skyforce. There is nothing like serving Beathra and The Whisper." Duke said, reminiscing of his time in the military.

Duke finished sorting the mail to send out first thing in the morning. He saw several letters from the Skyforce headquarters and knew most of the young gidgies they were being delivered to. Duke wondered what The Call letter read. Had he known, he would have been moved by Pockets inspiring words and would want to re-enlist right then and there; bad knees and all.

Dear Residents of Havengothy,

I am hereby informing you The Call has been activated. Havengothy faced a dark day during the Bloom Festival. The attack from the wicked enchantress was intended to strike fear in our hearts and paralyze us to doubt our King and The Whisper and have us question their love for us.

Neeradima will regret the day she touched the apple of Beathra's eye. She will fear the fierce army of Havengothy, who will bring her to her cowardly knees. We will rise together in unity and take back what she has stolen from us. We will rescue our loved ones, and we will retrieve our peace. We will not give her one more day of our joy. We will live in our freedom, and we will thrive in our home.

She is but an ant, and our forces will crush her; so, rise up inhabitants. Lift your voice with me and answer The Call. Stand in bravery. Sturdy your courage. We will confront this evil, and we will overcome! We will not back down! We will not cower from this challenge, but we will take ground and be victorious!

All who are able-bodied, of a sound mind and of a courageous heart, is beseeched to enlist. You will find an enclosed document to fill out and bring with you to the nearest Skyforce recruiting center. Thank you for hearing, answering, and acting on The Call.

Sincerely,
Corporal Anthony Garret
Assistant to General Dax

———————

It had been several days of interrogation, and finally, a glimmer of hope. Sylvia ran from the interrogation room in search of Moses. The liath was coherent and ready to talk and asking for the old council member. Moses was lying across the bench, snoring. His long beard draped over his chest, and it nearly hit the floor.

"Moses, darling, wake up." Sylvia nudged his shoulders with a little shake. "I'm awake! I'm awake!" he exclaimed as he jolted up. His beard snagged on part of the bench and jerked him back. Untangling himself, he stood up and asked, "What is it, sweetheart? Is everything ok?"

Sylvia grabbed his hand, "One of the liaths is awake. Now come inside, but be gentle, he is frail, and may not survive the night, but he wants to talk with you."

Moses walked in and saw the pitiful state of Milton. He was thin, and his skin was scaling and gray. A far cry from who he used to be, a lovely white-winged gidgie with an exceptional ability to train garden spiders. Nobody wanted the job, but Milton was remarkable with the creepy critters.

The other liaths lay knocked out by the potions Sylvia gave them. Their sufferings and vile speech were more than she wanted to handle. She double dosed them with her sleeping tonic. They were seething with hate and cursing her, Beathra, and all who lived in Havengothy.

"Milton laid still on the table. He was fragile and unable to lift his head, but his eyes caught Moses's, and he began to weep. "Moses, I'm sorry. I'm so very sorry." His soft cries moved even the angriest of hearts. With each drop of repentant tears, the color of Milton began to be restored. His lovely brown skin was like new, and The Whisper's presence was felt in the room with her warm breezy way.

Moses took Milton's hand, "Milton, we forgive you, but we need you to tell us what happened?"

Milton's voice was shaky, and he recounted the day he ran away. "I was herding my girls to a patch where a bunch of aphids had been seen. I was taking them to feast on the bugs when I was approached by a stranger. It was as if he knew me, knew my secret sadness I lived with. Few would risk getting close to me with my job. All except my sweet Ingrid. Oh Ingrid, darling, I failed you," Milton wailed.

Sylvia fetched Milton a small sip of her calming concoction, and he continued. "The stranger gave me something that was supposed to help with my heart sadness. I shouldn't have taken it; I knew it. But I did it anyway. I was just so tired of the heavy gloom. Then, I felt funny. Uneasy. Ashamed but exhilarated. I had to get away. I wanted to get away. I acted on every thought I had been harboring. I felt fearless and on fire. And I felt like everyone knew my horrible thoughts." Milton was shaking, and Sylvia placed a cold rag over his feverish forehead.

"Milton, do you know who the stranger was who tricked you?" Moses asked.

"And how did you get inside the garden without being seen?" Kody yelled.

Milton was afraid. "He will kill me if I tell. He will kill all of us." Milton shook and tried to get up, but his body was still too frail. He fell to the floor, and Kody lifted him back onto the bed.

Jo, Kody, and C.J. were growing anxious for answers. They had been interrogating the liaths for days, and this one was finally ready to speak, but he would only speak to Moses.

"This is nonsense, Moses. This vile creature has brought harm to our home, our gidgies! He's a traitor. I don't care if he is changing before our eyes, what he did is unforgivable." Kody vented.

Moses raised his hand in protest. "I agree with you Kody, he was a traitor, and he did cause harm, and it will not go without consequence. However, every wandering soul is always given a chance to come home by order of Beathra. We are his children, no matter how broken and deranged we are. Beathra wants to restore us." Moses then turned to Milton, who was fading fast.

"Milton, you are safe. No one is going to hurt you here. Now, it is crucial to us for you to give us the name of the gidgie who tricked

you. And you must tell us how your army invaded our garden."
Moses was desperate with his pressing for info.

Milton's breaths were growing shallow, "I can feel Beathra again.
I can hear his voice. Oh, how I missed it. Can you feel The
Whisper? She's here."

Milton was slipping fast. The Whisper's presence was near, and
the room was warm. There was a soft wind that was felt inside the
root as if a window was open.

Kody grabbed Milton by his ratty clothes and shook him, "Milton,
do not leave this world until you tell us who and how!" He
bellowed.

Milton's body went limp. Moses put his hand on Kody to have
him stand down, "He's gone, son. The toxins of Neeradima took his
life, but Beathra restored his soul."

The Whisper whooshed through the secret root room, ushering
Milton's spirit to the Great Ghost Warrior.

"I don't understand Moses, how can The Whisper and Beathra
act like Milton never did anything wrong? How can you say you
forgive him?" Jo and CJ were just as curious, but Kody was the one
who voiced the question on all their minds.

"Son, Milton's life was snuffed out at a young age. He missed out
on marrying the love of his life with his betrayal. The last years of
his life were lived in an environment of hate and rejection. The final
minutes of his life were filled with tormenting fear. Ahh, but the last
few seconds belonged to his creator. The one who has been longing
for him to come home. The one who wept from Milton's betrayal.
Milton may have lived these last years out of the presence of safety
and love, but tonight, he died in it. And that is what grace is: love
that has open arms, waiting, no matter what."

Sylvia added, "Milton's crimes are not without consequence. He
lived in his consequence. If you can call it living. He will not be
buried with the dignity of a Havengothy resident. He has missed out
on the wonderful and beautiful long life that is given to us as
gidgies. But Kody, who are we to say who is forgivable or not?
These questions can only be answered by the one these crimes were
committed against."

The room was quiet. No one could contest the wisdom that came
from Moses and Sylvia. However, the questions were still lingering
in the air. Who is the traitor, and how did they invade the garden?

Prince the skypony

Chapter Eighteen

A wedding and a funeral

Ruby and Sebastian were walking hand in hand around Ginny's pond. Spring was fading fast, and the warmth of summer could be felt. Duke was busy building an arbor for Ginny to cover in flowers for their wedding. Seb and Ruby stopped at the dock and dangled their bare feet in the water. Ruby didn't know what to say to Sebastian. She wasn't mad at him. Leaving early was out of his control, and the Skyforce was his dream. How could anyone ask someone to give up their heart's desire?

Ruby wasn't angry at the Skyforce, she knew this was necessary. Loved ones were still missing, and Havengothy needed heroes. What she felt; was cheated. Cheated out of a summer of being with Sebastian, and fearful something would happen to him in the days to come. They were finally able to confess their feelings to each other, and it made their moments together precious, and now, she must let him go.

"Ruby, you're awfully quiet, are you gonna say anything? I told you this news days ago, but you seem to be acting like it's not happening." Seb asked.

When he told Ruby about his early leave at dinner the other night, he expected her to get upset or cry. But she didn't say much at all. In fact, she pretended as if it didn't bother her that he was leaving three months early.

If he didn't know her so well, he would have misconstrued her passivity as a lack of caring for him. However, Seb knew she was a processor and needed time to wrap her head around disappointing news. But now he needed her to talk to him.

Ruby leaned against Seb's shoulder in the warm afternoon air and breathed in the smells of summer coming. "I'm sad we will miss our summer. This was supposed to be the best time of our lives. Swimming in Ginny's pond, taking long flights to the edge of the forest to spot migrating Atto-gliders, holding hands..." Ruby stopped and looked up at Sebastian, "But now, it's about survival and preparing for a coming war. It's about our garden, and everything around us is changing. Will you be home for the Harvest Carnival before you leave for advanced training?" Her voice caught in her throat, and Seb heard the quiver of Ruby choking back tears.

He pulled her into his side a little closer, "I will have two weeks of leave before I head out to the Broad River Island for my task force training. That will make it just around the Harvest Carnival. And I am going to need all the time with you I can get before that grueling ordeal. It's known as the crucible. It purifies and filters out the bravest of souls. It will be one of the hardest things I will ever do in my life, but it's worth it, just to be able to rescue our lost or fallen. But we still have over a week left to make some memories. So how about we start some of them now." Sebastian shoved Ruby into the water and then jumped in after her.

Ruby gasped from the shock of the cold water, then she charged at Seb in an attempt to dunk him. She never could though, he was way too fast and strong. The giggling could be heard by all on the farm. Duke looked up from his project and wiped the sweat from his brow and smiled when he saw the two splashing in the pond.

Ellie heard the ruckus being carried across the lake and came running out of the garden gate. "Hey, we were all supposed to go swimming after lunch!" She yelled, she then dropped her small gardening spade and ran towards the pond. At full speed, she dashed down the long dock and did a perfect cannonball with a giant splash.

The three friends swam and sunbathed and swam some more. They chatted and dreamed, and for a small moment in time, everything was normal again. There was no fear of the coming days. No letting go. No war. No liaths. Just best friends, spending a warm day splashing and laughing. It was just what they needed to lighten their hearts and encourage them for what was impending.

General Dax was still searching for Captain Roland. The task force team had returned with six of the thirty-four abducted gidgies. They were at the Healer's station being cared for by Julia and Sylvia. Sylvia called for Melia to come and use her mind healing powers on the troubled fairies. Raymond, the young man that was near Yoli, shared how she saved his life.

"Her last words to me were to not stop speaking to Beathra, that he was our only hope for rescue. So, I just kept talking to him. Even when they forced us to eat their poisonous rations. I kept speaking to Beathra, and it made the pain a bit more bearable. It didn't take it away, but I felt hope. And then, I could hear Yoli singing with another prisoner. And it inspired others to sing. Man, did that make the guards mad. They moved Yoli and the other guy because they were too much of an influence. But it was too late, we realized singing helped alleviate the agony."

"Did you see where they took Yoli and other prisoners?" Jo asked as Julia attended to Ray's cuts. She also gave him a special potion to purge him of Neeradima's toxic provisions. Raymond wanted to help as much as he could to recount all he knew of the dark caves of Darphea. He was sitting up to tell Jo what he could remember when the healing serum started churning inside his stomach; he was about to throw up.

"I think we need a bucket over here!" Jo called out. "And you better hurry!"

Julia made it just in time to catch the projectile vomit spewing from the pitiful Ray, "You are one of those. Usually, the potions work through one's system and purge them out the other end." She wiped Raymond's mouth and gave him a sip of cold water. Then she turned to Jo, "Sir, are you about done with your questions? I think this young man needs to rest."

Ray interrupted her, "No, ma'am, I want to keep telling the First Sergeant what I know. But can you leave the bucket, just in case?"

"As you wish, but I am only giving you ten more minutes, and then the First Sergeant here will have to come back later." Julia gave them both a nod and then went to attend to the others.

"You are a brave little fellow, Ray. Now, you were about to tell where you thought they took the other prisoners." Jo anxiously waited for the answers.

"I only saw them take them deeper into the mountain. The ones that refused to bow to the evil queen are used for slave labor. That is where they were moving us to, when we were rescued. Yoli went deep into the mountain, but we could still hear her song, though. It drifted up the tunnel, and those dumb liaths could not silence that brave lady. But there is something that guards the prisoners down there or someone. I overheard one of the liaths arguing about who's turn it was to feed it. But I don't know what 'it' is." Ray finished.

Ray was feeling nauseous again and grabbed the bucket. "Oh, one more thing, sir, five of the captured gidgies, willingly gave their wings to Neeradima. Leon, Mildred, Cho, Juan, and Amy."

"Did you see Barney, the twin? He was one of the guys who ran the Ferris wheel at the festival." Jo asked as he was about to leave.

"I didn't. He wasn't with the group. I gave you all the names of those I knew, there was only thirty of us. I counted. Barney wasn't one that was captured."

With that last bit of information, Raymond vomited once again. Julia came to attend to him, and Jo thanked the Healer for the extra time.

Jo relayed the info to General Dax, "Thirty-four are missing, but only thirty were carried off to Skawlterrin. Five of those captives chose to betray the King, and we rescued six. This sounds like a bad math word problem. I think the other four may be in the wilderness or injured somewhere between Havengothy and Skawlterrin."

"I think you're right, Jo. Let's contact the Captain of the Skyguard and request he put a unit together to comb the grounds and the tree limbs for any fairies that may have fallen from the claws of the flying beast." General Dax instructed, "We still have not been able to find Captain Roland. Did Raymond say if he saw him with the abducted?"

"No, sir, I gave you all the names Ray relayed to me. Raymond did share a disturbing piece of news. Neeradima has creatures guarding special prisoners deep within the caves. This is where he thinks they took Yoli and another captive. Do you have any idea what those creatures are?" Jo asked.

"They're her pet naffagrahns," The General answered. "She has been raising them in her wicked forest since her banishment. Outside of Skawlterrin, they would look like a wild boar in the Hyperion Mountains, but in her deranged land, they are a hideous and violent beast."

Naffagrahns have a round face and a broad mouth filled with yellow, jagged, needle-sharp teeth. Their fangs drip with acid saliva that burns their victims. They have a dragon-like skin that is hard to penetrate with swords or arrows. And their claws are as a serrated knife, so it rips and tears the flesh of its victims. They are the guardians of Neeradima's most precious or most dangerous captives.

It was the day of the wedding. Miss Kitty was at the house early that morning fitting Ginny for her gown and putting the final touches on

Ruby and Ellie's bridesmaid dresses. Ginny was a picture of perfection. Her white dress had a garnet ribbon in its hem to match her hair and the garnet's flecks in her wings. Her hair was in a loose bun, and she wore the highest heels she could walk in, nearly making her reach Ruby's chin.

It was a small ceremony with a handful of friends there to celebrate. The service was to be held near the water. Ginny had laced the arbor with a variety of spring and summer flowers; daisies, marigolds, delphiniums, and peonies, just to name a few. Her bouquet was simple, tiny white baby breath sprigs with wild red roses that matched her hair and ribbon.

Moses and Duke waited at the pond near the lovely arbor. With Sebastian and Jo standing next to him. White rose petals lined the path from Ginny's root to the lake. Ginny peeked out and saw all the guests, it wasn't a lot, but it was enough to make her feel nervous.

"It's going to be fine, momma; you have done scarier things than this. Like, raise me all by yourself. You deserve this day, and I couldn't love Duke more." Ruby hugged her Ginny. "Now, let's get this party started, shall we?" Ruby went to fetch Prince, Ginny's favorite skypony. She would ride him down to the pond and then hand the reins to Ruby once she was there.

Ruby was leading Prince from the stalls, and he was prancing and flying. He was excited to be part of Ginny's big day. Ginny went to her porch to wait. As soon as Prince saw her, he pulled away from Ruby and galloped to Gin and nuzzled her with his soft muzzle.

"Steady boy." She said and grabbed a sugar cube that she had tucked into her bouquet. Ginny climbed on Prince's back, ready to say her forever promise to Duke.

This was Ellie and Ruby's cue; it was time to start walking the path toward the pond. The violinist saw the two girls begin their descent and started playing.

Sebastian saw Ruby and had to catch his breath. She was wearing a pale pink dress, and her hair was swooped up, but like usual, it refused to obey all the bobby pins Ellie had shoved into poor Ruby's head. The girls strolled down the petal lined path and took their place on the opposite side of Seb and Jo. Seb was smiling his ridiculous cute smile that melted Ruby's heart every time.

Prince was prancing, proudly carrying Ginny towards her groom. Duke saw Ginny for the first time in her flowing white gown that draped over Prince. The large stout Skyforce veteran had small tears of admiration and love, flowing down his face. If Ruby had any doubt at all about Duke, those tears washed them away.

Ginny reined Prince in and stopped him just in front of Moses and Duke. Duke walked towards Prince and lifted Ginny from her skypony. Gin handed the reins to Ruby and stood on a little stool so she could somewhat look Duke in the eyes when she vowed her love and life to him.

It was a stunning ceremony with dancing and feasting. Lava lanterns were hung out by the pond so the party could go on into the night. Ruby had only broken two glasses and dropped one tray of raspberry cookies. Seb teased her that it was a good night for her if there were only a few cleanups.

It was during the crashing of the wine glasses that Ruby sliced the palm of her hand. "Darn it!" she exclaimed. Sebastian ran to help her clean up the glass when he noticed her hand was bleeding.

"Go sit down Rubes, I will pick up this mess. Here, put this towel on your cut, and I'll help you bandage it up when I'm done with the cleanup."

Ruby flew out to the small bench that faced towards the pastureland and watched as Prince and Piper grazed in the lava light glow. Sebastian picked up the bits of glass, then went and found Ginny's first aid kit and joined Ruby on the bench near the pasture.

Seb was wrapping her hand in bandages when he stopped and looked up at her. She was as pretty as ever; the sunny days were causing her freckles to spread across her nose, and her hair finally gave up and was falling down her shoulders and back. And that silly crooked smile that he had grown to love made her even more beautiful.

Ruby looked at him and smirked, "I know, I'm always breaking something, I'm a klutz," just as she was saying she was a klutz, Sebastian got the nerve up and leaned towards Ruby and kissed her. The kiss he had been waiting to give her since the day she pulled him behind the tent. The kiss he was dying to give her at the Bloom Festival before the invasion. The kiss he wanted to plant on her in the pond before Ellie's cannonball.

He placed both his hands on her face and pulled her close. Ruby responded with wrapping her arms around his neck, kissing him back. It was an epic kiss. It was a first kiss that was made for the record books. Prince looked up and saw the two in an embrace; He snorted and grunted in disgust, then went back to grazing.

On the other side of the garden was a different scene. There was no dancing and no celebrations. Milton's funeral was a quiet one. A tall, slender gidgie stood, dressed in black, shoulders slumped, weeping.

The warm night with the summer fragrances seemed unfair. The world should have stopped for this moment. It should be raining and frigid, and the atmosphere should be bitter. But instead, the only cold and bitterness that was felt was inside the grieving woman's heart.

Kody walked up to the tall fairy and handed her his hanky. She began to speak with soft cries "I read about Milton's death in the paper. I can't believe he was liath. I can't wrap my mind around him betraying our King," she wept deep gasps of anguish.

"How did you know him?" Kody asked.

"We were engaged. Milton was the sweetest, odd fellow you could ever meet. I knew he struggled with fitting in, and he had a sadness that ached inside his soul, but I thought I could make him happy. We met under the strangest circumstances. My name is Ingrid Milton, and he was Milton Ingrid. Our mail was mixed-up, so I went to his spider farm to exchange it, and he was so impressed I wasn't afraid of his eight-legged girls, he asked me to dinner on the spot. And that was that. I didn't mind his occupation, and he didn't mind I was a head taller than him." Miss Milton smiled as the tears freely fell.

"So, you never got to marry him," Kody said as more a statement than a question. He then placed a bouquet of wildflowers on Milton's stark gravesite.

"We were supposed to get married. Milton would tease me that my name would be Ingrid Ingrid once we wed. I had planned the most beautiful ceremony of all. Miss Kitty designed my dress, and we even hid a small stool at the altar for Milton to stand on. But the hours ticked away, and he never showed. I thought all this time, he had jilted me at the altar, and I guess in a way he did. I was so angry with him. I never imagined Milton being targeted by the enemy. I should have reported him missing. But his soul sadness made him withdraw for days occasionally. So, I just assumed he backed out. I was more concerned about my humiliation and my own broken heart…" Miss Milton could not finish her sentence, the sobs choked her, and she felt guilt, anger, and grief mixed into one giant knot in her stomach.

Kody put his arm around her and gave her a gentle hug. "Ingrid, I know for a fact, Milton did not jilt you. He was tricked into running away. It's hard for me to understand that he chose to betray our King, and not trust him, but what I do know now, is fear can grip a being clean into his soul and squeeze out any courage that may have been there. Milton may have lived in torment, but he died in the King's presence."

"How do you know this? The Havengothy Times said nothing of his repentance, they only identified him as the spider farmer who betrayed our land and was one of the liaths that attacked the Bloom Festival. I knew it was Milton. I don't understand; how could he leave? How could he betray us? How come I wasn't enough for him to stay?" Miss Milton's tears could not stop, they even caused a few to fall from the burly, Sergeant Major's eyes.

"I know this because I was there when he died. Honestly, I didn't understand how Beathra and The Whisper could forgive him, until I saw you, your heartache, and your sorrow. Grace wasn't just for Milton, it was for you, so you would know, his last breath was carried away by The Whisper. And it was magnificent." Kody was watching Ingrid process this new information.

"It does bring me great comfort to know he did not die alone, but was in the presence of kindness," Ingrid said as she calmed her sobs.

Kody remembered shaking Milton for information, "I would love to say that kindness came from me at that moment, but I was angry. Fury was all I felt, but it was Moses's words that have been burrowing in me like a corkscrew. He said, 'Milton may have lived these last few years out of the presence of safety and love, but tonight, he died in it. And that is what grace is: love that has open arms, waiting, no matter what.'

"I came here tonight to see if there was anyone that would miss Milton, and I saw you. So, you see, grace is at work, healing everyone Milton came in contact with. It showed me no one is beyond the reach of Beathra's love."

Ingrid wiped her nose with Kody's handkerchief and took a cleansing breath. "Thank you, Kody. I think you and I are both alike in this situation. I couldn't forgive Milton for leaving me, and you couldn't forgive him for his betrayal. But if our King can forgive him, so can we. I think tonight is a lovely night for letting go."

Ingrid took a ring from her small purse and set it on the insignificant grave marker that read, "Milton Ingrid," There was no honor, no tribute, no love, just a name.

Ingrid and Kody were leaving the graveyard when they heard a whimper. "What was that?" Miss Milton asked.

"I don't know, but I want you to stay here," Kody said.

He grabbed his sword and was cautiously walked towards the grove of trees that lined the graveyard when suddenly, Barney came bursting out of the trees.

He was bloody, delirious, but alive. Kody ran to Barney to help him up, and Ingrid quickly came to assist. The two carried Barney to the Healer's station when Ingrid had a thought, "You know Kody, if we weren't there to say goodbye to Milton, we wouldn't have been there to rescue Barney."

Ingrid took comfort in knowing that Milton's death may have saved a life. It was a small comfort, but it was there, nonetheless.

She was right. Barney's injuries were substantial, and he was saved within hours of death.

Chapter Nineteen
Going home

Neeradima's plan was a success. She called the attack a "fear strike" with the intent to stir up terror and doubt in the hearts of the inhabitants of Havengothy. She could do more damage with fear than she could with any other weapon. For fear burrowed into the minds of those who she desired to control and stripped them of hope.

It gripped hearts she could never get her physical fingers around. And if she could unhinge their minds, they would doubt their King and The Whisper. They would question their shelter and the love of their makers. If Neeradima could get them to wonder *why* Beathra would allow such things, she could fracture their faith in him, and then draw them to her.

The mood of the garden was a strange environment. It ranged from those who wanted to hide, and others who wanted to fight. Neeradima's plan was cunning; fear was ruling many of the forest residents. After the Spring invasion, several protests rose up, questioning the competence of Moses and his leadership.

The Havengothy Times reported dreadful accounts of gidgies leaving on their own volition. The terror drove a handful of them to surrender to the evil queen. They thought that if they went willingly, raising a white flag, they would avoid the dread of being snatched or the horror of being tortured. A large group of gidgies left to live in the Hyperion Mountain Range with the wild gidgies, hiding in its thick forest. They chose not to engage in the battles to come but instead, avoid all conflict.

———————

Sebastian left for cadet school. His sendoff was small, but the love and celebration were grand. Duke made Sebastian's favorite, a millie fruit upside-down cake. Ginny made iced and hot pinkle pepper brew, adding whipped vanilla cream to the cold beverage. Jo, Duke, and Kody gave advice on how to survive the rigorous training regimen. Ruby gave Seb a lock of her hair to keep with him. It was a hard goodbye, with tears and lots of promises to write every day.

———————

It was a warm summer that unfolded gradually. Ruby stayed with Duke and Ginny and helped on the farm. She hadn't decided where she was going to live. Vine was still quiet, and the hope that Havengothy usually felt, was now tangled with a presence of panic. Gidgies stayed inside for fear and apprehension of abductions. The normal summer activities were scaled back. The laughter that once filled the air was only heard on occasions, and it was brief.

Mothers kept their younger ones indoors or close to their roots. Along with living with a presence of fear, families were adjusting to life after The Call. Ruby even tried to enlist, but she was too clumsy to pass the obstacle course. It was just as well; Ginny was not ready for Ruby to leave her sight yet.

Duke and Gin made a small apartment root on the farm for Ruby and Ellie, and the two of them grew a fantastic garden just outside of it. Ruby used the mystical melody to flourish her garden. It would prove to be an abundant harvest, enough to feed several families that may need a little extra help due to family member's absences.

Duke finally got his hands on The Call letter, and it was so moving he tried to re-enlist to fight the monsters who struck fear in his beloved homeland. He was disappointed with his knees. They could not endure a refreshing course. The letter truly made him hungry to fight the enemy. And once again, Ginny was relieved.

The summer with Ellie helped Ruby alleviate the pain of missing Sebastian. Ruby wrote Seb six letters a week, compared to the one she would receive from him.

Ellie and Ruby would write their fella's every night, and hand them to Duke in the morning. It was convenient living right next to the HB network, and it made it easy to send Theo and Seb letters and packages. The difficult day came to help Ellie pack for her next adventure. In just four days, she would be starting her education to become a professor. It was a long flight to the East Branch, and it would take Duke and Ruby, plus two skyponies, to transport Ellie and her belongings.

"Is that everything?" Duke asked as he put the last crate on Prince.

"That should do it. I have all my books, clothes, favorite blankets, a pile of parchment paper, and a bouquet of scribble sticks for writing." Ellie answered.

"Perfect! I'm just waiting for one thing." Duke said and looked to the air. On schedule, Jo arrived.

"Jo will be escorting you two to the branch and making sure Ruby gets safely back home." Duke informed.

"I don't understand, aren't you coming with us?" Ruby asked, disappointed,

"Nah, I don't want to leave Gin here without me, so I asked Jo here, to do the honor of escorting the two of you," Duke shared.

Ginny looked surprised. "What are you talking about Duke? I told you I would be fine. I refuse to live in fear. We must live life as normal as possible. We can't give that troll the satisfaction of us shrinking back."

Duke put his finger to Ginny's lips to hush her. "This is not fear sweetheart, its precaution. This ensures the girls are safe in their travels, and you are safe in our root. I don't care if it's been a quiet summer. That wretched 'troll' is about to meet our military's fierceness, just you wait and see. But until then, I want to make sure my girls are safe."

Ruby was touched by Duke's care and concern for all of them. Ginny didn't protest, she saw that Duke was resolved in his decision. She hugged the girl's goodbye, and Duke brought out a brown bag full of fig and honey tarts and raspberry cookies. "Snacks for the journey. The tarts are still warm, so be a little careful."

Ellie gave Duke and Ginny one last hug, "Thanks for allowing me to crash with you guys this summer. It meant the world to me."

"It was our pleasure, dear, and our root is always open," Ginny said with another squeeze.

Duke and Ginny lived on the furthest west side of the garden, near the edge of the Darphea Wilderness. The East Branch of Havengothy University was all the way on the other side of the garden. It would be a two-day flight, flying eight hours a day with breaks. A Skyforce soldier could make the trip alone in one long day. However, with the skyponies weighed down, and stopping for bathrooms and meal breaks, the journey added an extra eight hours of travel round trip.

On the long flight toward the east branch, Ruby shared what she had heard from Sebastian, and Jo relayed his letters. They were excited that Seb was a few days away from coming home, just in time for the Fall Festival.

Havengothy's summers end was stunning. As the three flew over their land, they could see the subtleties of autumn coming. Leaves had already begun to change, and some were drifting in the air.

The fall fragrances were permeating the atmosphere with the faint scent of cinnamon, cardamom, and cloves. The spice trees were beginning to shed their red bark, and harvesters were weeks away from gathering the curls of the tree's skin or the seeds from the spicy pods.

The vanilla orchid farmers were draining all the milk from the last of the blooms, storing them in barrels for the winter. The spicy scents swirled with the vanilla, and the air smelled like apple pie and ice-cream.

"This is my favorite time to fly in our garden, the air smells like Yoli's apple cider. She always put extra cinnamon in her recipe." Ellie remembered fondly.

"I loved her caramel apple pastries because she put double caramel in them," remembered Ruby.

"She would always say things like "extra sweet just like you, or extra spicy just like me.' I sure do miss her. Jo, have you heard anything new with Yoli's search?" Ruby asked as she reminisced about all the kind things Yoli did for them as students.

Jo shook his head, "I'm sorry Ruby, there is nothing to report. We have rescued seven more fairies, but the wicked liaths are continually moving the prisoners. I think they are trying to drain all hope from them, intending to make them surrender to the vile queen. One fairy was beaten pretty badly when we found him, just for saying the name of Beathra. Neeradima's punishment is brutal if there is any mention of The Whisper or our King."

"That's horrible," Ellie said in surprise. "What is she afraid of when they mention their names?"

"We know that their names give us shivers. So, I would imagine it feels like the zap of an atto-glider hoof to Neeradima's head." Jo chuckled. "Their name alone can remind Neeradima of her fate, that a new world will arise, and all evil will be destroyed once and for all." Jo shared.

"That's an old prophecy Jo, for it to be fulfilled Beathra will be destroyed, our world will be demolished. How can that prediction ever be fulfilled without our very destruction? Plus, do you really think Neeradima can destroy Beathra? That prophecy was written in a different dimension, a different world." Ellie responded emphatically.

Her studies of history were thorough. And she could not see how the prediction could come to pass without the destruction of them all.

"Well, I do know that things are changing, and our world is readying itself for what is approaching," Jo said with confidence.

———————

Sebastian was finishing his final stretch of cadet school, and then he would be considered a Skyforce soldier. He and Billick were in the same unit and shared the same barracks. Their childhood friendship grew into a confident trust in each other. As a soldier, you had to know you could rely on your brother or sister in arms, and there was no room for pettiness in the ranks. If there were conflicts, they were addressed, and the quarreling parties were isolated until it was resolved. Seb and Billick only had to be separated once, and they learned quickly, it was time to grow up and put away their boyish competitions.

The two were returning from drills when they noticed they both had an envelope sticking out of their lockers. "What do you suppose this is about?" Seb asked Billick.

"Beats me. I guess we should open it and find out. Let's hope it's not a rejection letter." He answered.

The news was not a rejection, it was exciting and a little disappointing. It read:

Dear Cadets,

We are proud to announce that with your excellence in training, you will be advancing to Special Operations training camp the day after graduation. This letter is to serve as preparation for the coming days and to inform your family that you will not be home for leave. I am sure they will celebrate your accomplishments and be ready to see you this coming spring.

Congratulations on your qualifications and promotion.

Sincerely,

Penelope Hayward
Assistant to Commander Sidney

They both looked up from reading the letter with huge grins, "I can't believe it, we are leaving for the Broad River Island for spec op training in a few days. I have only heard stories of the island. I hear it will refine you to your soul," Billick said with a nervous smile.

"Yeah, I'm in shock too. It's called the crucible for a reason, Bill. I was hoping for those two weeks with Ruby, but she'll understand. At least I think she will. We better get to the HBN and get our letters out ASAP. Our families will be expecting us in a week." Seb said as he reached in his locker to grab his paper and scribble stick.

Inside the door of his footlocker was a letter from Ruby and a lock of her hair. He ran his hands over the rose gold curl, and said quietly, "I'm sorry Rubes, I'll be home soon." And then quickly wrote a letter to share his excitement for his expedited training and disappointment to not take her to the Harvest Festival.

———————

Ruby was helping Ellie settle into her dorm, while Theo and Jo carried in the crates from the skyponies. The head professor was a short, round woman named Judith Cline. She popped in to see if Ellie was settling in and gave Ruby permission to stay the night.

"Good afternoon, ladies, I see you are making yourself at home. Miss Winn, is there anything I can get the two of you?"

"Thank you, Professor Cline. I can't think of anything that I need. I love my room and view. I never imagined the East Branch was actually in Beathra's furthest reaching branches. I can see glimmers of light sparkling off the Broad River from my window." Ellie answered with delight.

"Professor Cline, I appreciate the offer to stay, but I traveled with two skyponies and a military escort," Ruby said with a chuckle.

"That is no problem for us. I have already spoken with Theo, and he has offered Jo to stay with him. And the skyponies can board in our stables. The stablemaster will make sure they are well cared for and ready for the journey home. Will that be all, ladies?" asked Professor Cline.

"Yes, thank you, professor. I look forward to starting my classes," Ellie replied nervously.

"Well, classes begin Monday. Enjoy your weekend, it will be the last one you see in a while with all your studies." Professor Cline smiled, but there was no joke in the work ahead for Ellie.

Jo and Ruby were headed home early the next day. Ruby mustered the courage to ask Jo for a huge favor, "Jo, remember how I told you about Vine, and how I could communicate with her?

"Yes, what about it? Has she said anything to you lately?" he asked curiously.

"That's just the thing, I have not heard from her. I spoke with her at the first of summer, but she was weak and told me not to come to her, and that it was dangerous. And now she is not saying anything at all. Would you mind if we swung by there before you took me home? I just need to see if everything is alright." Ruby asked pleadingly.

"I can't take you there, Ruby. For one, Duke would not appreciate me putting you in harm's way. And two, you just said yourself, Vine told you not to come because it was dangerous." Jo declined Ruby's request, but she was not done begging.

"Please, Jo, maybe you could go by and see what's going on. What if there is another one of those evil shrubs popping up, or a liath scoping out the place?" Ruby asked persuasively.

"All the more reason not to go. I'll tell you what, I will do a distant fly by, and if I see anything suspicious, I will report it to the General. And we will go back with a team. But I will not investigate the area without support." Jo negotiated.

This satisfied Ruby, but she had one more request. "Will, you at least tell me if she is ok?"

"I will," Jo said with a smile.

Jo and Ruby made it back in record time. The skyponies were swifter because they were not weighed down with their flight, and Ruby was a remarkable long-distance flier.

When they arrived, Duke and Ginny met them outside. Ginny took the skyponies to the barn to feed and brush them down. Prince and Piper were excited to see their master. They pranced and pounced all the way to the barn for their treats.

Duke invited Jo inside to rest for a few minutes. He made them both a pot of lava java. "This will help you finish the last leg of your journey headed home," Duke said with a chuckle and handed Jo the dark muddy drink.

"Think I could get some of that sweet vanilla pod milk Gin has?" Jo asked sheepishly. "I like it a little sweet and creamy. Her Bloom Festival drink converted me." He laughed with his confession.

"Sure, if you want to froof it up," Duke teased but handed him the carafe of sweetened vanilla pod milk.

Ruby was about to head to her little root apartment when she asked Duke if she had any mail. "The bees haven't come yet. You can check the crates to see if they have arrived while we've been visiting." Duke suggested.

Ruby ran out to Duke's hive to check for mail, and the bees were just arriving. She sat down on a honey barrel and watched as they buzzed by dropping letters and packages in their assigned crates. They really were magnificent to watch. Being twice the size of a regular honeybee and equipped with double stingers, they could look intimidating, but they were passive and dutiful.

Ginny was walking back from the stalls when she saw Ruby sitting on a barrel, watching the bees drop the mail. She flew by to sit next to her girl.

"Hi, sweetheart. Are you waiting for one of Seb's letters?"

"Yes, I'm glad Duke and Jo told me how hard it was for them to find time to write with all their training exercises, or I might have felt a little hurt by his lack of letters," Ruby admitted with a grin.

"Well, how about I help you sort the mail while we look for Seb's letter?" Ginny offered.

It didn't take long for Ruby to find Sebastian's letter; the cadet school had a special envelope with the Skyforce emblem watermarked on the corner. But she wished she would have waited until morning to check the mail. That way, she could have had one more day of believing she would see Seb soon.

Ginny sat with Ruby in the quiet. All that was heard was the low buzz of the bees. Then Ginny spoke. "Ruby, gidgies are given wonderful long lives, with the ability to love deeply. And when you love deep, it hurts more when you are separated. You are very young, and at the beginning of something precious, that can last for centuries. But darling, girl, you will need to sturdy your heart for the times ahead."

Ruby held the letter close and then looked at Ginny. "This growing up business stinks. I feel like I've aged ten years in the past four months."

"I know, but you are doing it beautifully. If ever there was a girl who could handle the hardships, it's you. Don't lose your song or your joy, sweetheart; instead, let them be your strengths and gifts you offer to those who are discouraged. Our land needs your silly, more than ever." Ginny knew that Ruby's love of life would be a light during the dark days to come.

"Well then, let's go bake something sweet and eat until our belts burst off!" Ruby said with a smile.

––––––––––––

Training on the Broad River Island during the fall and winter months were filled with vicious and grueling drills. It ensured the soldiers' determination and secured courage that could only be forged in the Refiner's Forest. A metamorphosis transpired for all who made it to the end of the crucible. They would never be the same after the Broad River Island experience. Only those who braved it to the end would be entrusted with the charm to cross the Darphea Wilderness.

The days to come would be a testing and crucible for all. The lighthearted, hope-filled land was preparing for battle. The success of the wars to come rested on the shoulders of young gidgies who were willing to contend for peace. If the inhabitants could withstand the troubled days ahead, they would see a victory like no other in Havengothy. They just needed to trust the voices that were leading them towards their triumph and conquer the fear that was trying to choke out their courage.

Chapter Twenty
Vine's identity

After Sebastian and Billick graduated from the three months of Skyforce Cadet schooling, which entailed physical training and knowledge testing. The next step of their education would be for Special Operation; this had three more months of grueling exercises. Starting first with endurance testing and then finishing with mental challenges. This last leg of their schooling was in the Refiner's Forest; a magical terrain that played tricks on the mind and made each subject that entered it face their worst fears.

There was also a part of the forest preparation that is never spoken of afterward. It is only a piece of common knowledge to all who completed the task of surviving the Refiner Forest. All task force members had to complete the last step of the transformation, or they would never be able to contend against the evil that they were called to fight.

It would be weeks of frigid weather, icy terrain, and several unknown factors that Billick and Sebastian would endure. But if they made it to the end, they would be transformed into a weapon for their King. For it is in the Refiner's Forest a warrior is fortified in a hope that can only come from the struggles they will face in the mysterious territory. And a new level of trust will surface as well, due to the obstacles they overcome.

Sebastian stood at the entrance of the forest. It was veiled in a thick denseness that he could only see past the first few rows of trees. Looking at the darkness that lay within it, he touched his hand to his pocket that held Ruby's lock of hair and said, "I'll see you on the other side, my silly girl." He then entered the thickness of the forest and disappeared into the shadows of its foggy, unknown land.

Jo did as Ruby asked and went to the site of Vines location, but the news he would relay to her would be devastating. Vine was destroyed. He convened with Moses and General Dax about the uniqueness of Vine and shared with them Ruby's connection. Moses was the only one who knew who and what Vine was.

She was the Empress of Ivy, a one of a kind that The Whisper created for sheer delight. Like Neeradima, she was made to beautify

Havengothy. Her actual name was Gabriella. Her job was as an encourager and guardian of the land. She was designed to speak life-words to all things living, and she was made to complement Neeradima's work.

Gabriella's duty was to protect young growth, shade it from the harsh sun, and to be watchful of pestilence. She would hover over seedlings and stay with the dying. The Forest Spirit and the vine were more than friends, they were like sisters. The two crawled and floated throughout the garden as emerald garland, growing, flourishing, and expanding Havengothy.

The difference between Neeradima and Gabriella was quite vast. Like The Whisper, Neeradima floated, and like Beathra, Gabriella was rooted. And though she crawled, she was still grounded. Neeradima had envisioned Gabriella overthrowing the garden with her, but the true vine would not revolt.

Gabriella grieved the loss of her friend. She refused to follow Neeradima, and instead, protected young gidgies in her greenery, hiding them during the Banishment War. Neeradima felt betrayed by Gabriella and raged against her. But the Empress of Ivy held fast in her stand in loyalty to Beathra and The Whisper.

With Neeradima's banishment, Gabriella slept. The harnessing of her magic was not to punish, but hide, protect, and preserve her powers, until the day the warrior arose. The one who could undo the damage that Neeradima inflicted. The warrior would work with Gabriella to sturdy their land and lead the inhabitants into victory, against the wicked queen.

Who would destroy Gabriella and why, was the question the council discussed? The new information about a young fairy named Ruby, who woke the vine from her sleep, piqued their interest and confused many council members.

"She can't be the chosen one, she is small, too weak and too young. I heard she was raised by a single mini fairy. And if that isn't all, she is from the west side of the garden. How can this possibly be? The prophecy speaks of someone great, with a heart of courage. The warrior should come from a prominent family, with a balance of a father and mother. None of this single parenting business. This girl is a bumbling garden fairy, subpar in her studies, and a bit of a troublemaker," announced Morphesis.

He was twelve years younger than Moses but was highly regarded in the circle of leadership. He was under the impression the chosen one would be a strong, mature man, from a family who lived in a root near Beathra's trunk, established and highly regarded. Not some single, unknown mini farmer who rescued creatures and gathered eggs for a living.

"You and I both know that Beathra and The Whisper are not impressed with outer appearance. If this is the warrior to arise, it is because of her heart, not her physical strength, or the family she was raised by." Moses interjected.

The council was divided, and Moses presented a solution to their disagreement. "If the girl is the chosen one, it is to be. And if the warrior has bloomed, this can only mean one thing; We are in the last days of what we know of our beloved Havengothy. I suggest we secretly assign guardians to watch over her. This will ensure her protection. If she is the one, we will know when it's time to train and equip her. I will venture to the wizard who lives in Hyperion Mountain. He will advise us as to how we should respond and what we should do."

The council agreed to the idea. Moses met with the General to decide on those who would covertly be assigned to Ruby. The rule: she could not know she was being protected. They did not want to self-fulfill the prophecy.

"Moses, I am assigning C.J. to accompany you on your journey to see Melchizedek. His training and skills are exceptional and can survive nearly any environment. Plus, he has that little critter, that may be a service to you on your adventure." General Dax did not ask Moses if this sufficed, the General simply told the elder it was what he was doing.

"Very well, General, I should enjoy the company and the help on the journey. At least tell me the boy can cook." Moses teased as he conceded to the General's decision.

———————

Ruby sat in her small root apartment reading for the hundredth time, the letter Jo sent her. Explaining what he found out about Vine, her name, and that she was now destroyed. If the ground wasn't frozen and covered in snow, she would fly to her and speak the charm in hopes of bringing her back.

Instead, she was burrowed in her tiny root, waiting. She felt helplessness, overwhelmed her, and stuck. All her hopes of starting a new life after school was dashed. She was in her own place, sort of; it was part of Ginny and Duke's root that they graciously created for her. Ruby felt like she was regressing.

Sebastian was training, and his letters were few and infrequent. Ellie was buried in her studies, and the possibility of getting together for Christmas was looking slim.

Ruby sat in her cozy chair, sipping her spicy pinkle pepper brew with extra honey, and nibbled on popcorn. She put the letter from Jo down and grabbed a scribble stick and parchment papers out to write Sebastian. Her loneliness was gobbling her up, and she had to do something to shake her sadness.

Dear Sebastian,

I hope all is well and you are surviving your training. Jo and Duke both have told me how difficult it is for cadets to get a chance to write with all their drills and lack of free time. Ginny, Duke, and I started decorating for Christmas. Their root is filled with evergreen, red ribbons, and small strands of lava lights. Father Christmas would feel right at home.

Ginny harnessed a sled behind Prince and Piper, and they loved prancing through the snow. I've cut a small tree, and I am going to set it up in the corner of my sitting room. It was a lot of fun playing in the snow and sipping hot cider and pinkle pepper brew. Duke brought a pile of his baked goods, and I ate so many I had to unbutton the top button of my pants.

This time of year, makes me miss you something fierce. I think of our last Christmas when we were all together. Ice skating on Ginny's pond, snowball fights, and drinking hot chocolate by the potbelly stove in her parlor; what fun we had. This year there is a lot more snow than usual.

I can't imagine what it must be like training in this freezing weather. Do you guys put up a tree or celebrate the holiday? The three of us cut trees for other gidgies who weren't able to get out of their roots or were too afraid to leave. Plus, we took them small packages of cookies and cakes that Duke and Gin made. Those two really are perfect for each other. They both love to take care of their neighbors. We are all planning on going to the Winter Festival.

Ginny has been developing two new drink formulas for her booth. One is a peppermint and chocolate lava java drink served with creamy marshmallow sauce. And the other, a spicy pumpkin with chocolate sauce and vanilla pod milk. The pumpkin one was a massive hit at the fall festival, she calls it a Punchilla. Clever huh? It's probably my favorite one she has created yet. The peppermint chocolate lava java is good too, though. I love to have one in the early mornings while checking on the HBN.

All the mail bees have their winter fuzz now. They are so cute looking all wooly. I can't help but want to scratch their little heads. I am even gaining a bit of favor with a little girl I like to call 'Baby.' She flies to me when she sees me and will sit on my shoulder if she's in a good mood.

I think that's all I have to share for now. I am enclosing some of Duke's marvelous cranberry scones with millie fruit jam. I know all of you like to share your care packages when they come, so I included extra. Be careful with the millie fruit jam, the last scone I had with it tasted of cranberry and creamed onions. I nearly lost my lunch. I scraped most of the jelly off my scone and tried again and got a tasty apple-flavored millie fruit jam. I could barely taste the lingering effect of the onion.

I miss you, Seb, and I look forward to Spring and dancing with you under the lava lights.

Love Ruby
P.S Instructor Kay is singing at the winter festival. I will be wearing my earmuffs you got me last year for more than warmth.

Ruby slipped the parchment into an envelope. She decided to not wait until morning to mail it and bundled up in her coat and boots and braved the cold evening air to take it to Duke. She knew he may not be at the hive, but she could leave it in the outgoing bin for the morning.

She was crunching through the snow when she heard voices coming from the hive barn. She slowly approached, unsure if she was intruding. As she got closer, she could see that it was Sergeant Major Kody and Jo talking with Duke and Ginny. Ruby didn't want to be rude and eavesdrop, but she didn't want to intrude either. The cold made the decision for her. She entered the barn, and the four older gidgies all stopped what they were discussing and greeted Ruby.

Ruby noticed they all ceased chatting, and she felt suspicious. "There is no need to stop your conversation on my account. I just came to drop a letter to Seb," she said, sounding a little offended.

Ginny looked at Ruby, sensing she was hurt. "Good evening, sweetheart. You are not interrupting anything. The boys here were popping in to mail a few letters and ask Duke about sending packages that were top secret." Ginny said as she glanced at the men to agree with her.

"That's right. We were dropping off a couple of packages, and we needed Duke's top letter carrier to deliver them," Kody said in his most convincing tone.

Ruby wasn't buying it. She knew they were discussing something important, but there was nothing she could do about it. If they didn't want to include her, they didn't have to. She was more hurt that the four of them were fibbing to her.

"Whatever. I just came out to drop this letter off to Sebastian and see if Baby was in her hive," Ruby announced as she plopped her envelope in the outgoing bin. Then she went and gave the wooly little bee a scratch on her head.

Ginny wanted to go to Ruby and tell her the conversation wasn't a bad one, but she was not permitted. Their discussion was confidential. The four gidgies waited for Ruby to finish petting the fuzzy bee, making small talk about Christmas and the winter festival. This piqued Ruby's interest, and she joined in on the conversation.

"It's weird celebrating such a festive holiday during these uncertain times. The harvest carnival was the slimmest I had ever seen in my lifetime." Ginny mentioned.

"We gidgies were designed to celebrate life and all its seasons. And the best way for us to not bow to that wretched witch is to keep celebrating. Our Skyforce and Skyguard have never been tighter and more efficient. This attack from Neeradima was intended to cripple us in fear, but her plan has backfired. It has made our garden stronger." Kody said with conviction.

"What about the gidgies that defected? I read that those that ran away to the Hyperion Mountains give up their ability to fly. Why would they choose to live a life of hiding and give up their gift of flight?" Ruby asked.

"They don't give up their ability to fly; they can't fly. The altitude, even in the lower foothills, is higher than the highest peak of the Darphea Mountains. No creature who is not from the mystical Hyperion Mountains can fly. And when a gidgie leaves Havengothy's shelter, they go wild. They have to fight for survival in pretty harsh terrain. Those who left our land in fear of war did not want to fight for the peace of Havengothy, only their survival. It's selfish, really." Jo said emphatically.

"We can't believe what the Havengothy Times is putting out these days. They are an infectious voice rather than an influential one. Those old ladies writing about our garden are nothing more than gossipers who are trying to make headlines. They were wrong about Emmet being a traitor, and they are wrong about our garden being afraid. There are more of us willing to battle than run away." Kody said with his arms crossed over his chest.

Duke suggested they all take the conversation inside where it was warmer, but Jo and Kody had to leave. Ruby was waving goodbye to Jo and Kody as she walked towards them, tripped over a stick, and ran into the doorframe. She quickly corrected herself, rubbing the bump on her head that was forming, and gave a wave that said, "I'm ok!"

Jo looked back at Ruby with the oddest expression, almost with pity. Ruby didn't know what to do with that look. She just smiled her crooked smile and waved awkwardly. Jo shook his head then quietly said to Kody, "We've got our work cut out for us."

"I am not sure I am totally convinced she is the chosen one. But I will do whatever is needed to protect that little girl. If the same ones who destroyed the vine know of Ruby's whereabouts, they will put it together that she is special." Kody mentioned as Jo, and he flew in the cold.

They picked up their speed to HQ to confess to General Dax that they shared with Duke and Ginny the possibility of Ruby being the chosen one. They figured it was better to ask for forgiveness from the General than permission for sharing the intel. The two felt the parental units needed to know how to stand watch over Ruby. They swore Duke and Ginny to secrecy to not tell Ruby of the extra attention she would be getting from the Skyforce.

Ruby said her goodnights to Duke and Ginny and then gave Baby one last scratch on her head. She knew Ginny wasn't going to share the conversation she and Duke had with Kody and Jo. All she could do was guess what it was. Ruby figured it was either military discussions or more liath sightings. She hated this in-between place of still feeling like a child but knowing she was an adult. Ruby felt the older gidgies were keeping things from her due to her age and ability to handle specific information. She made up her mind that night, come summer, she was moving out.

Ginny was quiet as she and Duke went to bed. She sat down at her vanity and brushed her long garnet hair, counting the strokes. Duke was lying in bed reading a book, then looked up at his wife. He couldn't imagine what was going through her mind.

Duke never raised a newly bloomed gidgie, so he didn't feel what Ginny was feeling. He loved Ruby, though, as if she was his own. And he would do whatever was needed to keep her safe. Tonight, Ginny was gut-punched. Jo and Kody delivered news that was far beyond Duke and Ginny's imagination.

"Sweetheart, are you going to brush your hair all night? Do you want to talk about it?" Duke asked carefully.

"I'm sorry darling, I was lost in thought. What did you say?" Ginny answered quietly.

"I know you're processing the information from Jo and Kody, but if she is the one to right-the-wrongs in our garden, she has been raised by the perfect mother. You have taught Ruby to be brave and true to herself and to love her garden and all who dwell in it." Duke said, trying to encourage his wife. "You've imparted compassion and respect from the smallest creatures to the largest ones." He finished.

Ginny climbed into bed, her tiny body barely making a dent in the soft mattress. Duke pulled her in and held her close. "I knew she was special. I knew there was something she was called to do for our garden, I just never imagined this was the 'special' thing she was bloomed for. Ruby trips over her own shadow, and her heart is generous and kind. What will war do to my silly, innocent girl?" Ginny said with concern.

"Jo and Kody risked a lot giving us this information. They wanted us to know so we could be part of the preparations for whatever comes her way." Duke encouraged.

"I understand that they bent the rules to include us in what they perceive to come, but I am having a hard time wrapping my mind around it. How is it that my girl is the chosen one? My little girl, who giggles and snorts, and sings to her garden. How is it she is called to be a warrior? And not just any warrior, the chosen one to confront Neeradima and rectify what that witch inflicted on our land." Ginny wasn't crying, she felt anger and fear. However, her voice was catching, and the lump in her throat was growing.

Duke just held her as she vented her thoughts. "Jo says the council thinks she may be the chosen one, that's why they have been assigned to just watch over her for now. That is a good thing. Right?" Duke asked.

"What will it look like Duke? How will my little girl fight that wicked enchantress?" Ginny asked. Now the tears were beginning to fall.

Duke's hands lifted Ginny's tiny chin, "I don't know what it will look like, but I do know what it will be. Miraculous. If Beathra chose her, then Beathra will gift her for her purpose. Snorting, bumbling, giggling, tripping, and all. "

Ginny curled into Duke's arms and slept restlessly. Her dreams were littered with war and fires.

The Hyperion Mountain Range

Chapter Twenty-One
The wild gidgies

The Hyperion Mountains were filled with unknown creatures, and though it was not an evil place, it was also not safe. Moses and C.J. had made it through the Darphea Mountain Range and were now into the foothills of the magic mountain. The wizard was the watchman of the land. He stood guard over the terrain and knew when the atmosphere changed by the presence of strangers. He could tell if they were good, evil, or neutral. It was his graciousness that allowed runaway gidgies to dwell in the lower foothills.

Without the gift of flight, Moses and C.J. would need to walk. They were approaching an area that made C.J. feel uneasy. He looked at Gertie to see if she was sensing any danger or evil, but she was snuggled in his oversized coat pocket, sleeping.

"Something isn't right here, Moses," C.J. mentioned.

"We are in the territory of the wild gidgies. They are watching us as we walk through. They are hidden in the trees, bushes, and ground." Moses whispered.

"How did they go wild so fast? I thought they just ran away a few months ago," asked C.J.

"There has been a colony of wild gidgies for hundreds of years; since the Banishment war. Their leader is still somewhat civil, and he is the one we will need to speak to if we want permission to pass. They are not warriors, they are survivors, which can look similar when they fight. Except a warrior is fighting for freedom and victory for others, and a survivor is fighting for self-preservation. Both are fierce, but wild gidgies adhere to their own rules." Moses warned C.J. and recommended that he be prepared for the unexpected.

The two slowly approached a grove of trees. C.J. could feel eyes on him, but he could not see anything. The wild gidgies were hidden well. Moses continued slowly and then looked back at C.J. and said, "Sorry, son. I have to do this." He then took one more step, and a snap was heard. Moses tripped a trap on purpose. The whipping of rope was heard zinging through the air. A net sprung from under them and captured both C.J. and Moses.

The two gidgies dangled from the net. C.J. grabbed his small blade that all Skyforce soldiers kept on their belt and was going to cut them out of the predicament, when Moses took his hand and said, "Wait and watch."

C.J. stared at the trees waiting. His intense gaze adjusted to the scene, and he began to see shrub covered creatures emerge from the forest. They practically blended in with the background. As they walked out of the thickets, they carried spears, and other hunting weapons. Their faces were painted in camouflage, and their wings hung behind them as wilted, shriveled limbs. They were chanting an unfamiliar rant and slowly drawing close to their captives with their spears.

"What are they afraid of?" C.J. asked.

"They are afraid we will make them come home. The wild gidgies live in fear and feel that outsiders are a threat. And they are untrusting of us because we are from a land they felt did not protect them. But do not worry, they don't want to hurt us, only scare us. They are passivists." Moses answered.

He then raised his hand towards the approaching tribe and said, "I would like to speak with Cornelius, your leader."

The small tribe started pounding their spears on the ground, and their chants got louder. Moses took a brown bag and a growler of liquid from his pack, "I have brought gifts for your leader. It is millie fruit, and Meredith Barry's merrybare berry bush brew."

The chanting stopped. This was the peace offering that would get Moses an audience with their leader. At that moment, a small fairy emerged from behind the wall of wild gidgies. Cornelius was a mini gidgie, but that did not mean he was a small leader. He loved his tribe, and he led them with great courage and authority.

Cornelius looked to the wild gidgies that were in the trees and gave them a sign to cut the captives down. Moses and C.J. fell with a loud thump. The first thing C.J. did with his free hand was check on Gertie. She was at complete peace. This gave the lieutenant comfort, but it also confused him. These savage gidgies seemed dangerous, but the pompadour's sensory gift was not affected.

Once they were free of the net, they stood up, surrounded by a hostile tribe. Cornelius approached Moses and, with the slightest nod, indicated to his clan the strangers were welcome. He then turned away from them and walked towards a tiny hut hidden in the shrubs. Two wild gidgies began to push Moses and C.J. towards Cornelius to follow.

"I have never been in this part of the mountain, or maybe I have, but just didn't see the wild gidgies. I never had to confront them. My last mission was to scout the terrain and do recon for a fellow soldier who was missing, but he was never found." C.J. mentioned as they followed the small fairy to his hut. C.J. noticed Cornelius's back; he was missing one of his wings.

The three sat down in the grass home, and Cornelius placed a plate of unknown meat in front of them. He then pounded on the table for Moses to set his offerings down. Moses brought out the millie fruit and the growler of Merrybare brew. Cornelius's eyes lit up. This was his favorite drink in all Havengothy when he and Moses served together in the Skyforce.

Cornelius suffered deeply after the Banishment War and decided he would never fight again. He ran to the Hyperion Mountains with what was left of his family, and a few Skyforce members followed him. Their minds and hearts were troubled, and they wanted to escape the pain. They struggled with adjusting to life after the war and chose a life of isolation instead.

Cornelius offered what he called a "Sanctuary" to those who wanted a life free of conflict. If he was going to fight, it was going to be for his food and nothing else. He would never again take a life unless it was to feed himself or his tribe. They put on a fierce front to scare others away, but they were actually peaceful beings within their colony.

Moses poured his old friend a glass of the bright pink brew. It fizzed, and Cornelius smiled. He missed the taste of home but not enough to return to it. Moses passed the beverages out and waited for his old friend to drink in the joy-inducing brew. Cornelius sipped the bubbly drink at first and then gulped down the rest and pounded his glass for another. C.J. was growing impatient but knew what Moses was doing; he was loosening up the governor to be able to communicate with him peacefully.

It worked. One glass in and Cornelius was smiling. He began to chow on the millie fruit but spit out the first two bites due to the rancid taste of moldy potatoes. But the bites after that delighted him, and he gobbled up the watermelon flavored millie fruit. Moses smiled at C.J. and said, "Once a gidgie, always a gidgie."

"Cornelius, my friend, it's been a long time since we have seen each other. Your community has grown. I see you have quite a few new residents. Many of which have refused to answer The Call that was put into effect in Havengothy recently. So, I am sure you have guessed; Havengothy will be going to war soon," Moses said in a matter a fact tone.

Cornelius was in a good mood, but the mention of war darkened his demeanor. He growled, "Don't expect me to be part of this next war. I already paid a high price in the last one." He was speaking of more than his wing. He was speaking of his peace, his mind, and a lost love.

"We're not here to ask for help, we are here to ask for safe passage to the Wizard, Melchizedek. I know you have the arrangement to dwell in his foothills, but we need an audience with him. We would like to pass through your land with your permission." Moses wanted the favor of Cornelius more than his permission, and catering to his authority would get both.

"You can pass through our land, but you are not to speak to my dwellers. They want nothing to do with the war to come. They just want to live a life away from Neeradima and her threats." Cornelius grumbled in a rough tone that sounded low and gravely.

"Cornelius, you know you are welcome to come home anytime and do not have to fight. You can live in peace in our garden." Moses kindly said.

"Peace? What Peace? That evil witch will never stop trying to hurt Beathra or his children. She will always threaten our world. I want nothing to do with a peace that comes from war." Cornelius was raised his voice, and Moses poured him another glass of the pink brew.

"How can you sit here, hiding? The peace that our world needs will come because we will fight against the one who is trying to instill fear and rob us of our peace. You sit here speaking that you will not fight, yet you trap and instill fear in strangers. You are fighting for peace; rather, you admit it or not. It's just that you are fighting alone. But if you fought with us, you would have an army that would protect your peace." C.J. spoke passionately with his voice slightly elevated.

Cornelius looked at Moses and said, "I see you have a passionate young soldier that feeds into the logic of war, Moses. What you don't, understand young man, is my fight here in the mountains is only a fight to survive. And I would rather fight the wild animals of this land than the forces of evil that come from Skawlterrin." Cornelius slammed his empty glass of brew on the table in annoyance.

"Then you will always be a survivor but never a victor. And to hide from a fight is cowardly," C.J. accused.

"Don't you call me a coward, you stupid fool. I fought for the freedom of Havengothy. I contended with the darkness. I watched my brothers and sisters fall to their death for the freedom and peace of our garden. I lost my wing, and I came home to a war-ravaged land that wept for their Forest Spirit, who betrayed them. I am no coward!" Cornelius yelled. He then went quiet and continued, "I am tired. And I want to be left alone." Cornelius had tears running down his cheeks, remembering the war, the price, and its trauma.

"You have safe passage, Moses. But do not ask me to help you if you find yourself in trouble here in the mountains or in Havengothy. I will not come. And I think the brew you brought me is a dud." Cornelius escorted the two out his door and assigned two tribe members to accommodate his guest for the night and to guide Moses and C.J. through their land at first light.

The morning came, and Moses and C.J. were packing their gear when Moses saw Cornelius at his hut doorway. Moses went to thank him and say goodbye.

"Cornelius, my friend, Sylvia, sends her love and says we always have a room for you." Moses gave another piece of millie fruit from his own supply to his friend and then slipped his pack on his back and began the journey through the wild gidgies land.

As C.J. was following the two guides out of the village, he looked back and saw the soldier he was sent to rescue last year. The now wild gidgie stood and watched as his Lieutenant walked backward, staring at him. C.J. turned around and pulled his stocking cap over his ears and shook his head in disbelief.

"I searched for that guy for over a month in these mountains, and he was probably hiding in the wild colony the whole time. I fought two liaths that gave me this scar down my face during that search. Only to leave these mountains without Quinton." C.J. mentioned to Moses.

Then C.J. paused and gave Gertrude a little head scratch, "Come to think of it; it was during that mission I found little Gertie here, and she's been rescuing me since that day. And now she saved our garden. So, I guess the search was for little Gertrude and not, Quinton." C.J. realized, thinking, that maybe the mission was more about rescuing his pompadour so she could be a rescuer to his land on the night of the attack.

Then he added, "After all, you cannot rescue someone who does not want to be saved." C.J. reached into his pocket, pulled little Gertie out, and let her ride in the front of his winter jacket with her tiny face poking forward.

The land was covered in snow, but C.J. noticed how well the wild fairies cultivated the lower foothill. They farmed what they could and gardened what would grow, and the rest they hunted or scavenged for. They had created a community that protected each other. They were surviving, but were they thriving?

"Moses, who did Cornelius lose in the war besides fellow soldiers?" C.J. asked as they trudged quietly through the thick snow.

Moses reflected back on the day he had to tell Cornelius of his wife's death. Cornelius's wife was a Healer with Sylvia. The two ladies were best friends. Allison died protecting the wounded. The Healer station was under attack. Sylvia, Allison, and several other Healers circled around the infirmed. Allison laid her life down to protect her patients. Sylvia used every healing tonic and her oracle gifting to heal Allison, but it was unsuccessful. While Cornelius was fighting the liaths during the Banishment War, the Healer's station was left vulnerable. Cornelius felt guilty for not being there to protect his wife.

Moses shared the story with C.J., and the young Lieutenant felt ashamed for being so harsh with the grieving warrior. "Is that why the main Healer's station is at the Skyforce headquarters now? Because of the attack?" he asked.

"Yes, Neeradima's army thought the sick and the injured would be an easy target. They did not expect to meet my wife, who is trained in Gidjidsu." Moses smiled. "But, even with the Healer's fighting ability, they could not hold the enemy back. Healers are created to heal, and Allison fought hard to save her patients. By the time a squad was able to get to the station, Allison was fatally injured.

"After the Banishment War, we knew the liaths would search for easy prey like the sick, wounded, and unwell. So, we moved the main Healer's station to headquarters to secure the safety of our injured soldiers. And any others that may need protection while healing."

"Are wild gidgies still considered Beathra's children? If they ran away from Havengothy, did they run away from Beathra?" C.J. asked in genuine curiosity. He didn't know what to think of these savage-like fairies, who looked similar but behaved so differently.

"They did not denounce Beathra, and living in Havengothy doesn't make you a gidgie, being connected to Beathra, and The Whisper does. The wild ones still carry their fire seed. They still love their King, but they may not trust him fully. Their fear, hurt, or heartache has caused them to run away. But they didn't run to the enemy, and the wild ones are not our enemy. They are our brothers and sisters who have distanced themselves but not fully disconnected themselves. There will come a day that they will need us, and we will come." Moses answered.

C.J. and Moses journeyed through the land for a full day, until they reached the end of the wild gidgies terrain. The two tribal members stopped at their perimeter and then turned around to walk back to their village. They never said a word to either Moses or C.J. and left them there alone in the cold.

The next level of the adventure would be harsh and even more unpredictable than the first leg of their journey. The two made camp for the night and opened a lava bean pod to heat themselves and cook their dinner. They slept, but it was a light and uneasy sleep.

The next morning, the Lieutenant broke camp and took Gertie for a walk. The pompadour was sniffing around the land when she yipped and came running to C.J. "What is it, girl?" he asked as he pulled his sword from his sheath and went to investigate.

Gertie was pink, so he knew she was nervous, but he wasn't sure what was causing her to feel so shaky. He slowly walked toward the forest of trees that were lining the wild gidgies land. As C.J. entered the snowy woods, he heard a low, throaty growl. Suddenly, he felt a hand on the back of his arm.

Moses whispered, "Back up slowly, C.J., we must wait until the lioness is done hunting before we enter. If you are in her forest during her prowling, you will be her breakfast."

C.J. slowly backed away from the entrance of the forest. He watched as the shadow of a giant beast moved to and fro in the blades of sunlight that cut through the snow-covered trees. In one sudden move, the enormous creature pounced on a wild boar and gave a deafening growl. Then the lioness carried her prey away, disappearing into the thick forest.

"Well, that was fortuitous. Now we can just follow her footsteps to the plateau of the mountain. That is where we will find the wizard, Melchizedek." Moses announced. He slapped C.J. on his back, tightened his backpack, and began trekking through the wooded hunting ground.

"What was that, Moses?" C.J. asked.

"That my boy, was the great Hyperion Lion. They are the fiercest creature that dwells in the mountain. And though they are wise and good, they are also dangerous and unpredictable. Now, let's be off, shall we?" And with that bit of information, Moses began the long hike towards the wizards dwelling place.

C.J. was excited. If he survived this mission, he would witness what only a handful of gidgies have ever seen in their lifetime, the dwelling place of the Mighty Lions.

The Diatone tree elf

Chapter Twenty-Two
Yoli and Jermaine

Yoli and Jermaine were hidden deep in the caves of the farthest side of the west Darphea Mountains. They hung in cages over a pit that housed Neeradima's pet naffagrahn's. There was a prison guard who stood watch over the two singing gidgies. He was a horribly deformed creature that was once a tree elf from the Diatone forest. A land where the king treated all his people fair and kind. The generous king shared his harvest and his treasures with all his subjects.

However, the prince was not happy with the arrangement and felt he deserved more than the peasants. When the king denied his son the wealth he was looking for, the prince went to Neeradima to request help to overthrow his father. The land was a considerable distance from Skawlterrin, so she asked what the prince would give her if she assisted him.

The wicked prince offered half of his people for her slaves; in exchange for support in taking the kingdom from his father. The elf king got word what his son was planning and dispatched a messenger to Moses seeking help. Neeradima thought she would be entering a peace-loving land, so she sent a handful of her strongest liaths to kill the king. The king hid his people.

However, Neeradima's army was greeted by one hundred and forty-four, elite, skilled warriors, known as the Beathra Brigade.

Trained in the Hyperion Mountains by Melchizedek, the wizard, these mighty warriors were not your average soldiers. The liaths were unprepared for such a fight and retreated. But not without the prince. The prince was now a permanent resident of Skawlterrin. He was deformed and filled with acid hate and was the perfect guard of the hopeful gidgies.

"Shut up! I am sick of your singing!" he screamed. The vile elf threw a rock at Jermaine, and it just missed his head. Yoli looked at her husband and said, "I can't believe you have endured this for seven years."

"Keep singing darling, it strengthens us and weakens them. If they could kill us, they would have by now. The fact that they are trying to hide us is a good sign that Neeradima's nervous." Jermaine smiled his toothless smile, and it made Yoli shake her head in unbelievable love and admiration.

She belted out her songs all the more, and Jermaine joined in. The old prince put his hands over his ears and screamed. "Stop!" but the two brave souls continued with their melody. Even the naffagrahn's put their paws over their head to block the joyful noise.

Neeradima was down by her marsh, checking on her monster that was formed in the swampy waters. And though it was a harsh winter, the swamp steamed and gurgled with sulfur gasses that put out heat and a scent that curled the nose hairs.

The creatures she was cultivating in the marshland were an experiment. If her plan worked, she would have a fierce aquatic army to invade Havengothy from the east through the Broad River. But they needed time to incubate, and she was not going to attack her former land until her water beasts were ready.

Torn landed next to the wicked queen and bowed low. "My queen, the vine I destroyed, has not grown back. It is covered in ice and snow. I do believe it is dead."

"I don't care about that wretched vine. Gabriella means nothing to me. Has there been any sign of the fairy who spoke my charm?" the queen screeched.

"No, your majesty, she is hidden. It is unpredictable to tell which grotesque winter festival she will be attending. There are several of them throughout all of the enemy's land," Torn informed.

"I know how that bloody garden celebrates." The queen bellowed but Torn stayed bowed low.

Neeradima knew full and well that the Bloom Festival was for all the garden inhabitants to come together and celebrate new life. The rest of the year, there were smaller community festivals that spread about Havengothy. She hated their joy. She hated their faith. The spring strike was a perfect hope crusher because it caused many of the gidgies to live in fear and doubt their King, and she benefited from their distrust.

The fearful ones who surrendered felt like a bonus. And when Neeradima heard others were running away to the mountains, she didn't care if they did not belong to her, as long as they did not serve Beathra, it was a win in her eyes.

"There is no need to watch over the vine, she is dead. I want you to continue with your search of the reckless fairy that stole my charms." Neeradima ordered. "And send me that oaf of a general." She screamed.

Torn mounted her hawk and flew into the forest in search of Ominous. The queen had a job for the general's informants.

The west side winter festival was at the Christmas tree farm ran by Haans and Agatha. The frosty magic in Havengothy was sacred. Father Christmas visited each festival, delivering unique gifts from Beathra and The Whisper. Even those who were in hiding ventured out into the cold weather to enjoy the winter carnival.

The lava light strands against the winter sky look like diamonds. Havengothy's air smelled of peppermint and pine. The festival was simple, with a few games and food booths. But there was no Ferris wheel at the celebrations.

Prince and Piper pulled the sleigh that was filled with all of Duke and Ginny's wonderful treats to sell at the winter carnival. Next to their booth was a caramel corn cart ran by Angus, a kind fat fairy who overindulged in his product.

Ruby had a fresh bag of his delicious popcorn. She was shoving an entire handful in her face when Joseppi walked behind her and startled her with "hello." Ruby jolted and lost half her bag of caramel corn with her shocked response, "Hellooo, Jo." she said with a mouth full of the popped kernels.

Jo apologized and offered to buy her a new bag, but she declined, "That's not necessary, Angus gave me the bag for free. It was his first batch to get his popper heated up. What are you doing here, anyway? Shouldn't you be running some recruiting booth or standing guard or doing something soldiery?" Ruby asked as she shoved another handful of popcorn in her mouth and offered Jo some.

Jo grabbed a fistful and informed her he had the night off. "Nope, no soldiery stuff for me tonight. The General gave me the entire week of Christmas off. I am having Christmas dinner with all of you at Duke and Ginny's. I even think Kody might be there."

Ruby looked suspicious. Of all the years Ruby has lived with Ginny, they never had company for Christmas. The two of them always took dinner to the elderly or the lonely. "Perhaps it's because of Duke and his Skyforce buddies," Ruby thought.

"Well, that will be a first for us, we never really made a Christmas dinner for a crowd. We always delivered them to the lonely or shut-ins." Ruby informed with a sideways look at Jo.

Without missing a beat, Jo added, "Oh, she's still doing that, but we will be helping you. I'm kind of looking forward to it. I usually just sit around at the Skyforce playing cards and eating Christmas cookies until I'm sick. It will be a nice change. I might even bring my famous bean dip." Jo added as he tossed a caramel covered kernel in the air and caught it with his mouth. He crunched it up and smiled at his success.

Ruby and Jo saw Buck and Barney enter the festival. Barney was thin and could not fly just yet. Buck carried him whenever they left their root, which was seldom. This was Barney's first big outing aside from the Healer station checkups, since the Bloom invasion.

Buck wrapped Barney's wooly scarf around his neck that was slipping and then carefully walked him to the covered sitting area near Duke and Ginny's booth. Jo and Ruby went to sit with the twin boys and see how Barney was faring.

Buck was situating Barney and putting a warm blanket over his thin legs when Ruby and Jo sat down with the twins. "Buck, we can sit with Barney while you go get something from Ginny's booth. Make sure you try her peppermint chocolate lava java with marshmallow sauce. Tell her it's my treat," Ruby said as she sat down next to Barney and pulled his blanket over his lap.

"That would be mighty kind of you Miss Ruby," Buck said. He then looked at his frail brother and asked, "Would you like one of those chocolate peppermint things or one of Ginny's creamy pumpkin drinks?" Buck asked.

"Barney smiled; I like the pumpkin drink. And can I have one of those gooey pastries Duke makes?" he asked childishly.

Ruby looked at Jo surprised with how childlike Barney was.

"Barney buddy, how's that bump to your head doing, Kody said you had a pretty big gash on the back of your noggin?" Jo asked and then looked to Ruby, hoping that explained Barney's behavior. It did. Her eyes filled with compassion, and she felt tears pooling, but she pushed them back. She was glad Barney was alive, whatever that looked like. And he was still just as sweet and smiley. In fact, he was even more cheery in his childish way.

"I have a big bump on the back of my grape. At least that is what Lewis says. I like him. He always gives me candy when I go see him and Sylvia. Do you want to feel my bump?" Barney asked.

Kody saw the three sitting in the covered picnic area and went to join them. "

Somebody needs to put a few more lava beans in the stove here." He said as he stoked the heat and added three more hot beans to the barrel. "That's better," he then sat down next to Jo and saw Barney across from him. The last time Kody saw Barney was at the Healer station, and he was still in a coma. "Barney, how ya doing pal? You look great. A whole heck of a lot better than the last time I saw you." Kody said with a giant grin.

Barney answered Kody in his little boy way, and Kody understood immediately what was wrong. He personally saw the gash on the back of Barney's head, and it was terrible. Barney was lucky to survive such a fall. Kody smiled at the new Barney, and then lowered his conversation just a tad to speak at Barney's new level. "I sure am proud of your bravery, Barney boy. And you're just as handsome as ever. Even with that big bump on your head." Kody said.

Barney smiled hugely. "Do you want to feel my big bump on the back of my head? Lewis calls my head a grape. I think that is funny." Barney said with a giggle.

Right at that moment, Buck returned with a platter filled with drinks and baked goods for everyone. "Ginny took care of us, alright," Buck announced.

Ruby glanced over at her mother and mouthed the words "Thanks," and Ginny smiled. Buck had explained everything to Ginny and Duke as he waited for his order, and Ruby could tell it moved Ginny's heart of compassion.

"Here's your pumpkin drink Barney and stop asking people to feel your bump. It's weird." Buck teased.

"I'm sorry, brother, but Kody said he was proud of me, and I wanted him to feel my bump so he could feel more prouder of me." Barney was thrilled that Kody felt pleased with him, even though he did not remember it was Kody who saved his life.

The small group of gidgies visited and ate under the tent the entire night. Ruby shared with Jo that she hadn't heard from Sebastian in a while. Kody and Jo both told her she wouldn't receive any letters during his last three months of training.

"I guess that's good to know. But I am still going to write," Ruby announced.

The festival evening was winding down, and it was time to close the booths and head home. There was still one more night at the festival, and then it would be Christmas. Jo and Kody helped Duke and Ginny clean up, and then they all trudged through the snow with Prince and Piper pulling the sled.

When they reached the root, the men unloaded the sleigh, and Ruby and Ginny took the skyponies to the barn to feed and brush them. Prince laid his head on Ginny's shoulder and rested as she combed his mane. Ruby was throwing extra straw in the stall to treat the ponies for all their hard work. She then gave them both an extra scoop of sweet grain. Piper pranced in and rolled in the fresh straw.

Duke invited Jo and Kody in for a glass of cinnamon whiskey. The three men sat around the potbelly stove, laughing and reminiscing about Skyforce cadet school. The girls came in from the cold night and joined the guys with a hot pinkle pepper brew with extra honey and a splash of the whiskey.

It was a perfect winter night. The warm root and the loud laughter eased the pain in Ruby's heart as she missed Sebastian. She was thrilled to have a letter from Ellie to read when she went to bed. When Ruby got up from the floor by the stove, Jo, and Kody both decided to leave for the night as well. She was a short flight to her apartment root, and Jo and Kody followed her as she went home. The two Skyforce gidgies waved goodnight as they watched her enter the small door into her root.

"Do you think she suspects anything?" Kody asked.

"Ruby may be young, but she is no fool. She will start to put it together eventually, that we are watching over her." Jo said as they flew to their housing.

Ruby went into her tiny root and uncovered her lava bean lamp to light her sitting area. Next to her overstuffed chair was a basket with parchment paper and scribble sticks. Ruby wrapped up in a blanket and nestled in to read Ellie's letter.

Dear Ruby,

It feels like a lifetime since we have seen each other. Thank you for the care package of homemade cinnamon shortbread cookies and Ginny's homemade plum jam. It was just what my late-night studies needed. I ate the whole tin in two days. I did share with Theo, but not much.

Things are going well with him. He is a second-year at ALC, so his schedule is different than mine, but we spend our Saturdays together studying. We are both staying here at the school for Christmas and will be joining a small group of friends in the large common area branch for a potluck meal. I offered to bring cheese and crackers. You know how much I hate to cook. But Theo is roasting a fitternick fowl.

Boy, did I get lucky with him. He is nothing but a gentleman. I wouldn't mind if he tried to kiss me though, but he seems to be taking his time. Oh, well. Have you heard from Sebastian? I have written a few letters, but I have only received one from him. I hope he is surviving the treacherous training. I have only read bits and pieces about the Refiner's Forest. It is all so hush-hush. I also read they emerge a different fairy, but I have no idea what that means.

Theo and I are planning on meeting everyone at the Bloom Festival this year. And I believe Theo volunteered to do security one night. It's strange to think we have to perform all these safety protocols. But I guess it's better than hiding in fear. Tell Duke and Ginny hello, and Merry Christmas!

I miss you, Ruby, and look forward to summer break spent with you on the farm.

Much love, Ellie

Ruby placed the letter in her basket that held all her writing items. She was tired from the day's events and decided to write Ellie back in the morning. Ellie knew nothing of poor Barney's brain damage, only that he survived a fall. Ruby fell asleep in the giant chair, thinking of all the things she was going to write Ellie come morning.

"Ruby, it's time to rise." A voice whispered into her ear. Ruby jolted from her sleep. It was morning, and she saw Ginny out by the barn hitching Prince and Piper to the sleigh. Ruby rushed to get ready to help Duke and Ginny with their food cart. She slipped on her warm boots and ran to her mother. In her rush out the door, her coat hooked on the doorknob of her root and jolted her back. Ruby fell over backward, doing a small summersault. Duke was walking by as Ruby fell back. "You all right, Rubes? There's no fire." Duke said, teasing.

Ruby giggled at her own blunder and answered, "You and I both know I don't need a fire to fall on my face." She unhooked her coat pocket from the knob, noticing she tore it a little. She then ran to Ginny to apologize for not waking up when she called her, "I'm sorry you had to wake me. I fell asleep in my chair and didn't wake up until I heard you say it was time to rise."

Ginny was buckling the bridle to Prince when Ruby was apologizing for sleeping in. She looked at Ruby, confused, and said, "I didn't wake you up, dear. You must have been dreaming."

"Wow, it sure felt real." Ruby snorted, "Since I am up, what can I do to help?" Ruby asked.

The three packed the sleigh with all the goodies for their food booth. Duke had brought Ruby a large mug of pinkle pepper brew with extra honey to warm her. She snuggled into the atto-glider wool Afghan that was draped over the bench of the sleigh. It was a perfect winter day.

Havengothy had a fresh dusting of snow the night before. The sun was out, causing everything to glisten and reflect the bright daylight. Christmas Eve felt marinated in hope, and it was just what the inhabitants of the land needed to cling to.

Duke looked over at Ginny and asked, "Did you see Ruby take a tumble out the front door?"

Ginny looked at Duke with a furrowed brow and sighed, "Yes, I saw the summersault."

Duke chuckled and teased, "Well dear, the fate of Havengothy rests in your little tumbleweed." He smiled.

Ginny was not amused.

Havengothy's Giant Winter Butterfly

Chapter Twenty-Three

The Christmas butterfly.

Christmas morning came, and Ruby was carrying gifts to Duke and Ginny's root when she saw the oddest-looking bird flying towards her. As it got closer, she realized it wasn't a bird at all, but a large butterfly. Havengothy's giant winter butterflies were rarely seen due to their midnight migrations to the Hyperion Mountains.

They were the size of a hawk with vibrant shimmering icy blue wings, but few ever had the privilege to view their majesty. On occasion, one would see them as a caterpillar in the thick ivy.

This magnificent creature was flying directly towards Ruby. She didn't want to move or speak for fear of scaring it off. To yell for Ginny and Duke to come to witness the spectacular creature would risk startling it. So, she stood as still as a statue and watched in awe as the colossal butterfly got closer.

It landed directly in front of Ruby. With its long fuzzy antennas, the butterfly held a book. Ruby gaped at the giant blue eyes of the winter butterfly, and the stunning creature stared back in wonder. Tilting her head back and forth to study the pink winged fairy, she approved of Ruby.

The book was entrusted to her as a caterpillar, from the Empress of Vines, Gabriella, with instructions to find the pink winged gidgie and return the book. The young caterpillar cocooned herself with it, hiding the precious book for Ruby and from the enemy.

Ruby was speechless. She carefully reached out and took the book from the velvet antennas. She tucked it in her jacket and stood there staring; bewildered as to how the creature came to have it. She reached out to touch the furry head of the gorgeous beast. At that same time, Ginny came out of her root porch to yell for Ruby to come in from the cold. The door shutting behind Ginny startled the glorious insect, and the butterfly launched from the ground, stirring up snow with each flap of her wings.

Ginny and Ruby watched the sky until the beautiful blue wings could no longer be seen. In unison, they both began to speak, over-talking each other with the wonder and magic of the moment. In all of Ginny's years dealing with wild and mystical beasts, she had never witnessed a giant winter butterfly.

Ruby and Ginny went inside and told Duke all about the incredible moment. Duke was curious but then said, "They may be gorgeous and mysterious, but my bees have brains. Can that butterfly make honey and read an address?" In Duke's mind, there were no higher creatures than his honeybee mail carriers.

The three had a delicious Christmas breakfast that Duke prepared, of sausage gravy over fluffy homemade biscuits, sweet preserves, and millie fruit juice. The silly fruit gave them each a gift of a different flavored drink, all sweet and tasty.

After breakfast, they began to prepare holiday dinners to deliver to the root-bound and shut-in fairies. Duke and Ginny hitched up the sleigh to Prince and Piper while Ruby started to load the baskets of meals. Jo and Kody arrived as the three were about to leave.

The five of them traveled all over the west side of the garden, passing out the delicious meal of roasted fitternick fowl with curcillium mushroom stuffing, smashed purple potatoes, and cranberry fickle fruit relish. For dessert, vanilla pod cheesecake with millie fruit preserves on top.

Each recipient was more than grateful. Some giving Ginny and Ruby handwritten notes. Others gave homemade preserves, and Duke even received a red knitted sweater from the cranky widow who never left her root.

Their last stop was a surprise visit to Buck and Barney's farm. Ginny had told Duke the night before she felt they needed to check on the twins. Duke whittled a skypony out of pine for Barney. Ginny made him a stuffed atto-glider using its actual wool to cover it in, and Ruby made the twins a large tin of sweets.

Duke held the enormous basket of food, and Ginny knocked on the door. They were all ready to sing carols when the door opened. The sight of Buck took their song away. He was in an apron, covered in flour, trying to make a Christmas dinner. Barney was having a bad morning. He had a headache and was crying. He was also upset because his scribble stick had just broken, and he was trying to color a picture for Father Christmas, who gave him the art kit.

Ginny went right to work, sending Ruby to calm Barney down, and the rest of them helped Buck clean up his attempt at dinner. Buck sat down, defeated. He began to share with them his struggles.

"Normally this would have been Barney's job to cook Christmas dinner, but since his injury, I have to do everything. I take care of him, run the farm, cook, and clean and take him to the Healer's station for checkups. He has nightmares of being snatched that keep us both up at night. And when he is having a day like today, it makes everything ten times harder. I feel like I'm failing. It's like I'm a single parent, but Barney's my brother and my best friend. I just never pictured my life like this, but I want to do it right. But how?" Buck was on the verge of tears, but he held them back.

The older gidgies listened as Buck shared the hardships of caregiving and the struggles he was having with Barney. Ginny set the table of the lovely dinner and made a giant pot of pinkle pepper brew for sipping on while Buck let them in on his hardships.

Ruby had calmed Barney down with the Christmas presents they delivered and was coloring him a picture of the giant winter butterfly she saw that morning.

"Ruby, guess what? I had a remember," Barney said.

"Do you mean a memory, Barney?" Ruby asked.

"Yes, I had a memory," He smiled.

"I hope it was a good one," she chuckled.

"It was the day I fell from the sky," Barney said in a whisper and then felt the bump on the back of his head.

"Barney, I am so sorry you had to remember that. Do you want to tell me about it?" Ruby asked as she went to sit next to him, as Barney played with his wooden skypony from Duke.

"I will tell you because you are my friend and I like you. And you bring me presents and candy," Barney shared in his childlike way. "My remember was when a bad guy yelled to drop me. He said, I was a twin and was off lemons." Barney said in a hush.

"I think you mean off-limits. Have you told Buck this memory yet?" Ruby asked as she pretended the stuffed atto-glider was flying.

"No, my remembers make Buck sad. I don't like it when he is sad," Barney said in a down tone.

"Well, Barney, we need to tell the others this memory. Do you mind if I tell Jo and Kody, or would you like to tell them?" Ruby asked but was already determined to tell the two Skyforce soldiers either way.

"I don't care. Can you color some more pictures of the butterfly?" Barney asked, already bored with the conversation.

"Sure, Barney, how about after dinner? I think it's time to eat. Let's go join the others in the kitchen, shall we?" Ruby got up from the floor, and the two cleaned up the sitting room and then joined the others at the table.

They all enjoyed a wonderful Christmas dinner with lively conversation and were utterly entertained by Barney's childish ways. It was endearing. Barney showed his guest what Father Christmas had left him, a box of art supplies. It was remarkable and kind for Father Christmas to leave a present for Barney, even though he wasn't technically a child physically; he was mentally and emotionally since the fall.

After dessert and clean up, they sat in the sitting room for the last of the pinkle pepper brew. Ruby looked at Barney and asked if he wanted to share his memory or should she.

"I'm tired. Can I just go to bed with my new toys?" Barney asked. While Buck went to help Barney get ready for bed, Jo asked Ruby what Barney's memory was.

In a low, hushed voice, she began, "He remembered the night he fell. He said one of the liaths, well, he called them bad guys." Ruby smiled at the tender moment and continued, "He said he heard one say, the twin was off lemons, but I am sure he meant limits."

"That's strange. Why would a twin be off-limits?" Kody wondered.

"Who knows with that witch. It could be because she either wants them as a set or not at all." Duke stated.

"I think it's worth a mention to the General," Jo added.

Buck entered the room after helping Barney put his pajamas on and caught the last end of the conversation. Ginny brought him up to speed, and Buck's head went low.

"My poor brother. I can't imagine his horror. Being captured, dropped hundreds of feet, crashing through branches and then suffering for nearly a week in the woods with a broken wing, beaten body, and a cracked head." Buck put his head in his hands and sat quietly. Still, no tears fell.

Kody put his arm on Buck's shoulder and said, "I will always be grateful I was at the right place at the right time. And Praise be to Beathra that Barney's life was spared. He is a delight to all of us, Buck. Had we known about your struggle, we would have come sooner. But from here on out, you are not alone in this. We want to help with your needs as well as Barney's."

At this act of love, Buck allowed his tears to fall. He had held them back for six months. Never allowing himself to focus too much on himself. After all, it was Barney who was the injured one. But knowing that others saw his struggle, his hurt, and his helplessness touched his heart, and the tears could not be stopped.

The sleigh ride back to Ginny and Duke's root was filled with Christmas carols, snacking on leftovers, and organizing help for Buck.

Jo and Kody saw the three back to their homes and then left for their barracks. Come morning, they would find the General and inform him of Barney's memory.

A blizzard moved in on New Year's Eve and snowed several gidgies in. The ones who could get out of their roots were digging out fellow neighbors. The Skyguard was training recent graduates from the academy with service to their community. Taking provision to the snowed-in, shoveling walkways, and breaking the ice from the Havengothy streams for water. It was hard work, but the new Skyguard's were anxious to help their garden.

Duke and Ginny spoke with the Captain of the Skyguard and informed him of Buck and Barney's situation. The gracious Captain enlisted a squad to come alongside the twins and help Buck with the winter chores. Ginny made sure they were well taken care of with fresh baked goods that she and Duke made.

Barney was Ginny's official sampler of new recipes she was practicing for the Bloom Festival. He was blatantly honest with his opinions, and Ginny appreciated it. Some of her new concoctions did not make the menu for the Bloom Festival due to Barney's truthful reactions.

Ruby was perfectly content being snowed in. She spent her days writing Seb and Ellie and studying the book the great butterfly brought to her. She knew, come spring, she would return it to the Professor, but until then, decided to write down, word for word, every charm from the relic. One particular spell she loved was protecting new seedlings and tender shoots from pestilence and creatures. Young plants were easy prey that animals and bugs loved to chew on their soft roots and sweet leaves.

Ruby practiced it on her herb garden in her window, but it didn't seem to work. She then read in a later chapter; the protective charm would not be successful if performed in a safe environment. There had to be a reason to quote it, an obvious threat being one of those reasons. That made sense: her basil was in a safe windowsill, flourishing in the winter sunlight.

The book felt living and magical. Ruby had forgotten how she felt when she read it. The author described beautiful events and moments that have never been shared in school, as far as Ruby knew. The book detailed the fall of Neeradima, her corruption of the garden, and the deep grief The Whisper felt with the banishment.

Ruby had enjoyed reading all the spells, but the ancient history in the volume surprised her. Every time she re-read a chapter; she would catch something different. It felt like it was speaking to her and about her. The book read like poetry, prophecy, history, and mystery.

She wrote down as much of the book as she could, often needing to borrow parchment from Ginny and Duke. As soon as the snow melted, she was returning this precious treasure, and she wanted all of its mysterious wisdom she could copy.

———

Meanwhile, in the Refiner's Forest, Sebastian was facing some of the most terrifying moments of his life. He entered a part of the woods that would test his nerve. He would face monsters he had no idea existed. Seb pulled his coat over his neck and flew into the icy wind.

The next creature he would combat was one of Neeradima's secret weapons for the sky, a flying serpent. It was a cross between a snake, lizard, bat, and a hawk. This hideous dragon was one of her evilest creatures. It guarded the treetops and the canopy of Skawlterrin and nested deep within the Darphea caves. It had low stamina for flying long distances, but what it lacked in flight it made up for in speed with slithering.

The demon-like creature had the face of a serpent with a jagged beak. A fan of scaly skin surrounded its face and flared out like a mane. Its wings were similar to a bat's arms, but it had claws on the ends to help it climb the trees. Its tail was a powerful weapon used for whipping or constriction. It spit poison that temporarily blinded its enemy. This creature crawled the ground, patrolled the sky, and instilled fear in all who crossed its path.

As Seb flew over the tops of the trees, the snow was blowing fiercely. He never saw the tail of the creature flash from the trees. The blow knocked him out of the sky. He tumbled down, crashing into branches until he sunk into the deep snow below. Feeling shocked, he shook it off and bolted from the indention of the snow, to see the serpent-like hawk flying overhead. Its wings whooshed in the air stirring up a blizzard-like storm, making it hard for Sebastian to see. That's when its tail grabbed him and began to spiral around him, crushing Sebastian's lungs and squeezing the breath out of him. The evil snake flew to a treetop and perched itself on top as it suffocated Sebastian.

Seb was pinned with his arms alongside him. He could barely move. He squirmed and inched his arms towards his belt and wiggled out his small knife. The scales of the monster were tightly formed together like an armor. They were also smooth, cold, and clammy. Seb turned the knife outwards, and using all his strength he could muster, dug the blade into the side of the beast, digging his sword between its iron-like scales. The snake whipped its tail in pain, and that's when Seb made his escape.

As he flew upward, he could see the blind spot of the creature, the top of its head, behind its fleshy mane. If he could get to its head, he could drive his sword through and kill it. Without second-guessing his plan, he flew at top speed, racing alongside the length of the serpent so as not to be seen. He drew his sword and in one move, thrust it into the skull of the snake. A haunting screech came from its mouth as it fell from the sky, but before it hit the ground of the forest, it faded into the atmosphere.

Sebastian hovered in the winter sky staring at the bare ground where the creature should have landed with a thud. He then had to remind himself it wasn't real. It was only a drill.

Training for the unexpected in the Refiner's Forest played with the mind, and equipped soldiers to face monsters bigger, stronger, and fiercer than themselves. Courage was a powerful tool in the heart of a gidgie. And with the right weapon and training, a

Skyforce soldier could contend with and even kill one of these beasts.

Sebastian performed several exercises where he flew over the cursed valley to rescue the lost or abducted. He had a job to do as a Special Task Force member, and he could not give in to fear and allow anything to interfere with his mission. The Refiner's Forest made sure soldiers could combat the enemy, and all that Neeradima would throw at them.

The six-month journey in the unpredictable woods was forging in Seb, a warrior. But the real transformation happens at the moment that is never mentioned outside of Special Task Force members. Each fairy enters the Refiner's Forest as a soldier, but they emerge as a weapon. The final step was the metamorphosing, and Seb was entering it on Christmas day.

The last three months were a mysterious transformation. Deep in the heart of the forest was the Cave of Conversion. It was in this dark hall they journeyed towards the end of the cavern and met their last teacher, Octavio. He would instruct them in their final step. It was in this secluded place that they were cocooned.

For nearly twelve weeks, they would face mental battles that had to be played out in their head, for it was in their dreams they were given visions of their life as a soldier, exposing where they were vulnerable and where they were gifted. Sebastian was learning his Achilles heel, Ruby.

He relived one nightmare over and over, the death of Ruby by the hand of Neeradima. And no matter how hard he fought against the wicked queen; it always ended the same. Ruby died.

His fear of losing her caused him to confront the "what if" and to train past it. He had to do a job, "even if" he lost Ruby. Even if he couldn't save her, he still had to finish the mission of saving those he could.

Three months of the same dream ended the same way, Ruby dying and Sebastian falling. It wasn't until the final week of his cocooning that he had victory. He was finally able to save Ruby, but it was at a significant cost. He would never be able to shake the dream; it would be his motivator and his monster.

Chapter Twenty-Four
The book return.

Spring came gently with a slow thaw of the land. The atto-gliders migration back to Havengothy was a spectacular sight. It was during this time that Ruby and Ginny journeyed to the edge of Havengothy to watch the wooly beasts return. The lighted hooves left streaks in the sky like northern lights.

Ruby brought the ancient book with her in hopes of stopping off at Professor Hill's root to return it. She knew he wouldn't be there because school was still in session. It was a perfect opportunity to right a wrong without him knowing it was her who took it. She hoped Hill would think it was in his root the whole time.

As they got closer to his land, it had that strange feeling Ruby experienced when Gabriella took her to Emmet's root.

"I think there's a liath shrub in this area," Ruby mentioned.

"How can you tell?" Ginny asked.

"Come closer, and you will feel the temperature drop, and this icky feeling of hopelessness linger. But why in Havengothy would Professor Hill be living near such a horrid plant?" Ruby looked around but could not see it anywhere. If it was near his property, it was hidden well.

"Perhaps he is a watchman like Emmet was," Ruby thought. As they approached his root door, the atmosphere changed, and the warm spring air was felt again. Ruby tapped on the small arched door and waited. She did not expect an answer; she was just being polite.

"What are you dropping off again?" Ginny asked.

"A book I sort of borrowed from him last year," Ruby explained.

Ginny glanced at the old, tattered volume and thought she recognized the author's name but couldn't think of where she heard of him.

"Wow, good thing Hill's not a librarian, you would have late fees that put you in the poor house, and your card would be revoked." Ginny teased.

Ruby cracked the door to slide the book inside the Professor's root. His home was dark, and it smelled musky. She peeked inside a bit further and could hear snoring. If Professor Hill was at school, who was sleeping in his home? Ruby slowly entered the stinky root and put his book on a side table near his dingy sofa.

She looked around the filthy root home, it was covered in trash and empty bourbon bottles. Professor Hill's place was nothing like his tidy, organized office. His root reeked of wizard weed and alcohol, which was obviously from his root guest. As she was tiptoeing out of his root, she tripped over a single black boot lying on the floor. She stumbled into the bookcase and knocked several items from its shelves, creating a thundering crash. Ginny heard the ruckus and peered in to see if Ruby was alright.

"What is going on in here?" Ginny whispered.

Ruby was about to fall into a giggle fit, and Ginny was close to joining her. Ruby quickly righted herself and looked in the direction of the stranger, who was still sleeping, making sure he did not wake up. He never moved. Both the girls began to snicker, and they had to put their hands over their mouths and jet out the root before they burst into laughter.

Ruby tumbled over more garbage. Unknowingly, knocking the book, she just returned, directly into a pile of lava bean skins near the furnace. She darted out of the root but not without seeing a painting of a beautiful young woman that hung over Hill's hearth. It was a larger picture similar to what Sebastian had seen in the Professor's office. Ruby quickly thought of that moment in his office, when Seb was telling her about the painting.

"Did Professor Hill have a wife?' Ruby thought questionably.

Ruby and Ginny bolted from the ground in a full belly laugh. Ruby's snort could be heard echoing through the forest.

"You can't blame my clumsiness for tripping in Hill's root. Did you see all the debris in his tiny home? How could I not stumble over all that trash?" Ruby asked while she was still giggling.

"Um, you tripped on the only thing that wasn't trash, a lone boot in the middle of the floor. The bottles were your second stumbling obstacle." Ginny laughed out her answer.

"Gosh. You think you know someone. I wonder who is living in Hill's root? Do you think it was his wife?" Ruby asked.

"Phineas doesn't have a wife that I know of, but he is a lot older than most of us around here. Maybe Professor Hill doesn't know that he has a root guest. Perhaps it a squatter taking advantage of Hill's empty root while he is working. I think we should tell Jo when we see him Saturday at Sebastian's graduation." Ginny suggested with a grin.

Ruby practically blushed. She was counting the days to see Seb. She had her clothes laid out that she wanted to wear and had been practicing how to do her hair. Her calendar was covered in x's marking the days off as they went by, with a giant circle on Saturday, March 28th, with stars all around the words, "Sebastian's ceremony."

Sebastian was ticking his calendar as well. His countdown was more subtle, with March 28th holding a small heart in its box and nothing else. Taskforce graduation was one day away. He would finally see Ruby. He wasn't sure how he was going to explain his transformation. His wings had changed color due to his time in the cocoon and were now a dull, smoky blue, and they were more muscular in appearance. The cocoon was a top-secret transformation, only known by those who finished their stint in the Cave of Conversion. And all were sworn to secrecy when they emerged from the three-month metamorphosing.

Billick entered Sebastian's barrack, "Tomorrow's our big day bud. Did you get your orders yet?" he asked.

"I did, I will be stationed at the Skyforce headquarters. Which will be nice because it's actually only a couple hours from Ruby's root." Seb answered with a smile.

"Me too. I think most of us who finished the Refiner's Forest will be stationed at H.Q. General Dax is assembling the troops. I think we will be deployed within a few weeks of our settling in, but at least we have two weeks of leave before then." Billick said, excited about the prospect of deployment.

Sebastian thought of his time in the cocoon, and the nightmare he had to conquer, "Yeah, I am looking forward to kicking some liath butt and bringing our gidgies home." He said with a lackluster tone. He was excited to rescue those who were still enslaved to the wicked queen, but he was afraid of not being around to protect Ruby.

The fear of anything happening to her was always on his heart. He had been watching out for her since they were kids. But something seemed different, he had this feeling Ruby was a target of the evil queen. He couldn't let his mind go there. If he did, he would become anxious.

Seb knew Ginny and Duke loved Ruby just as much as he did, and with her living with them, he felt better about not being around. Sebastian knew nothing of Jo and Kody's watchfulness of Ruby. Had he known, it would not have comforted him as one would think, it would only prove his suspicions.

The two Skyforce task force members packed their belongings and prepared for the next phase, their stationing at Headquarters.

Neeradima was pacing her chambers. Her winter had been quiet, and she was feeling stir crazy. The thaw in her evil forest was taking longer than she wanted. She was ready to strike. She knew the Skyforce was building an army, but so was she. She was preparing for an assault that would terrify the garden for years to come.

Ominous had been busy with his informants searching to recruit other traitors. Torn was still trying to track down the pink winged gidgie. Had Torn communicated with Ominous, he would have told her one of his informants knew precisely who she was. But the two liaths were enemies and hated each other. Everything they did was for their own ego and gain.

Deep in the caves, Yoli and Jermaine continued to sing, and it was their melody that inspired others to not lose their song. Jermaine was growing weak, the last beatings from the Diatone tree elf took him days to recover. Yoli hung in her cage in the center of the mountain and sang for both of them. She refused to give up hope. The more she hoped, the more she could feel hope rise.

Her voice was sweet and filled with adoration and love. The lyrics drifted through the darkness and echoed through the caverns, and though the horrid tree elf would beat Jermaine, he would not touch Yoli. It was becoming clear; he had a growing infatuation with the lovely gidgie. Jermaine could see the tree elf look fondly at his wife and worried. If the evil creature was falling in love with her, the elf would kill him. However, it may be just what is needed to allow Yoli's escape.

Ruby bolted awake; it was the day of Sebastian's graduation. It was half a day's flight to the ceremony. The task force graduation was held in the center of the garden where most special festivities take place. It would be a smaller group of fairies that would be receiving their Task Force pin.

Several cadets rang a bell to escape the Refiner's Forest, unable to finish the grueling trials and training that was involved. It was no surprise; the brutal terrain of the mystic forest can cause a faint heart in many. The ones who "rang out" went on to serve in other areas of the Skyforce, and they would have another opportunity to try again. Those who graduated received a silver pin engraved with a sword, that represented the warrior, a heart that represented courage and the fire seed that displayed devotion to their King's cause.

Ruby put on her prettiest dress for Sebastian's big day, her pale-yellow chiffon she wore to the Bloom Festival. It had been nine months since she had seen his face. All she had to hang onto during those long months were his short, infrequent letters. But those scribbled papers of Seb's were filled with hope for the days to come.

He promised dances, moonlit strolls, and adventures to the atto-gliders nesting grounds. The spring months looked hopeful. Ruby tried sweeping her hair to one side, but it looked like the mane on a skypony. She gave up on her attempt of a fancy hairstyle and instead let it fall down her back with a simple bobby pin to sweep her bangs out of her eyes.

Ruby missed Ellie as she prepared herself for the ceremony. It was moments like these, the girls laughed and dreamed together as they got ready for events. Ellie was always willing to fight Ruby's thick curls in an attempt for a new hairdo.

Duke and Ginny were finishing the morning chores around the farm and hives. They gave Ruby the morning off, and Ginny gathered the eggs from the fitternick fowls and gave little Baby a scratch on the head. Ruby spoiled the farm animals with extra attention and treats, and now they expected it.

Prince and Piper were stomping and snorting, upset that they were unneeded for the day. Prince especially hated it when Ginny left for long periods. He loved adventures, but Ginny kept the two skyponies in their stalls for the days outing. And Prince was clearly unhappy.

"I'm sorry, boy, we will be back tonight, and we can fly the night sky together," Ginny said, trying to comfort the devoted pony. She gave him a sugar cube and lavished both the skyponies with extra leaves of hay.

Jo and Kody landed at Ginny's farm in their finest uniforms, with all their medals pinned on their chests. They were proud Skyforce members, and Jo was excited to be the one who pinned Sebastian into his Task Force career.

Duke tried to wear his old uniform for Seb's graduation, but his pot belly would not allow him to button his jacket. He decided to wear a button-up shirt and his favorite pair of suspenders.

The four-hour flight to the center of the garden was filled with excited chatter. What life would look like for Sebastian after today was the main topic.

"Will he be able to spend time with me on the weekends, Jo?" Ruby asked.

"If he doesn't have guard duty or isn't on assignment, he should be able to spend some weekends with you," Jo answered.

"How long are assignments, and what do they entail?" Ginny asked before Ruby could get the question out.

"It's when a Task Force is deployed. They are not allowed to discuss the mission, but generally, it can be several days, weeks, or even months, depending on the job they are called to do. Moses and C.J. have been gone for nearly three months on special assignment, so you can see, it all depends on the duty at hand." Kody answered.

The trip went quickly with a short stop for drinks and lunch at a favorite pub called The Branch and Bloom. It was in the small branch restaurant that Ruby saw Trixie and Lewis having lunch. They were also going to graduation. Ruby went to the table to say hello, but Trixie saw her coming and jumped up to give Ruby a hug.

"Ruby, it's so great to see you, where have you been? What are you doing with yourself? Tell me everything." Trixie grabbed Ruby and drug her to the booth where she and Lewis were eating.

Ruby sat down at the table and thought about how to answer. What was she doing? She wasn't even in her own place. She was embarrassed to answer the question; instead, she shifted the conversation.

"Lewis, we've been visiting Buck and Barney and helping them out here and there. Barney talks about you all the time. He absolutely adores you."

Lewis smiled at the compliment from Ruby. "I think he's a pretty special guy. Sylvia has allowed me to sit in on Barney's exams because he likes me so much, and he's kind of grown attached to me. I like telling him stories about school. He seems to enjoy all my snot and booger moments that my allergies gave me and were the cause of all my tormenting. He gets a big chuckle out of them."

Trixie grabbed Lewis's hands, "I'm so sorry I was such a toad to you, Lewis," she said apologetically.

"You don't need to keep apologizing. That was forever ago. Besides, I knew why you terrorized me and others, but you have changed, and so have I. And today, we are going to see Billick graduate and celebrate his win in his life." Lewis comforted Trixie with his answer.

"Always the Healer, aren't you Lewis? I'm still sorry." Trixie said with a smile.

"Stop with the apologies, Trix. Why don't you tell Ruby how your sentinel training is going?" Lewis suggested. "She is in the top ten percent with the knowledge tests." He said, bragging on Trixie.

"That's only because you have been such a great tutor," she replied.

Trixie was a different fairy than she was in school. The bully was truly gone in her. Her humility and willingness to give another praise were refreshing and inspiring to Ruby. Lewis and Trixie were an odd couple that displayed what forgiveness and second chances looked like. Ruby looked at Trixie and said, "I want to hear more about your studies Trix. Are you truly the only woman training to be a sentinel?"

"I was the first to enlist for it, yes. But since I have joined, two other girls are in training now. They are older than me, but they said, I inspired them to go after a dream. Can you believe that? Me. A dream inspirer." Trixie said with a smile, "It's nice not being the only girl in class. Some of the guys are not too keen on a female watchman, but most think it's pretty cool. We've been doing a lot of defensive combat exercises, and I have to fight both male and female. We do wear our armor, and it's heavy, but it helps with some of the blows that come. Especially from the more competitive ones who still despise my presence." Trixie informed with a smirk.

"And she holds her own just fine too." Lewis bragged.

"Enough about us, Ruby, tell us how you are doing. Did you get that little root you were hoping for? How's your little plot of Havengothy doing? I bet you are flourishing the whole west side of our land." Trixie asked with a genuine interest in Ruby's life.

Ruby didn't want to answer any questions right now or ever, for that matter. She looked over at her table and saw Ginny signaling her that her order was ready.

"Welp, it looks like we will have to save those questions for another day," Ruby got up from the table, relieved she skirted all of Trixie's questions, "My sandwich just arrived, and Ginny is waving me over. I will see you guys at the ceremony."

Trix gave Ruby another hug and said goodbye. She then sat back down and asked, "Lewis, was it just me, or was Ruby avoiding our questions?"

Lewis's healing gift could sense Ruby's feelings. He could feel her embarrassment. He knew she felt uncomfortable and ashamed that she was not advancing in life like her friends. She didn't go to an Advanced Learning Center. She didn't join the military or Skyguard. She was comparing herself to others, and it was highlighting her insecurities and what she thought were inadequacies.

Lewis also felt something else; He couldn't quite describe what he was sensing. It was strange. Almost like he could feel a magical strength and gifting stirring inside of Ruby. But Ruby was unaware it was there. True to his Healer's code, he held what he discerned and answered Trixie's question, "She just needs our encouragement right now, Trix. Let's finish our lunch and get out of here, shall we?"

Chapter Twenty-Five

Graduation

Sebastian stood on the stage, scanning the crowd for Ruby. He could see Ruby looking for him, but his appearance had changed so much she didn't recognize him. He was broader, his wings had changed color, and his hair was very short, and he was wearing a blue Skyforce beret.

"I can't see him. Can anyone see where Seb is? I can see Jo up on the stage, but he's talking with the General. Where in Havengothy is Sebastian?" Ruby asked, frustrated.

Ginny could not see anything; everyone was taller than her. Duke looked at the small group on the platform but couldn't recognize Seb, either. It was Kody who found Sebastian and pointed him out to Ruby.

"There he is, standing near the end of the graduates, the second one in on the right." Kody pulled Ruby near him and directed her gaze towards Sebastian. And there he was, with his giant dimpled grin that melted her heart. He was leaner, but his shoulders looked even wider. She smiled and waved, but Seb could not wave back. He did give her a wink, and Ruby's heart leaped.

"Why does he look so different?" She asked Duke and Kody.

"It's the training on the Broad River Island. It changes a soul. Their inner transformation is seen outwardly. Sebastian is a soldier, and that will forever be part of him now." Kody answered.

The music began to play, and the ceremony commenced. General Dax was the speaker and would announce the soldiers and their rank. As usual, Billick's family sat on the front row, sitting tall and proud. Ruby always wondered why they seemed so full of themselves. To her, they acted like they thought they were better than everyone. Which might have been the reason Billick was so arrogant in school.

Ruby leaned into Ginny and whispered, "Why do I always feel like pond scum when I am around Billick's family? They bloomed from Beathra, too, right? Why is it that they seem superior to us common fairies? Perhaps they bloomed from the top branch." Ruby snickered.

"Barron and Bonny are perfectly nice fairies; they are just a bit more confident than most, that's all," Ginny whispered, trying to explain Billick's parents and their conceited behavior. Still, she, too, felt that they were a tad pompous, but Ginny would never say that to Ruby. Ginny wanted to be a good example.

General Dax stood at the podium, he cleared his throat and began his speech. "Families and Skyforce members, today is a special day. Before you stands a fierce group of gidgies, who endured some of the most grueling conditions known to our world. Their physical and mental training has groomed in them a Havengothy hero. To be a Skyforce member means to put your life on the line for your land. It means you are ready to fight and defend our world.

"These graduates have sworn an oath to protect and guard our remarkable garden and its inhabitants. Their lives as servants to our land is not without gratefulness. They have chosen to live a life of sacrifice, and we are thankful for their courage and bravery. Please stand to your feet and give the honor that is deserved to our Special Task Force graduates."

The small crowd jumped to their feet and clapped, whooped, hollered, and whistled. Ruby and Ginny did their finger in the mouth whistle that was louder than any yell or cheer. General Dax gestured for the crowd to be seated, and he began to announce the graduates.

"Specialist, Billick Baily," Barron Baily jumped to his feet to pin Billick with the task force pin.

"Corporal Cynthia Daniels," Jo placed the pin on Cynthia and saluted her.

Four other names were read until they finally reached Sebastian.

"Specialist, Sebastian James," Seb stood tall, with his shoulders back looking straight ahead. Jo took the silver pin and punched it through Sebastian uniform collar, he then stood back and saluted Seb.

Jo quietly said, "I am proud of you, son," for Seb's ears only. Sebastian saluted back and smiled.

"Thank you, sir. I wouldn't be here without you."

The General finished announcing the last three names and then closed the ceremony with, "Ladies and Gentlemen, I present to you the newest task force team of Havengothy's Skyforce Military. May Beathra always be by their side and The Whisper ever guiding them.

Stand once more with me and give these Skyforce soldiers a round of applause."

Once again, the small crowd bolted from their seats to cheer the newest servants of the garden. Ruby was yelling the loudest of her group. She was immensely proud of Seb.

The multitude of fairies began to disperse to find their soldier, and Ruby was shoving her way through the crowd to look for Sebastian. She was scanning anyone in a blue beret. Sebastian found Ruby first. She was in that yellow dress that made him lose his breath. She was thin. When Ruby was under stress, she didn't eat.

A buddy and fellow task force member came up alongside Seb and said, "Who is that babe?" Sebastian looked at him and smiled. "That *babe* is my girl." And he left the soldier standing there and snuck up to Ruby.

From behind her, she felt two hands go around her small waist. She turned to see Sebastian, but before she could get any words out, he pulled her into him and kissed her. Lifting her up from the ground, she dangled in his arms. Still holding her, Sebastian said, "Nine months is just too long. Never again."

Ruby was elated. She could hardly get any words out. Putting her hands on his face, she saw a more weathered Sebastian than the young boy from months ago. "You have worry lines. What are you worried about?" Ruby asked.

He didn't dare share with her his nightmare in the cocoon. He just knew he would do whatever he had to do to keep her safe.

"Eh hem," came a small voice from behind them .

"Sebastian dear, could you put my daughter down." Ginny paused then said," so I can hug you." she smiled.

"Yes, ma'am." Sebastian gently put Ruby back down and then bent low to hug Ginny. A small crowd assembled around Sebastian. Jo, Kody, Duke, Ginny, and Ruby were all talking at once, asking him about his training.

Ruby ran her hands over Sebastian's wings. They were incredible. They seemed thicker, stronger, but the biggest transformation was the color. Their once brilliant blue was now a smoky blue.

"I can't get over the change. You're so different," she whispered.

"And you have gotten too skinny. Our first date will be a giant picnic by the pond. Duke, would you mind whipping up some of your tasty pastries? Ruby needs to put on some weight." Sebastian asked as he put his arms around Ruby.

"Not at all, Ginny, and I would be happy to pack you both an entire basket of treats as soon as we get home," Duke announced.

"Perfect. I need to go gather my things, and we can get going. Hey, by the way, thanks Duke for letting me stay at your old root. I am ready to sleep in and eat real food. All I had to eat while on the island were those G.E.M.'s that we call gems," Sebastian informed. Then he quickly gave Ruby a small kiss on her cheek and flew to the room where his belongings were being stored.

"What are G.E.M.'s?" asked Ruby.

"They're a little premade package of food that stands for *gidgies emergency meals*. You have them when you are on a mission, some of them are pretty nasty. The joke is they are called gems, but they are far from it. But the desserts in them aren't too bad, right, Duke?" Kody said with a nod toward Duke.

"As you can see, I am not too picky about food." Duke slapped his belly a couple of times and chuckled.

Sebastian was in a small tent where the soldier's backpacks were being stored. Billick was already grabbing his rucksack when Seb flew in.

"Hey Sebastian. Congratulations. Ruby looks good. I bet she was happy to see you." Billick said, trying not to sound jealous.

"She's always looked good, Bill. We're headed home, I guess I'll see you in two weeks at H.Q." Sebastian threw his pack over his shoulder and dashed back to Ruby.

Billick watched as Sebastian left the tent. He felt confused about Ruby. When he saw her in the audience looking for Sebastian, all he could think was, "I wish she would look for me."

The nine months changed everyone, but Ruby especially looked different, more mature. Her hair was longer, and her body was small and petite, and her crooked smile had somehow turned endearing. He shook his head to shake his thoughts from his mind and flew to meet his family.

Sebastian landed next to Ruby and grabbed her hand, "As soon as Jo is done visiting with General Dax, we can hit the sky and head home. I have two weeks of R and R, and I don't want to waste another moment." Sebastian smiled.

Jo and General Dax were discussing the latest rescue mission. The recently deployed task force team brought home three more fairies from the Skawlterrin forest. They all had the same report; the evil land was still covered in ice, and though it was quiet, Neeradima was plotting something.

"Sir, one of the rescued gidgies, mentioned Yoli. They could still hear her song, but the other voice that sang with her has been quiet. We can only assume the worst with this info. We have got to figure out where the enemy is hiding her and the others. But each one we rescue has no recollection of the mazes of the caves." Jo mentioned.

"That witch is clever; she moves them around, and the Darphea caves and caverns are endless. Neeradima has had centuries to memorize the belly of the mountain. I know she is plotting something; I can feel it. But you can be darn sure we will be ready for her this time. Because this time, we will strike first." General Dax stated with emphasis.

"Yes, sir. Kody and I will escort Ruby and her family home, and we will see you in the morning." Jo saluted the General and was off to find Kody.

Jo landed near Kody, and asked, "Are we ready to get this caravan in the sky?"

"More than ready," Sebastian replied before Kody could. Still holding Ruby's hand, Seb bolted from the ground.

The flight home was filled with stories about Sebastian's training, all the goings-on of the garden, and Buck and Barney. "I feel so bad for them. It sounds like it might be harder on Buck because he is caring for Barney. Barney sounds like a happy kid. Will he ever get better? I mean, is his brain always going to be young?" Sebastian asked.

"The Healers say he *could* make a full recovery, but the brain takes time. And though they can do a lot with broken bones, sickness, and even troubled minds, Barney has a brain injury, and that's entirely different." Ginny answered.

"We just have to be there for them, so they know, they are not alone. Caring for someone by yourself is rewarding but can also be very isolating." Ginny was speaking from experience raising Ruby. She had no one to lean on. No one to help her through the hard days. Ruby's sleepless nights or her flight lessons all rested all on Ginny.

Ruby smiled at her mother. "Remember that one time I ran away from school and flew back home when I was about five or six? Only for you to drag me back to school the next day. I am so glad you didn't return me to Beathra or throw me in the pond. I am certain I deserved it."

"Or abandon her, that's what my folks did," Sebastian said with raised eyebrows.

The conversation quieted, and the small crew enjoyed the view of the beginnings of spring in Havengothy. The fragrance of winter was dissipating, peppermint was fading, and jasmine was beginning to fill the air. The snow was still piled in areas with fresh grass growing around them. Tender buds of green were being seen on the tips of branches and bushes. Havengothy was going to have a beautiful spring. The daffodil field looked like sunshine had spilled and flooded areas of the enchanted garden.

It was just after six when they all landed at Duke and Ginny's. Duke invited everyone in for something to eat and drink, while Ginny ran out to check her animals, let Prince and Piper out of their stalls, and take them for a short flight.

"I'll take care of the food, Duke, if you want to help Ginny finish up outside," Ruby offered.

"That would be most appreciated, Ruby." Duke handed Ruby the jug of water he had in his hand to make a pot of pinkle pepper brew. By the time Duke and Ginny were done outside, Ruby had a full spread of food on the table. Seb had thrown a few lava beans in the furnace, and Jo and Kody were slicing bread and cheese. Duke and Ginny walked into a warm home that smelled of Christmas.

The six gidgies all sat down together, and Ginny said, "I would like to give thanks to Beathra for our crazy crew. Our King has woven you all into mine and Duke's hearts, and we are so very grateful." She lifted her mug of pinkle pepper brew, and they all cheered.

The night was joyful but was coming to an end quickly. Jo, Kody, and Seb were out on the deck saying goodbye in the cold spring night. Frost was beginning to spread across the ground, and the sky was a black velvet with the stars on display. Sebastian gave Ruby a small kiss goodnight. "I'll see you tomorrow, I promise."

Ruby, Gin, and Duke cleaned up the dinner mess, and Ruby went back to her root. She had to write to Ellie and tell her everything.

The great wizard of the mountain,

Chapter Twenty-Six
Melchizedek

Moses and C.J. wintered in the Hyperion Mountain Range with the great wizard, Melchizedek. The mountain had an unusual secret for those who trained and lived in its harsh elements, a tropical forest. To enter this warm and humid place, one first had to have permission from Melchizedek. Secondly, they must pass through the eye of the mountain, a cave that was more of a tunnel, ushering travelers to the Fire Forest. From above, the canopy of the Fire Forest was covered in snow. Beneath it, orchids bloomed, tropical fruit flourished, and exotic butterflies and birds made their home.

Moses and Melchizedek sat in the balmy forest, discussing the journey back to Havengothy. "It appears, the young lieutenant has fit in nicely here in my mountains. He has asked to stay and train with the Beathra Brigade. I have told him I was fine with him staying, as long as you did not need him to return with you." Melchizedek shared.

"Yes, I have noticed his interest in the training exercise. It was my hope he would wish to enlist in the brigade. He has shown a special knack for the distinct combat that you teach here, Melchizedek. And he is a natural in my Gidjidsu technique. He shared yesterday with me; he was able to fly. I didn't have the heart to tell him I could fly this whole time. He would wonder why I didn't just fly here to see you. But then, I would have missed the necessary conversation with Cornelius." Moses said as he bit into a juicy tropical fruit called a roopalar, tasting of banana and coconut pudding.

"I wish these little morsels grew in Havengothy. I would eat them every day," Moses said with juice dripping down his chin as he devoured the last bit of the spotted, round fruit.

"Cornelius still has no idea the brigade watches over his tribe. We try to keep it a secret. His pride would not be able to handle the protection we covertly offer. Last week, while the shepherds were herding their small flock of shimalins, my brigade protected them from a band of liaths hunting for new creatures for Neeradima to distort." Melchizedek mentioned to Moses.

A shimalin is a spotted black and white goat-like creature with long silky fur used for spinning into yarn. The odd little animals do not fly but hop like a rabbit. They lay brown-spotted eggs that are collected for food, and the wild gidgies use the shells to make utensils and tools.

"I loved scrambled shimalin eggs, they were some of my favorite foods to eat while serving on the brigade," Moses remembered fondly.

Suddenly, a beautiful, giant butterfly landed near Melchizedek and leaned into whisper in the wizard's ear. "Well, this is interesting. Delphi tells me she delivered a book to a pink winged gidgie. She says it's the fairy we have been discussing. The book was entrusted to her by Gabriella, the Empress of Vines. What's that girl?" The wizard asked the butterfly. The lovely insect informed Melchizedek what she witnessed.

The kind wizard relayed the info to Moses. "She says here, a liath with a scar across her eyebrow returned with a cloaked fairy and chopped Gabriella down from the trunk, looking for a book. One of my books, in fact. When Gabriella was dying, she gave the book to Delphi while she was still a caterpillar. She took the book and quickly covered it in her silk. Delphi says she delivered it to the girl before she migrated here to my mountains." Melchizedek informed Moses. He then took a piece of roopalar and held it out for the beautiful butterfly to drink of its sweet juice.

"The book only has power in the right hands. I have no idea why Neeradima would want it. Unless she thought she could twist the mind of the one who could still recite the spells with love. Is that even possible?" Moses asked.

"Are you asking if someone can use an ancient spell of love and growth and twist it for their own good if they think they are doing the right thing?" The wizard asked Moses.

"That is exactly what I am asking," Moses answered.

"Yes, it could be possible, but their heart would need to still be pure, even if their mind is manipulated." The wizard sat on a giant rock and thought more in-depth about the question.

"This fairy named Ruby; she is the one who can wield the charms in my old book, you say? The prophecy speaks of the warrior to arise, and my scrolls tell of a secret weapon that Beathra and The Whisper will use. Could it be, Ruby is the secret weapon? It is written that Beathra loves to use things that look foolish to confound the wise and confuse the enemy. This very well could be such an incident." Melchizedek said as he remained in deep thought.

"She is unique and pure-hearted. And she is utterly unaware of the greatness that lies within her We have assigned guardians to watch over her. At this point in time, we believe Neeradima does not know who Ruby is. But we do believe, she knows that someone can use the book. That is why Gabriella was destroyed." Moses said. This interrupted the wizard's deep thoughts.

"I perceive there is more than the two guardians watching over her. In fact, there is one who will do anything to keep her safe. Now come, Moses, we have discussed much, and winter is nearly finished, we need to inform C.J. he has been permitted to stay, and I will send you an escort home. Your flight to Havengothy is long, and you have much to do when you get home." Melchizedek jumped from the large rock and began to walk the long tunnel back to the training ground.

C.J. was practicing combative skills with a lieutenant in the brigade named Callie. Callie had just swept her legs under C.J.'s feet, knocking him backward when Moses approached him. Landing in the old councilman's arms, Moses threw C.J. back into the match with a chuckle. C.J. then flipped head over heels landing behind Callie. He grabbed her from behind with his arms around her throat, thinking he had won the match. However, Callie was quick, and with an elbow to the gut and a head thrust back into C.J.'s nose, he lost his grip. Callie hooked her legs behind C.J. and knocked him backward on his bum. She then put a sword to his throat and declared herself the champion. Helping him to his feet, she said, "You're getting better, this altitude is incredibly difficult to train in. But you have adapted well."

Moses joined the two lieutenants, "Hello Callie, I see you have done a marvelous job training C.J.. I was just with Melchizedek, and he would like to speak with you." Moses informed.

Callie smiled at Moses and grabbed her gear, "I'll see you tomorrow C.J. unless you're tired of getting your butt handed to you." Callie threw her pack over her shoulder and went to find the old wizard.

Moses surprised C.J. with the information that he was permitted to stay and train to become part of the brigade. With sweat running down his brow, he wiped it off with his forearm, "That's great news, sir. I am learning so much here. Captain Ming has said I have a lot of potential." C.J. informed breathlessly.

They sky went dark for a few seconds and the two gidgies looked up. It was the great Hyperion Lioness flying overhead, casting a large shadow. "That's Phoebe, she was the one hunting that winter morning. I think I am growing on her. She didn't try to eat me during our last encounter. Her mate is Gabriel, and he is magnificent but a tad more terrifying." The lieutenant said with a smile.

"I love these marvelous beasts; they were an instrumental part in the victory in the Banishment war," Moses said as he admired the giant lion as it flew over. "C.J., I am leaving in the morning, and Melchizedek is sending with me an escort home. And though you are staying to train, you will be sent back to Havengothy this summer. Your service and skills will be needed for the impending war."

"I understand, sir. Who is escorting you home?" C.J. asked.

"Lieutenant Callie. We leave at first light." Moses answered.

C.J. looked disappointed. He was growing fond of Callie and did not have the heart to tell her he let her win the last match. He was willing to take an elbow to the gut every day if it meant sparring with her.

General Dax was standing on the Skyforce deck, looking out over Havengothy and into the Darphea Wilderness. The night was frosty, and though it was the beginning of spring, the air had the chill of winter. All of a sudden, the General could see a frail gidgie approaching the secret entrance of the Skyforce headquarters. He dispatched the guards to meet the stranger in the air. Who the two brought back was an unrecognizable Captain Roland. He was emaciated, his hair was long and filled with knots, and he stunk of liaths.

Ushering him to the Healer's station, Julia did quick work attending to the weak Captain. The Captain reached for the General and grabbed his shirt in desperation, and said, "I escaped the dark forest, be ready, a ground assault is coming." And then, he passed out.

The General left the Healers station and flew to find Kody and Jo. It was nearly midnight, and two Skyforce soldiers were on duty for the weekend. They were standing near their lockers talking about the Task Force graduation and reminiscing about their time on the Broad River Island.

"I thought I was going to die for sure." Jo shared laughing about the event.

"I feel ya. My biggest test was during cocoon time. I relived the same event over and over; I lost my wings. It was a different battle each time, but the end was the same, I was flightless. That was a mental war if ever there was one." As Kody was finishing his story, General Dax entered the locker room.

"Sergeant Major Kody, and First Sergeant Joseppi, might I see you in my office when you have settled in?" The General ordered.

"Yes sir, we are nearly finished unpacking for the weekend," Kody answered. The General left with a nod and went to his office to think. He needed to discuss his suspicion, and Moses was still in the Hyperion Mountains. He trusted the two Skyforce soldiers and their instinct.

Jo closed his locker door and sat on the bench to lace up his boots. "What do you think this is about, Kody? Did you forget to sign the duty ledger?" he teased.

"I thought it was about you and your weight gain. You are looking a bit pudgy." Kody harassed.

They entered the General's office quietly. The ever dutiful, Pocket was sleeping on a cot near his desk. His hands were in his pockets, holding a set of keys to the file cabinet. Kody closed the door gently and sat in one of the black chairs in front of the General's desk. Jo leaned against the wall with his arms crossed. Not in judgment but curiosity about the midnight meeting.

"Gentleman, we have had an unusual incident happen this evening; Captain Roland flew into the secret entrance of the Skyforce HQ, starved to skin and bones, smelling of liaths, claiming he had escaped from the evil queen. He informed us that Neeradima is planning a ground assault." The General shared, watching Jo and Kody's expressions.

"Wow, that's amazing he escaped. Has he said anything more? How long has he been missing anyway?" Kody asked. Jo stood stoically, doubting every detail of the Captain's story.

"He is at the Healer's station being attended to by Julia. He has been gone since last year's Bloom Festival." The General answered, still watching Jo for his response.

"You say 'claiming he escaped.' Does this mean you don't believe him?" Jo asked.

"The evidence is all there that he was a captive. He is emaciated, smells of the enemy, and he has intelligence of a secret assault. But something is not setting right with me, and I wanted to discuss it with the two of you. Would you both be willing to interview the Captain when he is awake? I do not want you to hint of my suspicions, instead, act as if you believe every word he tells you."

The General then looked at Jo. "Jo, trust your instincts. If the Captain is lying, he has gone to great lengths to convince us of his capture. I just have no idea of his motive to betray our land," said the General.

"Sir, last year you had said he was angry with you about something. Could that be his motivator?" Jo asked.

"What was he angry with you about? Kody questioned.

"He was denied a promotion. He felt that with his team leadership of rescuing the missing gidgies, he should have been advanced to Colonel, but I denied his submission. At this moment in time, I have no proof of his collusion with the enemy, just a gut feeling," the General answered.

"I think he was part of their abductions. He was creating a situation where he could be a hero for self-advancement. He may not be the mastermind in all the gidgies that have gone missing, but I would put a pile of gold on the fact he was behind the Bloom Festival invasion." Jo said sharply.

"I know how you feel, Jo, this is why I want you and Kody to 'interview' him. I do not want him to feel questioned. We must make it look like we believe him while we investigate the past ten months of him missing in action. If you cannot hold back your anger towards him, I will need to assign another Skyforce member," warned the General.

"I can hold it back, sir. I want to nail this guy and his traitorous hind end to the wall," Jo answered.

"When would you like us to begin the interrogation... uh, I mean, interview, sir?" Kody asked.

"As soon as the Healers give us the go-ahead," the General replied.

"I have an idea, sir, and it includes using the young Healer named Lewis," Jo suggested.

"I trust you, First Sergeant, discuss it with Sylvia to make sure she approves of your plan. In the meantime, not a word of what was deliberated here. You're dismissed."

Ruby and Sebastian sat on the pond dock, soaking up the warm spring air. Duke was true to his promise. He filled a picnic basket with sandwiches, cubed cheese, cookies, and small millie fruit pies and Ginny put two jars of her lavender java drink in the basket.

The pond was too cold to dangle their feet in, but it was a bright sunny day, and the water was crystal clear and showcased all the remarkable creatures that made the small lake their home.

"I leave for my first mission a week after I check into the Skyforce HQ. I am excited to put my training into action." Sebastian said as he bit into a fitternick egg sandwich.

"I would be so nervous. Do you have any idea what to expect on a mission?" Ruby asked as she sipped the lava java.

"All I know is to be ready for the unexpected. Speaking of unexpected, I got something for you." Sebastian pulled a small box from the picnic basket.

Ruby's heart skipped a beat. She opened the box, and inside of it was a tiny root with a young ivy leaf attached to it. Then she saw a delicate gold ring with a silver leaf on the top and a small diamond on each side of the stem. The band itself had little leaves circling halfway around each side. On the ring, there was a note tied to it.

"Dear Ruby,

This ring is a promise to always love you. To always protect you. And to always cherish our friendship. The vine root is a piece from the special one by our fort. May it remind you of your incredible gift to make things grow and how remarkable you are to me. I love you, Rubes."
Always yours,

Sebastian.

Ruby slid the ring on her finger, but then she held the small root to her heart. "Sebastian, how did you ever find a piece of her?" Ruby asked.

"I snuck over there on my way here and dug deep down into the dirt. I have no idea if she can be fully revived, but I figured if anyone could do it, you could." Seb smiled as he admired the small promise ring on Ruby's finger.

"You know what Ginny says a promise ring is, don't you?" Ruby asked with a smirk.

"No idea," Seb said, smiling as he took her hand.

"It is a promise for a bigger diamond." Ruby giggled with the lifting of one eyebrow.

"I can live with that." He chuckled.

Chapter Twenty-Seven
New life

Kody and Jo sat outside Captain Roland's room, waiting for him to wake up. He was ashen skinned and had black circles under his eyes. His nails were long and filled with dirt. The two soldiers had acquired the Captain's belongings. His clothes were covered with holes and smelled of body odor, liaths, and a faint hint of alcohol.

Kody held the bag of Roland's belongings and threw the Captains' shredded pants to the floor in disgust. "

Where would one possibly get a bottle of bourbon in Skawlterrin?" He asked Jo in a whisper.

"Nowhere. My guess: Roland is the uninvited guest in Phineas Hill's root that Ginny and Ruby told us about. They said the floor was covered in empty bottles of bourbon, and there was a stink of liaths near the Professor's root. It sounds to me that the ol' Captain has been conspiring with the enemy and has taken advantage of Hill's absence and hid out in his root. Think about it, the time frame fits his absence." Jo said with distaste.

"And in my opinion, he was drowning his shame of being a traitor with the alcohol." Jo added.

"We must be clever in our questioning. If Roland is the traitor, we need to trap him in his own words. That Lewis boy should be here with Sylvia any time now. Why did you want him in with us in the questioning Jo?" Kody asked.

"The kid has a special gift. Sylvia has mentioned he can read the emotions of a soul. I want him to quietly sit in the 'interview' of the Captain and get a read off him. From what I am told Lewis can detect the reasoning and mood of a being. He just needs to be near the one he perceives from." Jo explained.

"That is a wild talent. Sounds like Sylvia and her oracle gift." Kody said in admiration.

"Well, we will see if Lewis can confirm my suspicions of Roland," Jo mentioned as he peeked in the window of the Captain's room to see if he was awake yet. He wasn't. He had been sleeping since he returned five days ago. Today, however, Sylvia and Lewis would be under the disguise of care while Jo and Kody questioned the Captain.

Sylvia arrived just before noon. "Hello gentleman, the General has explained my role for today and what you are hoping to accomplish. Lewis is unaware of what our motive is with the Captain. All he knows is he is coming to get a read off a gidgie who escaped Skawlterrin. I trust his instinct, he has not disappointed since he has been tutoring under me this past year."

No sooner had Sylvia finished speaking when Lewis came around the corner. "Hello Jo, good to see you. I'm not sure how I can help you today, but I will do my best." Lewis said as he extended his hand to shake Jo's.

"Lewis, this is Sergeant Major Kody. He will also be in the room as we talk with the Captain about his traumatic experience. We would like you to sit in and make sure the Captain is doing alright. He has mentioned he escaped from the wicked forest and has been held prisoner for nearly ten months. He has also shared he knows of a few plans of Neeradima." Jo mentioned as Kody reached out and shook Lewis's hand.

Sylvia added, "Lewis, do what you do when you are in the room with Barney or other traumatized fairies. Listen with your heart and trust what you feel."

"I will do my best, ma'am," Lewis said nervously.

The four fairies entered Captain Roland's room. He was still sleeping deeply, due to the healing tonics Julia administered. Sylvia took a small cloth doused in fragrant oils that smelled of spearmint and held it under his nose to stir him awake. Roland's eyes slowly began to open. He saw Jo, Kody, and Sylvia. He did not see Lewis, who was sitting in the corner, observing.

"Good afternoon, Captain, we are sorry we had to wake you. First Sergeant Joseppi, and Sergeant Major Kody, have a few questions to ask you. I will be here if you begin to feel unwell. Can I get you some pillows to help prop you up in our bed?" Sylvia asked but began to prop the Captain up anyway. She then gave him a bright yellow elixir to help wake him up.

"Thank you, Sylvia. I am happy to help Jo and Kody in any way I can. What is it you guys need to know?" The Captain asked as he pushed himself upright in his bed and sipped on the sour yellow drink that gave him the shivers from the shock of the tartness.

In a tone of respect and compassion, Jo began, "Captain, I am sorry to hear of your ordeal in the dark forest. Can you remember anything about the caves or where you were held? Even the slightest hint or memory could help."

"It was pretty dark and smelled horrible. We were constantly being moved. The caves twist deep into the Darphea Mountain Range. It's hard to even know where you are going," the Captain answered.

"Yes, I understand. We have heard that from others who have been rescued. The General mentioned you overheard the enemy's plan of a ground strike. Do you know when this is supposed to happen?" Kody added to the question.

"I have no idea when they will strike. I heard two liaths discussing a ground assault. To me, it sounds as if they are going to send out Neeradima's beast and then her army of liaths. If I was in charge, I would prepare a team to confront the monsters in the valley." Roland advised.

"We will share this info with the General. Can you recall anything else about the caves? Maybe certain gidgies who have been held captive?" Kody asked.

"I am sorry, gentlemen; it has been a difficult ten months in the enemy's territory," Roland said, sounding distraught.

"Yes, I can only imagine. How did you escape from the intense security?" Jo asked, trying incredibly hard not to sound suspicious.

"It wasn't easy. I was in a dark cave for months, not too far from the other prisoners. I finally had my moment when they changed guards. I took my chamber pot and hit one of the liaths over the head, and then made a dash down the tunnel. It was a miracle I found my way out of the caves," the Captain answered in a persuasive tone.

Kody looked at Jo with the eyes of one who was believing the story. Jo then said, "One final question, and then we will let you rest; what did you hear in the caves? Did you hear weeping, screaming, or was it quiet?"

"I only heard suffering. The anguish from the caves was distressing," the Captain said with a shudder.

"Yes, I could imagine. The last thing one would hear in those miserable cells is singing, eh?" Jo nonchalantly mentioned as he wrote the Captain's last answer down with a brown scribble stick.

"You're absolutely right, Jo, no one is singing in the caves of such anguish. Look at me. I am a bag of bones. A soul can't find their song in a place filled with pain and torment," the Captain emphatically said.

Kody turned and looked at Jo with both eyebrows raised in shock, but Jo kept his cool.

"Well, Captain, it's clear you have been through a horrible ordeal. I am sure there will be some sort of recompense coming your way for your traumatic event. We will leave you now to get some rest." Jo saluted the Captain. It was painful to perform an act of honor, especially since Jo felt that he caught Roland in a lie.

The Captain had no knowledge of Yoli singing with the other prisoner. Had he known it was a frequent report from those who had been rescued from the dark land, he would have changed his story.

Sylvia gave the Captain a sleeping tonic and adjusted his bed and pillows. He drifted quickly off to sleep, and the four gidgies exited the room. Roland never saw the young Healer in the corner.

Lewis looked utterly confused as he followed the three older gidgies to Sylvia's office. The old Healer poured all of them hot mugs of pinkle pepper brew and sat at her desk. She began the conversation, "Well, gentleman, did you find the answers you were looking for from the Captain?"

"I believe we did. Lewis, is there anything you perceived from the interview that may help in this situation?" Jo asked, curious as to what the young Healer discerned.

Lewis squirmed a bit, this was new for him. The interviewing of the Captain made him feel uneasy and even a bit nauseous. "Sirs, the Captain seems to be under the belief you guys do not trust him. I could sense his suspicions of you as soon as we entered the room. But that's not the oddest part of this whole thing. He does not like you, Jo, and I sense you are not too fond of him either," Lewis carefully shared with a wince.

"You would be right in your perception Lewis. The Captain and I have had our differences. What do you think about his time in Skawlterrin? Is your perceiving gift feeling anything about his months as a prisoner?" Jo asked, still smirking about Lewis picking up on his dislike of Roland.

"That was odd. Captain Roland looked like a prisoner of war who had been starved. However, I believe he was lying through most of the interview. He wants to believe he is a hero, but he is sacrificing others for his own ego. I am utterly confused by him." Lewis said and then grabbed his head in pain. He had a scene flash in his mind that felt like a hot knife running threw his skull. He shouted in agony, and Sylvia, Jo, and Kody all ran to him.

Sylvia knew exactly what was going on; Lewis had his first fire sight vision. Healers with such a gift are rare; Sylvia and Allison were the only ones who existed until now. An oracles first fire sight vision always felt similar to a piercing migraine.

"What did you see, Lewis?" Sylva asked as she placed her hands over his head to soothe the pain.

With his eyes tightly shut, he watched a prophecy play in his mind. But he refused to say what he saw. He shook his head and repeated, "No, no,"

Sylvia tried to calm him. "Lewis, it's just a vision. Tell us what you see."

Lewis held his head in agony. "I see a battle coming. It's violent. The cost is high, but we have a victory. I see Captain Roland standing near the General, but I am not sure why he is there. The General knows Captain Roland is a traitor." Then Lewis paused.

Jo knelt down and said, "it's alright, Lewis, go on."

With eyes watering from the pain, Lewis continued, "I see, I see, I see friends; turned enemy hurting Jo and Kody." Lewis's eyes shot open in terror. His body was shivering, and he felt like he had the flu.

Sylvia wrapped Lewis up in one of her shawls and put the hot mug of pinkle pepper brew in his hands. She then pulled a piece of honeycomb from her desk and made Lewis nibble on the sweet, waxy morsel.

"Lewis, dear, is this your first vision of the future?" Sylvia asked.

"Yes, ma'am," he said in a trembling voice.

"Lewis, son, you have been given a wonderful gift. Beathra calls it *Fire Sight*, and you are the third of our kind to have such an impartation. You have been shown the possibility of the future, but also the treasure of preparing and warning our garden. Do not be afraid of what you saw, instead, tell us how to react to vision." Sylvia's wise counsel calmed the frightened Lewis down.

"Jo, you must not go to battle without your helmet and Kody; when you see a strange-looking liath, let it be. He is not evil. I don't know why, but I sense he still has good in him. I also see a chameleon covered in black stuff. Kody, he needs your help."

The three older gidgies all looked at each other. The detail and warning of Lewis's vision unnerved them. "A strange-looking liath? What are the possibilities of this being a miss-fired prophecy?" Kody asked Sylvia.

"Pretty slim. What Lewis saw was a forewarning to you and Jo to be equipped. It sounds to me that our garden is about to go through a shaking. We have been given tools to prepare for the days to come. I suggest you two make your way to General Dax and relay everything you have heard today. I will stay here with Lewis and help him regain his strength." Sylvia suggested as she put her arms around Lewis to quiet his trembling body.

Sebastian was on his first mission, and Ruby busied herself with the preparations of her spring garden and focusing on nurturing Gabriella back to life. She sat in her small apartment root with the little piece of ivy in a small glass jar. The vine was but a wisp of a root, no thicker than a strand of hair with a bit of stem connected, and a wilted leaf attached.

Ruby spoke the life charm every day for the past two weeks, and she was growing discouraged. Nothing had changed in the tiny vine. She pulled Gabriella from her kitchen window and spoke to her as if she could understand, then she remembered a spell she read in the ancient book about life revived. It was used to refresh perennials after a long, harsh winter, but she decided to give it a go with Gabriella.

"The winter's past, the frost is gone.
The nights are shortened, the days grow long.
Spring is here, and with-it life.
Shake off your slumber and be revived.
Your time has come to bloom once more.
This is the season you've been waiting for.
Stretch your stems towards the light.
Bust through the earth, with all your might."

Ruby recited the charm three times and nothing. Then a fourth, a fifth, a sixth. She felt ridiculous. "I have to admit defeat sometime."

She thought to herself. She went outside and sang the charm in her own tune around Ginny's farm.

The effects were extraordinary, small bluebells began to pop up out of the ground, crocuses, hyacinths, and tulips all began to shoot up and show their young stems and leaves.

"The charm works! I know it's not me quoting it wrong," she said to herself, out loud.

A warm breeze blew across Ruby's face, and she immediately knew The Whisper was near. She then could hear her fire seed begin to speak within her, "Ruby, where there has been much trauma, more love is required. Do not stop speaking life over Gabriella, or any creature you know that has endured violence by the hand of the enemy. It may take more time to see positive results, but with each word of love and life, it will unravel the curse of death."

Ruby stood and listened as the warm breeze of The Whisper circled her, and Beathra spoke through her fire seed. She leaned against an almond tree that was bursting in pink and white blooms from the charm and pondered what she was instructed to do.

Ruby did not realize she had been given extraordinary powers. The reviving magic, repetitively spoken, could transform even the darkest of souls. Ruby would feel the effects of the magical words, for it would revive areas that had been damaged by heartache in her younger years. The more she quoted the lines of the spell, and sang it over her garden, the more she would be transformed.

That is the preciousness of such a charm. Like a jar with honey being poured from it, the container would be coated in the sweet golden syrup as well.

The letter

Chapter Twenty-Eight
The love letter.

It was the week of the Bloom Festival. The spring was exploding on the farm, and Ruby's charms were flourishing the flower and vegetable garden. Duke and Ginny were busy preparing for the special event with experimental drinks, pastries, and cookies.

Ginny wanted to surprise everyone with a new beverage. She would, of course, offer her honey lavender, lava java. But recently, she created an orange and honey lava java drink with a touch of chocolate. Duke followed Ginny's idea using their abundant harvest of oranges and almonds and made orange marmalade and almond pastries along with his fig and honey ones.

They were packing their carts, for Piper and Prince to pull when Ruby and Seb showed up.

"Where have you two been?" Ginny asked with a smile.

"We just came from Buck and Barneys. You're not going to believe this, but Tobias and Timothy; the twins that graduated about five years before Seb and I moved next to Buck and Barney to help on the farm. But that's not the best part. They are going to help the twins run the Ferris wheel this year! Isn't that great news?" Ruby said excitedly.

"That is amazing news. How wonderful! Twins in Havengothy are unique, and though they aren't rare, they are still a bit uncommon. What are the odds of having two sets of twins living so close?" Ginny mused out loud.

"What made them think to do such a thing?" Duke asked.

"I guess Toby and Tim's parents both serve on the Skyguard, and they were telling the twins how hard it's been to find crews to continue helping Buck with the farm," Sebastian informed.

Ruby excitedly interrupted Sebastian's story, "Toby is such a compassionate gidgie, and he wanted to do something to help. But it was Tim who suggested they just move close by," she said, rapidly speaking.

"They wanted to start a small farm and grow groves of Camillicent trees, so this was the perfect fit." Sebastian finished racing Ruby to the end of the story.

They were both giggling and elated with the spectacular news. "Praise be to Beathra!" Ginny declared.

"Those two boys deserve the kindness of Tim and Toby. Duke added.

"Ruby, will you come and help me with Prince and Piper to get them ready for the festival? I want to do something special with their mane and tail." Ginny asked.

"Absolutely. In fact, I have ribbon leftover from your wedding I can put in Piper's mane!" Ruby said excitedly as she and Ginny flew to the barn.

"When is your next mission Seb?" Duke asked as he threw a barrel of Vanilla Pod Milk in the cart for Prince to pull.

"I leave Saturday, but I will have Friday night to take Ruby to the festival.

I have a lot of dances to make up for and prizes to win her for missing the Fall and Christmas carnivals." Seb answered as he helped Duke load jugs of honey and sacks of ground lava beans into the cart.

"Yes, you do. That's all we've heard about while you were training. Ruby talked about all the things you two were going to do when you got home." Duke teased. "How is rooming with Billick going. You had mentioned to me he was a bit sweet on Ruby. Do you think he still is?" Duke asked.

"It's hard to say, sir. If he still is, he keeps it hidden. But I see the way he watches her. Not like a creeper, but he does look at her as one would admiring a girl they liked. But he is respectful and has not done anything inappropriate." Seb said, assuring Duke that Billick was a nice guy and not to worry about Ruby around him.

"That's good to hear, but he sure was a puke to her for a long time. Especially for someone who supposedly liked her. I will always keep my eye on him because of that." Duke said in a fatherly tone.

"Ha, Jake, my foster dad used to call me a puke. But it sounded much worse coming from his mouth than it does yours. He usually had a few swear words behind his nickname for me." Sebastian said with a chuckle. The pain of his family's rejection did not hurt him like it did when he was younger. He had found his family and a place he belonged with Ruby's family and Jo and Kody.

"Son, you don't need to think about that rat, Jake, he missed out on seeing you grow into a fine Skyforce soldier," Duke said proudly.

"I have duty tonight, but I have all of Friday off. I will see you at the festival first thing Friday morning to help you and Gin set up. Plus, I want to spend as much time with Ruby as possible since I leave on a mission early Saturday. It's a bummer you can't figure out how to get your wagon to fly behind the skyponies, eh?" Sebastian said as he flew off to find Ruby to tell her goodbye.

Ruby and Ginny were in the barn discussing the festival. Ginny stood on a stool grooming Prince and braiding his mane, while Ruby was putting the garnet-colored ribbons in Piper's black mane and tail. The two skyponies loved getting to go on adventures with Ginny. They didn't mind they had to pull a cart instead of fly. As long as they were with their master, they were content.

"Ruby, I noticed you've been singing around the garden, and I can't help but observe that when you sing, things tend to flourish a bit more. This wouldn't happen to have anything to do with that old book you returned to the professor's root, would it? I saw that it was written by Melchizedek. Would you mind letting me in on your little secret?" Ginny asked.

Ginny was careful with the question. She had been watching Ruby work in the garden and noticed that the orchard production was more significant. The veggie patch was thriving, and the flowers had never been thicker or more vibrant. Plus, she had more oranges than she knew what to do with.

Ruby stood with her head down, focusing on weaving the ribbon in Piper's mane. She did not know how to explain the magic of the book and its charms. Ruby had no idea who the author was. She just knew it was a magic book. "Do you know who Melchizedek is?" Ruby asked.

"I have only heard stories, more like fables, of an old wizard who lives in the Hyperion Mountains. It's said he keeps past and future records of all the worlds. When I saw the tattered book you had of Phineas Hill, I didn't think much of it, until I remembered an ancient legend of the magical wizard of the mountain.

"My mother told me years ago about a grumpy wizard who ruled the mystical mountains. She made him sound like a monster who would strike me with lightning if I didn't go to bed when I was told. I realize now, it was to get me to obey." Ginny said and then giggled at the thought of it.

Ruby laughed; grateful Ginny never used scare tactics to make her obey. "A wizard wrote the book? Holy Havengothy!" Ruby quipped out loud, but more to herself.

"Before I returned the book, I copied all of its charms and spells and most of its stories. After seeing the power of its pages, I have no doubt that the wizard exists. I do not think he is a grumpy or cruel wizard, not by what I have read. He seems just as loving as Beathra and The Whisper. The pages are filled with The Whisper and Neeradima's charms and how they worked together. It also has warned of some of Neeradima's more evil creations. Well, not exactly creations, she does not have that kind of power. She only has the power to corrupt." Ruby explained.

She felt a twinge of guilt that she had kept this magnitude of a secret from her mother, but how does one really begin to explain it? She would first have to admit she stole the book. That alone would disappoint Ginny. But then Ruby would have to try and explain the charms and how they worked. It all seemed so far-fetched to convince another. But here Ginny was, interested in the magic that the book contained. And not just curious, she believed in it.

"I think we should keep this to ourselves right now. It could put you in harm's way if someone knew you could employ the spells that were written. Who all knows about the book?" Ginny asked.

"Seb and Ellie know, but so does Jo, Moses, maybe General Dax. Possibly Captain Roland. Hmm, maybe Kody. Oh, and now you." Ruby said with a grimacing smile.

"Holy Havengothy, Ruby. Did you ever plan on telling me?" Ginny asked, hurt.

"I'm sorry, momma. I didn't know how to tell you. It was difficult enough explaining it to Seb and Ellie, and if it wasn't for the death of Emmet, I might have not told Jo."

Ruby began to explain everything to Ginny about the book, all the way back to the earthquake when Gabriella woke from the life charm, up to today, quoting the reviving spell over the vine.

Ginny sat down on a bale of hay, processing all Ruby was telling her. She thought back to the night Jo and Kody shared with her the special guardianship they would be doing secretly over Ruby.

Ginny remembered watching Ruby as a young girl, gifted with growing a garden. Ruby would sing over everything she planted. She would talk to a carrot with the same love and admiration she would speak to Prince or Piper. Her little girl always had a way with Havengothy's foliage.

It was all beginning to make sense. All except why Beathra chose her to raise Ruby. Now, her daughter was possibly the chosen one to defend their world against the wicked enchantress. Ruby was gifted with magic and authority to grow her garden, but was she given the same abilities to fight for it? Ginny's mind was reeling from all the information when Ruby sat next to her on the hay.

"Mother," Ruby rarely called Ginny "mother." When she did, it was out of sarcasm or sass. Like when she was upset for being grounded, or teasing Ginny that she looked like an old lady. Ginny was a young single mom who toted little Ruby everywhere she went. The two were as tight as any mother and daughter, but also like sisters. However, today, Ruby saw Ginny as the mother who always fought, taught, and encouraged Ruby to dream. Unknowingly, she was seeing the pride, fear, and worry a momma has when a child is called to great things.

"Mother, I am sorry I never told you about the book. First, because I stole it from Hill's office, I never borrowed it. And secondly, because it was magic, and it felt crazy to even mention such a thing. From here on out, I will do my best to tell you everything. In fact, I have been reciting a reviving charm over the bits of the vine that Sebastian gave me. Gabriella has begun to sprout, and even produce a few leaves!" Ruby said excitedly.

"Well, it's all water under the bridge now. Let's get these ponies to the carts. I have plans for all those blasted oranges our grove produced because of your charms." Ginny hopped off the bundle of hay and jumped bareback on Prince and flew out of the barn, expecting Ruby to follow.

Sebastian entered the barn as Ginny thundered out of it, nearly knocking him over. Ruby was jumping on Pipers back when she saw Seb.

"Hold on, girl, we will go in a minute," Piper was annoyed at the delay and stomped her hooves. Ruby gave her an apple, and this seemed to appease the skypony.

"Hi, Seb. Are you on your way back to headquarters?" Ruby inquired.

"I am, I just wanted to tell you goodbye, and I will see you tomorrow at the festival. I'll meet you at Duke and Ginny's cart around one. That gives us plenty of time to help them set up and maybe check a few booths out before the evening festivities begin." Seb said as he reached for Ruby's hand.

"That sounds wonderful. What time do you get off duty tomorrow?" Ruby asked.

"I have duty from eight pm to four am. I am hoping I can get a small nap, and then, I will head toward the center of the garden and find you. I promise we will be the first on the dance floor tomorrow night and dance until our toes bleed." He gave Ruby a small kiss and left.

The carts were overflowing on the journey towards the center of the garden, but Prince and Piper did not complain. Duke and Ginny checked in with the coordinator of the event, Mr. Vargas. Their assigned area for their booth was close to the twins.

"This is prime real estate!" Duke declared. As the ponies pulled the carts, they passed by Buck, who was setting up the Ferris wheel with the help of Toby and Tim. Barney was sitting on a bench playing with his stuffed atto-glider Ginny had made him.

"Ginny, Ginny! Hi Ginny! Ruby! It's me, Barney! Buck, can I go with Ginny and Ruby?" Barney bellowed.

Buck looked up from the rope he just tied to a stake to secure the base of the big wheel. "If it's alright with Ruby and Ginny." Buck shot a glance at Ginny, and she gave him a nod of approval. Barney saw Ginny's gesture of "yes," before he heard Buck's permission, and ran to Ruby and grabbed her hand.

Barney was a head taller than Ruby, but he walked alongside her holding tightly to her hand and clutching his green wooly atto-glider under his arm.

"Buck won't let me out of his sight. He is afraid I will get snacked again," Barney shared with Ruby.

Ruby knew he meant, "snatched" but she didn't want to correct Barney. "He is a good protective brother, Barney. You can help us set up Duke and Ginny's cart. I bet Duke will let you sample some of his new baked goods," Ruby looked at Duke and smiled.

"Only if he pulls his weight," Duke said with a wink.

Barney did his best to help with setting up the booth and tent but would often get distracted. Ginny asked Ruby to take Barney to the picnic area to play. Ginny piled a plate full of Duke's sweet pastries, a meat pie, and a jar of an orange, vanilla pod milk just for Barney.

She made Ruby the chocolate and orange lava drink that Gin called, "Orange you glad you tried it." It was a long title, but she got such a giggle out of it, there was no talking her out of changing the name.

Just after one o'clock, Sebastian landed at the center of the garden. It was buzzing with gidgies setting up for the kickoff of the night's activities. Skyguard's and Skyforce were already a strong presence, and there was more to come as the sun dropped down. C.J. would be missed, along with his little creature Gertie and her talent of changing color.

The General was confident in his soldiers and felt all precautions were taken to ensure a safe festival. His spies and those who have been rescued have all relayed similar information; Neeradima was plotting something, but she was not quite ready. This info did not relax security and canceling the Bloom Festival was out of the question. Gidgies would never consider it. They were created to celebrate life, and the Bloom Festival was just that.

General Dax had asked all off duty Skyforce members to wear their uniform and carry their weapons. The Commander of the Skyguard's did the same. Sebastian was wandering around the carnival when he found Ginny and Duke. They were busy trying to be fully set up for the opening at six o'clock. Ruby helping with Barney delayed them a bit, but Ginny would never say anything about it.

Duke looked up, carrying the poles that held the awning and saw Sebastian in his uniform, "Hey bud, are you working?"

"No, and yes. The uniform is a precautionary measure to ensure the safety of our residents. Where's Ruby?" Seb asked as he looked around and couldn't find her.

"She is helping Buck out a bit by keeping an eye on Barney. But while you are here, do you mind helping me with these posts to prop the awning up?" Duke asked.

By three o'clock, Duke and Ginny's 'Treats and Drinks' booth was nearly ready to open for business. Ginny was busy writing the menu down on the sandwich board, and Duke was hanging his signs overhead.

Sebastian wiped the sweat from his brow, and Ginny brought both him and Duke a large glass of a reddish-orange drink. One sip and Seb knew it wasn't just orange juice. "What is this, Gin?" Seb asked in shock at the first drink. "We had a huge harvest of oranges this year, so I am being creative. It's whipped vanilla pod milk with orange juice and a splash of cranberry juice for color."

"It's good. I like it. Duke, if you don't need any more help, I think I will try and find Ruby." Sebastian informed.

Duke thanked Seb for his help and gave him a plate of pastries. Seb looked at the gooey, orange marmalade and honey pastry. "More oranges, eh?" He chuckled and then yelled back. "It's good. I like it."

Ruby heard Seb yell and looked up from the picnic table she and Barney were playing cards at. Sebastian was in his Skyforce uniform, his black hair was a little messy, and he was trying to eat one of Duke's pastries without letting it drip on the front of him. She smiled at the sight. He had never looked more handsome to her.

One of her favorite things about loving someone she knew as a child was watching him age. Sebastian felt Ruby's eyes on him and looked up from his bite. She was smiling and looked absolutely adorable. She was still wearing her work clothes of overalls, and her hair was pulled back with a bandana. She sat at a table covered in paper, scribble sticks and cards.

Seb joined the two for a few minutes when Buck came and gathered Barney. "Thanks for keeping an eye on him, Ruby. I truly appreciate it. Lewis and Trixie promised Barney to take him around tonight. We are gonna clean ourselves up before the festival opens. You and Seb have free rides tonight on the Ferris wheel." Buck took Barney's hand, and Barney told Buck all about the yummy food Ginny and Duke fed him and how he beat Ruby in cards a billion times.

Ruby flew back to the small tent behind Duke and Ginny's booth, where the three of them stay during the festival. Miss Kitty altered Ruby's pink dress she wore at Gin's wedding and made it into a cute romper. Ruby emerged from the tent, and Seb was eating another of Duke's pastries. "

If you're not careful, you won't be able to fly to headquarters tonight or fit in your dress blues." Ruby teased.

Sebastian's eyes fell on Ruby, and he stopped his chewing. The pink one-piece romper with her wild rose gold hair, and hot pink wings made her look like a picture. Ruby blushed at Sebastian's speechlessness.

"Come on, dork, let's go find Ellie and Theo. They are meeting us at the trunk of Beathra at four."

Ellie and Ruby chatted a mile a minute, excited to finally be together. Sebastian was not enjoying his time as much. Theo was awkward and had become a bit full of himself with his recent honors at the East Branch. Seb found it challenging to hold a conversation with him, but he did his best for Ellie's sake.

The four sauntered around the festival as booths finished setting up. Sebastian bought a large bag of caramel corn for all of them to share, and a small bag of plain, buttered popcorn for Ruby.

The lava lights were beginning to glow against the dusk sky, and the band started tuning their instruments for the first dance of the night. Ellie looked at Theo in hopes of a waltz, but he declined her request.

"Ellie, you know I can't dance. I am all legs and two left feet." He said. "How about a Ferris wheel ride instead?" he offered. This appeased Ellie, but Ruby saw her friend's disappointment.

"I don't care if you're a lousy dancer, we are cutting a rug. I waited too long for this moment." Ruby teased as she grabbed Sebastian's hand and flew towards the dance floor.

"I wouldn't think of refusing to dance with the prettiest girl in Havengothy," Seb answered.

The two were the first on the dance floor, but it quickly filled up. Ruby and Seb saw several couples from school join in. Trixie and Lewis were in a dancing circle with Barney, then Seb and Ruby joined them.

Suddenly, Todd and Barb jumped in. Elizabeth and Colin saw the fun, and Liz yelled out, "You can't dance the Beathra Bop Boogie without us!" Lester and Katie saw the enthusiastic dancing crew and joined in as well. It was a wild conga line with giggles bumbling into one another ,and Ruby tumbling and tripping over Seb's feet as Barney led the line.

After a long evening of dancing and laughing, Seb and Ruby left to play a few carnival games and grab something to eat at Duke and Ginny's. Sebastian won a stuffed unicorn and a cheap plastic ring.

"I don't think this is what Ginny meant when she said a bigger diamond." Ruby laughed as she put the ugly ring on her finger.

"I have something for you too, Seb." She said with a smirk.

Ruby took a small gift from her clutch. It was a piece of parchment paper folded several times over until it formed a little square package. She tied it with a thin red ribbon. On the front, it read, "Because you believed in me."

Sebastian held the tiny present, confused. "This is as light as a feather. Is there anything even wrapped up in this. If it's a gift of goodwill, it doesn't count?" He joked.

"Open it," Ruby ordered, smiling her crooked grin.

Seb untied the paper and unfolded it carefully, unsure as to what he would find in the crinkled paper present. As he opened the last bend, a small green leaf laid gently within the parchment.

"Is this from the vine?" He asked in shock.

"It is. Turn it over." Ruby said.

On the backside of the leaf was a small, penned message that read.

"I have loved you since the day you made me laugh. Your love restored my smile and has helped me grow into who I am today. I love you, Seb.

Forever yours,
Ruby

Beathra

Chapter Twenty-Nine
The heartache

The first evening of the Bloom Festival went late into the night. The presence of the Skyforce and Skyguard was profoundly felt. But did not dampen the spirits of those who were enjoying the festivities. Billick was not on duty, but he still spent the night watching others. He observed his friends flash mob dance with Barney and watched as Ruby and Seb rode the Ferris wheel. He sat in Meredith Barry's, merrybare berry bush brew booth, sipping lemonade, and surveyed the carnival fun while it whirled by him.

The loneliness that Billick felt was heavy. He hated that he felt so alone. "Get it together, Bill. You're pathetic." He said to himself.

He and Sebastian had to prepare for a mission first thing the next morning. He decided to pop in on Seb and Ruby and remind Sebastian they had to fly out soon. He landed next to the couple as Seb was tucking the parchment, wrapped leaf in his pocket.

"Hey bud, we have an early day tomorrow. I thought we should head back soon." Billick said. He watched as Ruby looked disappointed, "Well, I guess we could wait another thirty minutes or so," Billick added.

He's right Ruby, I should probably say goodnight now. I'll be back soon. It's not supposed to be a long mission. Right Bill?" Seb looked at Billick, wanting him to reassure Ruby it was all going to be alright.

"Oh, yeah, yeah. Basic patrol, search, and rescue. We should be home in a few days." Billick said convincingly.

Sebastian held Ruby's face in his hands. "I'll be back sooner than you think." He then gave her a small kiss on the lips.

Billick looked away, his hands in his pockets, trying not to feel uncomfortable. The two Skyforce soldiers launched and made their way back to the H.Q.

"We don't even know how long our next mission is Seb, the General is briefing us on it in the morning," Billick said, confused.

"I just don't want her to worry. Ruby hasn't been too keen on me in the Skyforce, she's always anxious something will happen to me. What she doesn't realize is I have the same fear about her." Sebastian confessed.

It was a spectacular Bloom Festival that ended with a lava work show. All the vendors stayed an extra day and enjoyed serving each other in their specialties. They made Monday, a vendor only celebration, and it was a party all to themselves. There were no newly bloomed gidgies this year, but all the residents felt it was coming soon. Duke, Ginny, and Ruby took their time going home, relishing the warm spring.

It was late Tuesday night, and Ruby and Ginny were brushing down the two skyponies as Duke unpacked the cart. The three were tired but elated from the success of the festival. Ginny's orange drinks were loved by all, and Duke's fig and honey pastries were a best seller. The carts were light, and Prince and Piper pranced with delight with the ease of pulling them home.

Ellie had confided in Ruby that she was having doubts about Theo but didn't know what to do. Theo was changing. He was offered a position as a professor's aid at Havengothy Gardening University when he graduated next year. However, his ego was more than she could handle, and she wasn't sure if she could make it another year.

Ruby suggested that she kick Theo to the curb, but Ellie wasn't ready to commit to such a radical idea.

"Ginny, if you were in love but were having second thoughts about someone, what would you do?" Ruby asked.

Ginny looked at Ruby in shock. "I thought you and Seb were doing well!" she exclaimed.

"Not me, a friend. Ellie is feeling a little on the fence with Theo." Ruby explained.

"I noticed he was a little different this year. He was kind of..." Ginny searched for the words, but Ruby knew precisely what to call him.

"A skypony's behind." Ruby finished. Piper and Prince looked at Ruby, insulted. "Sorry, guys." Ruby apologized.

"Well, yes, I guess he was a bit full of himself. But perhaps it's just a phase." Ginny said, trying to sound encouraging.

"I told her to drop him like a bad habit." Ruby declared. Ginny raised her eyebrows.

"Ruby dear, you need to be cautious with such advice. It could backfire on you. They could work things out, and then you're the enemy to their relationship." Ginny suggested.

"I just don't like seeing Ellie so weighed down by him. At the festival, Theo stopped suddenly when we were all walking, and I ran into the back of him. Ellie and I started laughing, but he gave her a look like she was a new bloom and needed to grow up. It reminded me of the look I.K. would give me when I made mistakes or failed my spelling test or existed in his presence. I wanted to hit Theo in the throat right then and there." Ruby declared, suddenly feeling the emotion of I.K.'s rejection and cruelty.

"Ruby, walk cautiously through this. You don't want to hurt your friend. Keep writing to Ellie and encouraging her with studies. Share your life, your time with Seb, but darling, if she wants Theo, you will need to step aside and stand by her in her choice and stand by her if she decided to break it off. That's what friends do." Ginny's advice was hard for Ruby, but she knew her mother was right.

Jo and Kody landed on Duke and Ginny's porch dressed in their uniforms. Duke was carrying another empty jug of honey to his hives when he saw the two Skyforce members on the patio.

"Hey, fellas! We are all out here by the barn unpacking." He yelled.

Jo and Kody flew to Duke and asked where Ruby was. The look in their eyes was not good. Jo looked sick, and Kody was taking the lead in the conversation.

"What's going on, Kody? Why are you both here so late in the evening? It can't be good news." Duke said nervously, feeling bad news was coming.

Ginny and Ruby came around from the stalls and found Duke talking with Jo and Kody. Duke looked up and saw Ginny, his eyes were filled with tears. Ruby saw Jo and the stress on his face. He was a wreck and could barely look her in the eyes. Right then, Ruby knew: something horrible happened to Sebastian.

Ruby's stomach dropped, she felt like she was going to throw up. Her mind began to realize what her body was responding to, "Noooooo!" she screamed. "No, No, No. Not Sebastian. NO!"

She crumbled to the ground, unable to stand under the heaviness of shock and grief. Her ears rang, and her vision began to go black, she couldn't breathe. She was going to pass out. Jo wanted to fall with her.

Ginny knelt down by her and held Ruby as she wept, "Kody, what happened?" Gin asked through tears.

The pain she had for her daughter gutted her. Ruby was in the dirt, knees bent, and tears were falling hard, hot, and fast. She held herself up by her hands as the rivers of sorrow gushed from her eyes. Mud was already beginning to form from the volume of tears that fell. Kody and Duke wanted to run to Ruby.

"What happened?" Ginny yelled.

"We got word they found Yoli. A recent task force member returned with her location. He was unable to rescue her. Billick and Seb volunteered to be part of the team of six. They practically begged the General to be part of her rescue because she was so special to them. It was actually Seb who found Yoli.

"He was deep in the caves of Darphea. Sebastian had surprised a tree elf who was guarding Yoli and another prisoner. Seb knocked the tree elf out and was able to free the two gidgies. He sent Yoli and the other in front of him towards the team that was in the cavern hall. That's when Sebastian was jumped from behind by a liath.

"The team's first duty is to those they are sent to rescue. They rushed Yoli and the other out of the caves to Commander Sidney, while two of our own chased down the liath who captured Sebastian. They invaded cavern after cavern, killing liaths, and even rescued a forest elf, but Sebastian was nowhere to be found. It was like he disappeared," Kody choked on the last bit of his story.

Jo was holding his head with both hands as if he was trying to keep his skull from splitting in two.

"What about Billick? Did he make it out?" Duke asked as he bent down to Ginny and Ruby.

"He did. He's pretty beat up and shook up with the loss of his friend. He's at the Healer station right now with Lewis. The General is with him as well. Yoli and the other victim are in real bad shape, he may not survive. Sylvia is doing all she can to save him." Kody finished. "The team is debriefing and will be going in to find Sebastian as soon as we have a solid plan. We will rescue him, Ruby," Kody added.

Jo bent down to the ground where Ruby was. She was doubled over, with her face in her hands, buried in her lap.

"Ruby honey. I am so sorry. Had I known Sebastian wanted to take on such a mission, I would have gone with him." He said, trying to soothe her.

"Ruby looked up at Jo. Her face was red and blotchy. "Why does he always have to be the hero? Why did he join that stupid Skyforce? I knew something bad was going to happen. I knew it! Jo, you never should have let him!" she yelled.

She didn't mean it. She was proud of Sebastian, and she loved how Jo loved him like a son. She was in shock, grieving, and angry.

Jo was hurt but tried to understand. In his pain, he sat in the dirt with Ruby and let his tears fall with hers. He cried because of her grief and his. He wept because he felt responsible and helpless.

Jo didn't know how long he was knelt down. His knees hurt from being bent. One knee was resting on a rock that was digging into his kneecap, but he refused to get up. Ginny was still there with Ruby, quietly soothing her, pulling her hair back and holding her around her shoulders. Kody and Duke stood silently watching over those they loved, grieve.

Jo finally found the courage and the words to speak. "Seb is well trained. I have complete faith in his survival and his rescue. And I have complete faith in Beathra and The Whisper. Yoli survived an entire year in that hell, so I know Sebastian is going to make it." Jo did his best to sound confident. He would not allow himself to lose faith.

Ruby had no response. Her soul felt empty. The four older gidgies circled around her as she wept until her eyes ran out of tears.

"I just don't understand why." She whimpered in a faint cry. "Why did Beathra let this happen? Why didn't The Whisper help him? Why Seb?" Her legs felt heavy, and her shoulders burned. Even if she wanted to stand, she couldn't.

Duke lifted Ruby up from the ground and cradled her in his arms. "Oh, honey, 'Why' will always be part of our life. We will never understand certain things and *why* they happen. But we are going to help you through this until the answers come. And we will believe in Beathra, regardless of the why."

Ruby buried her head in Duke's chest. She was spent. Her body hurt from grieving, and she was tired. She wasn't sure if she passed out or fell asleep. Duke carried Ruby into the root, and Ginny tucked her into her old canopy bed. She kissed her little girl's forehead while burning tears ran down Ginny's face.

"Oh Beathra, I have questions too. Is this why you have called her, for a time such as this? Is this the beginning of my nightmares? Give her the grace and strength to face the days to come. I know there is a warrior in her, so let it rise from her." Ginny prayed.

Ruby slept deep. Her dreams were confusing. She saw wars, fires, battlefields covered in carnage and evil creatures she had never witnessed before. She could hear Sebastian calling her name. Then Ruby saw herself in her dream. She rose from a pile of rubble, dressed in armor, holding a sword in one hand, and a small, strange dagger in the other. Then the faint call of Beathra and The Whisper was heard and felt like a warm breeze.

"Ruby, your time as a gardener has been training you to become who you are designed to be. You, child, have been made for such a time. It's time for you to see yourself as we see you; it's time for the warrior in you to arise."

Ruby tossed and turned in her bed violently, kicking her covers from her. Then she heard The Whisper speak to her in a calm, gentle voice, "Speak the reviving charm over Barney. You will see then; you have been made for more than growing oranges."

Ruby bolted awake with sweat pouring from her. She sat up in her bed and looked out the window. She suddenly remembered Sebastian was missing, and her throat felt tight with the sadness of it all. She wasn't sure if it was morning or evening. She sat on the edge of her bed for a short time, then took a deep breath. Ruby told herself, "You need to face the day." She wrapped herself up in a blanket and walked out into the sitting room where Duke and Ginny were.

"Where's Jo and Kody?" she asked as she entered the room.

"Jo and Kody left two days ago, honey," Duke answered.

"Good morning, sweetheart," Ginny said as she put her knitting down and jumped up to make Ruby a large mug of pinkle pepper brew that was simmering on the stovetop. She loaded it with honey and added a splash of vanilla pod milk.

"I slept for two days? I don't suppose there's been any news on Sebastian?" Ruby asked.

Ginny handed Ruby the spicy drink and then sat on the arm of Duke's chair next to him.

"I may have added something to your tea last night to help you rest. As for Sebastian, there is no news. We did hear that the other fellow rescued with Yoli was her husband, Jermaine. I guess he had been missing for a long time. When Yoli was abducted last year, she was thrown into the same prison cell as Jermaine. Isn't that crazy?"

Duke informed.

"Jermaine has been missing for over eight years. Yoli always said she knew he was alive." Ruby said, pondering on Yoli's faith. Ruby felt her hope grow a bit at that moment.

"I know this sounds strange. I feel a little nuts for saying this, but I think I need to go see Barney." Ruby said.

"Barney? I thought you might want to go to the Healer's stations and check on Billick or Yoli." Ginny asked.

"I do want to go see them; I just feel I am supposed to go see Barney first. I told you it sounds crazy. But I had a dream that I needed to go see him and..." Ruby stopped and looked at Duke, then Ginny. "Does he know about the book?" Ruby asked.

"I tell him everything, dear. Husband and wives are horrible that way," she said with a wink.

"Good. I am glad you know, Duke. The Whisper told me to speak the reviving charm over Barney. I am not sure what will happen. And I will feel absolutely foolish if nothing happens, but I have to try."

"Darling girl, we know you are made for more than just gardening. Perhaps, you were made for such a time as this." Ginny said with a smile.

Ruby looked at Ginny in shock. She practically quoted Beathra and The Whisper. "Why would my heartache be the catalyst to my destiny?" she wondered to herself.

She then felt Beathra speak to her through her fire seed, "Your destiny has been etched out for you since the beginning, Ruby. However, you have always thought of yourself as unimportant, unqualified, and unaccepted. The need to rise up and rescue the ones we love will cause a sleeping warrior to wake."

Ruby sat down on the couch across from Duke and Ginny. She blew on her drink to cool it and thought of the dream of her in armor. She took a sip and then looked at her mother and Duke, who was beginning to feel like a father to her and then announced, "I think I am supposed to join the Skyforce. I am going to find Sebastian. And if he is found while I am training, great. But if he is not, I will be ready to fight for him!"

At that exact moment, Duke and Ginny looked at each other, remembering back to Jo and Kody's visit. Ginny felt fear rise up in her heart, realizing the end of life as they knew it was crashing all around her.

Duke took a big swig of his lava java drink as his bushy mustache soaked up the bitter beverage. He put his lower lip over his mustache that hung over his upper lip and sucked all the black liquid from it. He slammed his mug on the table a little harder than he intended and announced, "I guess we should start preparing you to pass the obstacle course then, because girl, you trip over things that aren't even on the floor."

Ruby went back to her apartment root that evening and wrote Ellie the devastating news of Sebastian missing in action. She also shared with her the plan to enlist in the Skyforce and join the Special Task Force team.

When Ruby sealed the letter, something inside of her felt different. She could sense courage and bravery to answer the impossible and aim for the incredible. She ran outside to drop the letter in the bin for the HBN to go out first thing in the morning. On her flight towards the barn, she looked up at the sky, then closed her eyes and said, "I'm going to find you, Seb." Just as Ruby opened her eyes, she plowed into the barn door.

Neeradima threw a mountain goat into a bottomless pit. "Hello, my pet. I brought you something special. I need you to keep your strength, I have big plans for you soon."

The bleating of the goat could be heard crying out in distress and echoing throughout the mountain caverns. All who listened to the pitiful moans of the goat knew its crying would not last. And when its bellowing stopped, it only meant one thing; the monster in the pit was fed.

A shadow slithered back and forth in the dark hole, slowly zigzagging, watching the small critter panic with nowhere to go. Then in a sudden move, a giant mouth opened as if it unhinged its jaw and rose up above the poor creature and then plunged down and in one bite, swallowed the goat.

Neeradima laughed in wicked delight. "Those stupid fairies will not know what to do with the likes of you." She glided through the caves viewing each captive as a trophy. As she was staring down a long canal, Torn updated her on a recent victim.

"Your Majesty, the prisoner you have taken an interest in, is ready to speak with you. He appears to be willing to negotiate." Torn said in delight.

"What makes you think he is ready to give up his fire seed?" Neeradima hissed.

"He is the one who rescued the singing gidgies. He had dropped a letter of sorts when he invaded our caves." Torn said.

"What kind of letter?" Neeradima screeched.

"It is a love letter written on a piece of ivy with a girl's name. He is in a position to barter for his little love's freedom. I may have led him to believe we captured his sweetheart." Torn said, taking much delight in the situation.

"Where is this letter?" Neeradima screeched.

"It fell from my hands when I was running from the stupid ferries that were trying to rescue the poor chump," Torn answered.

Well then, let's go see who this soldier is sooo in love with, shall we? What's the girl's name so we can con this idiot out of his wings and fireside?" Neeradima laughed as she made her way to the prisoner.

"Ruby." Torn snickered.

It had been weeks since Seb rescued Yoli and Jermaine. Torn hit him on the back of the head with a rock and dragged him into a secret tunnel the liaths used for shortcuts in the mountain. While Sebastian was imprisoned, he scratched the days down on the walls. It had been forty- two days. He was strong and resisted the interrogation of Ominous and Menace. The beatings were violent, but this is what he trained for on the Broad River Island. He never divulged the plans of the Skyforce. Even with the poisoned provisions that wracked his body with pain, he held the secrets of the military deep within him.

However, he had forgotten Ruby's letter was in his jacket the morning he left for the mission, and the toxic rations clouded his thinking. He remained steadfast in his resolve to not give in to the mental warfare. His determination to endure was deep. It felt like every fiber of his body was on fire, and his head was throbbing with the foulest headache.

Seb resolved to not bow to the wicked queen. However, when Torn began to taunt him about his girl Ruby, he felt his resolve weaken. If Torn was telling the truth, he was in trouble.

He was dragged to Neeradima's chamber to meet with the queen. She continued with the lie that they captured Ruby. She threatened Sebastian that they were about to begin the process of feeding Ruby the torturous morsels of Skawlterrin.

"Your little vine loving girl came looking for you, she must really love you." Neeradima laughed. The liaths in the room circled with delight as buzzards waiting for something to die.

"I have no use for your little girlfriend. If you just give yourself up, I will release your precious Ruby. Neeradima hissed and sat on her granite throne, awaiting his answer.

Sebastian felt sick. If he had any doubt that the evil queen had Ruby, the mention of her love of vines sealed his belief. If Sebastian failed to cooperate with Neeradima, she would kill Ruby. His heart failed him. His determination began to leak from him as if he had been filled with holes. His hope was draining. Everything he feared was falling on him.

He remembered the time in the cocoon and knew there was only one way to protect Ruby; he had to sacrifice himself. But to save Ruby, he would need to betray his King; how could he stay faithful to one to save the other?

Secret Weapon

Epilogue
The Battle

Eighteen months had gone by since the Bloom Festival invasion. Since that day, all of Havengothy's leaders had been building an army to attack Skawlterrin, to avenge those who had been lost and rescue those who had been abducted. The building of the strike teams was secret, with only the highest of council and military knowing the fullness of the war strategy. Intelligence came forth from a Beathra Brigade member; Neeradima planned an assault on Havengothy at dawn.

Captain Roland stood on the Skyforce deck near the General. Though no evidence could be found to prove the Captain a traitor, the General would not allow the Captain away from his sight. The Skyforce army lined the sky. Weapons in hands, they waited quietly as the sun still lingered beneath the horizon. It was an icy winter morning that had sparkles of frost in the air. There was an eeriness to the atmosphere as the army waited.

The weight of an impending war hung in the sky like the fog. Jo, Kody, and Billick were with their units, hovering in the sky. Their hands were on their weapons and their eyes on the terrain of Skawlterrin. Jo's helmet was attached with an extra strap, and Kody was scanning the sky for an unusual liath, whatever that may look like.

Nervously, Captain Roland looked at the General. "Sir, I'm certain the enemy will be making a ground attack. We should have troops below. Allow me to lead a unit across the Darphea Valley!" he said, trying not to sound panicky.

"The General grabbed the Captain around the shoulders and pulled him close with a forceful tug, "I wanted you here by me to watch your information play out, Captain. After all, you have played a huge part in this moment right here." The General said as he let go of the Captain.

Captain Roland stumbled back from the dismissive shove of the General, into two guards. Two sentinels came and stood on both sides of Roland. The Captain looked at them nervously, realizing his betrayal to the garden was realized.

Roland was shocked to see a woman sentinel watching over him. Trixie met his gaze with an icy glare. The Captain looked away in shame and watched in horror; his plans were about to crumble.

The enemy began to rise from the wicked forest trees, like black smoke lifting from the land. Their evil chants could be heard as growls or low rumbles that got louder as they advanced. An army that rode on corrupted creatures just as vile as the riders, rose from the darkness. Hate upon hate, they aimed toward the upper atmosphere, contradictory to Roland's intel.

General Dax yelled for his soldiers to holdfast. He flew back and forth in front of the sea of Skyforce soldiers shouting, "Today, we avenge our land! Today, the wicked enchantress will feel the wrath of a good King! Today, we bring our loved ones home and crush the enemy! This is the day we put these foul creatures under our feet!"

The roar of the Skyforce army shook the leaves of Beathra and rumbled across the Darphea Valley like rolling thunder. The enemy felt the boom of the roar and became enraged. Ominous sat on his buzzard and scanned the sky for General Dax.

He spotted the General in front of his army. Ominous squinted his yellow eyes and raised his creped skinned arm. With his sword held high, he yelled through his rotting teeth, "ANNIHILATE THEM!"

The flapping of the wings of the wretched beast that the liaths flew, made an echoing, crashing sound, and wafting the vulgar smell of the liaths under the noses of the Skyforce soldiers. Jo looked at Kody, "How can they not smell their own stink?" he asked jokingly.

Kody smiled at his friend and shook his head. Jo took the words to heart from Lewis, to wear his helmet; going the extra mile, he added a second strap, just to be on the safe side.

"Let's disinfect the sky, shall we?" Kody answered with a grin.

General Dax rose above his army and shouted in a ferocious growl, "Kill them if you must! Capture them if you can! Today is our day of vengeance! Today, the enemy pays for the trouble she has brought on our world!!"

The Skyforce army rushed fearlessly at the enemy. The liath's flying creatures were using their talons to capture the Skyforce soldiers. Still, the Skyforce soldiers were equipped with razor-sharp daggers, slicing feet, claws, or toes from the wicked beasts. Ominous was zeroed in on General Dax with one agenda, to cut off his head.

Kody and Jo fought alongside each other, knocking liaths from the sky. There were Skyforce and Skyguard's on the ground fighting the liaths that were rushing from below. The enemy was crawling from secret areas into the garden, in hopes of a surprise assault. The battle on the cursed land was vicious. One by one, liaths and Skyguard's fell to their death.

The hours went by slowly. The morning turned to evening, and the fight was dark and bloody. Seventeen hours later, and the enemy was still coming from the evil forest like someone kicked an anthill.

Up on the deck of the Skyforce headquarters, the two sentinels stood watch over Captain Roland. He stared at the battle that played out before him. The General knew all along Roland had lied about the ground assault. The Captain looked at Trixie and had a thought, "Surely, I can take a woman." And he began to plot his escape from the guards.

The Darphea Valley was crawling with evil beasts. Neeradima could be seen at the edge of the Skawlterrin forest. In the daylight, she seemed almost transparent. But when the night fell, she was a dark shadowy presence. Alongside her stood two of her naffagrahns. The wretched creatures looked at her, waiting for her command. They were hungry for her to set them loose.

The sun rose on the second morning of the great battle. Kody saw a small creature crawling near the edge of Skawlterrin. The poor beast was covered in Tragedy Tree seeds. It was Emmet's chameleon, and he was helping to lead out a small group of enslaved gidgies. Kody called for backup. His petition for help got the attention of a strange colored liath named Stain, that rode on a small black raven.

As Kody flew towards the small gathering of lost gidgies that the little chameleon was rescuing, the unusual liath saw where Kody was headed. If Kody took those prisoners, Stain would pay a high price at the hand of the wicked queen.

He yelled at his raven, Galax, "Stop that fairy!" Galax torpedoed toward Kody.

A team was dispatched to help Kody with the fight. As Jo flew to help his friend, Menace, a commander in Neeradima's army, saw the approaching Skyforce soldier. Menace chucked a giant rock from his slingshot at Jo's head, knocking his helmet sideways and leaving an enormous dent in it.

A strap sprung loose from the collision, and Jo's ears were

ringing from the impact. Jo immediately thought about Lewis's warning to wear his helmet and was grateful he took heed. Billick flew quickly to Jo's aid and to draw the enemy away so Jo could continue his plight towards Kody.

Stain finally made it to Kody and jumped from his raven. Like a cat sliding down curtains with its claws out, Stain dug his sword into Kody's right wing and slid down it, tearing it open as one would fillet a fish. The liath looked Kody in the eye as it slashed his wing wide open. Kody was shocked, first by the excruciating pain but also by the look of terror in the enemy's eyes.

He wasn't your typical liath. And even in Kody's pain, he felt pity for the creature that was once a gidgie. Remembering Lewis's prophecy, Kody looked deep into the eyes of the liath looking for what Lewis prophesied. The two were spiraling to the floor of the valley when Galax swooped under Stain to catch him as he fell from Kody's wing. The raven rushed the liath away.

Kody was spiraling down toward the ground when suddenly, Jo tucked himself under Kody's arm to rescue him. In the process of sliding under Kody to lift him, Jo knocked his helmet off.

"What about the gidgies that are trying to escape with the chameleon?" Kody asked Jo.

Holding his friend up, Jo looked back and saw the rescue team that Kody had called before his injury. A team from the Beathra Brigade and a small crew from the task force immediately flew to meet the helpless chameleon and assist him in attempting to rescue the escaped prisoners.

Two Skyforce members named Layla and Thomas lifted the suffering lizard to carry him to safety. This was a dangerous task. The tragedy seeds were barbed all around him and could harm anyone who touched the poisonous black kernels.

Layla threw her coat over the pitiful animal, and Thomas took his jacket and put it under the suffering lizard, creating a sort of hammock. The two task force members carried the creature to the Healer's station. The other gidgies from the Beathra Brigade lifted the small group of fairies trying to escape Skawlterrin during the chaos of the war. Some team members carried two over their shoulders.

Jo answered Kody's question, "They are being rescued as we speak." It was a long flight to the other side of the valley, and Jo had to avoid as many conflicts as possible. The seasoned First Sergeant flew low to the ground, to prevent dropping Kody from a long fall.

Out of nowhere, a club with a boulder fastened to its end, struck Jo's head, and split his temple wide open and slightly concaved his skull. With a gaping wound to his head, Jo valiantly flew with Kody as far as he could before he fell to the ground, going in and out of consciousness.

Kody had to act fast. He gathered Jo up and threw him over his left shoulder. In pain, he ran for the safety of Havengothy. Kody gave a high pitch whistle for the Skyforce to come to his aid.

Injured, but determined, Kody held Jo tightly over his shoulder as he fearlessly fought three liaths with his sword. A Skyforce team arrived just in time and drew the fight from Kody and Jo while Commander Cinders called her team to assist in getting the wounded to the Healer station.

Menace was living up to his name. It was he who struck Jo the second time. Enraged that the liath had injured Jo, Billick took his anger out on the vile commander. The sound of their crashing swords was loud. It was wrath, rage, hate, and vengeance that collided on the floor of the cursed valley.

Suddenly, a dark enormous shadow began to cover the valley floor. It wasn't a cloud but a giant flying serpent. Riding the wretched snake was Torn. The dragon like snake let out a screeching hiss that pierced the ears of all who were in its path.

Torn's mission was to find the secret entrance to the Skyforce headquarters. Captain Roland had given her instructions on how to invade the concealed platform of the headquarter. As the serpent began to rise up toward the Skyforce platform, Trixie and six other sentinels met the giant beast at the entrance. The whip of its tail knocked two of the guardians from its post.

Ominous caught view of the General aiming towards the H.Q.'s entrance. The liath directed his buzzard toward General Dax. The quick reflexes of the General saw the bird of prey coming at him and dodged the collision. He then made it to the Skyforce entrance and stood with the sentinels to hold off the serpent's attack and the invading liaths.

Ominous hovered on his buzzard, contemplating if he should engage in the battle at hand. He withdrew from the conflict and let Torn and her flying beast have them all. He chose instead to chase down a group of Skyforce soldiers aimed towards the Skawlterrin borders.

Captain Roland watched in horror as the tail of the serpent wrapped around a guardian and began to squeeze the life out of him.

The cowardly Captain began to skulk away, but Trixie caught a glimpse of his retreat. She quickly flew and landed in front of him.

"Don't think you can bring this trouble in our world and not pay for it!" She yelled.

The Captain looked at her, as to size her up and mocked her attempt to stop him. "What do you think you can do to stop me? You are nothing but a woman trying to do a man's job." He said in a condescending tone.

Trixie raised her eyebrows at the arrogance. Reaching behind her to draw one of the two swords she carried, she skillfully wielded the weapon, poised to take the Captain's head if he dared to run. But the Captain met her gaze with hatred and distaste of a woman warrior.

"Go home, little girl. You don't belong here," he taunted.

Trixie glared at the prejudice of the Captain. "Oh. I am home," she said, and then charged at the coward.

As she lunged towards him, with her sword, the Captain took his razor-sharp dagger, hidden in his belt, and threw at Trixie. The blade plunged deep in her thigh, causing her to stumble and drop her weapon. If she pulled the knife out of her leg, she would bleed to death for sure.

"I will not be beaten by a cowardly weasel," she yelled. She pushed herself up while Roland ran towards her with the intent to tackle her. The two tumbled and rolled on the floor. The fight was brutal, with fists to the face, head, and gut.

Nearing the entrance of the H.Q., Trixie saw the serpent hovering. She grabbed the Captain by his shirt, and with every ounce of strength she had left, she yelled, "Your master is calling you!" And she threw the Captain toward the flying creatures mouth. In the conflict of it all, the blade fell from her leg, and the wound began to gush blood.

The serpent saw the falling fairy, and with his mouth opened wide, he swallowed Captain Rolland in one bite.

General Dax watched as Trixie stumbled from the loss of blood. "Tyler, get Trixie to Healer's, now!" He ordered.

Tyler, a Skyforce armor-bearer, who was bringing new weapons and arrows to the front-line soldiers, rushed Trixie to the Healer's station. However, he stopped long enough to tie his belt around Trixie's thigh in hopes to stop the bleeding.

The commotion was wild. Tyler cradled Trixie as he flew as fast as he could. The blood loss was astronomical. The Captain had hit the main artery, and the brave sentinel was fading fast.

A young Healer named Erin was directing traffic at the H.Q. Healer's station. She organized the injured soldiers by the severity of their wounds. As soon as Tyler arrived with Trixie, she was as white as paper.

Erin yelled, "We have an urgent one, Sylvia!"

The graceful Healer looked up from caring for Kody, "I'm sorry, Kody, I will get Lewis to come and finish with your stitches and brace." Lewis arrived just as Sylvia was mentioning his name.

"Go ahead, Sylvia, I will finish up here," he said, not knowing the emergency Sylvia was rushing off towards.

She hurried to Tyler and saw Trixie. She then looked back at Lewis, who was busy caring for Kody, and her heart sank.

"Oh, Beathra, give me the wisdom for this moment right here." She finished her plea to the King then ordered, "Take her to healing room three and get me, Julia."

Trixie was being carried to the operating room on a stretcher, passing Kody and Lewis. Lewis looked up as Tyler and Erin carried Trixie. He felt the emotion that was coming from Trixie like a wave. She was dying, and she knew it. Lewis froze.

Kody, still in extreme pain, put his arm around Lewis and said, "If you need to go to her, I can wait." The young Healer didn't respond, he just left Kody and ran to Sylvia.

"No, Lewis, you cannot be part of this, you are too close. I will do everything, and I mean everything I can do to save her life. The rest is up to Beathra." Sylvia said as she held Lewis back.

"Let me see her, please, Sylvia." He pleaded with tears.

"We are on borrowed time, son, so be quick," she replied desperately.

Lewis grabbed Trixie's hand and remembered the day they both laid in the Healer station recovering from their abductions. That day then led them to this day now. He bent over her pale face that was lined by her dark purple hair, and he kissed her.

"You're gonna be ok, Trix. Better than ok." His voice caught in his throat, but he continued, "I love you, and I will be right here waiting for you." Lewis's tears were streaming down his face, and he could feel Trixie's love for him being returned. It was only a matter of seconds that they had the interaction, but it felt like a bubble in time that went quiet just for them.

Sylvia rushed past Lewis, and the door shut. He was left standing there on the other side, feeling helpless. Kody quietly came and stood next to Lewis. He didn't say anything; he just stood alongside the young Healer as he leaned his forehead against the door and quietly wept.

The battle continued. The giant flying serpent needed to be brought down. When it wasn't flying, it was crawling on the ground, whipping its tail across the valley floor, and wiping out liath and Skyforce alike. C.J. had a crazy idea. He found Callie and quickly explained his plan to destroy the snake.

"His skin repels the arrows. We have to find a way to kill it, and I think I know how, through its eyes. If you can draw his gaze in one direction, I will take my spear and pierce that dragons brain. When it fans it wicked mane, it creates a blind spot. This should generate an opportune time for me to sneak up on it. I just need one thing."

C.J. looked at Callie and grimaced. Callie shook her head in disbelief, "You want me to draw its attention, don't you?" Still shaking her head.

"I do. Watch its beak; right before it spits its poison, it fans its scaly hood thing." Before she could protest, C.J. took off. Callie looked at the casualties the wicked beast was leaving behind, and she knew this was the only way to stop it.

She bolted towards the snake with a small prayer to Beathra. Torn saw Callie rushing towards her and turned the snake's attention to the approaching gidgie. The snake was spewing its blinding venom when the acidy liquid hit a Skyforce soldier in the face, causing him to fly directly into the serpent's waiting mouth.

Callie caught a glance of C.J. with the giant spear and knew she had to hold the gaze of the snake until she saw it frill its neck. She calmly faced the beast and Torn, ready for whatever was to come. In one bold move, Callie flew directly toward the enemy. Torn kicked the flying snake as one would a horse, "Kill the stupid fairy!" She yelled at the beast.

As the creature lunged with its beak open to gulp down the brave gidgie, C.J. came from the side and thrust the spear through the eye of the snake paralyzing it, but not yet killing it. Driving the weapon into its brain, its mouth snapped down just missing Callie, and it began to spiral downward.

Landing on the floor of the Darphea Valley, the flying serpent made a sickening thud. C.J. and Callie rushed to the snake to cut off its head.

Callie was met by an enraged Torn. She charged at Callie, but the seasoned brigade member flipped over the head of the irate liath and landed behind her. C.J. was standing over the dragon-snake and began to chop off the head of the menacing creature.

Neeradima could be heard from the edge of the dark forest. "Stop him!" She screeched.

She unleashed her pet naffagrahn's to attack all and any who dared to kill one of her secret weapons.

The monsters were headed directly towards C.J.. Billick spotted the wild boar-like creatures and aimed his bow to stop them. Raining arrows, he filled the backs of the beast. Other Skyforce soldiers saw the naffagrahns running across the valley floor and began to join Billick in stopping the charging creatures.

Torn had retreated, so Callie was able to join C.J. in cutting the head of the beast off. The naffagrahns reached the two brigade members just as they swung their final blow of the sword. They flew away as quickly as possible, covered in sprays of blood. The liaths were falling back; defeat had to be admitted.

The beast they had put their hope in was dead. The naffagrahns began to devour the monster and feast off its belly. The Darphea Valley was covered in bodies once again.

The Whisper's presence was felt throughout the war, guiding the soldiers in strategy, and gathering souls who lost the fight.

As the snow began to fall, the enemy retreated and the wicked queen withdrew to her hiding place, humiliated, and enraged.

———————

The Skyforce sent a recovery team to gather the fallen soldiers that lost their lives. The search and rescue team braved the frigid weather while shoveling snow and enduring bone-chilling winds. They refused to leave their brother and sisters bodies behind.

Havengothy lost 150 Skyforce members during the battle. And

though that would be considered a low number, the price was high, and the entire garden grieved.

The three-day war was known as The Great Liath Battle. There were several casualties, and the H.Q. Healer station was overwhelmed. Many of those without life-threatening injuries were sent to the healing rooms at the Gardening University. Jo stayed at the H.Q. Healers station, in a coma. He had a giant bump on his head and several stitches across his temple.

Kody stayed at the Healer's station for nearly a month to recover. He searched for the chameleon that was being treated, and he watched as the Healer's performed their magic on the pitiful lizard. Meredith Barry's merrybare berry bush brew was used to remove the Tragedy Seeds that the chameleon suffered from.

The response of the joy-inducing drink colliding with the trauma-inducing seed was phenomenal to behold. The colors that the chameleon changed were otherworldly. Vibrant colors flashed like lightning, and then the chameleon's curly tail went stick-straight and fell completely off. Leaving him with a tiny nub and the last color that he flashed, a cantaloupe orange.

Kody adopted the chameleon and named him Scout. The two would sit with Jo for weeks until it was time for Kody to leave the Healers. His wing was too destroyed to fly home.

Duke, Ginny, and Ruby arrived at the Healer's station to pick the wounded soldier up to take him to his root. They hitched Prince and Piper to their cart, unsure if Kody was able to fly. The three entered the Healer's station in search of Kody and to visit Jo.

Kody was in the lobby with Scout lying at his feet. Ruby ran to him and hugged him. She could hardly look at his wing. She didn't know what to say to him. The battle took a toll on him, and his countenance was full of sorrow.

"Kody, why don't you stay with Duke and Ginny for a few days before you go straight home. Duke would love to practice his new recipes on you." She knew it was a lame attempt to make conversation, but she had to say something.

"I'm good, Ruby. I just want to go home. Besides, I have this little guy to keep me company," he answered. Kody did not want pity.

They all went to see Jo in his room. Jo was still lying in a coma. Julia was in his room, giving him his healing tonics and changing his bandage on his head. She looked up at Jo's visitors and smiled. Ginny saw Jo lying on the bed, appearing as if he was lifeless.

"We should come back another day," Ginny said, overcome with the sight of her friend.

"Visitors are good for him. Come in and say hello." Julia directed.

Ginny put her basket of goodies on Jo's side table and watched as Julia forced liquids down his throat. "I was such an idiot bringing this basket. How in the world is he supposed to eat anything in this?" Ginny whispered to Duke.

"Ginny, love, we came to see our friend and show him we care about him. Plus, Jo could wake up tomorrow and be grateful to have our basket of treats instead of this Healer's goop they're shoving down his face." Duke said reassuringly.

Julia left the room, and Ruby followed her out. "Julia, do you know where Lewis is?" Ruby asked.

"He may be in the garden. That's where he spends most of his day, since…." Julia's answer trailed off.

"Which way to the garden?" Ruby asked. Julia pointed downward, and then she entered another room to see her next patient.

Ruby popped into tell Ginny where she was headed and then flew outside to the garden to find Lewis. She walked around the frozen ground until she spotted him sitting on a bench alone. Ruby stopped and stared at her friend for a short moment. She didn't quite know what to say, but she knew she needed to see him. Taking a deep breath, she flew to sit by him.

"Hi, Lewis," she said softly.

Lewis looked up at Ruby, his eyes were bloodshot from lack of sleep. "Hi Ruby, what are you doing here?" He asked, with a gravelly voice from exhaustion.

"I wanted to check on you. I heard about Trixie. Oh, Lewis, I am so sorry. My heart is broken. I can't say that I know exactly what you are going through, but I do know what it is to lose someone you love." Ruby put her arms around his shoulders.

He dropped his face in his hands and began to weep. "I don't know how to keep going, Ruby. Trixie had such life in her. How can she be gone?"

Ruby comforted her friend as he cried. His tears steamed in the cold air. Ruby knew this pain. The loss. The empty heart. And she also knew, Lewis would learn how to live again, without Trixie.

Sebastian had been missing for months and the not knowing was killing her. However, like Ruby, Lewis needed to hurt until he healed. He would never feel entirely whole, but he would find a way to live again.

The two friends sat in silence for close to an hour. Ruby's teeth began to chatter, but Lewis didn't feel the cold.

"I'm sorry, Ruby, let's go inside and get you warm." He got up from the bench and reached down to help his freezing friend up.

Lewis looked down at Ruby, who just froze her fanny off to sit with him. "You know, Ruby, I think there might be a Healer in you somewhere," he said with a smile.

Ruby hooked her arm in Lewis's arm and said, "Nah. I am training to join the Skyforce," she answered.

"Really? How's that going for you?" He asked.

"Mmmm, not so great." Ruby giggled.

Lewis laughed; he knew exactly what that meant. Her clumsiness would be her biggest obstacle. The two gidgies entered the Healer's station, laughing about Ruby's fiascos.

"Thanks, Ruby. It feels good to laugh again." Lewis said as they entered the lobby.

Ginny saw Ruby and ran to her and Lewis, yelling, "He's awake. Jo's awake."

All images purchased through Adobe Stock

Art credit

Chapter one- The book- © Dr. N. Lange

Chapter three- Pinkle pepper © Na.Ko.

Chapter five- The liath shadow © vladorlov

Chapter eight- The Darphea Wilderness © Maxim B

Chapter nine- Young Neeradima © syberianmoon

Chapter ten- The vine © Ekaterina Glazkova

Chapter eleven- The cloak © Kaselmeyk

Chapter fifteen- The bloom festival © ikonacolor

Chapter sixteen- Darphea Mountain caves © jamesjoong

Chapter eighteen- Prince the Skypony © Ariana

Chapter twenty- Gabriella © gaihong

Chapter twenty-one- The Hyperion Mountains © storm the Hyperion lion

Chapter twenty-two- The distorted Diatone elf © Andreas Meyer

Chapter twenty-three- The winter butterfly © aboard

Chapter twenty-eight- Ruby's love letter © Jean-François DESSU

Chapter twenty-nine- Beathra at the bloom festival © Kevin Carden

Epilogue- The flying serpent © photosvac

Made in the USA
Middletown, DE
14 June 2023

32610899R00158